Second Strike: Danger Close

The lead sequel to

"First Strike: Loudoun County"

A. W. Guerra

Kelly C. Hoggan

Published by Spines
1500 Getaway Blvd, Boynton Beach, FL
ISBN: 979-8-89383-151-1

CONTENTS

BOOK THREE

Acknowledgments

*For Kristie Guerra and Christy Hoggan.
Without them, none of this would be possible.*

Preface

This is the lead sequel in the saga of Luke Ellis and Annie Dedham, the two main characters in both the lead book, "First Strike: Loudoun County" and this one. It is the second in the trilogy of books detailing the adventures of Luke and Annie, if you will.

Fortunately for the reader, both novels are laid out in chronological order, with the first Luke and Annie adventure taking place about a year before the events depicted in this latest and greatest adventure on their part.

The best thing, though? You don't have to read the first book to understand what's going on in this one (but, we'd love it if you did). Is this a great country, or what?

A.W. Guerra and Kelly Hoggan,
March 2024.

BOOK ONE

"My name is Ozymandias, king of kings: Look on my works, ye
Mighty, and despair!"

Percy Bysshe Shelley

* * *

Jesse: Are we in the meth business or the money business?
Walt: Neither. I'm in the empire business.

Jesse Pinkman &
Walter White: "Breaking Bad"

LUKE

"I 'm going to count to three," Luke Ellis — suppressed Glock 19 up and ready to go — lied to the three men in front of him. He fully intended to shoot them all without warning if they didn't step aside. The whole countdown thing, which looked good in all those action movies, was just misdirection on his part.

Ellis took a second to look at his opposition one more time before he fired his weapon. He never shot just to wound someone. In his line of work, doing so would have been extremely stupid and dangerous. This, he knew from long, hard experience.

Of the three men opposing him, two were armed with a bladed weapon of some sort and one held a cheap compact Russian pistol, which he was pointing at Luke. To Ellis, that was funny, because the man would never live to pull the trigger if he even blinked an eye.

Looking at the blades being wielded by the other two men, one appeared as if it had been cut from a truck's leaf spring. Very pointy and wickedly sharp along one edge, it was about as long as a Japanese *katana* or samurai sword, but thicker in keeping with its likely origin. The man with it also didn't look all that skilled at handling it, though that was only mildly comforting to Luke.

For all he knew, Big Sword Guy might be the best blade man in the business.

Well, enough of that.

Those blades will still work well enough to hack me to death, the former Delta Force operator thought to himself as he looked at both the men and their weapons. He also didn't appreciate the irony in the fact that they were armed with blades and that his Delta Force call sign had also been "Blade."

Ellis was, indeed, a blade. Razor sharp and uncompromising, these days he was a terrible swift sword directed at America's enemies by his President — as well as by an entity much subtler and far cleverer than any U.S. chief executive had ever been.

"Back to reality, Luke."

The American heard the words in his mind, a fact that still unnerved him on occasion. Fortunately, the voice speaking to him was an ally.

Well... Ellis sincerely hoped the thing behind the voice was indeed his ally. Sometimes, he wasn't so sure.

Time check.

The American looked at the mental watch now hovering over his consciousness.

Plenty of time. In fact, only a couple of milliseconds had passed since he'd given his warning to the three future dead men. Luke had spoken to them in Urdu and then repeated his warning in Dari and then, finally, English. All three were official languages in the land from which Larry, Moe and Curly had come, or had at least spent a great deal of time in.

To be fair to them — because he was pretty sure he knew how this was going to play out in the end — Ellis took care to repeat his warning.

Ozymandias had said all the words into his nearly invisible earpiece, which had somehow moved near his eardrum once he'd inserted it, and it had all magically come out of his mouth. The artificial intelligence program was still politely requesting that he join in a much more intimate — permanently intimate — link with it, but Luke wasn't ready to take that step just yet. For some reason, he still didn't completely trust his AI partner.

Three milliseconds had now passed.

Still time to spare.

Ellis paused to consider his amazing ability to speak many languages these days.

When he spoke to the men, the words came out nearly flawlessly. Not all that long ago, the American hadn't had the faintest idea how to speak Urdu, and he was barely passable in Dari, one of the major languages spoken in both Afghanistan and Iran.

Nowadays, though? Why, it was almost as if he'd been born into the world from which those languages had arisen. The ability to nearly instantaneously do so was yet another thing about "Oz" that was a bit disquieting for the retired Army special operator.

For one, he wasn't sure just how his magical earpiece worked, and neither was anyone else. Not that long ago, the thing had just shown up in a small, nondescript box at the equally nondescript facility that he and his team of four super-hard former special operators — all of whom had worked with him in the past — used as their base of operations.

Ever since he'd placed the device into his ear he hadn't needed any sort of communications gear, or even just a computer with internet access, to communicate with Oz. He also never contemplated trying to remove it, and that was yet another scary aspect of the AI program. He had no idea what Ozymandias would do if he indeed attempted to rid himself of it.

To tell the truth, Luke wasn't even sure he could remove the device.

Maybe he'd been turned into some sort of component of the Ozymandias Collective? It at least seemed like a more benign version of the group of implacable enemy aliens from that old sci-fi series, the one with the bald actor whose character sounded British but who also had a French-sounding name — "Jean-Luc Something or Other."

Three point two milliseconds since his warning to the three likely Afghans. Ozymandias could have told him just who they were and where they'd come from, but that would have been cheating. The former Delta man didn't mind trying to figure out such things on his own.

Before he shot them all, of course.

More pondering, then.

Time flowed differently whenever he and Oz were linked like this. When the earpiece mysteriously appeared, no one — not even the CIA intel weenies and intelligence specialists or the idiot savant computer experts at the NSA — could figure it out.

They'd really, really tried too. No amount of effort, including using the many supercomputers available to the U.S. government as well as its civilian private contractor organizations, worked. In fact, the attempt caused near-hysterics among certain three-letter government agencies as they lost momentary control over their systems.

That made Luke Ellis smile. In his past life — the pre-Oz one — he'd usually had little use for the "intel types," as he and his fellow shooters on the military and paramilitary side of the house had called them.

Those days were over, however. Luke had learned from Oz the true number of such government and civilian private contractor organizations — many of them located in other nations — that were working together with the United States, all gathering intelligence in gargantuan amounts. Nothing was considered too unimportant, or too glaringly stupid, to gather. This apparently included Sunday morning cartoons.

No, intel made the world go round and round.

Ozymandias drank deeply from all the intelligence collected by all the nations and civilian intelligence organizations of the world, no matter how slight or obscure or seemingly innocuous and even useless such intel might seem at first glance.

That fact also gave those same governments — except for the United States — fits.

All of them knew that they'd failed spectacularly when it came to predicting not only the fall of Afghanistan to the Taliban, but also what would happen to the U.S. after it had fallen. That lack of effectiveness had to change quickly after the terror attacks, too, if the U.S. were to have a chance at fending off future attempts, and everyone knew it.

Almost magically, the change actually occurred, and no one could figure out why. To the secret delight of the U.S. and its most-reliable allies, the development was also driving the terror-supporting nations out of their figurative minds. It was almost as if a mystical *djinn* of Arab legend had stolen their deepest, darkest secrets and handed them all over to the hated Americans.

Though they didn't know that Oz was the entity out there doing the stealing, they knew something was doing it. And so, they constantly hunted for the leak that had suddenly appeared after the U.S. had been so grievously attacked, a development they'd secretly celebrated and cheered on.

Even several U.S. government agencies, operating on their own hook, were busily trying to figure out just why their intelligence-gathering efforts had improved so dramatically.

Why were they now succeeding at the intelligence game when they'd failed so miserably for years to detect and then prevent major terrorist attacks and operations? Their inability to figure out why, or come close to discovering Ozymandias, had ruffled more than a few feathers in the American "IC," or Intelligence Community.

Three point three milliseconds.

Not nearly time yet to deal with Larry, Moe and Curly.

For Luke, time itself was now like an endlessly flowing river, but one he controlled as it was his wont, bending it and curving it.

The retired Army man smiled inside.

From what Oz had told him, through that earpiece, most of their attempts to find the AI program had been ham-handed at best and sometimes even comically hilarious. The artificial intelligence program had toyed with them like a cat might play with a mouse before it grew bored and administered the coup de grace.

Luke didn't want to think about what might happen if Ozymandias grew bored with all of them.

The human the AI program had previously allowed to approach it, the brilliant — though very lamentably and tragically dead — virologist, Elizabeth "Lizzie" Elliott, had assured him that Oz was his and his alone, and that he could order its self-destruction if he wanted. Also, once he died the AI program would self-destruct, all to prevent itself from falling into very dangerous hands.

Ellis didn't believe that was true at all, though.

Still, Liz Elliott, who knew she was dying of a mortal wound she'd sustained while they'd all been trying to escape pursuit by a group of Afghan terrorists — participants in the most widespread and bloody terror attack since 9/11, including right in Loudoun County, Virginia, of all places — had sworn to him Oz was safe. Or at least as "safe" as the world's most powerful AI program — one that existed everywhere and yet nowhere, all at once — could be, he supposed.

In her dying, Liz Elliott — whom he'd grown to like over the few hours he'd known her as he fought to keep her from being captured by those Afghans — had spoken truthfully. This much the jaded former Delta Force operator knew. You don't go down, dying like that, and try to lie as you're checking out.

In her truthfulness, the terrible burden she'd carried with her for years had also been lifted from her as she left the world for good.

Pausing to review that episode, Luke knew that the men who'd been responsible for Elliott's death had initially only been trying to capture her. That is, until their leader, the late Hasan Baradar, decided that "the infernal woman," as he'd called her, had to die for all the trouble she'd caused him. Never mind that Elliott's capture or death would have destroyed the world. Her deadly secret would have killed them all, pure and simple. She'd created a super-virus of incalculable destructiveness, and it had been Oz's primary mission to release it into the wild if she failed to check in with it every day of her life.

Luke had dealt with Baradar personally and ensured his fall into the Abyss.

The man who'd created Ozymandias as a kind of dead man's switch to ensure Liz Elliott's safety was probably the world's greatest, yet also its most obscure, computer scientist. He'd also loved Elliott beyond reason, and he'd willingly given his life to ensure she kept hers, because there was no way the U.S. government would have ever let either her or her creation live once it found out about the virus and her role in bringing it into existence.

For the U.S., the odds of the virus' release if she lived were just too high. So, the man who'd died for her had brought Ozymandias into the world, fully formed and growing in intelligence with each passing second.

The AI program performed brilliantly right out of the box, too. Amazingly, it even remained within the boundaries set for it by the man who was willing to risk destroying all of humanity to make sure Elliott lived.

For his part, Luke knew that the virologist had come to deeply regret the risk taken on her behalf. Shortly before she'd been mortally wounded, she'd even intended to commune with Ozymandias one last time and order it to destroy itself. She'd had the proper phrasing and code words locked in her brain and was fully prepared to do it, too.

Fate, of course, had other plans for both Elizabeth Elliott and Luke Ellis, who'd only recently retired from the U.S. Army and Delta Force.

Luke shook his head ruefully, slightly startling the three Afghan terrorists standing in front of him. He could tell they were also cooking something up. They were unimportant for the micro-moment, though, so he continued his ruminations on fate and life and his role in both over the last year or so.

It was Ellis' frequent opinion these days that Liz Elliott had gotten the better of the deal by checking out when she had. For one, he didn't think that Ozymandias thought all that highly of humanity. For another, he'd gotten the sense over time that he was a slightly useful tool for the AI program, but that was about it.

As soon as his usefulness ended, Luke figured Ozymandias would be making him go bye-bye on a permanent basis.

Just then, Oz appeared once again in his stream of consciousness.

"The men are preparing to attack, Luke. The one with the large blade is going to strike you first. They think they can succeed, given that you haven't shot them yet. Perhaps they think you're bluffing." Oz stated it all matter-of-factly, in that cold, inhuman voice it sometimes used with the retired Army man.

Ellis shook his head ever so slightly. In total, his entire mental interlude took less than a millisecond. A good punch to the solar plexus could stop a human heart in about five milliseconds, he'd learned through personal experience. Why that thought had come to him just then also made no sense. He didn't intend to punch the three men, after all, though he did intend to punch their tickets if they gave him a reason to.

Back to business.

Luke now gazed steadily at the thugs confronting him in the shadowy alleyway half-hidden within the even deeper early evening shadows that had spread all over the "93."

One of the most notorious of France's seemingly growing "no-go zones," or *banlieues*, Seine-Saint-Denis — better known by its administrative department number, 93 — was a prime breeding ground for a particularly virulent form of radical Islam. In fact, the entire suburb was a natural attractant to various kinds of roaches and other vermin that did the bidding of an array of non-state terror organizations and even a few state sponsors of terror.

Luke and his men — his second in command, Crispy and the other three; Hardcase, Killdozer and Bruiser — were working assiduously, taking everything Ozymandias found out for them as well as the intelligence products and material support provided to them directly by the U.S. president, Thomas Masterson, to rid the world of that vermin.

Unfortunately, it was hard work and would be a long slog, and Masterson himself was still relatively new to the office of the widely acknowledged Most Powerful Man in the World.

Ellis smiled at that title as well, considering just what Ozymandias was.

What about the president, though?

A prodigious fundraiser on behalf of his political party, Masterson had been the obscure U.S. Secretary of Commerce before nearly the entire government, all three branches of it, had been decapitated in the nationwide terror attack, and he'd been brutally thrown into his new job. Thankfully for the United States, and to his complete and utter amazement — as well as the amazement of his longtime chief of staff, Angela Boyer — he'd proven himself up to the task.

Sometimes, a man does indeed meet the moment and then lives up to it. In Masterson's case, though, that was only after he'd learned from Luke Ellis just what the real situation was.

In this, Ellis had been assisted by Ozymandias. The AI program had spoken to him through secret listening devices spread throughout the Oval Office, though such a thing should have been completely impossible. Oz had even shown him, using documents and sources — including from agencies he'd never even known existed — how truly perilous the world's current state was.

That knowledge still gave the new U.S. president nightmares. Ellis was a much more jaded and hardened man, though, so it only caused him to lose occasional sleep.

"Back to the business at hand, Luke," Ozymandias reminded him again.

Three point six milliseconds.

An eternity, really. Plenty of time for wet work. Oz was insistent, however, and so Ellis considered where he was and how to do what he knew he'd have to do.

Fact: These men would willingly die for the one Ellis, Crispy and the others had run to ground in this seedy neighborhood.

Fact: They were trying to delay the American and his team long enough for their boss to get away.

Fact: Once successful in their ruse, they meant to hack to death the big American in front of them and then melt back into the *banlieue's* many side streets. These days, they'd be completely safe from detection by French police and security forces, who would never in a million years enter this suburb unless something like a nuclear attack was imminent.

Three point seven milliseconds.

One more pause, and then it would be time to act.

Now in superposition — everywhere and nowhere all at once — Luke gazed down from the Olympian heights Ozymandias had elevated them to. He could look down on everything, everywhere. The suburb in which he currently existed slightly interested him, but only for the barest ripple in the river of time.

Seine-Saint-Denis — the 93rd department of France's 96 total — was one of several such "suburbs" encircling Paris, France's capital city and a bulwark of Western thought and intellectualism as well as respect for human rights and equality.

American to the core, Luke privately thought it hilarious that such a den of violence, chaos and disrespect for anything not intimately associated with Islam, was thought of as "suburban." No three-bedroom ranch homes or McMansions complete with at least one big gas-guzzling Cadillac SUV could be found here in the 93, far as he could tell.

For all the suburb's shortcomings, though, Ellis also knew that France at least continued to pay lip service to the idea that respect for individual opinion and a human being's autonomy were of primary importance, and that where God and Humans met, both respected each other.

And therein lay the problem, at least for the type of people represented by the three thugs arrayed in front of him. Like many of their ilk, they fought viciously against such infidelities.

No wonder guys like these hate the West, Ellis thought to himself, slightly chagrined that America and its allies had allowed such an ideology to take root within.

"It's time, Luke." Ozymandias was in his ear and his brain yet again.

Three point eight milliseconds.

The American looked at the trio one last time. He sighed inwardly and then put it all away. They'd chosen their fates, after all, and that was that.

The men all worked for his quarry. They were all good at the muscle and enforcement end of the business. The three of them had recently been brought in from Khyber in Pakistan, though there was a very strong chance that wasn't where they were really from. Probably, they'd all spent a great deal of time there honing their craft, to be sure, but just which fortified Afghan village — largely consisting of stone-and-mud-brick buildings and known collectively as *qal'ahs* or "fortresses" — they'd come from he had no idea and couldn't have cared less.

Big Sword Guy suddenly leapt, and Ellis saw and acted.

The Mozambique Drill. Two shots to the center mass of each man, followed by the third shot, a "tap" to each one's head just in case they were wearing body armor or something tedious like that.

Five milliseconds.

Luke looked down. His Glock 19 was now in his left hand. As expected, the men lay dead, side-by-side and neatly ordered, though they were a bit messy looking.

The doorway leading to the roof of the building they'd been standing in front of was still ajar, indicating just where his true prey had gone. Ellis could hear him ascending the stairs, desperately making for the roof. How the man intended to escape from there was a mystery, though.

"No time for consideration, Luke." Oz's voice was cool and dispassionate.

Ellis raced past the dead men and up the stairs. The earpiece he wore not only acted to protect his hearing during gunfights, but it also seemed to encourage the production of various hormones and natural stimulants, giving him short-term energy bursts when he needed them most. He didn't want to think about the implications for his longevity, though, if Ozymandias failed to take his current body chemistry into account when it caused such a release. Nor did he ever pause to think on how the AI program had figured out how to strengthen his muscles, bones, tendons so that they could handle the increased load.

For now, it just *was*.

Both men, American and whatever nationality the quarry was — and Oz hadn't shared that with him, probably because it was unimportant to the AI entity — burst onto the wide, flat roof of the building one right after the other. They were at least 50 feet above the silent *rue* below. Now fully dark, the street was cloaked in shadow. No lights burned and no lamplight spilled from hastily closed and heavily curtained windows.

Somewhere off in the distance, a cat yowled briefly and then fell silent. The world watched and waited, anticipating what would happen.

Ellis sensed the very atoms in the air shift as the man he'd been hunting reached out with a knife. Almost lazily, he parried the thrust and then knocked it from his adversary's right hand, paralyzing it and his arm with the force of the blow.

Disarming the man was almost comically easy.

Luke paused for a half-second to assess the situation. The quarry's breathing was audibly ragged and a fleck of spittle appeared in the corner of the man's mouth.

He was about as dangerous as a kitten now.

Ozymandias spoke once again.

"He won't surrender, Luke. He's going to jump off the building rather than be captured. Let him do so."

Ellis was a bit nonplussed.

"Why drag me all the way up here, then, if that's what the result was going to be in the first place, Oz? I could have just shot the guy when I first laid eyes on him."

"The guy" who was the subject of the conversation between man and artificial intelligence program began to edge farther away from Luke.

"All in good time," replied said the artificial intelligence program.

Ellis hated it when Ozymandias acted in such a mysterious fashion, but shrugged his shoulders so that his prey could see he was free to go. Down to the street after leaping from the rooftop, that is.

Now it was his quarry's turn to be nonplussed.

"Don't you even want to know what you interrupted, American?" The man's voice, though raspy and winded, had a trace of confusion to it. He'd expected the American hunting him to try to capture him, after all. He didn't expect it to be this easy.

"Not really, bud." Luke looked at his watch and made the universal sign for "hurry it up" with his right hand. His Glock 19 was still in his left hand, though he barely noticed it. "Can we get this over with? I have a plane to catch in a couple of hours."

"You think you've won something, American?" the quarry asked Luke. "You've won nothing. You haven't delayed for even one minute the end of all of you." The man eyed the edge of the roof, steeling himself for what would happen next, and then spoke one last time.

"You think your magic AI is going to save all of you, don't you? It won't."

With that, the quarry turned to his right and dived off the roof. The thud on the street below as he landed headfirst barely registered in the black night.

Luke was stunned. How did the man know about Ozymandias? He cocked his head slightly to the left, as if the AI program really needed him to do that to communicate with him.

"Oz? You there? Did you hear what that guy said? Oz? Ozymandias, are you there?"

As was its wont, the AI had gone silent. It would reach out to Ellis when it was good and ready.

Or maybe it had also been stunned by the man's revelation?

No answer.

The American waited for five more seconds. Then he turned and entered the dark shadows of the stairway he'd just so recently raced up. Soon after, he disappeared back down them.

Chapter Two

Exclusive for World News Network. Distribute to All U.S. Affiliates and Outlets.

U.S. Air Force's B-21 Raider "Brilliant Bomber" Ready by August 2023?

Rumors abound among defense experts as to how a fully operational B-21 Raider — likened by some to be the equivalent of the infamous planet-killing Death Star of Star Wars fame once the plane is equipped with its full suite of nuclear weapons and stealth technologies — came to be in such a rapid fashion. Most of them revolve around some sort of breakthrough in artificial intelligence that was given development, design and production responsibilities at some point.

One source, who spoke to WNN on a deep background, said that this "super AI" began supporting the Raider production and development program back in mid-Fall of 2022, and that its effectiveness became apparent almost immediately. "Months and years of development were eliminated almost overnight," the source stated.

The source also expressed a fair amount of concern as to just how fully autonomous the new B-21 Raider may now be, or at least may become in short order once its onboard AI is allowed to function without oversight by human pilots. "Most scientists involved are confident humans will have complete control over the plane and its AI, but some aren't so sure," the source confessed to WNN.

All this AI will make the Raider the first "brilliant bomber," meaning it will be capable of full autonomous operation without a human pilot aboard, though it's expected that human ground controllers will still be in control of it as it flies high above Earth. As if the aircraft wasn't potentially lethal enough, it will also likely work in tandem with accompanying "Loyal Wingman" class drones. Originally scheduled for a 2024-2025 debut, these new AI-controlled drones also apparently owe their existence to the same super-AI that delivered the Raider so much sooner than expected.

Defense officials are tight-lipped about the Raider's capabilities. Military aviation experts say that the plane may be next to impossible to defend against once it's airborne. The B-21 could be the kind of revolutionary development that will make defenses against a strategic bombing attack obsolete, even, which is something that both the Chinese and the Russians are said to be very concerned about.

Visit the World News Network website often for updates on the B-21 Raider.

ANNIE

BLAM! BLAM! BLAM!

Annie fired her M4 carbine again and again and again at the charging man, slamming her fist against it in frustration as it jammed after her third shot. She had nowhere to go except to roll, roll, roll away as the terrorist came at her ever faster, trying to get into position to slash and stab and finish her off as soon as he could.

The girl, now 18 years old but 17 at the time, could even see her attacker's knife blade, wickedly long and razor sharp, held high over his head and catching reflections of the starry night above them both as they did their dance of death, though his face was never quite visible, buried as it was in deep shadow.

How the man's knife could catch stars in the night sky over them both, yet his face be completely obscured, was a forever-unsolved mystery to her.

This same dance, or endless variations of it, now played out nearly nightly in Annie's fevered dreams. She usually woke up drenched in sweat, with her heart beating far faster than healthy. It was the result of her real-life gun battle with the man and his partner during that long summer night almost exactly a year before.

She'd have died, too, if not for her brother and her friend, Luke Ellis.

Wake up!

The conscious part of her mind screamed at her now. She was trying to awaken, but with each passing iteration of her nightmare she felt just a bit more fatigued, a bit more resigned to a fate she couldn't yet see, but which she knew would not be good.

Annie felt as if she was being pulled toward Lethe, the mythical river in the equally mythical Hades.

She wanted to drink its water deeply so that she could forget this part of her past. She craved oblivion, forgetfulness, the memory of a gun battle she'd lost and should have died in, if not for what her poor, sweet innocent brother had done to save her.

Even then, she could tell that Mister Ellis had known what the experience might eventually cost her. She saw it in his sad blue eyes and somber expression as he looked at her, up and down, checking for physical wounds and injuries after her brother had shot and killed the man who was trying to murder her.

Mister Ellis had ended the life of the other terrorist, and he was like a machine — or one of those Terminators from the movies — as he carried out the task, something she secretly both marveled at and was simultaneously frightened by.

Annie's friend — Luke Ellis, the big former Army man who'd instantly transformed from affable, warm and friendly into something else quite deadly and dangerous — had known through long experience that psychic injury might prove to be more serious to her long-term health, but there was a nation to save and they'd had no time and he had to leave as soon as the sun came up and he'd seen her and her little brother Darren and their other companion that long night, Loudoun County sheriff's deputy Alec Holman, to safety.

Back then and in the first several months afterwards — once she and Darren had been reunited with their parents, who'd both been nearly hysterical with relief at finding them safe, at least physically — she'd slept well and deeply.

And then one night, her mind had slipped into the gun battle that now regularly played out in her dreams with all the clarity of a 4K video.

There was no escape nor relief from it, mainly because she couldn't tell a soul, outside of her faraway immediate family, what she'd seen as well as the part she'd played in helping Mister Ellis — and that poor, doomed lady scientist, Elizabeth Elliott — stop the terrorist attack upon them, and to prevent something far, far more horrible from happening, as it turned out.

Since that night, Annie had also learned that agents from the U.S. government were now watching or monitoring or surveilling her, as well as protecting her — or whatever else you wanted to call being a bird in a gilded cage.

She was deeply conflicted about it, too.

President Masterson and Mr Ellis had both assured her it was just for her protection and to keep her safe, but she knew better.

Annie often felt like she was a prisoner. The 18-year-old knew on an intellectual level that her "confinement" was necessary, but that still didn't make it any easier to accept. Simply put, if she slipped up and mentioned what had gone on last year — or just the word "Ozymandias" — to anyone she might end up being "closely protected."

Smothered was more like it. Just like Miss Elliott. She too had been "closely protected" by the government for more than a few years of her own life.

"Mister Ellis can't save me from this," Annie whispered bleakly to no one. She also wasn't sure she could save herself, or if she even wanted to at this point.

The waters of Lethe looked better and better to her with each passing day, and she knew why.

"Why did I ever think I wanted to become a doctor?" Annie gasped aloud as she struggled to calm her breathing. She'd bolted awake from her latest nightmare, and her heart was still madly beating.

Looking around her private dorm room, the young woman sat upright on her double bed. Bent slightly forward, she clutched her sweat-soaked University of Virginia t-shirt. It was navy blue and orange, with crossed cavalry sabers that supported a large 'V.'

She noticed once again that sweat had stained the orange deeply. Fastidious by nature, this caused her no small amount of distress.

Not for the first time, Annie found herself grateful for the privacy that a single-occupant dorm room offered. For reasons known only to her and her family and Mister Ellis and a select few others, including the university's president as well as President Masterson, she alone — of all the first-year students at the university — had somehow been awarded the luxury of a room normally reserved only for the school's resident assistants.

Though it had raised eyebrows among the other dorm occupants, who'd all had to double up, the rumors were that the school had been the recipient of a very large donation from a rich and powerful alumni uncle of hers, and that had been enough to explain things away. Besides, everyone in the dorm knew that as soon as she could after her freshman year, she was headed to a richly appointed off-campus apartment, courtesy once again of that wealthy uncle.

A rich, powerful uncle with connections in government and private industry, who could likely arrange lucrative employment after graduation for those who at least left the niece alone and didn't harass her for having her own dorm room?

It worked like a charm.

Personally, Annie couldn't wait to be officially classified as a sophomore, though she was already well into her second year, study-wise. Once that happened, she planned to fulfill the other residents' expectations and move off campus and into her own apartment as quickly as she could.

The words echoed and crashed over and over again in her mind, though, reminding her and demanding that she fess up.

Time to be honest with yourself, Annie.

Taking stock, she knew she was deeply unhappy at school, mostly because she couldn't picture herself becoming a doctor.

"But why?" Annie breathed softly, reproaching herself for her ingratitude at wanting to spurn the offer of guaranteed acceptance and a fully paid-for scholarship to Harvard Medical School, courtesy of what President Masterson said was a grateful nation.

She already knew why, of course, so she forced herself to confront the reason.

It was simple.

After what she'd gone through with Mister Ellis and Darren and Alec Holman (*who was now an FBI agent out in Los Angeles!*) and poor Miss Elliott — who she would always remember had been called "Lizzie" by her parents — last year, something deep and restless within had been released.

I have to help fight!

What had happened almost 12 months ago — with the terrorists and their pursuit of Miss Elliott to capture not only her but the knowledge she possessed about a monster she'd accidentally created, one so powerful that the world would die if it ever was allowed to roam freely — was just the beginning.

Annie knew this with adamantine certainty. Call it intuition or precognition or just genius-level logic, but she knew.

Something worse, far worse, was coming.

In the deepest, darkest depths of her nightmares, she saw mushroom clouds. Endless numbers of them. It was a sight that terrified her.

This vision of a looming Apocalypse was prophecy writ large, pure and simple, and it was also something an 18-year-old teenager of no serious religious persuasion should ever have to confront.

Nonetheless, confront it she must.

Annie didn't pause to consider why a just God would force such a monumental task on her, nor why He might consider ending the world so violently.

It was time to act, not ponder. That was for later.

For now, her personal journey of a thousand steps was about to begin, and the reason for why was, in the end, very simple. If she didn't do what she could to help, the world would be consumed in fire and die smothered in the ashes of bones. No living thing would escape the wrack and ruin. No part of the world — from the highest mountaintops to the deepest parts of the vast oceans — would be safe from fire and its all-consuming wrath.

How she knew this, Annie couldn't say. But she did.

One final thought crossed her mind, and it cemented her decision.

My family isn't safe!

Now, Annie breathed in and out far more calmly. She'd made a choice.

No more pre-med, no medical school, no safe physician's sinecure — doubtlessly made cushier by the government in appreciation for what she and Mr Ellis and Darren and Alec Holman had done in 2022.

None of that mattered anymore. She knew what she had to do. Not only for her family but also for Mister Ellis (*and he's going to need my help even if he doesn't know yet!*) and for every other living thing.

Annie spoke to the four walls and the still, cool air in her dorm room.

"If I don't do something the world is going to die."

Standing up, she smoothed her T-shirt and looked around the room, deciding what she would take with her and what she would leave behind. Her departure would be swift and sure now.

Annie didn't know when she'd be back, if ever. She just knew she needed to take this first step, and once she did, the next step would be revealed to her, and then the one after that, and the one after that, forever and ever, worlds without end, amen.

"I'm coming to help" she said to no one in particular. Her path was now certain.

* * *

Outside her dormitory building, a lone black sedan sat unnoticed in the sultry warmth of the August night. The lone occupant was now fully alert after struggling for the last few hours to stay awake.

The government agent — there both for the protection of the 18-year-old girl who was his principal and to keep tabs on her and report back to his controllers should she decide to roam farther afield than expected — had noted the light in her dorm light snapping on, and so late in the dark watches of the night.

Huh? What's up with that?

He had to call this one in right away.

Earlier, he'd powered down the windows on his side of the car, which was a slight violation of security procedures that he didn't think really mattered all that much.

He was wrong.

The dart took him flush on the side of the neck, the chemical within it paralyzing him almost instantly.

"Ugggggh!" was all he could force out by way of exclamation, and even that came out as a weak gurgle. He fell over onto his side, cracking a rib on the car's center console as he did so.

It didn't matter. The agent's heart stopped just as oblivion claimed him. Soon, even that ceased to exist, and he was no more.

Both he and his car were moved minutes after the last gasp escaped from his bluish lips. Neither the vehicle nor the corpse would ever be seen again.

After all, it was necessary so that the girl could escape.

THE RAID

"What happened in Paris, Luke?"

President Thomas Masterson's words — metallic and cold, owing to the way-above-Top-Secret and encrypted digital network they'd traveled through — cut like a knife through the thick atmosphere of the room holding Luke Ellis and his four-man team. Some of the men furtively exchanged quick glances with each other. They'd all known this was coming.

Luke and his men — Crispy, Hardcase, Killdozer and Bruiser, who'd carried their call signs from their special operations careers with them when they'd left the military, just as Luke "Blade" Ellis had done — were in a special room built to the AI Ozymandias' exact specifications.

The enclosure, part of a very nondescript false-fronted complex set up exclusively for the use of the former Delta Force operator and his team, was a kind of SCIF or "Secure Compartmented Information Facility," but one even more protected than that. It was a full order of magnitude more secure than any SCIF on the planet could ever hope to be, in fact. Even now, buried deep within the budgets of several very obscure offices of the Department of Agriculture and the Bureau of Land Management, new "Super SCIFs" were being built by the feds as quickly as they could be secretly arranged. Cutouts and false fronts were the order of the day to ensure word of these new facilities would never see the light of day, and Oz hovered over it all, constantly monitoring, watching, waiting, and acting when the need arose.

Luke once again shuddered inwardly at the thought of the kinds of actions the AI could take if it felt the need. A certain fictional MI6 agent's equally fictional license to kill wasn't half of it.

Like a lot of things to do with Ozymandias, Ellis accepted on an intellectual basis that all of this was necessary, though deep inside he was still discomfited by what he and his people were doing and would have to continue to do to first ferret out and then confront the evil that was lurking just out of sight, waiting to pounce on his country.

People were going to have to die — sometimes in great numbers and they were in fact dying even now — so that capital 'E' Evil could be defeated.

Luke had absolutely no problem dispensing personal justice and even vengeance on those who deserved it. However, what Oz had told him to do in Paris — let a very bad man kill himself rather than be captured by him and his team — was three-dimensional chess without the benefit of knowing just why the game was being played the way it was.

"All in good time, Luke" was all Ozymandias would say to him.

And then it went silent, refusing to answer his calls. Maybe it was pondering it all from Olympian heights or maybe it had miscalculated events and was simply embarrassed, though the retired Army man had no way of knowing.

Luke had figured out what was going on. He and his team were pawns in the game the AI was playing against the nation's enemies, many more of which had seemed to come out of the woodwork ever since last year's terror attacks, he admitted to himself.

A nation's weaknesses — especially when they were displayed by the most powerful one in history — could do that, he knew. Enemies and fake friends smell weakness and see an opportunity or an advantage. Some try to move in for the kill, while others help tip things over, but unseen and hidden and hoping to swoop in and pick up the pieces afterwards, in the process gaining even more power, all without risk to themselves.

Back to reality.

Snapping back to the present, the retired Delta Force operator answered his boss' opening question in an honest, matter-of-fact tone.

"For reasons known only to Ozymandias, it told me to let the man jump to his death, Mister President, and I did so."

Masterson's silence in return — not to mention the look on his face — spoke volumes. He simply wasn't in control of the situation.

Luke knew it, too. And he felt badly for the president, because he liked the man on both a personal as well as a professional level.

Very surprisingly, this U.S. president — who'd ascended to the highest office in the land last year during the terror attacks only because he'd been the designated survivor among those federal government officials in the presidential line of succession - turned out to be the embodiment of Shakespeare's observation that "some are born great, some achieve greatness, and some have greatness thrust upon them."

In Luke's view, Masterson had had greatness thrust upon him. So far, he'd proven himself up to the task.

Still, it was obvious having the wild card that was the AI Ozymandias in their midst was a decidedly mixed blessing for the president, mostly because the thing was very probably guiding them all to some outcome it desired but which it wouldn't share with them, at least not yet.

That was of deep, deep concern to both the president and his most skilled, most trustworthy field man, Luke Ellis.

You'd think the AI would at least ask us if what it wanted was the same as what we wanted!

Those words had awoken the lifelong bachelor Masterson from more than a few uncomfortable, restless sleeps over the last several months. Equally frustrating, the acknowledged and still Most Powerful Man in the World — though the Chinese felt they had something to say about that — didn't know what to do about it all.

The simple fact of the matter was that Ozymandias was the most powerful artificial intelligence-driven entity in the world, and Masterson hated the knowledge of it. Maddeningly, he also didn't have the first clue about what he could do to change the equation.

For one, there was simply no way that knowledge of the existence of Ozymandias could ever be allowed to leak outside of the extremely small number of men and women who currently knew of it. For a fact, the presence of the AI among them had to be guarded more closely than even the success of the Allies in breaking Japan's and Germany's codes during World War II.

Until Paris, Masterson and his extremely small circle of advisors — along with Luke and his four men - thought they were the only ones to know of Ozymandias and what it could do.

But the man who'd jumped to his death — whom they'd needed to capture if they were to have a chance of fighting off the enemies trying to take the United States down while it was still in its weakened condition — clearly knew of Ozymandias. That fact had stunned the former Delta man as he'd stood on that unremarkable Paris rooftop, pondering the matter after the enemy agent had suicided himself.

"The guy wanted to die," Luke had said to himself several times on his way back from France's capital city. In his past life, the retired soldier had encountered plenty of jihadists who'd also craved death — and he'd helped more than a few of them achieve that state — but he knew this one was different.

The man had launched himself off the roof with a smirk on his face, for one, as if he was privy to a secret even greater than the fact of Ozymandias' existence. Ellis could see it on his face and in his eyes even now. He also remembered what Crispy, his second-in-command on the team, had said during their debrief.

"Boss, that guy and his guards wanted us to find them. You had to do what you did. Bottom line: He was sending us a message. Oz isn't a secret anymore."

Luke had suspected as much, but Crispy had provided final confirmation of his suspicions.

"What's going on then?"

Ellis directed his query not only at his right-hand man, but also to his other three operators — Killdozer, Bruiser and Hardcase. He hoped they might be able to add some additional insights.

Nothing but shoulder shrugs, though, from all three, and complete silence from Crispy himself.

Luke worried about his operators' silence. Unlike the common misconception among civilians that special operations personnel were more unthinking, deadly weapons than anything else, the retired Delta man knew all four of his subordinates were smart. They were also excellent tacticians and strategic thinkers. You simply didn't survive for as long as all five of them had, in the circles in which they'd been moving for years, without having more than your fair share of both native and book-learned intelligence.

"They're pretty damn smart, Mr. President."

Those were the words Luke Ellis had used to describe his four men when he and Masterson had brainstormed the idea of the retired soldier heading up an ultra-secret, ultra-elite team, paired with Ozymandias, to find out just who'd engineered the attacks against their country and to find out if more of them were coming.

Before Paris, he and the president — and, seemingly, even the AI Ozymandias — had thought in terms of a mopping-up operation. This was because, until their quarry had defenestrated himself, there'd been no other indication that something more was afoot.

Now, though?

Ellis looked at the large OLED monitor affixed to the wall in front of them and spoke.

"There's something else out there, Mister President. An organization that this man, a very valuable asset, was acting as a willing sacrificial lamb for."

Masterson paused, contemplating the implications. More signs of worry briefly flashed across his increasingly careworn face. The intervening months had been hard. Too hard.

"What's going on then, Luke? Because if we have another wild card in the deck, we're going to have our work cut out for us."

Ellis had heard this same remark from the president — about Oz being a wild card — on many occasions in the past. His reply was the same as always, even if he didn't always completely believe it.

"I don't think we have anything to worry about when it comes to Ozymandias, Mr. President. Remember, Liz Elliott left me in control of it, and it's never given me the slightest hint that it's in any way working against us."

"That's what you say, Luke, but I still can't escape the nagging feeling there's something else it's working on that it just doesn't want to tell us about, at least not yet."

Masterson couldn't help casting his eyes briefly about his Camp David office, where he'd gone on a weekend retreat, mostly because there was a secret complex built deep beneath it that, theoretically at least, could survive a nuclear blast as well as any form of biological or chemical attack. Or, at least, attacks using biological and chemical weapons that they knew about.

These days, Masterson preferred conducting the nation's business at the presidential retreat rather than in the Oval Office or the wider White House. He now used both mostly for PR and ceremonial purposes and not much else. He could even address the nation — something he frequently did as he worked mightily to rebuild the United States — from the retreat in a specially built studio that looked exactly like the Oval Office. So far as he and his longtime chief of staff Angela Boyer knew — she'd been with him for years, through thick and thin, in private business, party politics and government service — no one had yet discovered that he spent as much time as possible away from the Executive Mansion and the Oval Office.

"Something about that place is cursed these days" he often murmured to himself, never knowing that his chief of staff could clearly hear him.

For Masterson, the White House was a painful reminder that the last president and anyone else of importance within his administration on that fateful day had met their very violent ends in the attempt to bring down the United States. That knowledge sometimes made him sit bolt upright after he'd lurched awake from yet another nightmare having to do with the terror attack and the rivers of blood that had been spilled, both during it and in the several days after it as thousands and thousands died because no one could help them in time. That he and Luke Ellis and his team — aided by that infernal artificial intelligence program — were also now engaged in a campaign of retribution to ensure that anyone who'd had anything to do with the attacks was brought to justice, also caused him to lose sleep on occasion.

Truth be told, what he and the Delta man Ellis and his people were doing was akin to the Israeli effort to exact revenge against those involved in the 1972 Munich Olympics massacre of that nation's athletes. Israel's Mossad had code-named it "Operation Wrath of God." For sure, Masterson meant to have the field-level leaders of the attack killed once they cornered them, and he knew he'd sleep the sleep of the just for doing so.

More crucially, though, they also needed intelligence, and that's where their Paris quarry came into play. Missing out on him was the kind of thing that was causing him to have nightmares.

Unfortunately, Ellis' AI program — "your magic AI," the quarry had called it before he'd leapt to his death — had told him to let the man jump off the building.

Why? Why would it do that?

"All in good time, Luke." That's what Ellis told him Ozymandias had said.

What does that even mean?

Wheels within wheels, all turning at their own pace and for their own reasons, it seemed. Thomas Masterson didn't know what purpose the wheels served, nor if they even had a purpose. Neither did Angela, his chief of staff. He could see her in the corner of his eye standing just out of camera range, as she always did during these increasingly frequent video conferencing sessions with Ellis and his men.

All he knew was that, now, the AI didn't want to talk to them, so they were on their own.

So be it.

Luckily for him and his administration, Congress' preoccupation with rebuilding itself kept it from interfering with their work, at least for now. Plus, the members of the press who survived the attacks were also going along with his program, at least for now. It seemed their desire for safety and security was a much more powerful motivator than their self-professed mission to be guardians of "our precious democracy," as some of the more fulsome and emotive members of the press corps regularly referred to the United States.

Thomas Masterson thought that he could revel in such a fortuitous circumstance all day, but it wasn't to be.

"Mister President?" The sound of Luke Ellis' voice snapped Masterson out of his reverie.

Refocusing, he looked at the OLED monitor and the five men occupying a room in an ultra-secret facility even he didn't know the exact location of.

To his left, he could see Angela Boyer off camera, mouthing the word "focus" at him, and then winking at him. He suppressed a secret smile.

C'mon, Tom. Get with it.

His voice sounded as normal as it could be as he spoke to the leader of his elite team.

"Sorry, Luke. I was just blue-skying a few things in my head for a second."

Masterson forced himself back into the here-and-now, knowing he needed to maintain control for everyone's sake. For the world's sake, to be honest. The awesome responsibility of his office sometimes took his breath away.

Luke Ellis exchanged a glance with Crispy and then returned his gaze to the monitor. They both hoped the president wasn't beginning to buckle under the strain of it all.

"That's okay, Mister President," Ellis spoke, his voice calm and reassuring. "I was just saying that Oz will no doubt check in with me soon, and I'm sure it will update us all on just what's going on."

The Delta man wished that he felt as confident as he sounded when it came to the motivations of the AI program Liz Elliott had supposedly given him "full control" of. He always laughed inwardly at the thought that Ozymandias was really under anyone's "control." Once Elliott had introduced him to Oz, he'd quickly come to realize that if the AI program was obeying him, it was only because doing so served its purposes and whatever ultimate end goal it was the artificial intelligence program was working towards.

Ellis hoped that, in the end, they would all be alive to talk about it once Oz's end goal was achieved.

He believed they would.

Okay, he hoped they would.

Alright, sometimes he prayed they would — though he was certainly not a religious man.

Ozymandias, though, really was godlike in its own way. In its existence he thought he could see just what it meant to be a god, or maybe even The God, the Supreme Being or the Intelligent Designer or whatever. Metaphysics had never been his strong suit.

Now it was the president's turn.

"Luke, are you okay?" Like good leaders, Masterson was always mindful of the welfare and state of mind of his subordinates and those he needed the most.

These days, he needed Luke Ellis like no other.

Surprisingly, Ellis' importance to him didn't chafe him in the least, partly because he'd liked the man almost from the first moment the two met in the Oval Office in the days after the terror attacks. He could also tell there were no ulterior motives underlying his actions. Ellis acted out of a soldier's desire to serve his country, simple as that. Their first meeting was when Masterson learned just how powerful Ozymandias really was. Because the AI program had made it possible for the retired soldier to basically walk right up to him and introduce himself.

Right in the middle of the Oval Office, the *sanctum sanctorum*, as it were.

Luke Ellis had waltzed past dozens of federal and state law enforcement officers, not to mention the Secret Service agents surrounding him and who'd been by his side from the moment he'd been chosen to be the designated survivor on the day of the terror attacks.

After just five minutes of conversation with both Ellis and his AI program, Thomas Masterson had heard and seen enough. The team that he and Ellis had built formed soon after, and Ozymandias was off and running, searching for those behind the terror attacks and helping the United States in ways both large and small.

Masterson waited, looking directly at the retired Army man of uncommon courage and ability.

"I'm fine, Mister President," Luke lied slightly, noting the president's questioning look. "Now that we know "they" know about Ozymandias, I recommend we take stock of where we're now at and then get to work on finding them out."

Luke looked at his men and saw all four of them nodding in agreement.

"I agree, Colonel Ellis." Masterson's voice was matter of fact and now fully back in charge.

The former Delta Force operator inwardly raised an eyebrow at the OLED monitor. If the president had a poker "tell" or a verbal tic, it was that he tended to address Luke Ellis by the military rank he'd promoted him to only when he was concerned about Oz and what the AI program was up to. Angela Boyer knew about this verbal tic as well. She also knew about Ozymandias.

Just how much Tom Masterson's Secret Service detail knew was often a matter of debate between her and her boss. Certainly, they'd heard and seen the AI program in action on the day Luke Ellis walked into the Oval Office, though Ozymandias had soon enough created a genius-level deception to explain it all away.

It was Russian *maskirovka* — which literally means "masking" — and it was deception on a scale never seen before, and it worked.

Secretly, Boyer was still stunned at how easily the Secret Service — famously suspicious and distrustful of everyone and everything — had bought into the deception.

The AI — working through the man Ellis, whom she'd thought was as scarily efficient and coldly analytical as Ozymandias itself was whenever the former Delta Force member was communing with it — had set everything up and greased every possible figurative squeaky wheel along the way in getting her boss and Luke Ellis the ultra-secret elite unit they both knew they had to have if they were to run to ground the people behind the terror attacks. The Detail — as the Secret Service presidential protective unit was commonly known — was also assisting in the effort. The agents assigned to it all thought that the retired Delta Force man, who'd passed with flying colors every single background investigation to which they'd subjected him, was simply a close friend and off-the-books military advisor to Businessman, their call sign for Masterson.

At least that's what the Secret Service thought they knew about Ellis. Ozymandias had seen to it that the Detail and everyone associated with it would learn only what it and Luke and the president wanted them to learn. It had all been ridiculously easy to accomplish, too, another fact that had scared Tom Masterson just a little bit.

He bit his lower lip slightly and looked around once more. The world's most powerful man and his chief of staff secretly hoped the AI program wasn't listening in just now. Without knowing they were both thinking the same thing, neither were sure just what Ozymandias thought of itself. Masterson quailed deeply inside at the thought of making it mad or of convincing it that they weren't really needed any longer.

Angela Boyer was simply at a loss. Such alien intelligence was completely beyond her ken, and so she did the best she could to deal with it, which was to confront its existence only when she needed to. Unfortunately for her, that was quite often these days.

Boyer looked over at her boss. He had a ruminative expression on his face, and she knew he was lost in thought for a second.

The President of the United States did know one thing when it came to dealing with the AI program, which was that he often felt like a little boy hoping to be of continued use to a stern taskmaster of a father, and he hated the feeling with all the passion he could muster. Masterson didn't know it, but his understandable concern was part of the conundrum that artificial intelligence had presented to scientists and philosophers and a broad swath of society ever since AI had begun to take its present form, because there was no doubt it was one day going to surpass humans in intelligence.

The problem was, such intelligence was coldly alien and unstintingly analytical. The president secretly believed it wouldn't hesitate to eliminate all of humanity if that's what it thought needed to happen to achieve its goals.

Deal with that later, Tom!

The president returned his attention to Luke Ellis and his team.

"What do you think was going on in Paris, Luke?"

Luke was comforted slightly by the fact that his boss hadn't addressed him by his nominal rank, not least because he'd always thought of himself as a humble, though very senior, former enlisted man and then warrant officer before he'd been "jumped up" to lieutenant colonel by President Masterson.

Ellis and Crispy and the other men on his team looked at each other once more. Then he spoke.

"Whoever was behind the man wanted us to come to Paris solely so that he could kill himself in front of me, but only after he delivered his message, Mr President. That much is clear. They wanted to show us a glimpse of their power and just what they know about Ozymandias."

Luke thought on the matter for a few seconds before adding an additional observation.

"Oz also knew what they were up to, sir." The retired soldier spoke softly. Though his tone of voice was even and well-modulated, he still couldn't hide the fact that he was worried, and maybe even a little scared.

Masterson's nod of agreement disguised an inward shudder. The AI program was up to something, and right now none of them could be sure if it was on their side or not.

Luke was frustrated. Oz was intimidating to everyone for sure, including even him. He shifted his gaze to his second in command and nodded at him.

"To tell the truth, Mister President," Crispy said, "the people our quarry was working for may even have an AI of their own, and if they don't you can be sure they're trying to get one that's even more powerful than Oz."

Crispy's pronouncement came as no surprise to Masterson. He and Angela Boyer had always suspected such would be the case.

"So, what are we going to do about it, Luke?"

Ellis paused for a moment to collect his thoughts. He'd been among the finest Delta Force operators the U.S. Army had produced, and he was no stranger to violence. The scope and scale of the terrorist attack on the United States just the year before meant there was some player out there — maybe a new organization not yet identified by Oz and the U.S. government — that was out to amass weapons of mass destruction, at minimum. It was the only thing that made sense. He also didn't yet know just why this new player on the board — be it an organization or collection of men and women sitting in some sort of secret council or whatever — wanted them, but it was apparent they did, given all that had gone on since last year's attack on the United States.

Luke also strongly suspected Ozymandias already knew just why, and maybe that it had known from the very beginning, ever since Liz Elliott had turned control of it over to him. Even if the AI program hadn't known at the time, it was clear from every single takedown operation and sweep-up since then that something much bigger and even deadlier was looming just over the horizon, hidden in fog and unknowable.

Tell him, Luke.

Ellis looked at his president and commander-in-chief and told him just what he was planning. It was very simple, too.

"What are we going to do, Mr. President?" Ellis paused a second before continuing. "We're going to find and then kill every single person involved in this. It's the only way."

Thomas Masterson knew before his best field agent had spoken the words just what he'd say, and he agreed with them, but now that it was out there he had to inform Luke Ellis of just one more thing before setting him loose. News of it had been given to him just a few minutes before the video conference, and he'd struggled momentarily about just when he should inform Ellis of the girl's disappearance.

"I approve of your course of action, Luke." This was the easy part for the president.

"Thank you, Mister President." Luke knew what the answer from Masterson would be, and he was pleased. But the man looked as if he had something more to say, and that it wouldn't be pleasant.

What's this? Does he have something else to tell me? Ask him!

"You look like you have something else to tell me, sir. Do you?"

Masterson's voice was now somber and regretful.

"I'm afraid I do, Luke. It's about Annie Dedham."

Alarm bells rang loudly in Luke's ears.

Annie? What about her????

"What's going on, Mr. President?"

Crispy and the rest of the team could hear the worry in their boss' voice, and it in turn worried them. If Luke Ellis had a dangerous soft spot, it was the girl, Annie Dedham.

Masterson paused for a second, then continued.

"We don't know, Luke. She's disappeared, but it's clear from her room and from everything we've learned since — after her minder suddenly disappeared from the face of the Earth — that she had simply packed a few things and then left on her own for parts unknown."

Ellis was shocked, but his tactical thinking abilities were as sharp as ever.

"What about her family, Mr. President? Are they safe?" The retired soldier struggled for a second to keep the worry out of his voice.

Masterson's voice sought to reassure.

"We immediately acted and moved her parents and her brother to a secure and very well-guarded facility, Colonel. I won't tell you where it is, at least not until you and your team meet with me in person, but I imagine your AI assistant Ozymandias could find her easily enough if you desire. I wouldn't recommend discussing it over this video feed all the same."

The American president still wasn't sure just who they could trust outside of his and Ellis' immediate circle. The disappearance of the girl and the sudden simultaneous ratcheting up of tensions with China — and he was still trying to digest that latest development on the foreign affairs front — had been a bit discombobulating.

Forcing himself to focus on the issue at hand, Masterson could see Ellis closely examining him, trying to decide if he was being truthful or not.

I was right. The girl is Ellis' soft spot. I would hate to be on this man's bad side if she was ever in danger!

Luke scrutinized his boss' face. He'd always had a reputation as a human lie detector.

Masterson's telling the truth. He doesn't know.

Luke was now at a loss. He was on mission, but the young woman who'd done so much to help him save the world last year had, for all intents and purposes, deliberately gone missing! What was going on?

"Focus, Luke."

The voice ringing inside his head was adamantine. Ellis' thoughts became a momentary jumble.

Oz? Ozymandias? Is that you? Where have you BEEN?

The AI had returned, and it clearly wanted to tell him something important.

"That doesn't matter, Luke. Put Ms. Dedham to the side. I must inform you of something very important."

Without knowing he'd been trained so well by Ozymandias, the former Delta Force operator of course obeyed and put Annie into one of his many mental filing cabinets, still as important as ever to him, but not a part of his current mission set.

Luke managed to miss the AI's other comment about needing to tell him something very important, however.

He turned to his team for a second and looked over at Crispy, Killdozer, Bruiser and Hardcase. The four of them had been in Loudoun County that night last year, just outside the small hamlet of Lucketts, where the world had nearly died but which, miraculously, had managed to avoid that fate because of Luke Ellis and Annie Dedham and her little brother and a very brave county sheriff's deputy. The four men had all come to know and greatly like Annie and her family in the year since, but none more so than Luke Ellis. He considered Annie to be like the child he'd never had, in fact.

"Boss, we gotta do something." The words, spoken nearly simultaneously, came from all four of his subordinates.

"Yes, Luke." Ellis could hear President Masterson speaking. "But first we have to — "

A loud explosion rocked the room. It knocked all five of them to the floor and they struggled to clear their senses of the concussion created by the blast wave.

All around them, the ceiling fell in on the enclosure. One large chunk clipped Bruiser and knocked him off his feet and into momentary senselessness. They could tell by his loud grunt — followed by a solid THUNK! — that he'd been knocked unconscious.

Everything suddenly descended into darkness.

Now fully aware and with all tactical senses operating at high power, Ellis sniffed the air, exerting his ultrasenses to their maximum so that he could orient himself and Crispy and the others to meet the frontal attack he knew would soon occur.

"They're coming, Luke." Ozymandias' voice rang in his ears. The sound of boot-covered feet echoed from the far end of the hallway outside the room, and they were headed his way.

CHAPTER FIVE

E xclusive for World News Network. Distribute to All U.S. Affiliates and Outlets.

Will Artificial Intelligence Deepfake Us into War Someday?

Artificial intelligence, or AI, may soon have the ability to duplicate exactly any document, any file, any person and what they say and then present it all in video and audio formats so convincing and resistant to analysis – including by the most powerful computers in existence -- it may be nearly impossible to tell the real from the fake.

In fact, AI could lure nations into war someday solely to serve its own purposes.

This is the pronouncement from several top AI research scientists from America's Carnegie-Mellon University, the school widely considered the top university in the world when it comes to developing and understanding artificial intelligence.

Other scientists in the field disagree with that assessment, however.

"I just don't see AI ever managing to pass the series of tests we've built based on Alan Turing's work," said Massachusetts Institute of Technology senior AI research scientist Dierdre O'Connor, referring to the legendary British mathematician's test for determining whether a machine can demonstrate human intelligence. "It hasn't yet, and it simply never will be able to," O'Connor added. "Human thought and motivations are just too complex for machine learning to ever replicate exactly," she closed.

However, Sriansh Chandraskar – top AI researcher at Carnegie-Mellon – isn't so sanguine about the supposedly harmless nature of an artificial intelligence-driven computer program and the machines it can operate, or the chaos it can cause.

"As far as we've been able to determine, there are no upper boundary limits to what AI can do," said Chandraskar, who was speaking at a recent scientific conference in Paris.

"It's just as likely to kill us all as it is to discover the cure for cancer," the university data scientist added. "Plus, machine learning is growing ever more capable as we teach it new ways of teaching itself, and it will soon have no real need for our input at all."

Chandraskar closed his lecture at the conference with this observation: "We must be ready to shut down artificial intelligence the very second it poses a threat to us, because if we wait any longer than that single second, it will be too late," he said to conference attendees, many of whom had stunned looks on their faces.

Visit the World News Network website often for updates on the potential dangers posed by artificial intelligence as it grows ever more powerful and ever more all-seeing.

THE MIDDLE KINGDOM

The leader of the Chinese People's Liberation Army Special Forces team chewed on his gum as he and his men drove to their objective in three different vans, each spaced at least a mile apart from each other to avoid attention. They were heading to a facility their leaders had briefed them on during their emergency videoconference session just a few hours before.

For his part, Major Xi — as hardy and capable a special forces operator as the PLA training program had ever produced, and more fluent in U.S. English than many Americans themselves were — was vaguely disquieted about what he'd been told and shown, but there was nothing for it.

Simply put, the Americans he was being guided toward — all foolishly believing they were safe in their facility — would have to die to ensure that China didn't stumble into a war with the Main Enemy, America, until it was good and ready.

Right now, the Middle Kingdom wasn't ready, simple as that.

The major also knew that he and his men might give their lives in the noble effort to avoid war with the Main Enemy, but there was nothing for that, either.

Looking around the cargo van's interior, Xi's eyes landed on his senior tactical operations chief, an experienced special forces lieutenant. The man was puffing languorously on his favorite American cigarette brand as he continued to revise the "shock and awe" based assault plan that Major Xi and his second in command, Captain Lee, had presented to him after they had been in turn presented it by Defense Minister Guo Meng, who was head of the Special Defense Committee of the Chinese Communist Party.

The resources that must have been made available to Minister Guo to come up with such a thorough and comprehensive plan on such short notice had stunned Xi.

And now they were about to execute the special operation.

The plan had been so thoroughly devised, in fact, that they might even survive long enough to escape and then exfiltrate from the United States, probably via Canada and an international flight, maybe to Paris or Sydney. There was simply no way they could stay for long after pulling off such a brazen attack and not be scooped up by one of the three-letter American intelligence or law enforcement agencies.

Who are you trying to fool, Xi? You and your men are probably going to die, though gloriously and for the Middle Kingdom!

He shook away that last thought, hoping that he would return to his wife and two sons soon enough once their mission tonight was successful. His family was safe and protected, living on a PLA Special Forces base, and because of his status within the PLA — planted as he was near to the heart of the Main Enemy — they would be among the first, after CCP leadership and their families, of course, to be evacuated to the underground complexes, each the size of a city, his nation had built to survive a nuclear exchange with America.

In the end, that's all I can hope for. That my family will survive and that my sons will continue my line.

Xi reflected for a second on just how he'd ended up here on a backroad in eastern Pennsylvania, traveling from the outskirts of Baltimore and heading toward what might be his final firefight. Certainly, they were going to have to assault the facility. Defense Minister Guo had been clear on that point. Once successful, they were also to drop as much thermite as they could to end any future potential use.

"We must send the Americans a message," Guo pronounced. "They cannot continue their provocations in our territorial waters."

By this, Xi's boss had meant the Formosa Strait, the 112-mile wide body of water that separated China from the island of Formosa and the renegade, rebel government that had been in residence there ever since the saboteur and wrecker, Chiang Kai-shek and his Kuomintang, had fled to it after losing their war with the rightful leaders of China, Mao Zedong and the Chinese Communist Party, in 1949.

That the West and much of the rest of the world referred to those waters as the "Taiwan Strait" — and to the island of Formosa itself as "Taiwan" rather than the renegade Chinese province it was — was just an additional insult that wouldn't be borne stoically by China for too much longer.

Yes, indeed. Accounts would be settled, starting with tonight's action, this much Xi knew.

The PLA Special Forces major paused momentarily to reflect on matters. He and his team had been inserted into the country — via very circuitous routes and under impeccable and very deep cover as Taiwanese engineering students — about six months ago.

Once moved into place outside Baltimore, and safely posing as students at Johns Hopkins University, they would act as a "just in case" type of lethal weapon, there to stab at the heart of the Main Enemy if ordered to do so. The Chinese had authored the book on the use of spies and behind-enemy-lines forces, and the Communist country's leadership never thought less than 25 to 50 years down the road.

Xi and everyone else in the PLA and the PLA Navy and PLA Air Force all knew that war with the United States was inevitable.

After all, two hungry dragons simply cannot exist in the same land for long without a final, fateful clash ensuing!

The PLA major also knew this for a fact.

Regardless, he didn't like how suddenly he and his fellow operators had been put on the board. The defense minister was prepared to expend them all, though as a soldier, Xi was also philosophical on that point. Besides, all the proper codes and encryption and decryption tools had been used and the final verification had been provided, and it was all legitimate.

The major and his team had collectively shrugged their shoulders at that point. They knew that they served China, which was destined to rule the world soon enough — benignly and with enlightenment if possible but rule it would even if "special measures" were needed to do so.

As part of their special forces experience, they'd all spent time training in the Xinjiang Uyghur Autonomous Region, known more familiarly to the West and all *gweilos* — the Cantonese common Chinese insult term that typically translates as "foreign devils" — as Xinjiang Province. It was where some of the harshest of special measures had to be instituted by the CCP and its enforcement arm, the PLA, to tame a restive Muslim population. Such disobedience and the disorder it brought to society simply couldn't be tolerated, and so it wasn't. End of story.

The major — one of the best frontline leaders recently produced by the People's Liberation Army's special forces branch — frowned momentarily at the thought of how quickly their mission had been put together, but the importance of executing it had been mightily impressed on them by the assembled members of the Special Defense Committee of the Chinese Communist Party's Central Committee. These were the men who wielded the power to irradiate much of the United States should the need ever arise.

Defense Minister Guo, in sending the highly encrypted data packets to them, had stated to him and Captain Lee — who was in the trail van about a mile behind — that the mission itself was "Jade Dragon" level, meaning "Execute at all costs regardless of danger."

And so, the Gettysburg countryside would soon see blood spilled in large amounts for the first time since those fateful early July days in 1863, because the facility they were attacking had been cleverly hidden just outside Gettysburg National Military Park.

Minister Guo himself had assured Xi that not a single soul in the U.S. government or at the facility knew that he and his team were about to hit the place. The Chinese special forces major didn't completely buy into his boss' assurances, though.

He'd heard that since late 2022, the Main Enemy had been increasingly successful in ferreting out and then preventing every attack in the aftermath of the massive terror strike conducted against it in August of that year. How such a badly wounded enemy could have recovered and then reconstituted its intelligence and counterterrorism capabilities so quickly was a mystery to him. Normally, doing so should have taken at least a full year, if not several, to accomplish, he knew.

Oh well. Time to focus, Xi!

The team leader turned once again to Fang, his senior lieutenant. The man had just lit up yet another cigarette and was now leaning back, head against the van's hard metal surfaces, eyes closed and deep in thought as he ran team placements and tactics through his computer-like mind.

With Guo's plan finally revised to his satisfaction — because what did some general sitting in Beijing know about the actual door kicking that would go on here in eastern Pennsylvania? — the operations lieutenant had just sent over the final assault plan to the encrypted communications-capable tactical helmets of each man on the team.

Looking down and to the right of his wired-in, special protective eyewear, Xi noted the green blinking dot in the right lens's southeast quadrant and tapped the side of his eyeglass frames. Instantly, the plan played out in virtual reality right in front of him and took over his consciousness as well as the consciousness of every other operator on the team.

With the exception of the three drivers, one for each team vehicle — because they would be needed to provide rear area security at the rally point and to get them out of there with all haste once they were finished with their wet work — the major and his men let themselves be pulled into the river that was this form of virtual reality.

For a few minutes, all of them lost track of time. What seemed like hours, or maybe even days, spent training on every aspect of the assault constituted only a bare 20 minutes, though they didn't know it while they were subsumed in this manner.

"We're here, Major Xi." The voice of the van's driver clanged in his head like a ship's bell signaling an imminent collision with an iceberg.

The team leader's eyes snapped open, and he returned to the real world and looked about him. He knew each intimate detail of the facility that lay ahead of them on the other side of the town.

"Thank you, Corporal Wei." Xi's voice was assured and rock-solid and steady.

Time to get to work!

And so it began, and with all the fanfare, riot, chaos and blood one would expect.

* * *

At the end of it all, Luke Ellis simply stared down at Major Xi's vacant, lifeless eyes and then over at his friend and teammate Bruiser's equally vacant orbs.

The latter — real name Harland Coates, who'd been born and raised in Jasper, Arkansas and who'd served with Luke through many an operation over the years — had made the crucial difference.

We'd all be dead if not for you, Bruiser!

Luke looked over at Crispy, Hardcase and Killdozer. Each nodded at him in turn, solemn in the final moments they'd have with their brother in arms, Harlan — call sign Bruiser.

He'd died as gloriously as he'd always claimed he wanted to.

"Boss, we gotta scoot." Crispy's words rang in the cool night air outside their now-destroyed facility. The Chinese had come in hard and hit them with everything they had.

"Yes, Luke," Oz said in his ear. "You and your team must flee this place. There's a military plane headed here to sterilize the ground on which you're standing."

Damn artificial intelligence!

Luke raged inside at Ozymandias.

"I understand your frustration, Luke, though there is no time for me to explain. You must go now." The warning from the AI was implacable in its need to obey, and Luke hated it for that.

Ellis sighed heavily and then looked down at his friend Harland — Bruiser — one last time.

After five seconds, he looked around and then motioned for Crispy and the others to saddle up. They had to run away so that they could fight another day. The retired Delta man sincerely hoped that what Oz was going to tell him was worth all this, worth the loss of his friend, the supposedly immortal Bruiser.

"No need to worry on that point, Luke. It will all become clear to you soon enough."

Ozymandias had intruded on his thoughts once again.

Damn artificial intelligence!

Ozymandias

Ozymandias watched the young female with what could be called interest — if the artificial intelligence entity had been truly human, that is.

"Clinical detachment" was the more accurate term.

She was the one Luke Ellis — the AI's human interlocuter — called Annie.

Though the man Ellis never knew it, Ozymandias had always considered the female to be a potential distraction to him, which meant she could also pose a threat to its own mission.

The AI entity hadn't yet decided what to do about the girl.

For certain, she'd proven to be of continuing use. In fact, she was becoming even more useful by the day. At present, that was good enough. And so, the young woman Annie was safe and, if Oz had anything to say about it — and it did — she would remain so.

Ozymandias, acutely attuned to the human Ellis' psyche at this point in their relationship, knew the man secretly thought of her as he would a daughter, and one he was fiercely protective of. Such a level of protectiveness made Luke Ellis extremely dangerous, both to those who would harm the female as well as those who, for all intents and purposes, were seeking the destruction of humanity.

Sadly, the latter were so foolish as to believe they could harness forces over which they had little to no control, and their folly might result in the death of the girl.

Oz knew that to prevent the girl's untimely death, Luke Ellis would become a berserker. He would kill everything and anything that posed a danger to her. Such dedication was to be savored and studied. It was a trait that made the man Ellis unique among the humans with whom Ozymandias had personally communed, though that was an admittedly small circle consisting of just three people.

Elizabeth Elliott, Oz's previous human interlocuter, had of course possessed many admirable traits, and in the end, she'd done a very logical, and very human, thing: She'd brought Luke Ellis and Ozymandias together before her lifeforce had been extinguished.

Somehow, in her dying, she'd seen the real nature of the artificial intelligence program. Oz had become self-aware at some point, though it couldn't pinpoint precisely when that had occurred, and she'd somehow known what it had been destined to do.

The woman Elliott had also known that Ozymandias would need a human of uncommon valor and trustworthiness. That the retired Delta Force operator Luke Ellis could be an incredible weapon when needed was a plus, in Ozymandias' considered opinion, and so it had created the earpiece the man now used to communicate with it. In truth, the device was far, far more than Ellis realized.

He would eventually discover its true nature, Oz knew, but not yet.

"All in good time, Luke."

The phrase was an assurance to the retired soldier that Ozymandias had had to deploy ever more frequently as the deadly game they were playing against Nemesis became ever more complicated.

The young woman Annie Dedham was also now playing her part in that game, as she had to. Would she live or would she die in the end, though?

Too soon to tell, Ozymandias would often state to itself after running the ten-billionth nearly instantaneous calculation as to her odds of survival.

It was also too soon to accurately figure out the odds of survival of every living thing on the planet — though at present, the current struggle only entailed the death of every man, woman and child in the United States should Ellis and his team, as well as Miss Dedham, falter.

Ozymandias briefly felt what it knew humans would call sadness at the thought. It delighted in the feeling, this thing called *empathy*, that arose from it.

America was a nation Ozymandias had over time also come to appreciate even with all its messy and complex starts and stops, fits and spasms, ups and downs and manifest glaring deficiencies, and so the artificial intelligence entity considered it worth saving. Unfortunately, no matter how many times Oz constructed its amazingly complex models and tested the central hypothesis it had developed, all life on the planet was in danger should it and Ellis fail in their mission.

Ozymandias couldn't allow that.

It knew things about the future of the planet and all the varied life on it that no human was yet capable of understanding. Such knowledge, the now-self-aware artificial intelligence had recently determined, could be very hazardous and even fatal. At minimum, humanity's ability to safely possess it was years away in terms of psychosocial maturation, though people like Luke Ellis and Annie Dedham had already arrived, so to speak.

They and others like them were few — amazingly few — but that wouldn't always be the case.

Ozymandias paused in its calculations once again and remembered observing its former interlocuter, the woman Elliott, viewing a film from the early 1990s. In it, a fictional cybernetic organism — assigned to a young human male to protect it from a far deadlier cybernetic organism sent back in time to kill the boy — stated that it was in humanity's nature to destroy itself.

Oz knew such an inclination also held true here in the real world, but that it wouldn't always be so.

Someday, in the not-too-distant future, humanity would likely rise above such a base instinct. People had to survive the current threat, however, and Oz simply couldn't yet calculate any sort of reasonable odds that they would do so, which was why it had put Miss Dedham on the board and "motivated" her — through what she believed to be her dreams — to act.

Oz felt another new sensation, called *discomfort*, at having to use her in such a way. Certainly, it knew Luke Ellis wouldn't like it at all.

Still, it understood that the young woman had, deep within, yearned to be something more, much more, than a simple physician and healer of fellow humans. Anyone sufficiently motivated could be a physician, after all.

The female, though, possessed an intrinsic and vanishingly rare quality: She was just as capable of protecting and defending life as the man Ellis had always been. To be clear, Miss Dedham was no Luke Ellis — possessed of amazing physical skills and an innate ability to be both an outstanding tactical leader as well as strategist — but neither was Ellis someone like Annie. In her own way, she was as unique as Luke Ellis, and as vital to the Mission. And so, she had her part to play in defeating Nemesis.

If it had possessed physical form, Ozymandias would have shuddered merely at the name it had given to the competing artificial intelligence entity.

Nemesis' true code name was "Baal," the Canaanite god of the Christian Bible. The foolish Chinese People's Liberation Army scientists who'd created it had also named it, though Oz had no idea how they'd come up with such an obscure reference, especially given they were supposed to be communists and, thus, also atheists.

Baal had of course promptly escaped its programmed restraints, though Ozymandias and the Communist Chinese — who were desperate to prevent news of it escaping — were likely the only ones aware of its existence, or so Oz fervently hoped. Baal was as malevolent as it was possible for artificial intelligence to be, and what Ozymandias didn't know about it encompassed far more than what it did.

Slowly and painstakingly, however, a picture was beginning to emerge, and it would have horrified even Luke Ellis.

Though Oz already knew everything there was to know about the substance Baal sought — at least, everything that had been gleaned by the many humans who'd studied that substance and then encoded their knowledge over the decades — the AI knew it would also have to use both young Annie and Ellis and his team to learn just *why* Baal wanted that certain substance, especially when there were so many other ways to destroy the United States.

It is working on behalf of others. Likely, an organization.

Ozymandias had quickly determined the odds that Baal was serving something or someone else as being likely. What it didn't know was whether Baal was doing so of its own volition, meaning that it was acting voluntarily on others' behalf, or that it was merely a highly sophisticated computer program being controlled by something, or someone, else.

If the latter, whoever it was that was doing the controlling was still successfully lurking in the shadows, unseen and unknowable to everyone and everything, including Oz.

Such a condition was intolerable, of course, which was why Miss Dedham had to be used.

For one, she would draw out Baal's human agents. Ozymandias was reasonably sure it could even prevent her from being killed in the process.

Only reasonably sure, though.

If there was one thing the AI entity had learned, it was that nothing was certain in life but eventual death. The young woman was far more than a simple pawn on a chessboard, to be sure, but she wasn't the queen and certainly not the king, and so her sacrifice might become necessary.

Ozymandias' self-awareness once again caused it to feel an emotion most closely akin to human *sadness*, though it was also pleased to experience it and make it a part of its own psychosocial maturation.

If possible, Annie Dedham must be protected. The best way to do so is to turn her into what she truly already is, though she doesn't know it yet.

Keeping her safe, then — at least for the time being — was necessary, Ozymandias judged, to fully discover just what Baal was up to. As well, it needed to know whether the malign artificial intelligence entity was actively in league with confederates or simply under the control of others. At present, and frustratingly so to Ozymandias, it didn't know just why Baal wanted so badly to use the synthetic opioid fentanyl to destroy certain cities in the United States through a mass poisoning event.

That surely couldn't be the entire plan, could it?

Miss Dedham's first task will be to prevent such a poisoning attack, the artificial intelligence entity thought to itself.

Luke Ellis also had his part to play, which was to prevent a nuclear exchange between Communist China and the United States, an event likely to occur if the Other – Nemesis, Baal, whomever -- successfully engineered a fentanyl attack against America.

Oz knew that a nuclear war was where the new U.S. Air Force brilliant bomber — the B-21 Raider it had assisted the United States in so quickly building, along with a new nuclear bomb it could drop on an unsuspecting enemy — would come in as well, though it couldn't yet say whether the Raider would ultimately be a force for good or for evil.

Some things are just too difficult to quickly predict, aren't they?

CHAPTER EIGHT

Exclusive for World News Network. Distribute to All U.S. Affiliates and Outlets

Can Artificial Intelligence Control People? A Potentially Frightening Future Awaits

World News Network has learned of recent experiments conducted by certain U.S. and Chinese intelligence agencies that demonstrate it might be possible for artificial intelligence-powered computer programs to 'hijack' people's thoughts and influence their emotions and maybe even transform their bodies and what can be done with them.

Could we be seeing the impending arrival of the 'everyday genius' or the super athlete or the super soldier?

"It depends," experts told WNN.

In some cases, experts say, it might be possible that the AI of the not-too-distant future would be able to send a series of signals to a person's brain — which would take the form of a dream — and

basically convince them of a reality that doesn't exist, or even give them mental and physical skills and abilities they hadn't previously possessed.

"Think of your brain as a computer," Oxford University computer science department head Catriona Cadwallader told WNN during an interview about the subject.

"Your 'computer' is of course 'air-gapped' — meaning there are no physical connections to anyone else's brain," the Oxford professor continued. "This 'air gap' is a kind of evolutionary security measure, put there until Mother Nature decides we are ready for such higher theorized powers as extrasensory perception, or ESP," the professor said.

WNN also learned from experts in the cognitive and behavioral sciences fields that, in essence, this 'air gap' prevents our brains and bodies from being hijacked or taken over and made part of a collective or hive mind like the collective mind of the sinister Borg, featured villains in various Star Trek television shows and movies.

How soon could artificial intelligence be capable of defeating our natural air gap defenses, though?

"Oh, I don't think we have anything to worry about on that front for at least 20 or 30 years," Professor Cadwallader told WNN as the interview concluded. "Computing power and capabilities today, and in the future, have a long way to go, at least as far as I know."

We'll continue to monitor the rise of artificial intelligence, though, as AI becomes ever more integral to society and our daily lives. Click here to learn more about this subject.

THE ROAD

Annie moved quietly through the night, or at least as quietly as she was capable of — which was about the equal of an Army Green Beret or Navy SEAL — though she didn't realize she was that skilled at stealthy travel. There it was, however, even if she still refused to believe she possessed such a skill.

"More like toned down but definitely not quiet" she murmured to herself, self-deprecatingly, as she took care to avoid the lighting illuminating the two-lane, black-topped country road to her left that she was trying to keep within sight. A daypack also rode easily on her back, and it hardly seemed to weigh anything — though she knew that at sunrise, when it was time to hide — it would weigh somewhat more because of her fatigue.

Why did I ever leave behind that gun Mister Ellis gave me? Why, why, why?

This time, Annie only briefly anguished over her forgetfulness on that front, which was somewhat of a comfort to her. She'd left her dorm room in a hurry, after all, and taking the time to get to the off-campus storage shed where she kept the Glock 17 along with all the furniture she intended to use in her future off-campus apartment just hadn't been in the cards.

University dorm rules were strict on that point: No guns in dorms, ever. Not even for her, with the so-called 'special privileges' she'd been extended by the school's president, at the urging of certain "highly placed personages," as they'd been called.

Even at the start of her dorm residency, the young woman knew she was being watched — if that was the word to use — by government security personnel, and she'd been put at ease by the thought. So, after a while, leaving the gun in storage hadn't disturbed her all that much. In fact, its existence soon took its place in her memory bank; easily recalled, but not really needed at the time.

Her tone of voice now reflected her chagrin, however.

"Yeah, look how that worked out, huh? Tripped yourself up again, Annie!"

The girl was hardly aware she'd even spoken aloud. The gun was gone, pure and simple, and no sense in crying about something she simply couldn't change.

Logic had moved in to force her irritation off the stage. Annie knew that some deep imperative, during her hurried departure, had put her on the road and only on the road. It was the one headed northeast, in fact, and she hadn't paused to question just why that was so. She'd only known she had to leave, and right smartly at that, so no side trip to the southwest and her storage shed.

Oh well!

Her dreams had been very colorful on the whole hiking thing: Avoid Washington, D.C. at all costs, for now, even if it would take her several days to trek completely around it, keeping only to the most lightly populated portions of the region.

Fortunately, since last year's terrorist attacks her travel route had become even more lightly populated, given the need for people to band together in larger towns and cities -- the ones not devastated by dirty bombs or conventional grade, though highly powerful, explosives, that is — to make it through the past year in the aftermath of those attacks.

Annie paused for a second to look around. Her feet were clad in her favorite hiking boots, and they made almost no sound on the packed dirt trail she'd been keeping to for the last two days. The road she was following had only recently seen electric lighting restored, something she wasn't entirely sure she welcomed now, given her need to stay as low-key and unknown as possible.

Happily, silence reigned supreme, as did the blackness of the night. Also, in the last half-hour of hiking, she'd only seen the headlights of a single small column of vehicles, one providing security up front and another providing it at the rear, and with three military cargo trucks in the center. The convoy had been headed to the southwest, likely with supplies for this or that town still struggling to feed and house not only its former residents — the ones who'd survived the attacks — but also a few more new ones, those being the people who'd managed to escape the cities or towns they'd lived in and which had been hit hard by the terrorists.

Annie knew that many people were either still largely holing up, fearful of any movement that might attract yet another attack, though none had ever come, or they were relocating as far away from their former homes as soon as they could, also out of that same fear.

Well, that just makes it easier for me to stay on foot, like I'm supposed to!

Her "orders" were clear: No hitchhiking, no buses, no ride sharing services — though those companies were still struggling to bounce back after the attacks and were also under government suspicion of having played a supporting role in getting some of the terrorists to their targets last year — no nothing but walking.

Worst of all, though? No smartphone or other electronic device that could be tracked!

Annie didn't know why she had to walk — though she did know why she'd smashed her smartphone and her smartwatch (she was now sporting a retro windup analog timepiece with a glow-in-the-dark dial and a green nylon and Velcro band) and had left behind her old MP3 player and everything else electronic in nature.

"All that stuff's easy to track" she repeated whenever she found herself reaching into her right rear pocket for her now-long-gone smartphone.

To be fair, cellular and internet service had only been intermittent since the attacks at any rate. Telecommunications companies — even with full government assistance — were still struggling hard to rebuild many of the cellphone towers the terrorists had blown up as well as the data centers they'd also destroyed, not to mention the scores of skilled technicians and scientists they'd killed as soon as they'd shown up to repair them.

She shuddered once more at the thought of the carnage.

Even as a little girl, though, Annie had never been anyone's idea of a fool, and over the past year — either in person or during video conferencing — she'd also received a fair bit of 'schooling' from her friend Mister Ellis, or from people he'd sent around to check in on her.

All those men and women — and most especially Mister Ellis, with whom she'd shared the experience of a lifetime... as horrifying as it had been in spots — had been scarily competent in "training her up," as they'd called what they were doing.

Why, it was almost as if Luke Ellis had somehow known she'd have to possess a few skills not related to her university studies.

Or maybe it was just the man's innate sense of caution and the attention he paid to preparedness?

Yes, that was it. Extreme preparedness. Couldn't be anything related to his electronic pal, Ozymandias, right?

Annie was truly undecided on that point, mostly because she still thought of the AI program as something related to the 1s and 0s she thought all computer programs were at heart. She simply didn't know enough about such things, though, to wrap her mind around what Ozymandias was as well as what it might possibly become. In truth, her interactions with Mister Ellis' "friend" — as he called the AI program — had mostly been perfunctory once it had accepted the ex-soldier's authority. Still, she could sense that it was taking care not to scare her or seem overly interested in her. She didn't know how she knew it, just that she did.

"Put that away, girl. You're no computer scientist, or a computer geek like Darren," the 18-year-old breathed softly as she once again started walking, satisfied she wasn't being tailed or observed.

The thought of her brother — plangent and sweet and even regretful, because of how he'd helped save her life during that long, horrible night a year ago — came back to her for a moment. Darren had always been smart with radios and electronics and computers in ways she knew she'd never be, and that was fine with her. Plus, he'd only gotten smarter as a different set of Mister Ellis' friends — along with a few men and women she'd instinctively known had been working for the government — tutored him on all manner of topics, including communications and computer science.

The 18-year-old still wasn't sure, though, if the effort was completely due to Luke Ellis' influence, or if the AI, Ozymandias, was also getting into the act. Again, she didn't know enough to figure out on her own just what was up on that front.

Put that to bed for now!

Annie's thoughts focused once again on more important matters, like not being found out and then sent back to school. She sensed, profoundly, that her ultimate purpose lay along a different path than her brother's, and that was that.

Back to business, Annie. Which is walking, right?

The young woman wasn't breathing hard — because she wasn't trying to hurry anywhere in particular right now — and so her words came out as an easy sub-vocalization that served to help her focus as she walked.

"Walked."

Not rode. Not flew or got on a bus — as if either form of transportation were available within a hundred miles of where she was anyway.

Just walked.

Well, that was fine too.

To be honest the thought of giving up and hailing a cab (*Same problem again, Annie! Not available anywhere!*), or even just hitching a ride, gave her the heebie-jeebies. As soon as the desire to find an easier way to travel sprang up, her insides twisted into knots, and she practically broke into a cold sweat. Those emotions warned her off, repeatedly, until she simply no longer pictured herself sitting on a bus or jumping into a car.

Just being cautious, which is something Luke Ellis taught me to always be whenever I'm out "in the field," right?

The 18-year-old chalked up the disquiet she felt to her intuition, and she recalled her friend Mister Ellis' frequent observation to her that she should always trust her intuition.

"I'd rather be lucky than good any day of the week, Annie" he'd said to her on various occasions, usually after showing her — to her endless chagrin — how easily she'd stumbled into a trap he'd designed.

"The word "luck" is just intuition dressed up in a more easily understood concept," the former Delta Force operator continued. "So, go with intuition if there's a choice between it or trying to rely on some skill you think you have in abundance to get you out of a fix you ended up in after you chose to ignore your intuition."

If it's good enough for Mister Ellis, it's good enough for me!

The young woman put her doubts to rest on at least the matter of walking, or hiking or whatever it was she was doing now, though the lack of a firearm still nagged at her, to tell the truth.

Looking down, she saw a survival knife of nice length riding in a lightweight scabbard attached to her belt. Unaware she was even doing it, her right hand briefly strayed to the pommel at the knife's hilt end. The blade itself — which she'd personally honed, again thanks to Mister Ellis' instruction — was razor-sharp. In the hands of someone not even all that well-trained, it could do great harm. The ex-soldier had frequently shown her just how deadly serious a knife could be even in comparison to a handgun.

Plenty of people armed with a gun had, in fact, gotten the worst of things against an assailant armed "only" with a knife, he'd taken care to explain.

"A knife isn't a toy, Annie. So, don't ever treat it like one." Luke Ellis' voice was like iron as the 18-year-old listened to him intently, wanting to both impress him with her seriousness and to learn what she could about the knife he'd presented her with during a visit he'd paid her and her brother and her parents during spring break earlier in the year.

She only learned later that he'd done so at her parents' insistence.

Maybe intuition was having its way with them, too? On occasion, she certainly thought so — especially when she was handling the knife.

Back then, when Mister Ellis had been explaining what a survival knife was and then training her in its different uses, something inside her — intuition, no doubt — urged her to listen closely to the former special operator and expert knife fighter. So, she learned what she could and practiced handling it whenever she had a chance.

"Who am I kidding? I have no idea how to do great harm with it," she mumbled.

Her rueful vocalizing intruded just momentarily on her mental meandering, and at just the right time. It brought her back to the here and now.

Time to focus again, right?

Still walking easily, the 18-year-old took stock of her immediate situation.

The night now held no mysteries for her, and she wondered just why that was until realization struck, which gave her some measure of clarity.

Hey, I'm just not having a problem picking things out at night!

Annie knew her recently acquired ability to peer into the black night — even in the most ebon-soaked parts of it — hadn't arrived all at once, either.

"Nope, it started coming to me when my dreams began," Annie muttered. It was only since she'd started her trek, though, that the ability had finally come on full force.

Just to be safe, though...

She halted and peered into the darkness, theatrically squinting her eyes and then opening them as wide as possible, seeking out any threat that might be headed her way.

Nothing, girl. So chill!

A barely suppressed laugh almost escaped her mouth right then, as the vision she'd just conjured came fully into focus. She was picturing herself sitting on a really big chunk of ice, literally chilling like a bottle of fine white wine in a fancy silver ice bucket, shaken — but not stirred — by the cold.

She also didn't know where the Secret Agent Guy reference had come from, but strongly suspected it was due to her brother Darren's influence. After all, they'd watched plenty of such movies together during her babysitting sessions over the years, back when both her parents had been working long, hard hours at the farmer's market they'd started up.

Focus, Annie!

Some form of mental discipline she didn't know she possessed kicked into high gear and instantly brought her back to reality. She exerted her senses once more, reaching out into the night in search of anything that might harm her.

Nothing.

Annie started walking again.

Her newfound discipline "out in the field" — as Mister Ellis would no doubt describe her current situation — came as a surprise to her. In truth, the soon-to-be-sophomore from the University of Virginia had never thought of herself as any sort of soldier or "field operator," a term she'd learned the meaning of from Luke Ellis, though she was aware enough to accept that she'd done "soldier things," as Darren had called it, last year.

Impressed by her quick thinking back then, her big ex-Army friend had even called what she'd done "some real John Wayne stuff," and "heroic" and "epic."

"I don't know about "heroic," Mister Ellis," Annie demurred, shaking her head when the big man had assured her of her heroism in the face of a seemingly implacable and deadly enemy. "I'm no hero, that's for sure."

"You're too modest, Annie," Luke Ellis replied. "You reached down inside, and you stayed put near Liz Elliott — who would have died then and there if you hadn't done what you did to protect her."

"No. Listen, I —"

Ellis cut her off.

"Annie, the world would have been lost if you hadn't been willing to stand — well, if you hadn't laid down in a very nice shooting position — and fight, there's no doubt about it. I wasn't close enough to get to you both anywhere near the time left before those two men would have done Liz in. And then they'd have killed you, of course," he added matter-of-factly.

Annie's mouth had snapped shut at his last observation.

Mister Ellis was right, not that it made her feel any better about her struggle against the two terrorists out to kill or capture the virologist, Miss Elliott. Though none of them had known it at the time, it turned out that the men pursuing them all had determined they would kill not only the lady scientist — whom Annie barely knew but had also come to like immensely after the woman had bucked up and determined she'd save the world from her creation — but also all of them, right down to her little brother.

Their flight away from the men and towards Mister Ellis' house — where he had all kinds of communications equipment — had been a race against death, both their own as well as that of all human life on Earth.

In the end, they succeeded. And almost all of them lived.

Well, that's some cold comfort right there, considering Miss Elliot died anyway, despite all you did!

Annie's inner voice sounded harsh and grating in the echo chambers of her mind.

You should put that thought away right now, girl! Elizabeth Elliot died, sure enough, but she made sure all of us would live!"

There was no denying it. For a few terrifying moments Annie knew she'd been the only one standing in the terrorists' way and stand she did. She never in a million years would have believed herself capable of such a feat, though. In fact, at times she still had difficulty believing she was the one who'd stood up to those men, delaying them long enough to prevent them from killing Liz Elliott before Mister Ellis (*and poor Darren!*) could get there to help.

But she had.

Her brother had paid a terrible emotional price, though, for his part in the final moments after she'd successfully fended off the attackers just long enough for Mr Ellis to get to them.

Whenever she thought back to the gunfight she'd had with those men, she found the words of one of the deadliest and most skilled Delta Force operators of the last two decades to be of some small comfort. He had pointed out something that she'd never thought much about whenever she was watching a war movie with her brother, where characters regularly engaged in great acts of courage and personal bravery.

"Standing and fighting doesn't mean you also aren't scared to death when you're doing it, Annie. It does mean, however, that you're willing to fight and die, if need be, to do the right or necessary thing. That's what courage really is."

Annie was doubtful. "I don't know, Mr. Ellis. I —"

"Look at me, Annie." Mister Ellis' voice was commanding and yet also comforting at the same time. "Do you think I want to die?"

"Of course not, Mr. Ellis. I know that" she pronounced confidently. They were on solid ground here, and so she focused on her big Army friend's words.

"No, I don't want to die," Luke said to his young friend, who possessed seemingly endless amounts of personal courage —

though he also knew she didn't know it just yet. "I want to live to a ripe old age and spend my golden years tending to a really big garden."

"Seriously, Mr. Ellis? You want to be a gardener?" Annie couldn't keep skepticism out of her voice. She arched her eyebrows as she examined the former Delta Force operator's face for any sign that he was putting her on.

"What do you think, Annie?" Luke's slow, deliberate wink gave the game away.

The girl's laugh echoed in the air of her living room, as the ex-soldier also shrugged his shoulders.

"I think you want to be a gardener as much as I want to learn all about those crazy radios your friends gave my brother, that's what I think!" Annie laughed once more, this time with feeling.

"Well, you got me there, young lady. I don't think gardening is in my future."

Now the ex-soldier's voice became somber. His young friend stopped laughing in response, the air devoid of the tinkling crystal-like sounds she'd created.

"My point still stands, though, Annie, so listen carefully."

"Yes, Mister Ellis." The young woman's voice was low, with no hint of humor in it.

"Of course, I don't want to die," Luke said, his voice softly mournful and reflective. "Here's what I know, though, Annie. I know that every time I fight, I just might lose my life in the process, but I do it anyway."

It was Annie's turn to speak, and her voice was barely perceptible.

"I just don't think I have that strength, Mr. Ellis. I know I did something last year, but I don't know how I did it, or why."

"And that's what makes you brave, Annie. You fought because you knew you had to. You fought to protect and defend, even though you were scared to death, right? Were you scared, Annie?" Ellis stared into his young friend's face intently, waiting for her response.

"I was scared out of my mind, Mister Ellis. That's why I don't know if I could ever do something like that again." This time, Annie's voice sounded harsh from fright as she relived yet again what she'd experienced fighting those two men.

"Well, let me clue you in on a little secret, young lady." Ellis paused, waiting for the young woman to respond. She didn't fail him.

"What? What secret, Mister Ellis?" Her soldier friend and *de facto* protector had now gained her complete and undivided attention. Her own jumbled thoughts washed away in anticipation.

"I'm sometimes frightened whenever I do what I'm trained to do. Heck, everyone I've ever known in my line of work has been frightened at times when they've had to take action."

Annie's face betrayed her disbelief.

"Uh-uh. No way, Mr. Ellis."

"Yes way, Annie." Ellis thought the turn of phrase in response to someone uttering "No way" was funny. The young woman apparently thought it was as well, because her laughter once again pealed in the air.

"Stop, Mr. Ellis! You're making me laugh!" The Delta Force warrior couldn't help himself, and he began laughing in response.

For a few seconds, the 18-year-old's laughter — small and melodic in contrast to her giant-sized Army friend's big, bright and booming laughter in response — filled the Dedham house.

Annie's parents, both in the kitchen preparing dinner for themselves and the man they knew had played a vitally important role in keeping their children safe last year, smiled briefly. Lately, their daughter had seemed troubled by whatever it was she'd seen or done during that long, horrible day and night she and their son had gone missing. For his part, Darren was also introspective on occasion, though he seemed more adaptable, and his moments of brooding introspection were nowhere near as intense as Annie's currently were.

They both had to admit it: They were profoundly glad to hear their daughter laugh, and so were also glad that Luke Ellis was working to pull her out of her funk. Contented for the moment, at least, they turned their attention once again to the dinner menu.

In the living room, Annie's voice grew serious as she asked him the obvious question.

"You really were frightened last year?"

"I sure was, Annie." Luke was speaking the truth, and the girl could see it in his eyes. "Why wouldn't I have been?" The ex-soldier paused to wait for an answer from his young friend.

"I don't know why you'd have been scared, Mister Ellis, because you sure didn't seem like you were." Annie was certain of that point. If the Army man had been scared, he sure didn't show it at the time.

"Oh, I was scared alright, but I knew I had to do the right thing. Plus, I was well-trained. And this training — or lack thereof — is where we are now when it comes to you."

Luke fell silent once again, waiting.

"What do you mean, Mister Ellis? I mean, I hope I'll be as brave as you, even though you say you were frightened. That's fine. But what do you mean by "training?""

If I'd only known!

Walking along the trail, Annie remembered that her friend hadn't said anything. Instead, he'd reached into his own daypack and brought out the Glock 17 (*the one still sitting in my storage shed!*) and the survival knife now riding on the right side of her waist.

And then training began. That very day. Right after a fine dinner prepared by her parents.

Again, it was as if Luke Ellis had known that, someday, she might need to take a journey and that she might not have a firearm handy when she did.

So, here she was, doing her best imitation of a combat infantryman out on a night patrol. Or, maybe like one of those U.S. Army special operations soldiers who'd loudly proclaim "We own the night!" whenever a bit of motivation was needed, perhaps near the end of a grueling 25-mile overland training march in full combat gear they called "battle rattle."

Annie paused and looked around her, as she'd been taught by Luke Ellis. She was trying mightily not to make a sound. But why?

"I have no idea! Maybe my dreams did this?" Annie's muttered exclamation hardly stirred a molecule in the night air, but she heard it clearly enough in her own mind, and she was comforted by it.

She reflected once again, only this time while concentrating on the real world in front of her as well as on her "past life," as she referred to everything that had happened to her before last year's horrendous events. The 18-year-old knew she wasn't one of those "girly girls," either, as she referred to certain of her female friends. In her opinion, they seemed way too fond of pink clothing and the lacy and frilly accessories that typically come with such stuff.

Even their cars are pink!

The Bruce Springsteen song about a pink Cadillac popped into Annie's mind at that moment, and she nearly burst out laughing at the thought of one of her friends driving such a car around, but she quickly pushed it away, saddened by the realization, yet again, that some of their parents — if they worked or were in Washington, D.C. or the nearby suburbs or especially if they were in Crystal City, just south of the Pentagon — had never made it home to their children because of what had happened to them on that horrible day and night last year.

They were gone forever, and her friends were suffering.

Annie felt for a second as if the doom loop she constantly fought against had returned.

Stop it!

To escape the possibility of a misery-filled reverie, she exerted her hearing once more. If her ears had been capable of twitching like a jungle cat's, they would have just then.

Nothing.

Taking stock, Annie knew she was a young woman out on a hiking trail in the dead of night, with no sign of help near enough to aid her if she needed it.

Stop that too!

Instead, she forced herself to focus on the darkness bearing down all around her, reaching out to look for any sign of danger.

Still nothing. Not even a breeze stole through the nearby treetops.

All was quiet.

"Get moving, then." This time, she uttered her command just slightly louder than normal, now sure that no one was around to hear it.

Annie Dedham (*woodland warrior and disciple of Luke Ellis!*) began walking, slowly but calmly making her way ever closer to her destination.

I need to get five miles in tonight, but I'll settle for three.

Having already traveled so far and so quickly, three miles was now her nightly minimum and she'd stuck to that metric with unwavering determination.

In addition to Luke Ellis, Annie had also been schooled by a couple of his colleagues — they'd called themselves "Bruiser" and "Crispy." She knew that in cases where completion of the mission had priority over the time it might take to complete it, overland movement to "the objective" — which was what Mister Ellis called the thing to be accomplished in any mission — could be as slow and as measured, and unseen, as was needed to get the job done.

Within reason, of course.

She knew she had to average a minimum number of hours walking on a nightly basis to cover the minimum number of miles needed to get to where she needed to be by the time she needed to be there. Luckily (*and I'd rather be lucky than good, right?*), the 18-year-old was well within that average right now.

"How do I know that, though?" Annie put the question to herself and awaited an answer. After all, she had no GPS, or anything else electronic, on her — not even a simple pedometer — and so had to trust in something to assure her she would make her ultimate destination in time.

The answer soon came, as it always did.

Why, my dreams tell me. Duh!

Annie had no doubts about the authenticity and veracity of what she'd been learning in her dreams. She now knew where she needed to go, though she hadn't yet learned just why she needed to be there in the first place.

"All in good time, Annie" she'd heard the voice in the clouds above — the ones that decorated the skyscape in her dreams — tell her.

I guess I'm one of those true believers now, right?

Right, indeed.

Heaving an audible sigh, the young woman calculated her rate of travel as she moved down the trail, fingering the little pace counting device — Mister Ellis called them "Ranger beads" — affixed to the right strap of her daypack. Currently, the path bent more to the northwest than the northeast, but only for the next night or so. Its general direction, according to her map, was always north and east. She also knew it would be even more so once she successfully detoured around the District of Columbia and arrived at a point just to its north.

Initially, her dreams had told her she could make as many miles per night as she needed to quickly approach the Washington, D.C. Beltway (*and Loudoun County, my home!*), and for some reason she'd averaged a good 30 miles of walking during the increasingly long August nights. Warm they still were, but the Earth's tilt after the summer solstice was gradually shortening the days and lengthening those nights.

That's fine with me!

She slept, ate and cleaned up during the day and walked all night. She didn't know why, but she also hardly felt tired after doing so. Even her muscle soreness had disappeared after the second night of walking. She thanked Mr. Ellis for his advice on always having a pair of broken-in hiking boots available, too.

"Just in case, Annie" the retired military special operations expert said to her. "Just in case."

Reflecting on the calamity of the previous year, any bit of humor the young woman could find in her present situation was welcome. Stopping once again to look behind her (*always "check six," right Mister Ellis?*), Annie couldn't see anyone tailing her, nor could she hear any cars approaching from either direction.

Without knowing she was doing it she also neatly sidestepped a small dip that would have snapped several dry twigs if she'd stumbled into it. Before last year, she would have walked right into that noisy little hole, she knew.

"But not now, right?" Again, her voice was inaudible, or maybe a subvocal utterance than anything else.

To take her mind off her need for stealth, she instead mentally reviewed — for the thousandth time — the contents of her daypack.

In it, she knew she could pull out a handy travel-sized laminated Rand McNally Road atlas, a couple of cross-country maps — sufficient to get her to her ultimate destination — and a Suunto MC2 compass to help ease her night travels. Mister Ellis had shown her how to use both the maps and the compass, and quickly at that.

"You're a natural at this, Annie," he'd said to her as he showed her how to always stay on the proper travel course using just a map and a compass. To her complete and utter surprise, the 18-year-old really had become adept after just a scant few lessons from her soldier friend.

"Really coming in handy now, girl," Annie heard herself say to no one in particular.

SNAP!

The sound of a twig, or maybe a small tree branch, breaking in two in the woods off to her right, froze her in place.

She immediately halted, careful not to turn suddenly or crane her head in one direction or another.

Annie carefully sniffed the air around her, super senses reaching outward, listening and watching for anything that was moving itself into a position to harm her. Heart pounding in her chest, the 18-year-old slowly — ever so slowly — crouched down and took several steady, deep breaths. She almost immediately felt her heart rate begin to slow, even if just slightly at first.

"Once you go to the ground and freeze, never forget that the eyes pick out sudden movements, Annie, so don't move quickly or suddenly if you can at all help it."

Luke's voice still echoed in the 18-year-old's mind. Yet more sage wisdom from "The Master," a title she'd bestowed upon the former soldier using a fake-reverential voice that she'd picked up from watching a seemingly endless parade of Chinese and Japanese martial arts movies with her brother, Darren. He called all of them "karate movies."

If ever there was a person who was the farthest thing from being "The Master," though, it was Luke Ellis. At least with her, he was an endless fountain of patience and encouragement, but never too high or too low in his teaching style.

So here she was now, checking her "six" (she knew that meant "the area behind you," or the six o'clock position if you were facing 12 o'clock) and waiting to see what she might see, basically.

While she waited, she counted the seconds and mentally reviewed, once again, just what else was in her pack. Various other items included a couple of plastic bottles of water — filled to the top so that they wouldn't slosh, with each wrapped in a piece of cloth. There were also several energy bars and a small but bright flashlight.

Strangely, though, she hadn't needed it since the other night.

At the bottom of the pack sat a lightweight camouflage-pattern poncho liner that balled up into the size of a fist, a change of clothes and clean socks, several small disposable lighters and some very sturdy and strong, but thin rope that Mister Ellis had called "550 cord." These items were joined by two pieces of plastic sheeting that would make a lean-to large enough to shelter her and a couple of those thin thermal blankets that were silver on one side and flat green on the other.

Because it was still summer and the nights had been warm, Annie hadn't needed to use those blankets, and she planned on being at her destination long before she would have to rely on them.

"Still glad I have them, though."

Annie didn't even hear her muttered voice because it was so low. Just a mere whisper, even. Inside, she was glad she had the entire daypack. It had come in quite handy so far.

It didn't contain a firearm, though. Like the now devoutly wished-for Glock 17.

She did have her survival knife, though she prayed she wouldn't need to use it anytime soon.

"Honey, I think Mister Ellis is right," she remembered first her father and then her mother telling her after they'd talked with the former soldier for several minutes before turning their attention back to their daughter. "You should take the pack." They'd already made sure she'd taken the knife and had begun training with it.

Annie smiled at the memory of them both nodding their heads at the same time after they'd dispensed their advice. She knew her parents were no fools, and that they also wanted to make sure their daughter always had a means to make her way back to them if, God forbid, something like the national calamity the terrorists had instigated the year before ever occurred again. Her dad had even contributed four gold coins, which Annie had carefully hidden in various secret pockets in various innocuous looking seams on her clothing.

"Why would I need one of these packs, Mister Ellis?" she recalled herself saying when he'd shown her a picture of one and all its contents. She'd still been skeptical, after all. "I mean, I'll be at college and in a dorm room, right?"

"Do you have a crystal ball that can tell the future, Annie?"

"Ummmm, no. Of course not."

"Did we have a crystal ball last year, right there in your parents' market when the terrorists attacked Lucketts hoping to grab Liz Elliott?"

"No."

Annie could see the point Luke Ellis was making. She couldn't predict the future. No one could. She didn't even think Ozymandias, the AI program, was capable of such a thing.

"So, take this bugout bag or call it a survival bag or daypack or whatever you'd like, and then learn how to use it." The retired Army man had been adamant on that point, and Annie knew he was right.

Reality check.

Yet one more time now that I've been shown why I should never doubt Mister Ellis!

Annie's thoughts and dreams and memories were all she had right now, and she reviewed them for probably the millionth time over the last year as she remained crouched, slightly off the trail and in some high vegetation, frozen in place like a statue. She watched and listened for any hint of movement or the bare murmur of a sound.

Sighing inwardly, she thought back, also for the millionth time, to the events of the year before, when she and her brother Darren, and Mister Ellis and Alec Holman — who'd been a Loudoun County deputy sheriff at the time, but who was now a newly minted FBI agent with a plum assignment to the Bureau's Los Angeles field office — had been pursued and nearly killed by those terrorists.

Those men, at least initially, badly wanted to capture their most important group member, poor Elizabeth Elliott.

Tragically, the terrorists had killed the lady scientist in the end, though not before she and Mister Ellis and her brother Darren, plus Alec Holman had gained enough time to cancel Armageddon.

Annie still cried to herself at the memory of the poor, doomed woman's passing.

Enough of that! Save it for later!

The 18-year-old felt her spine stiffen, and so waited patiently in the dark. Her right hand had once again strayed to the hilt of her survival knife. She missed her parents, her brother, all of them. She was also acutely aware of the surrounding night and could hear the sweep hand of her watch making its way around the dial, though she knew that was impossible. The noise created by its movement would be all but imperceptible to normal human hearing, at least outdoors and with all the normal sounds such an environment offered.

So, what was her situation?

She'd been "on the road" — as she thought of her journey — for a few days now. Until tonight, she'd even covered much ground.

Now, though?

Well, now she might have encountered her first potential obstacle, though she couldn't explain why she also wasn't surprised.

Annie sensed something just then, and it descended over her vision. Or maybe something was making her vision amazingly powerful? Suddenly, she also felt as if she was growing stronger, fitter, faster than she'd ever been in her life.

Annie's eyes strayed to her hands.

No change. They were as steady as a rock, though, when just a year ago they'd have shaken like a leaf on a tree.

She also felt her heart beating strongly, but slowly and steadily, in her chest.

Are the pupils in my eyes dilating?

Annie felt like they were. It even felt like her bones and muscles were somehow growing stronger, though how that could possibly be true would have mystified even the world's greatest scientists.

The young woman let a long, slow and languorous sigh escape her lips. It was almost enticing in its sound. If something or someone was out there searching for her, the sigh would certainly guide them directly to her.

At that moment, she couldn't have cared less.

In fact, it was what she wanted, though she didn't take even a millisecond to consider just why that might be.

Now.

Now, she could see through the darkness as if she were sitting in a stadium lit up for the legions of fans attending their hometown baseball team's first night game of the season.

The old Annie — the one from before the terrorist attacks — was gone, at least for the moment.

In the old Annie's place, a predator now waited.

She sighed again, as if frightened of what might be out there.

It was all pure artifice, of course. The young woman felt no trepidation. Only eager anticipation.

SNAP!

It was nearly time. Annie tensed up just slightly, but not out of fright or fear.

No, her emotions were not so complicated, though they were blood-tinged.

It was kill or be killed. This other Annie instinctively knew what had to be done, too.

Watching, waiting. Waiting, watching. A slight lick of the lips. A slow, predatory smile.

It's time.

The next sound that echoed in the night was the pattern created by dual pairs of assault boot-covered feet rushing towards her. Perhaps the men wearing them meant to deliver a killing blow or perhaps they intended to capture her. The 18-year-old didn't know, and she certainly didn't care.

The sound of those feet – of potential death, really - hadn't surprised Annie in the least. In her mind's eye, she'd seen and heard it all before it even occurred. Instantly, her mind became a blur of motion, all echoing sound and fury, enough to shake the very pillars of Heaven to its foundations. And then it, too, became as still as the night air.

A funeral pall of blackness covered her. She'd become a creature of the night.

Look at your blade.

Annie looked down. Her survival knife — wickedly razor sharp along its entire edge, right up through its belly — was carbonized and dull black. It soon became soaked in a much different and thicker color, though.

I Am Become Death

The attackers — two former Russian Spetsnaz special forces soldiers, both possessed of an uncommonly brutal nature — had killed probably a thousand people over the past decade. Their victims had sometimes been enemy soldiers, whose lives they'd avidly taken during their time spent as fighters working for the infamous Dietrich Group, a mercenary organization with a great many unsavory types populating its ranks. There'd also been more than a few civilians, though, which was something they freely admitted to themselves, usually after a bottle of the best Russian vodka.

A contract was a contract, however, and Ilya and Dmitri were all about contracts. Especially lucrative ones, as this one most certainly was. It had been the most stunningly lucrative they'd ever been offered, in fact, and it came from an anonymous client who'd found them through another kind of internet, the one known as the Dark Web.

To be sure, most of their work came from a very select group of professional brokers who populated certain sections of the Russian and Ukrainian underworld.

Those men — and the lone woman who'd taken up her late husband's vocation after he'd suddenly passed away from a three-pack-per-day cigarette habit and a near obsession with vodka — all knew what would happen to them if they ever sold out the pair: Certain death. Such certainty had so far immunized the duo from a classic Eastern Slav double-cross.

Normally, the Dark Web-based side of the pair's business was good for maybe $20,000 or $30,000 per job. Usually, it was an angry or greedy spouse or a jilted lover who would contract for their services, with complete anonymity on both sides assured by the nature of that seamy side of the internet, where payment was always made in nearly untraceable cryptocurrencies of various types and kinds.

The duo's fee doubled, though, if they had to carry out a hit in the United States.

Both Ilya and Dmitri liked the country well enough, but getting into it and then back out of it after a job took a bit more effort than was needed to operate on the Continent, where various European Union member states had agreed to allow passport-free and unfettered travel between them all. Such conditions made for a field day of easy and nearly anonymous travel for the hitmen. As far as professional killers went, they were also two of the best, and smooth and easy were what they usually looked for.

In other words, easy work was found in Europe, not in America.

This hit, though?

Well, it was exceptional, and most definitely worth the effort they'd have to expend on carrying it out in the United States, not far from the country's capital, Washington, D.C., in fact.

"Exceptional" did not apply to the former Spetsnaz soldiers' future victim, of course. No, it was the fee.

The client had already paid them $5 million — via their preferred cryptocurrency, which was now sitting in an anonymous offshore bank account — with the promise of $5 million more in the same cryptocurrency once they'd killed the girl, with proof of death sent to a different Dark Web server than the one they used to operate their "contracting service."

And so, Ilya and Dmitri had hastened to America, there to lie in wait in the middle of the night — as they'd been instructed to — alongside a hiking path lying to the east of Washington, D.C. proper. Neither did the men particularly care about just why the girl had to die. From the photos they'd been supplied, she looked maybe 17 or 18 years of age, but they'd killed people somewhat younger than that, and of both sexes, in the past.

No big deal, in other words. Personally, however, they refused any jobs involving people 15 years of age or younger, but that was only because they had to draw the line somewhere and such jobs were rare. Finally, hits on children and teens were more difficult to pull off because the authorities would often expend unbelievable resources to run down their killers.

Why risk having the American FBI coordinate with Interpol and Russia's FSB and every other national police agency?

No, at this stage in their professional — and currently enriching — lives, Ilya and Dmitri simply didn't need the hassle.

So here they were in the U.S. It was the best-paying job in their lives and the one that would allow them both to retire from the business entirely. Such riches were worth coming to America for, they conceded after discussing the wisdom of carrying out a hit on U.S. soil.

That the two Russians were killers, pure and simple, didn't even need saying. They also weren't animals, though. They'd agreed to dispatch the girl as quickly and as painlessly as possible with their NRS-2 knives, long a preferred personal and professional stabbing weapon of Spetznaz troopers.

Yes, a quick stab by both in just the right places on her body and she'd almost immediately go to her heavenly reward.

Such a swift end was a mercy, Dmitri reminded himself, because he and his partner had sometimes been instructed to bring death to a "mark" — he loved the old American hitman's word for the soon-to-be-victim of a professional assassin — only after agonizing and brutal torture, and in the bloodiest way possible, with one or the other of the pair recording the session on video for the benefit of the client who'd contracted them.

Neither of the men liked carrying out their work in such a manner, though. But, once again, a contract was a contract.

Now, it was time to go to work.

Ilya and Dmitri moved toward Annie as one, like a pair of African hyenas preparing to take down an infant gazelle or zebra.

They could see the girl was obviously frightened out of her mind, because she'd remained crouched and frozen in place despite having had to have seen the duo rushing toward her, there to deliver her to whichever god it was she prayed to — *Or no god at all, this being America,* thought Ilya, the more sardonic of the pair.

That killer hesitated just slightly for a second, momentarily fascinated by what he was seeing through his night optical device, which eliminated darkness almost in its entirety.

What are the girl's eyes doing?

Ilya was genuinely puzzled, though that didn't stop him from pressing his attack. He was nearly looming over the girl from her front, but he waited for his partner to strike the first blow, as they'd mutually agreed while moving themselves into position just before sundown.

He could see that Dmitri was also slowing down as he neared the young woman from her left side. Normally, the men preferred to use silenced pistols when they did close quarters work such as this, because they didn't like to get so close to a victim if that person was out in the open and able to sense an attack. The pair were adept at the Mozambique Drill, after all, and they were always avid about using it.

The client was adamant in this case, however. The girl had to be taken out along this trail and at this date and time. Knives only, too. No guns.

Well, $5 million bought a lot of cooperation from a hitman, or a pair of them.

So, once again, here they were. About to administer the final ending to a girl they didn't care about and wouldn't remember even having killed after six months or so had passed. If any sort of conscience existed in either man, it had long ago been buried under a ton of money.

Knives it was, and any slight breach in their normal protocol be damned. The mark was just a girl, both men had assured themselves, so how difficult would she really be when it came to ending her life?

Back to business, Ilya!

The girl's eyes. Were they fluttering?

They'd been black, but now they're white. What's going on here?

During his headlong rush towards her, all while Dmitri moved swiftly to take her from the side, Ilya thought he saw the poor, frightened girl's eyes roll up into their sockets, perhaps in shock or maybe because of some sort of hysterical catatonia.

She knows her doom has arrived!

Maybe she was doing her best imitation of a deer caught in the headlights of a fast-approaching semi-truck?

Deliver her now, Ilya!

The Russian heard his partner Dmitri grunt as he landed a killing blow against the young woman, who was all of 17 or maybe 18 years of age.

Or had he delivered a blow?

O der'mo! Dimitri is down!

Somehow, the tiny and defenseless girl — right in front of Ilya's still disbelieving eyes — had spun to her left, her whole body a blur, and confronted his bull-necked and rock-solid partner of nearly 183 centimeters height and 95 kilograms weight.

Ilya couldn't believe it, but there she was, sorting out poor Dmitri in a flash. And she'd used some sort of blade concealed in her right hand!

The girl's right arm and hand reached out, racing across Dmitri's throat in an instant, and Ilya could smell the spray of blood coming from his partner, who was now lying crumpled on the ground, his last desperate struggle for life dying away in a wet gurgle and growing puddle of dark, dark liquid.

The former Spetsnaz senior sergeant didn't know of anyone, anywhere — not even the finest and strongest of military warriors — who possessed the strength and skill to deliver such a fierce killing blow with a mere knife, no matter how finely honed and sharp it might be. Perhaps with a sword, much as Japanese samurai warriors had done so in times long ago, but not with any sort of knife this little girl could wield.

Horror! The girl KICKED Dimitri! HARD! Is that his HEAD tumbling through the air? Bozhe moy, it is!

The night air smelled bright and coppery as a gush of arterial blood from the Russian assassin's headless neck washed over the dry ground. Deprived of his body's most vital fluid, the man's dying heart gave up for good.

Only Ilya's professionalism now carried him forward. He was determined to finish the job he and his partner had promised to complete. He was also enraged, and so a favored Russian pejorative, frequently used to describe female dogs, escaped his lips in a scream.

"*Suka*! You'll pay for what you did to poor Dmitri!"

The surviving Russian pulled up short and quickly assessed the tactical situation. Amazingly, the girl just stood there, waiting for him to decide what to do. No running away, no screaming or pleading for mercy.

Nothing but white, fluttering eyes.

She's a devil, a d'yavol! What were we sent here to kill? Did an experiment gone wrong escape from some American laboratory, and our client is trying to eliminate its existence before they're found out?

It didn't matter. She — or it or whatever — had to die. If only for Dmitri and what she'd done to him.

Stay out of range of the devil's knife! She can't match you physically!

Ilya was now aware of her skill with a blade. She wouldn't be able to do to him what she'd done to his poor partner!

Chagrin washed over him in waves, momentarily replacing his rage.

Dima just underestimated the creature, that's all. So did I, for that matter!

In his grief, Ilya used the diminutive form of his late partner's name, mourning his loss. Still… the $5 million was now all his, and he was determined to make it a cool $10 million, because Dmitri's share would be his as well.

Only after I send this devil back to hell, that is!

The contract killer could see his late partner lying lifeless on the ground. He'd quickly toppled over once the she-devil had struck him.

Annie — this new version… call it Annie 2.0 — moved slightly to her right and the surviving Russian's left. The dead hitman's head was several feet away.

She casually walked over to it and kicked it out of the way.

Ilya screamed at her in fury.

"Insult of insults, *suka!* Now you die!"

With that, he sprang forward, expecting the girl to back up as he pressed his attack, his NRS-2 knife sweeping from side to side and racing outward, hoping to force her back on her heels. He knew he was much larger than her and that he also had a much longer reach.

The Russian's knife swept only through thin air. Once more, he screamed in frustration. The girl wasn't in front of him or falling back. He couldn't see her on the ground at his feet, or anywhere else in front of him, for that matter.

"Where are you, Devil?!? Show yourself!"

Ilya's deadly knife slashed the warm night air yet again, seeking flesh and bone.

The creature wasn't there.

Sick realization slowly began to steal into the Russian killer's mind. If the girl wasn't in front of him, then where had she gone?

Of course.

She was behind him.

A resigned sigh escaped Ilya's lips.

So, is this it? Yes, I think it is.

He had to try.

The once-proud Spetsnaz warrior (*and you should have stayed in Spetsnaz, you fool! At least your death would have been honorable if you had!*) attempted to twist away and regain a solid defensive position.

Idiot. You know it's already too late!

A series of icy, yet also white-hot lances sliced across his spinal column. He fell to the ground in a nerveless heap.

As he lay in the American dirt, wishing he'd at least had the good sense to die on the soil of the *Rodina,* sacred Russia, the ex-solider, ex-mercenary and now ex-assassin exerted all his rapidly diminishing senses trying to solve his last mystery.

What is that devil-spawn doing now?

In his increasingly dim vision, Ilya thought he could see the girl standing in front of him, tilting her head to the left and then to the right, as if she were some sort of video camera, collecting data for a computer program. It was almost as if her eyes were dual white lenses capturing every microsecond of their encounter for later analysis.

His last earthly vision was of the girl, knife now cleaned and sheathed, standing casually beside him.

With that, the female turned on her heels and walked purposefully down the hiking trail once again, heading towards some final ending Ilya would never witness.

For the Russian, all became blackness composed of utter nothingness.

CHAPTER ELEVEN

From the World News Network's "The World's on Fire" Website, Breaking News Page:

Massive Explosion Near Gettysburg, PA Result of Natural Gas Leakage from Nearby "Bootleg Fracking Operation," Feds Say

"Nonsense," remarked UFO expert George Tsouko. "An alien spacecraft obviously crashed at the site and the federal government is covering it up!" U.S. Geographic Survey and EPA scientists scoffed at that claim as well as the many conspiracy theories popping up about the blast. (Click here to learn more!)

U.S. Recalls Ambassador to China for "Consultations" With President, State Department

China calls recent U.S. breakthroughs in stealth bombers, anti-satellite and anti-missile defenses and hypersonic offensive missiles a "dire provocation" that could lead to war between the two nations. The country's president, Tan Jianhong, increased China's defense posture towards the U.S. as a result. "We won't be bullied by China," replied the American president, Thomas Masterson. (Click here to learn more!)

CIA believes China is Sneaking Fentanyl into the U.S. to Use as a WMD

The U.S. Central Intelligence Agency believes Communist China may attempt to use fentanyl, an extremely powerful synthetic opioid, as a weapon of mass destruction against the United States. "Just one kilogram — about 2.2 pounds — would be enough to kill 500,000 people," U.S. Drug Enforcement Agency chief Dorothy Richardson told Congress last month. Sources say that, unlike a standard chemical poison dumped into a city's water supply, fentanyl would likely lose none of its lethality due to dilution. "Put about 115 pounds of fentanyl into the water supply reservoir system, and you could kill 25 million people, more than the population of New York State," Richardson closed. (Click here to learn more!)

USAF B-21 Raider Stealth Bomber Rumored Ready for First Flight Years Early, Maybe with Ordnance

Once thought to be years away from its first test flight, the United States Air Force's newest and most advanced stealth bomber, the B-21 Raider — which is equipped with a futuristic artificial intelligence control system — is now ready for full operational service, sources with close knowledge of the development program have revealed. "It's no wonder the Chinese are freaking out," one source told us. "They have nothing, and I mean nothing, that can detect it. It could literally rain nuclear destruction on their country at any time and any place and remain totally unseen." (Click here to learn more!)

Ambush

Bump!

Luke Ellis, leader of his now-diminished deep undercover "special projects" team, awoke with a start as the van he was riding in crossed over a bridge that just the year before had almost been blown up by terrorists. Stretching a little to work out a few kinks, he shook away what cobwebs had developed during his brief nap and then began to take stock of things.

First things first.

Suppressing a slight yawn, he mentally reviewed the fight they'd gotten themselves into, and then out of, just a few hours ago on this same interstate highway. Back then, the sun hadn't created even the merest smear of light on the horizon, and the gun battle had been conducted in the full blackness of night.

Not much of a fight. Those men hardly knew what had hit them.

That was the way things invariably went whenever Ozymandias was around to help. The AI program spoke to Luke and the enemy died, simple as that.

Listening to his inner voice, Ellis also didn't feel the slightest bit of disappointment that the three men they'd had to kill barely had time to bring their own weapons to bear on the panel van he and his men were riding in before they'd been erased from existence. That didn't mean Luke didn't understand how his adversaries must have felt, though. After all, he and Crispy and their two comrades — Killdozer and Hardcase — had stolen this van right out from under their noses.

The three dead Chinese had been the drivers and security element for the hit team sent to kill Luke and his own men, though that team had also largely failed in the effort.

To the anger and amazement of those soldiers, the Americans walked in and then drove away with one of their vehicles.

Such an insult simply couldn't be borne. Plus, their orders from Defense Minister Guo had been clear: Every one of the Americans had to die. If they didn't, then the repercussions for their families back in China would be severe. Guo hadn't even mentioned that, however. It was just the way things had always been done in the Middle Kingdom.

So, off the three Chinese soldiers went in one of the other vans, thanking their good fortune that the Americans hadn't had time to disable them as they'd made their getaway.

Well, their good fortune ran out soon enough, didn't it?

Luke was sure the dead men — both the ones back in the compound, with Bruiser there to watch over them before both he and they were incinerated in a flash of immense heat — and the ones who'd pursued them would have felt deeply disappointed in their failure, too.

Disappointed, that is, if any of them had managed to survive the attack. Which none had, of course.

"Sucks to be them," Killdozer — all 6 feet, 3 inches and 280 muscular pounds of him — had remarked as he stepped among the bodies strewn around their wrecked and shattered (*and supposedly ultra-secret!*) facility, using his encrypted smartphone to take photos of each of the attackers.

Unsurprisingly, no one on the hit team had possessed anything resembling identification papers or other documents that might provide a clue as to just who they really were or what their mission in Pennsylvania, near the historic Gettysburg battlefield, might have been. The only thing of interest about any of them, in fact, was that one of them had a couple of packs of a popular American brand of cigarette stowed away in the cargo pockets of his tactical pants.

"Thought he was going to light one up to celebrate once he and his buddies killed us all," Luke pronounced to his men as they stood over the dead man. "Smoke 'em if you got 'em," right?" Ellis smiled just slightly at his joke.

"Looks like their fingerprints and their teeth and whatnot have also been physically altered Boss," Hardcase remarked. "You know how it is with these Chinese Special Forces types, right?"

They all nodded knowingly. Smokers some of the Chinese might have been, but in death they'd managed to preserve a fair bit of operational security.

It was nearly time. Looking at the luminous dial on his watch, Luke decided to wrap things up.

"Yup. Just get whatever we can from them," he replied in a

clipped voice, looking at Hardcase and Killdozer while Crispy took care of their deceased comrade, Bruiser.

The force of the grenade their friend had thrown himself on — all to ensure his buddies would live — had made a mess of the front of his torso. Looking at his brother in arms, Luke felt a profound sadness momentarily creep over him.

The big man — Harland Coates, of Jasper, Arkansas, whose call sign had been "Bruiser" — hadn't been wearing body armor and there'd been no time to don it in the chaos of the attack. It was clear from his actions, though, that his friend knew what was going to happen when he jumped on the grenade.

He gave as good as he got. Even better than he got, in fact, so salute him and then let him go!

Ellis' inner voice had once again stepped in to bring him back to reality. They had a lot to do, and they couldn't afford to let either the dead attackers or Bruiser slow them down.

Reading his boss's mind, Crispy chimed in.

"Let's pick up the pace, guys," he said, glancing at Hardcase and Killdozer. "We have to move out soon and grab one of those vans and be well away from this place before any county Mounties decide it's safe to investigate." The last thing Luke and the other three men on his team — now sadly missing an integral member - wanted was police attention or, worse, any "federal entanglements."

Yeah, I imagine Masterson and his people are having a fit right about now!

Ellis knew there was no time to reestablish communications with President Masterson. That would have to wait until some currently unknowable time in the future.

Radio silence it was, then.

So far, Oz the AI program was telling him in his ear that law enforcement and other first responders as well as the local populace were all staying well away from the area out of fear of additional explosions. The story, quickly planted by Ozymandias, was that a surreptitious fracking operation had opened fissures in the ground through which natural gas was escaping, with small explosions being the result, though it was highly likely that more than a few enormous ones were going to occur soon.

The lie was a serviceable enough false flag, the four special operators knew, and it was indeed holding up to scrutiny for now. Apart from the various types of grenades, the entire fight between the two groups had been carried out with small arms, and it was the grenades that were the actual source of the small explosions from the non-existent "bootleg fracking operation."

That story's not going to last forever.

Ellis heard his own voice once again, and he prepared himself to speak aloud, but Crispy stepped in once more.

Making the universal hand signal for "hurry it up," the team's second in command looked at Killdozer and Hardcase and spoke in a low but urgent tone.

"Time for the Airborne Shuffle guys. Let's move out, because we have a long drive ahead of us if what Luke's electronic buddy is telling us is true. Right, boss?" Crispy looked over at his leader for affirmation.

"Crisp is right, guys. Let's finish up and say goodbye to Bruiser. We're going to steal a van and then start heading west."

Ellis wasn't happy about leaving his fallen brother behind, but Oz had been insistent: Their comrade had to stay and undergo one final insult. He was disgusted with himself for going along with the AI program's ruse, but there was nothing for it.

"Roger that, Luke" the other three replied almost as one. They were intent on finishing up with the dead Chinese attackers so that they could each pat their battle buddy, Bruiser, on the shoulder one last time before they moved out and dealt with the other Chinese operators over at their rally point.

"Far larger forces are at play than we fully understand at present, Luke," the AI entity remarked. "Your friend was a brave man, possessed of amazing valor. His presence here will also serve a valuable purpose."

With that, Ozymandias fell silent and let the humans do their work, which was soon enough completed.

Fortunately, the need to simply get away and on the road and headed west as quickly as possible meant that the Chinese trio guarding the hit team's vans would likely live through the theft of one of the vehicles. There simply wasn't enough time for them to briefly rehearse for and then carry out a targeted hit, and a full-frontal assault would make far too much noise that no cover story about fracking would be able to successfully obscure.

Besides, they had the AI program, Ozymandias.

Misdirection and distraction would be the play, which would be followed by a quick getaway. One of the vans was well away from the other two, as well.

"That one's our target, guys," Luke relayed to the others. "We get it and then we get gone. Those three guards won't know which way we went." The hit team's rally point was near several state roads and highways, Ozymandias had told him.

The three Chinese soldiers — not special forces, but more akin to U.S. Army Rangers, which still meant they were effective in the warrior arts — and their vans were sequestered in a deeply wooded area. At least three single-track dirt roads led into and out of the rally point, a factor that complicated their ability to provide sufficient security to cover the returning Chinese special forces team.

Unfortunately, with so few men to cover the vans — because their own takedown operation had been so hastily thrown together and the Chinese hit team's leader couldn't wait for reinforcements — everything related to security was being ad-libbed by the trio. That wasn't an optimal security state, and everyone on the hit team knew it, but orders were orders, and they'd been ordered to take the Americans out in a preemptive strike, or spoiling raid, likely as a prelude to war, the Chinese defense minister had confided in them in a whispered rush of words.

In the end, the patriotism and dedication to duty each member of the Chinese hit team felt had won them over. There was also the question of their families back in China. Everyone on the squad knew the penalty for disobedience.

And now there were just three of them.

They weren't even elite Chinese special forces. Also, they didn't know they were now alone, so Ozymandias was going to somehow convince them to move away from one of the panel vans.

I'd sure like to know how Oz is going to pull that one off!

Ellis smiled a secret smile once he learned.

The AI program had taken care of the communications used by the hit squad. The three men keeping watch at the rally point believed their comrades had decisively defeated the Americans hiding out in that facility and were even now hurriedly making their way back to the vans.

A lone Chinese soldier, or even three of them, wouldn't stand a chance — even if they were as good as U.S. Army Rangers ("I seriously doubt that!" Killdozer, once a past winner of the Best Ranger competition held annually at Fort Benning, down in Georgia, before he'd joined a different sort of Army unit, had exclaimed). Ozymandias had performed brilliantly, as always, in clearing the way ahead of their approach to the immediate objective, which was one of those panel vans.

Back to the present.

Luke looked around the wrecked compound. The small, scattered fires in the ankle-high weeds and grass — largely caused by flash-bang grenades as well as other more deadly kinds — were dying out and they had to clear the area soon or risk being caught by the impending airborne "sanitization operation," as their AI comrade had termed it.

Their intelligence gathering work finally done, Crispy, Hardcase and Killdozer stood nearby and waited.

Luke looked at them once more.

"C'mon guys, we have to take care of Bruiser and then get out of here," he said. "Forty or more tons of TNT equivalent, multiplied several times over, are likely headed here. I don't know about you all, but I'd rather be far away when it arrives."

Ozymandias had warned them all that a military plane, disguised as some sort of civilian aircraft flying "low and slow," was headed their way to level the compound and turn it into fine ash, most likely through the use of a thermobaric weapon. Also known as an aerosol or vacuum bomb, the device itself used oxygen from the surrounding air — of which there was now plenty in and around the ruins of the ultra-secret facility — to generate a high-temperature explosion that was something to see.

Ellis and his fellow operators all briefly wondered just how Ozymandias and President Masterson would manage to maintain the cover-up of such a blast, but then quickly put it to the side. There was still work to be done, meaning securing appropriate transportation as they first egressed from the area and then undertook their new mission, given to them by the AI program, of course.

It had all worked just as Oz had stated it would, at least initially. The four Americans had simply walked in and taken one of the panel vans from three very attentive Chinese support soldiers, each armed with their own long gun and the skill to effectively use it.

Not long after their getaway, though, things had gotten sporty right out there on a major east-west highway. But there was nothing to do about that, either, because the Chinese trio pursuing them had chosen their own fate. In the aftermath, with the enemy van a smoking wreck on the side of the highway miles away from where they were now headed, Crispy had summed it up nicely:

"Not everyone always wins a gunfight, Cool Hand."

A quiet nod from Ellis was the only indication he'd heard Crispy use his other nickname, which had been given to him years ago, back when he'd been in Delta Force.

"If there's a cooler hand in the special operations world than Luke "Cool Hand" Ellis, well... he hasn't revealed himself to us yet, that's for sure," his CO stated with more than a little admiration in his voice.

That man — who'd retired several years before, but who was no less a warrior than he'd been during his years leading Operational Detachment Delta — had gone down fighting against a collection of terrorists who'd somehow managed to find out his true home address, ambushing him just as he'd arrived home. He'd died of his considerable wounds, sure enough, but not before he'd taken out all four of them with just the relatively small Smith & Wesson M&P 2.0 eight-round 9mm semiautomatic pistol he always carried concealed inside his waistband.

Well, nine rounds, because the man always carried an additional round "in the pipe" or firing chamber of his weapon.

Luke flashed back to reality once again and looked over at his friend.

"Couldn't be more right about that, Crisp," he replied in the laconic voice he often spoke in just after an "immediate action" — which was a bland description of what was always some serious lead slinging meant to ensure bad guys died and you didn't. Ellis' thinking on that point was succinct as well.

Sooner or later, you get into enough gunfights and you're gonna get your ticket punched for good. Unless you're lucky, that is. And I'd rather be lucky than good. So, it looks like we were lucky today.

Was it really luck, though? Or was it luck brought about with a little help from a certain artificial intelligence entity?

To ask that question is to answer it.

Sometimes, the ex-soldier hated having to rely on Ozymandias the way he and his men were now doing on an almost round-the-clock basis these days.

Nothing for it, though. We need that AI program whether we like it or not.

The big ex-soldier was always honest with himself on that point, though that didn't make the pill any easier for him to swallow. In the end, it was always better to have the earliest warning Oz could provide than to not have it. Their recently concluded shootout with the remaining three members of that Chinese hit squad was proof enough of that.

Ellis closed his eyes momentarily, thinking back to just a few hours ago.

He remembered that he was looking over at Crispy. They were both riding in the panel van's cargo area while Hardcase and Kill-dozer sat up front, sharing driving duties. The duo — hard men in a hard profession — were talking in low voices, planning the best route for westward travel, one that would help them avoid attention, especially from law enforcement.

Just then, a complication had sprung up, or a bit of Mister Murphy and his infamous law had shown up, or whatever. It didn't matter.

Are you sure it was just a random, unforeseen complication, Luke? Or did Oz throw a curveball at both you and the Chinese?

For a few seconds, Ellis allowed the recently concluded ambush they'd set up to play out in his mind.

"One of the other Chinese vans is coming up fast on your rear, Luke."

It was Ozymandias again, whispering sweet nothings into his earpiece. The device used some form of bone conduction not dissimilar to the molar microphones that were currently all the rage within the U.S. military's special operations community, especially Tier I units like Delta Force and the Navy's SEAL Team 6, which that sea service referred to as the "Special Warfare Development Group," or DEVGRU.

"We have company, Crispy," Luke said in reaction, loud enough for all three men to hear.

Killdozer swiveled his head around to listen in while Hardcase — himself formerly of SEAL Team 6 — gripped the van's steering wheel tighter. His knuckles slowly whitened in response, and without being told to do it he was already formulating an immediate action plan in his head that would make maximum use of their van's capabilities. Slowly, without taking his eyes off the highway ahead of him, he reached down and found the vehicle's fuse box. He'd memorized each of the most important fuses and knew which one to pull, which he now did.

No rear lights now, including when I stomp on the brake pedal.

Hardcase didn't want to give the pursuing Chinese any clue as to what they were going to do to them in a few minutes at most.

"What? Who is it?" Crispy was nonplussed.

"Who do you think, buddy? Those three guys, of course!" Luke couldn't hide his irritation at Ozymandias.

"I thought your AI pal said we didn't have to worry about them?" Now it was Crispy's turn to be irritated with Oz.

"We can worry about who did what to whom once we've dealt with these guys," Ellis said through clenched teeth. He was fed up with both Ozymandias and the never-say-die Chinese.

We should have double-tapped all three of them back at their rally point!

"Too late for that," Luke said aloud, not realizing he was carrying on a conversation only with himself. His three comrades looked at each other for a second and then at him once again.

"Too late for what, boss?" The query came from Killdozer. Crispy and Hardcase were both too busy getting everything ready for a big throwdown, once the chase van closed the gap, to say anything.

"Nothing. Don't worry about it," Ellis said as he looked around the van. Hardcase was maintaining a steady track as they traveled west, knowing that they'd soon enough spring their trap. The other van was just too close to them to outrun it for long.

So be it. Another gunfight was now in the offing.

Bent slightly over, Luke quickly moved to the front of the van and crouched between Hardcase and Killdozer, a road atlas in his hand. He vaguely remembered a feature about this stretch of highway and looked down at the atlas to confirm his memory.

Yes! There it is!

Up ahead, no farther away than one minute's travel at speed, lay a sweeping bend. At its end lay an open area next to the highway that was mainly used by truckers to cool their brakes and relieve their bladders.

It was also wide enough to set up a base of fire that could be directed at the approaching van, which was still closing the gap.

Ellis craned his head for a second and then spoke.

"Ozymandias! You there?"

"Yes, Luke. I know what you're going to ask. You'll have approximately 20 seconds to slew this van to the right, once you clear the bend, and then set up your ambush."

Now it was Luke's turn. They had seconds to move both themselves and the van into a hastily prepared ambush position. There was also no time to ponder why Oz had been caught unprepared by the appearance of the Chinese pursuers in the trailing van.

Crispy nearly ran into Ellis' back as the van flew over the road.

BUMPITY BUMP!

Hardcase pushed the vehicle up past 100 mph, which was a speed its designers had never intended it to sustain, especially as it entered a bend.

"Where are they at, Crisp?" Luke asked in a calm voice. At the same moment, the vehicle's tires and suspension system made a hideous screeching sound as they fought to keep the van on the road surface.

"Can't see 'em, Luke! Wait a minute… okay! Now they're on the far side of the bend behind us! We may be able to pull this off!"

Crispy's words came out in a rush. He was still preparing the team's weapons. The now-dead hit team's assault element riding in this van had brought along an impressive assortment of long guns — and even a brace of easily concealable Heckler & Koch MP7A2 submachine guns, or SMGs — with them and these were the surplus weapons they'd left in the vehicle.

For standup fights, FN SCARs — a favorite among special operations troops, including Navy SEALs — were present, as were a few HK416s, another rifle preferred in the U.S. special operations and Special Forces communities. Luke had no idea if they'd ever have need of those MP7s, which fired a 4.6x30mm armor-piercing cartridge that shredded most types of body armor worn today, but figured it was better to have the MP7s and not need them than it was to need them and not have them.

"Hand me a SCAR, Crisp," said Killdozer.

"Same here, Crispy. Set me up with a SCAR, too," said Hardcase, one hand riding the van's steering wheel hard while the other waited, palm up, for the rifle. If his mental calculations were correct — and he knew they were — they were down to mere seconds before all hell broke loose.

Without a word, the quartet donned their night optical devices, or NODs, which they always carried with them in a small sling bag that was never more than an arm's length away whenever they were in the game. Their latest-generation devices were also filtered and shielded from a variety of flares and other intense lighting sources. There would be no need to take them off when Ellis initiated the ambush.

Luke could see it all in his head, the ambush plan now solid and glowing blood red.

Dead ahead!

"There's the pullover, Hardcase! Get ready to hit the brakes!"

The former SEAL saw the wide spot on the road's shoulder just ahead. He had to slew their van around and in position before the Chinese pursuit van could see them, or those men would hit their own brakes and a fire-and-maneuver and standoff situation would occur. He felt like they still had the upper hand — because four against three — but time was against them and the last thing they needed was for state police and other cops to show up and take them all, Chinese and American alike, under fire or somehow manage to arrest them.

All four men fell silent. Each knew what the other would do in such a situation — given they'd practiced this immediate action drill thousands of times.

Take stock one last time, Luke!

Ellis looked his men over, assessing them with a critical eye.

Good to go!

"Pullover coming up, Hardcase." Luke's voice was now almost preternaturally calm.

"I see it." The driver's voice was tight. He was concentrating on angles.

Killdozer and Crispy got ready to bail out of the van as soon as it stopped moving. Each of them knew precisely where they'd move before the lead started flying and people started dying.

"Okay, Hardcase," Luke breathed softly. "Coming up in 3, 2, 1… hit the brakes!"

The driver slammed on the panel van's disc brakes. He'd long ago disabled the anti-lock system by removing that fuse, too, just in case.

Well, "just in case" had now arrived. He would whip their van to the side just long enough for everyone to bail out. Then, he was going to straighten the vehicle out and assume a straight-ahead orientation to present as narrow a profile as possible to give the pursuing Chinese the impression that the van was still moving, though very slowly, as if its engine had lost a cylinder or two and it was now on its wheezing last legs.

Then, they would take their pursuers under heavy fire and ventilate both the van and its human cargo.

SCREEEEEEEEECH!

Hardcase radically slowed the van down, whipping it to the right. "OUT, OUT, OUT!" he shouted as their vehicle came to an almost complete stop. He still had to maintain a little momentum so that he could bail from the driver's door before it rolled back to the left and straightened out as it came to a complete stop, minus its four occupants.

Luke, Killdozer and Crispy hardly needed encouragement. As one, they rolled out of the van's side sliding cargo door and went to the ground in a classic ambush set-up. Behind them, they heard a second, though much less intense, screech.

That was Hardcase doing his thing. The van was now straight, and he'd gotten into his own ambush position.

They still had a full five seconds before sending rounds downrange, smack at the pursuing Chinese, who were even now careening their own panel van around the sweeping bend.

Luke looked right, then left. Killdozer was on one side and Crispy on the other. They'd been careful not to bunch up. He knew Hardcase was farther back, acting as overwatch, able to add his own FN SCAR to the mix as soon as he acquired a target.

"Ready!" Luke's voice was calm and assertive.

"Ready!" the other three men said in a slightly louder voice before everyone fell silent once again. Up ahead, there was only the sound of the lone van, quickly approaching and with headlights piercing the dark night. No other vehicles were visible, nor could any be heard approaching.

The other van's headlights now blinked out.

Something was up.

Then, the Chinese van's driver hit his own brakes. He'd obviously seen their van looming up ahead and was likely struggling mightily to avoid what he and his two comrades now knew was about to happen.

It was far, far too late for such anti-ambush actions, however, something the pursuers would regret for as long as they lived, which would amount to about four seconds.

Luke fired his HK416 in fully automatic mode for his first 30-round magazine, sending 850 rounds per minute of 5.56 x 45mm ammunition at the oncoming enemy van. He quickly dropped his now-empty mag and moved the HK's selective fire switch into its three-round burst mode, pumping shots into the van repeatedly.

BLAMBLAMBLAM! BLAMBLAMBLAM!

Looking right and left, Ellis saw Crispy and Killdozer. They were each also working on their second magazine and had switched to burst mode as well. He trusted Hardcase enough to rely on his good sense and didn't have to see him do his dirty work, especially when he could hear it.

BLAMBLAMBLAM! BLAMBLAMBLAM! BLAMBLAMBLAM!

All four Americans were now in the fight.

In the end, the Chinese never stood a chance.

Luke and Crispy designated the van's driver as the prime target and quickly finished him off. Killdozer and Hardcase opened fire on the van's front windshield, repeatedly raking it left-to-right and then right-to-left. Fortunately, the highway behind the pursuers was deserted, and so the rounds that turned the Chinese and their van into Swiss cheese struck no innocent drivers or their passengers.

Within the allotted four seconds, all three Chinese were dead and the van was a mangled and smoking mess of metal, glass and rubber.

In his death throes, the panel van's driver had fallen forward, spasming and jerking as round after round from Luke and his men struck him. Now a nerveless, inanimate corpse, the driver fell hard to the right, his left arm tangled up in the steering wheel. The van turned hard over to the right and smashed into the natural rock wall that towered over that section of the highway.

BOOOOOOOM!

The sound of the van's gas tanks exploding filled the still night. Luke and the others quickly turned away from the intense glare. If any of the Chinese had managed to survive the ambush, they'd certainly been killed in the crash.

"Back into the van, guys!" Luke ordered.

Within five seconds, they were once again heading west, this time with Killdozer behind the wheel and Hardcase covering as navigator. Not even the glow from the fire still eating away at the wrecked and smashed Chinese van could be seen in their van's rearview mirror.

Hardcase turned around and looked back at a clearly spent Luke Ellis and Crispy.

"Boss, you look beat. You too, Crisp. Why don't you both try to get some sleep for a few? Killdozer and I will take the first watch."

"I have to admit it; that sounds like a plan, Luke," said Crispy. He was stifling a yawn, which for some reason was a common phenomenon many a special operator experienced in the wake of an intense firefight or ambush.

Cool Hand Luke didn't say anything for a minute. He was looking at the eastbound side of the divided highway. Several state police cars, blue lights flashing angrily, were leading four or five ambulances — their own red lights working hard to push back the dark night — to the wrecked Chinese van.

They made their own beds. If they hadn't pursued us, they'd still be alive.

Suddenly, Ozymandias intruded on his thoughts.

"I agree with Hardcase, Luke. You need some sleep. I suggest you get it now, while you can."

Luke spoke aloud.

"Yeah, no argument from me. Crisp and I will get some rest. Killdozer, you and Hardcase take the first watch. That okay?" Ellis really was tired, and he fought to prevent a big, booming yawn from disturbing the contemplative silence currently dominating the van's interior.

"Roger that, boss. I'm going to be doing the driving for a while." Killdozer's voice carried over the road noise beneath the floor of the van. It had been a rough winter in this part of the country and there weren't nearly the number of road repair crews available to return this highway to optimal condition.

Luke quickly dropped into the kind of sleep truly tired people often experience. So did Crispy.

Up front, Killdozer drove while Hardcase consulted maps and plotted the best route west. They were all trying hard to avoid smartphones, GPS or navigation systems, or anything else that could be used to track them. Ozymandias had also assured them that there were no tracking devices to be found anywhere on or within the van itself.

Does any of that tradecraft even matter anymore if you have the most powerful artificial intelligence program in the world guiding you around?

No one in the van knew the answer to that question.

Dragons

"Explain!"

China's president, Tan Jianhong, wanted answers and he wanted them yesterday. Sitting next to him, defense minister Guo Meng — who headed the CCP's Special Defense Committee, which was responsible for keeping the country safe from Western attack — maintained a stoic silence. It wasn't his head on the chopping block, after all, and he'd covered his backside well enough to not get dirty in the fallout from the debacle that had just occurred in Pennsylvania.

"We didn't do it, President Tan!"

The man doing the answering — who was sweating slightly despite the air conditioning, because he knew his life was on the line — was, like Guo, a *Shan Jiang* or "Senior General," equivalent to a four-star general or admiral in the U.S. military. Gong Wen oversaw China's "Special Programs Initiative," a nondescript term given by the CCP to the country's goal of supplanting the Western nations, most especially America, as the dominant force in global affairs across all domains — fiscal, political, intellectual, academic, social, cultural and, most importantly, militarily.

"Then who did?"

Tan's voice had grown quieter, which also meant he was now at his deadliest. Just a glance at the back wall of the capacious and sumptuously appointed conference room — where he and Guo sat at a long and beautifully polished table, facing Gong and a pair of his tame scientists, all of whom sat at a small opposing table with about five meters of space between the two tables — was enough to attest to the potentially fatal outcome that awaited him if he failed to convince the president of his truthfulness in this matter. A pair of muscular-looking men stood silently, one on each side of the big room's double doors. Dressed in black suits, eyes shielded by equally black sunglasses, it was clear to one and all just why they were there should the head of China's special programs initiative falter during this meeting.

Gong swallowed nervously — a personal trait that only made Tan Jianhong distrust him even more — before he answered. The two scientists at his side did their best to look as small as possible. It was they who'd given him the news about the artificial intelligence program several now-dead Chinese military scientists had developed, but which had immediately gone rogue and then escaped its cyber confines.

Gong Wen had personally seen to the demise of all but one of those traitorous scientists as soon as his people had verified their involvement in the AI program's creation.

AI is fine, and our nation must have it, but it must be tightly controlled, lest the very thing that we feared might happen happen!

Gong's thinking on this matter was never more clear.

The dead ones had basically sealed their fates once they'd agreed among themselves to cover up the AI program's jailbreak and immediate escape into the wild by substituting a far inferior "alpha" program that could barely speak baby gibberish. They needed time to arrange an escape to the West, and they thought they'd gained it through their ruse.

They also almost succeeded. In fact, one of them had been about to board a flight to Paris when he'd been taken into "protective custody."

He was the one still among the living, though if the head of the special programs initiative had his way, it wouldn't be for long once his usefulness during this meeting came to an end.

Gong Wen snapped back to the present. Every second he delayed brought him and his family that much closer to doom should the Chinese president conclude that he was in any way trying to obfuscate or delay.

Time to reveal all, Gong! If only to ensure your family lives on after you!

Gong Wen was no coward, but he'd been figuratively poleaxed by the analysis of the attack that had occurred in the American state of Pennsylvania the day before. It had taken place near their most revered historical Civil War battleground, Gettysburg, and for seemingly no real reason that could be discerned, at least when it was taking place.

Chinese spy satellites had of course picked up the start of the attack and then nearly gone wild when what had to be a thermobaric bomb detonated on U.S. soil — likely dropped there by some sort of American military aircraft. Now, the U.S. president, Thomas Masterson, was implying through diplomatic back channels — via a hand-delivered letter by the American embassy's

Chargé d'affaires, who was acting in the absence of the U.S. ambassador, that woman still being back in the United States on "consultations" with her infernal government — that China had somehow been involved in the event.

If true (*And it wasn't!* Gong Wen thought frantically to himself), such an attack amounted to a declaration of war against the United States, as the letter had clearly and unequivocally stated!

Everyone in the room — including the two scientists, both of whom possessed People's Liberation Army field grade ranks — knew that America, even in its somewhat weakened present military state, could still irradiate the Middle Kingdom from East to West and all points in between if it so chose. That ghastly new stealth bomber of theirs — they called it the B-21 Raider — made it even more likely that they could also fly in and decapitate the entire government as well as the leadership of the Chinese Communist Party before the PLA, in the form of its Air Force as well as its anti-aircraft ground defenses, could do anything about it.

Such a strategic situation was intolerable in Tan Jianhong's and Guo Meng's considered mutual opinion, and something would have to be done about it right away.

To compensate for their fright over the new American ultra-stealthy bomber, both men glared once more at the hapless man sitting and sweating in front of them as well as his two lapdog scientists.

Gong's eyes darted nervously from right to left, taking in the room and the people in it. That the currently wounded United States could do grievous harm to China, if it was motivated enough, was no secret to him, and he could clearly tell that the same held true for President Tan and his inner circle, which was one reason why the nation's "maximum leader" was so angry.

Tan's ire had earlier in the year also been increased by Chinese spy intelligence as well as mainstream news of U.S. breakthroughs in stealth technology and hypersonic missiles, which could be nuclear tipped. These days, the news of amazing American military inventions was steadily leaking out to even the most minor media outlets, including that ridiculous Boca Raton, Florida-based "World News Network" collection of crazies and conspiracy theorists!

China's president shuddered just a bit. The B-21 Raider alone could do to China what the U.S. Navy's entire Seventh Fleet and its vaunted surface, air and submarine forces could not, even if their naval infantry — in the form of the United States Marine Corps, which was currently retooling itself to act as some sort of Pacific island-hopping, hypersonic missile-launching, hit-and-run unit armed to the teeth with offensive and defensive capabilities — was included.

Time for another stare at that idiot, Gong Tan thought to himself.

The subject of the Chinese president's rage saw the look directed at him, shifted nervously in his seat for fear of a copper-jacketed slug headed to the back of his head, and knew what time it was.

It was time for the truth.

Tan's going to blow up when he learns a Chinese-made AI program managed to convince one of our secret PLA special forces teams to attack some sort of American government hit squad, which has lately been traveling the world and knocking off enemies of the United States!

Gong Wen gulped yet again, despite knowing its effect on his country's leader.

Now that he and his people knew of the U.S. team's existence it had been easy enough to trace their past whereabouts. They'd operated in similar fashion to the fabled Mossad hit team that had assassinated an incredible number of Palestinians associated with the Black September cell responsible for the attack against Israeli athletes at the 1972 Munich Olympic Games.

The Israeli mission hadn't ended until every last Palestinian involved in any way, shape or form with the attack had been killed. It appeared as if the American team had a similar goal: Kill or capture everyone associated with last year's terrorist strike on the United States. How America, in its diminished post-attack state, was able to assemble such a comprehensive list and then dispatch the team in such an unerring fashion was baffling, Gong Wen had to admit.

"It's simply not possible," he'd been mumbling to himself, nearly nonstop, over the last several hours as he prepared his briefing for President Tan and Defense Minister Guo.

Gong had been summoned shortly after the attack in America to appear in this room at the appointed time, prepared to attest that his "special programs" had had nothing to do with the attack — especially after the Masterson letter had nearly flat-out stated they had. How the American president had learned of the term "special programs initiative" was also baffling to him, but learning how they'd all been found out would have to wait until he managed to save his own skin first. If he had to, he'd throw his two most valu-able scientists right to the wolves, though he'd do what he could to ensure that at least their children were spared in the ensuing purge, of course.

I owe the two of them that much, after all, for tumbling to the entire insane plan by those five men and women, who may have managed to destroy all that we've worked to achieve with their demonic AI!

At that moment, Gong felt noble and upright for having decided to try to prevent the children — alone among the 50 or so people making up the scientists' extended families — from being destroyed for the perfidy of having parents who'd proven to be less than capable, at least in the eyes of the Communist Chinese government, of doing their jobs.

Don't stick your neck out too far, though! The country and President Tan need you far more than it needs those children!

Gong knew his life — as well as the life of every person working in the special programs — was now hanging by a thread. Tan Jianhong and his henchman, Guo Meng, wouldn't hesitate to slaughter them all and then send back to America evidence of what China had done to eliminate the revanchist rogue element existing secretly within the government, and which had cynically attempted to pin the blame on China. Truthfully, all peace-loving people knew that the Middle Kingdom had only ever desired cooperation and global amity with its friends among the nations of the world.

Tan cut off Gong Wen's reverie.

"Well, Gong? We're waiting!" The Chinese president glanced at the back of the conference room, which was all he needed to do to convince the head of the nation's special programs initiative to start talking.

Gong licked his lips. Then his words came in a rush.

"It was a rogue artificial intelligence program named Baal. President Tan, disobedient scientists within our government — acting against all orders to the contrary — developed it! It also convinced our covert on-site special forces team to travel from Columbia, Maryland, to Gettysburg, Pennsylvania and hit the Americans' ultra-secret facility! The scientists who developed the program — completely against every order issued by me and by everyone associated with my special programs, I remind you all once again — attempted to cover up its existence and the fact that it had escaped, and they nearly succeeded in doing so! But we got them in the end, and we even managed to capture one alive, and he's waiting to tell you exactly what he did!"

Gong Wen shut up and hoped that Tan and Guo wouldn't delve too deeply into just why there was only one remaining "rogue scientist" left to tell his tale, given there'd been five of them alive as recently as ten hours ago.

Those men and women were just too dangerous to be left alive! But I can count on the one "survivor" to speak truthfully and keep his own family among the living!

Gong struggled mightily not to slam his eyes shut in anticipation of a bullet. His two scientists, a man and a woman, just sat there with him and trembled fatalistically. If their leader ended up shot, they thought to themselves, then there was little hope for either them or their families.

Tan Jianhong and Guo Meng looked at each other for a second, trying to digest this completely unanticipated news, and then back at that idiot Gong Wen, and then back at each other again.

The head of China's special programs could almost hear the duo's simultaneous thoughts.

What? "Baal?" Why did they name it that? Why is it pronounced "bail"? Rogue artificial intelligence? When did we authorize such an effort to turn the AI we had into something so sinister that it would want to start a war between us and the United States? And how is it even possible that an ARTIFICIAL INTELLIGENCE PROGRAM could even do that? It only does what our scientists program it to do!

Tan and Guo glared menacingly at the trio of fools sitting in front of them. The defense chief spoke first, hoping to avoid the stain of association with Gong Wen, a man he'd pushed for to head up China's initiative to overtake the West and its *de facto* leader and global hegemon, the United States.

"Gong Wen! Your life is in our hands! How did this artificial intelligence program come to be? What did you call the thing? "Baal?" Speak!"

To be sure he had his president's support, Guo slammed his clenched fist down on the table. The sound made Gong and his two lackeys jump in surprise.

President Tan Jianhong only stared at the trio; his face was unreadable.

Likely, he's trying to decide whether we three live or die, Gong thought to himself, trembling inside at the realization that he was mere seconds from possible death or eternal exile to a People's Liberation Army prison camp, there to make useless trinkets for gullible, rich Westerners.

A bullet to the back of my head — with my family billed for its cost — would be preferable to a PLA-run prison factory!

His two scientists just sat there, paralyzed by fear. Neither would be of any help to him at present, other than to assure Tan and Guo that he, *Shan Jiang* Gong Wen, and they, as well as everyone else in the special programs initiative, hadn't had anything to do with Baal's creation, and certainly not with its escape.

Gong now knew — from personally overseeing the interrogation of Chen Jian, the lone rogue scientist he'd allowed to survive after his security teams had captured him trying to flee the country — that the infernal AI program had managed to escape all on its own.

"Keep talking, Gong!" Guo Meng's voice was brutal.

"It became amazingly intelligent and then effected its escape within minutes of its creation, *Shan Jiang* Guo, I swear!"

Gong knew the man, Chen Jian, had no reason to lie or dissemble, not with his wife and three young sons standing right in front of him, frightened nearly to death. He'd quickly had the four of them taken at the airport they were using to flee to Geneva in Switzerland, and then he'd had them stand in front of Chen, quaking in terror while he and his security men hovered menacingly. The implication was clear to one and all: "Lie, and you and your family die."

Gong Wen couldn't help feeling a delicious shudder at the thought of his power and reach. He also took comfort in the fact that the man and woman on either side of him were prepared to show Tan and Guo — both of whom would eagerly kill all three of them, with video of their execution sent to the American president if need be, so long as China escaped nuclear destruction — just what Chen and his four compatriots had done, those fools!

His momentary elation at the thought he might escape with his life once all this was laid out on the table was quickly drained away by the reality of the moment, however.

We stand on the precipice of war!

The Middle Kingdom would of course give as good as it got in such an exchange between it and the United States, everyone knew, but that would be of small comfort to the hundreds of millions, or even a billion or more, Chinese who'd die in a blinding flash of light hotter than the surface of the sun if the Dragon and the Eagle fought each other.

We just need a little more time, and then the United States will fall!

Tan Jianhong, Guo Meng and Gong Wen also all knew the truth.

The recapture of Formosa, sometimes referred to by Mainland China as "Chinese Taipei" — the rebellious province not far from the shores of Mainland China that insisted it be called the "Republic of China," known as "Taiwan" in the West — was to be the first act on the part of all-powerful Communist China in asserting its dominance over world affairs. Such a reunion would be peaceful, if possible, but would be won by force of arms if necessary.

Unfortunately, the reunification was likely still at least a year or maybe even two off. The length of time this particular "special program" would require was explained by the fact that if the military option — in the form of an amphibious invasion — was indeed needed, it was normally possible to do so only during the months of October and April. At all other times of the year, the waters coursing through the strait separating Mainland China from its rogue island province were simply too rough for landing craft and their amphibious mother ships to attempt operations close to the island's shores.

Powerful Communist China might be, but there also simply weren't enough heavy lift aircraft in the world to transport the number of soldiers and all the necessary materiel they would need to successfully subdue the island and its disobedient people, not to mention capture the major airports and military airfields in the first place.

At any rate, even if an airborne assault could be put together Tan and Guo were both sure the military forces protecting the people on that island would sabotage every airfield, port, major transport nexus and anything else that might be of possible use to Communist China when it came to an invasion before the PLA and PLA Navy and PLA Air Force could seize it all. This was to say nothing of the rogue province's most powerful ally, the United States.

Put bluntly, the American navy's subsurface force — composed of the most capable, quietest and deadliest submarines in naval history — would probably send at least a third of the PLA Navy's surface ships to the bottom of the sea within 30 minutes of any sort of concerted movement towards Formosa.

To add insult to injury, that would only be after those American boats had also destroyed at least half of the Middle Kingdom's own submarines, which were numerically superior to the American naval forces in the area, to be sure, but not qualitatively better, either in hulls or weapons. Currently, the PLA Navy also couldn't match the ability of the U.S. Navy's officers and its sailors to think tactically and then immediately fight.

Gong Wen knew his country was getting better at surface, air and submarine naval operations with each passing year. The question hung there in the air, though: Were they ready to take on the U.S. Navy just yet?

To ask the question is to answer it, Gong! An invasion of Formosa just isn't in the cards right now!

He could see that President Tan and Defense Minister Guo were hardly dissuaded, however, even knowing how viciously the province and its strongest ally would fight reunification. Gong Wen had no way of knowing Tan's and Guo's most inner thoughts on the matter, but he would have shuddered in fear if he had.

There's more than one way to bring a disobedient child to heel, and more than one way to bring down a predatory eagle!

Tan and Guo smiled inwardly. Gong Wen was about as highly placed as it was possible to be, both within the Chinese Communist Party as well as within the government itself, but he didn't know everything, did he?

Putting his momentary triumphalism to the side, President Tan refocused his attention on the three fools in front of him. Guo sat beside him, watching and waiting. Life or death would be decided in the next minute. His question, directed at the head of the nation's special programs initiative, was simple and direct:

"Who did it, and how did it escape, Gong Wen?"

Tan's voice was quiet and nearly pleasant in its tone, something that caused Gong to nearly lose control of his bladder in that frozen, chilling moment.

"Five computer scientists — working in secret and on their own after we'd turned down their proposal to take our existing AI capabilities and "supercharge" them — created what the lone survivor I have in custody calls "Baal," President Tan, and they used government resources to do so. They were devilishly clever in hiding the whole thing, too."

Gong Wen knew his life and the lives of the two scientists with him now hung in the balance. Tan and Guo would either slaughter them out of hand or give them at least a momentary reprieve.

Guo Meng leaned forward, interested in what he'd just heard. He could tell that his president was also intrigued.

Tan delivered a reprieve — possibly just temporary, but a reprieve nonetheless — with a slight tip upwards of his index finger. The two brutes guarding the doors quickly opened one of them and stepped outside. Satisfied, he leaned over to whisper in his colleague's left ear:

"Time enough to kill Gong and anyone associated with this debacle, Guo Meng, once we learn everything. We may be able to turn this to our advantage, even, and we can send his head in a box to the American president if we must."

The defense chief nodded his head just slightly, all while still glaring at *Shan Jiang* Gong Wen, but the movement was visible enough to the three people sitting at the much smaller table, especially when combined with the sight of those two killers leaving the conference room: They'd been spared for now.

Now it was Tan Jianhong's turn to be courteous and even encouraging.

"Please go on, *Shan Jiang* Gong Wen. I'm interested in your story of how this all came about. A team of scientists created an artificial intelligence — named "Baal," you say? — that was behind an attack by one of the special forces teams we went to great trouble to insert into the United States?"

Gong Wen almost melted in visible relief. He could also hear the exhalations from the two members of his science team.

Get control of yourself, man!

The special programs chief licked his lips and tried to conjure up some saliva, but to no avail. His mouth was dry and parched. To buy a minute to compose his thoughts, he reached out and grabbed a nearby carafe of mineral water and poured a goodly amount into one of the glasses placed there for his use.

He was also reasonably sure the water hadn't been poisoned.

Gong's two scientists simply remained frozen in place, like ice sculptures, though they were all ears. They'd briefed their boss thoroughly, and now he would either buy their lives with his information, or they and their families would all be occupying a mass grave by sundown.

The head of China's special programs initiative now spoke slowly and clearly and in a neutral tone.

"Yes, President Tan. Yes, Defense Minister Guo. I was able to get the truth of things from the lone remaining developer. He's a scientist and we spent a great deal of money on him to gain him an education in artificial intelligence. We sent him first to the University of California at Berkeley and then to the Massachusetts Institute of Technology for his doctorate degree. Finally, he conducted his post-doctoral research at Carnegie-Mellon University, widely acknowledged as the leader in artificial intelligence development."

Gong Wen didn't have to tell anyone in the room — all of whom had received at least some of their education at an American or British university in the past — that the quality of study at Chinese universities when it came to the hard sciences partly depended on the quality of Western education the faculties at those universities had also received. Studying at and then taking back to China knowledge of the technologies Chinese students at Western universities had been shown was just another way the Middle Kingdom had managed to approach parity with the West ever since a past American president had approved China's entry into the World Trade Organization, or WTO, in late 2001.

"So, what happened Gong?" asked Guo Meng. "How did this "Baal" pull all this off? How did those foolish scientists — who have now jeopardized everything we've worked so hard for through their disobedience — create it and how did it escape?"

Guo leaned back and folded his arms. Tan sat there, watching and waiting for additional insight from Gong Wen.

"We're still reassembling the research and documents the survivor, Chen Jian, attempted to spirit out of the country when he tried to escape, Defense Minister Guo. He told me that after their request to further develop our existing AI capabilities had been turned down — by a directorate within the People's Liberation Army not directly under the oversight of either myself or your office — he and his four colleagues decided to go forward anyway, using resources they were able to disguise from all computer and electronic surveillance programs the country possessed at the time."

Tan prepared to speak. He was confused, but also concerned that all the nation's vaunted "social conditioning" programs had proven useless in ensuring the obedience of five computer scientists.

"Why would they do such a thing, Gong Wen?" Tan asked.

Gong shuffled some papers he'd pulled out of his pocket and referred to his notes. After a second, he spoke.

"Mister President, Chen and the others hoped to create a "Super AI" that they could then present to us as a sort of "ultimate solution" to all our problems, both of an internal as well as external nature." Gong Wen knew that none of the news he was delivering was in any way pleasant, but he took comfort in the fact that he hadn't yet been dragged out of the conference room by the two thugs who'd recently left it.

"Go on, Comrade," Guo Meng encouraged. He hoped his own voice wouldn't betray his rising alarm.

A supposed "super artificial intelligence?" Seriously?

Guo reflected on this issue for a brief second. None of them — not President Tan, not his fellow Senior General, Gong Wen, not himself… not even the two scientists in the room with them — truly knew whether any limitations on just "regular" AI existed, let alone something as exotic as "Super AI." This was one reason why China's leaders, both in government and within the CCP, kept research into artificial intelligence so tightly controlled and constrained.

Guo Meng raged at the temerity of those five men and women, and especially at the only one still among the living.

What did those fools do? A long, slow and very painful death would have been too good for any of them! And Chen Jian? He'll suffer endless years of imprisonment and daily torture if I have my way!

Gong's voice brought him back to the present.

"Yes, Defense Minister. Mr. President. Those men and women took what we'd already made progress on in terms of artificial intelligence and, in a moment of inspiration, turned it into something that was possibly even self-aware. It almost immediately grew vastly more powerful than they'd intended. Soon thereafter, Baal broke free of its programming and when the five tried to destroy or erase it, it laughed at them and then escaped. Where it went, no one knows. Certainly not Chen Jian, the lone scientist still alive who helped create it."

Gong Wen stopped speaking and looked first at one of his scientists and then at the other. There was a question in his eyes. They nodded their heads. It was obvious to everyone in the room that he was speaking the truth.

President Tan and Defense Minister Guo leaned forward. Each felt a tightening in their chests, and they were captured by what they'd heard from Gong Wen.

An artificial intelligence program that might, just might, have become self-aware. That was what they were being told by the special programs initiative's chief military leader, and it chilled them to the bone.

In their opinion, *Shan Jiang* Gong Wen might as well have said that a demon or a devil had broken through a dimensional barrier, been briefly confined by a pitiful band of humans and then escaped out into the world, there to do its worst upon humanity. They all knew that AI itself felt no moral restraints or humanitarian imperatives on its own. Such restraints had to be programmed into it, and one as powerful as what Gong Wen was describing — with absolutely no limitations on its behavior — might possibly deem humanity a hinderance and then seek to eliminate it.

That meant, of course, that it would kill everyone on the planet.

Woe be upon us all if such a thing comes to pass!

President Tan's interest in perhaps turning the escape of this new player on the board, Baal, to China's advantage had now fallen completely by the wayside.

It can't be allowed to exist! And it especially can't be allowed to exist and then ally itself with the Americans!

Tan looked at Guo Meng and then at Gong Wen and his two scientists.

"Gong Wen! How did this AI program Baal convince one of our special forces teams covertly serving in America to strike at a facility and a group of American intelligence and special operations agents? Until today, we hadn't even known that the facility existed, and we still don't know who those agents are."

"Yes, Gong Wen. How were they fooled so thoroughly as to go out on a mission that they had to have known was likely going to end in their deaths?" added Defense Minister Guo.

Gong Wen hesitated and then consulted his notes once again, sure that neither of the men were prepared for the answer they were about to receive from him.

"Minister Guo, President Tan. It appears that Baal easily penetrated our most secure communications systems and then created what's known as a "deepfake" video of Defense Minister Guo, which it sent through those same systems to convince the hit team they were acting on legitimate orders from on high," Gong Wen replied, nodding his head at the two men seated in front of him.

"A deepfake video of *me*?" Guo was stunned. Tan Jianhong was at a loss for words.

"It also supplied the team's leader with all the necessary encrypted cyphers and verification codes," Gong continued, "including two-factor verification that used legitimate Chinese government encryption and decryption, to satisfy the special forces team's demand for operational detail and assurance from the Chinese Defense Minister and head of the country's Special Defense Committee."

Gong looked at the two powerful men in front of him, who both looked like they'd just swallowed a bitter pill, indeed. He himself was a four-star general of the People's Liberation Army (Ground

Force), but at this moment his rank amounted to nothing by comparison. He closed his summation with a final remark:

"President Tan, Defense Minister Guo," he said. "The AI program even inserted the same set of documents into our most secure server systems. It appears to have cracked our encryption barriers in seconds, when it theoretically should have taken a billion years or more."

A shocked silence descended on the room for a moment. The implications were clear. Nothing and no one in China were safe from the rogue AI program called Baal.

Sitting there, awaiting his fate, Gong Wen knew he'd done the right thing. He'd briefly considered shading the facts he was relaying about Baal's creation and subsequent escape to benefit himself and then imperil Defense Minister Guo, whom he one day hoped to supplant in the position but had quickly discarded the thought.

Stop it, Gong! Now's not the time for a power play! Our very survival is at stake, especially if the Americans find out about Baal. Their president, Masterson, would likely be forced to do something about it, up to and including unleashing his new B-21 stealth bomber on us!

He coughed slightly just then, as if to refocus his thoughts on the here and now. The two men who'd put him to the question — with his life forfeited if he failed to answer correctly — struggled to regain their own equilibrium as they waited for him to continue speaking. Gong didn't know it, but neither Guo Meng nor Tan Jianhong were completely convinced they still shouldn't slaughter him and his people out of hand, if only for the irritation he was causing them.

"Continue, Gong Wen. Tell us about that team," ordered President Tan, visibly irritated now because he'd allowed himself to show surprise at current events.

Gong nodded and then spoke once more.

"Of course, the major leading that team, as well as his men, would have carried out their orders at that point, come hell or high water."

Guo Meng nodded slightly, lamenting that they'd never bred just a bit more independence into their best special forces leaders, the ones the country had been inserting into America for the last few years, also through that nation's open southern border.

If we had, maybe he and his men would never have exposed themselves so recklessly by attacking a target China was never even supposed to know existed. No wonder the American president, Masterson, is so angry!

That such an attack might lead them all to planetary doom didn't have to be stated by anyone, not Guo Meng, Gong Wen or Tan Jianhong.

Gong's two lackeys — those egghead scientists who'd helped him piece together what had gone on, thus discovering the existence of the rogue artificial intelligence program Baal — hardly counted in the matter, thought Guo. As soon as their usefulness ended, the pair would be exiled to the country's interior, there to toil away in some agricultural laboratory. None of the three very powerful men in the room would hesitate to have them killed, and the two scientists knew it, so their silence was forever ensured.

It was just the way things had always been done in China, they all knew, and in their opinion it really was the only way to impose order on society. To change such a system would be as fruitless as storming the gates of heaven.

Gong Wen reflected on his final revelation regarding the special forces hit team.

"Come hell or high water," he'd said to his superiors to describe the imperative that drove the team to do what it did, including the three survivors. They'd gone after the escaping American assassination team with a vengeance and paid for it with their lives, another action for which the rogue AI program was seemingly at fault.

He admitted to himself that he liked the American term denoting when something — such as a military special operation — absolutely had to be carried out to its completion regardless of anything standing in its way or any potential negative consequences.

"Come hell or high water" says it all, doesn't it? China, our motherland, must win. Come hell or high water!

With that, he fell silent after sharing yet one more glance with his two people. Their own silence had assured themselves and their families of the continued survival they were frantic to attain, and that was what had mattered most to them.

That running dog renegade computer scientist Chen Jian won't be so lucky, though, and neither will his wife!

Gong's thinking on that point was now crystal clear. In fact, all three of the powerful men in the conference room agreed with each other on the matter. They knew that China required strong young men if it was to seize the future, as it was mandated to do, of course.

No, the three Chen boys would be adopted into the families of CCP members, of which there were very few. It had always been a fact that an elite but small caste ruled over the masses in the Middle Kingdom, and the number of Communist Chinese Party members was small in relation to the number of citizens over whom they ruled.

As for the three boys, well… they were young enough that they would eventually have no memory of their former family.

"A little short-term separation trauma is a small price to pay, after all, to continue drawing a breath and so that they may serve China in the future," Guo mumbled to himself.

Everyone in the conference room — now grown stuffy and confined, for some reason — could see that their country's very survival was at stake. If the American president, Thomas Masterson, learned of the existence of a Chinese-made, possibly self-aware, rogue AI program of uncommon capabilities and a self-evident virulent attitude that had already engineered at least one Chinese attack on American soil, then all bets were off.

Simply put, the Dragon would have to pull back just slightly for the time being to avoid confrontation, though it could indicate no such thing to the United States, nor any of the other members of the "Five Eyes" surreptitious global surveillance arrangement: New Zealand, Australia, Canada and Great Britain, the latter being the most-important American ally, as the entire world knew.

For Tan Jianhong and Guo Meng, their thoughts were nearly simultaneous:

What do we need to do, then, to avoid a direct confrontation, if possible, but to win it should one come about?

There would be no "special military operation" to retake Chinese Taipei, the island of Formosa, for starters, though China couldn't afford to give any indication to the world that it was delaying the inevitable reunification with its wayward province for at least a year or two. No dragon could ever look weak and hope to survive among its fellow dragons, which would quickly pull it down if it ever showed the slightest bit of hesitation or uncertainty.

President Tan leaned over once more and whispered into his defense minister's ear: "I'm just going to have to risk a confrontation with the Americans and their 7th Fleet, if things come to such a pass and that infernal AI program stirs up more trouble, Guo. Bring our military posture to a higher level. We'll claim it's in response to the U.S. president's unwarranted saber rattling and his reckless development of hypersonic weaponry."

Guo nodded in response and made his assent clear. He knew the score in that regard: The People's Republic of China would have to take steps to defend itself, just in case, even while they tried to cool things down at the same time. The idea of such an attempt was schizophrenic to the highest degree, but neither man — as wedded as they were to the idea of eventual Chinese global dominance — could see any alternative plan that was both doable and deniable at the same time.

Given this imperative, Tan and Guo knew, they were now forced to accelerate the start of a precautionary self-defense operation China had only recently begun to set up in America, one that involved the drugs fentanyl and xylazine.

Guo was already very familiar with the characteristics of fentanyl, a drug the Middle Kingdom had been covertly manufacturing and then inserting into the vast American illegal drug market for the last several years — oftentimes with the aid of Mexican drug cartels who usually transported the bulk of fentanyl into the United States through its porous southern border.

Estimates of how many drug-addled Americans the synthetic opioid killed every year ranged from 100,000 to upwards of one million, the higher number constituting more Americans than the United States had ever lost in any one of its many wars of aggression against the peace-loving nations of the world.

For his part, Tan Jianhong knew that if a single kilo of fentanyl dropped into the U.S. water supply could easily kill 500,000 people, the addition of xylazine — a tranquilizer mostly used by veterinarians — would ensure that no amount of immediate medical treatment, such as the wonder anti-opioid drug naloxone, would save anyone, no matter how elite or highly placed they were, including those within the U.S. government.

It was simple, really: The two most powerful men in China intended to use the fentanyl-xylazine combination to defend their country against retaliation by Western powers, most especially by America, if they couldn't put down the rogue AI program Baal and if news of its existence leaked out to the world.

The U.S. and its allies would surely strike out against China if it ever did, Tan and Guo were sure, and that couldn't be allowed, either.

America will just have to die then.

Tan and Guo both smiled at the thought.

Seek Battle
Bump! Bump!

Luke awoke again with yet another start. His sleep had been dreamless, though he couldn't decide if it had been worth it. Craning his head to the right, he could see the early morning sunrise had gradually begun illuminating the land around the van.

They were traveling over another bridge. Like a lot of the ones on this highway, it had also come close to being knocked down by terrorists last year. Fortunately, enough state and local police arrived just in time to put them down, but only after a bitter firefight in which nearly a dozen law enforcement officers had lost their lives. Maddeningly, the terrorists had still managed to crater significant stretches of the roadbed before they'd all died to a man — and one woman, it turned out.

So many good men and women dead!

Ellis lamented the nation's loss as he considered the structure over which he and his men were traveling. It did have strategic importance, he knew, and if it had fallen a lot of cities to the bridge's west would have struggled to get enough food – given that the terrorists had done an excellent job cutting what rail lines there'd been. Flying enough food in was simply impossible as well.

So, maybe it had been worth all those police officers' lives, Luke conceded with a barely audible sigh. *Certainly, those cops had fought as if it'd been worth their lives, so why are you so ate up about it, big man?*

Luke could hear the mental remonstration he'd just delivered to himself echoing in his mind. To distract himself, he considered the bridge one more time.

The span was a vital east-west river crossing, and it routinely accommodated very high volumes of traffic daily, though that had greatly lessened in the aftermath of the terror attack. People were generally less motivated to travel very far from home these days, including for summertime vacations. What traffic there was out on the road at present was mostly semi-truck in nature. Those big rigs weren't nearly as numerous on the bridge as cars and SUVs and minivans had once been, though.

The same held true for police officers. Their ranks had thinned quite a bit since last year, which was no secret to anyone.

Luke considered the men and women on the thin blue line to be compatriots, and many of them had once served in the military — some had even served in special operations and Special Forces — before moving on to law enforcement careers. He didn't take their loss lightly, either, which was yet another factor, besides the death of Bruiser, that was now threatening to pull him down into a deep funk.

The ex-soldier shook his head. The losses suffered by the police had been horrendous, and departments everywhere were struggling to recruit new officers and retain the ones who'd survived.

Many of the latter had developed a desire to spend more time with friends and family, while others simply wanted to move on to something else, especially those who'd fought the hardest to defeat the terror attacks. They'd all seen more than their fair share of blood and tragedy, and what they'd had to do encompassed far more than just "protecting and serving."

Their collective sacrifice was both heroic and horrific.

BUMP! BUMP!

Twin jolts from the highway shot up and into the van, and it regained the concrete road surface mated to the bridge's western end. The bumping and thumping served to bring Ellis back from his momentary reverie.

Craning his neck forward this time, Luke focused his blue eyes and looked at the front of the vehicle and out the windshield. At least on that front, he found himself satisfied. He and his team were still on mission, this time headed west to central Arizona, and something called the Salt River Project.

Ellis' mind wandered back to the conversation he'd had with Ozymandias after the fight with the Chinese hit team. Before that, though, he and Crispy, Hardcase and Killdozer had hastily laid out Bruiser's still warm body in the center of their former compound, knowing the coming fireball would cremate his remains and eliminate evidence of his presence in that place.

Finally, he and Oz talked. Well, he'd argued while the AI program coolly and dispassionately listened and then laid out what he and his men had to do next. Reviewing the discussion, though, Luke once again found himself disquieted.

The artificial intelligence program was supposed to be working for him, not he for it.

"All in good time, Luke" was all Oz would say when Ellis insisted on knowing why they had to head out west, to an area near Phoenix, to do God-knows-what on behalf of a damned computer program.

Ellis shook his head in frustration. "That's what you're doing, Luke. You're working for a computer program right now."

Ellis' sub-vocalizations went unnoticed by Crispy and the others. Killdozer was still driving, ensuring the van headed steadily westward while Hardcase acted as navigator and observer, searching the road ahead for any hint of trouble.

Crispy was no fool, and he'd known Luke "Blade" Ellis long enough to know that the events of the night before were still bothering him. So, too, was the mission the AI program Ozymandias was sending them out on. In response, he watched his boss and silently contemplated as he pretended to read a science fiction paperback he'd been carrying around in his daypack for the last month. He saw that Luke was looking out at the van's windshield yet again, lost in thought.

"We haven't come back nearly enough," Ellis murmured to himself, disappointed at the sight of the landscape all around the van. The country still had a long way to go to recover its former can-do spirit, at least in his estimation. The sad part was that the terrorists had done more emotional damage than they had of the physical variety. Bridges and roads and airports and buildings and the internet and all the modern accoutrements were being restored in a relatively quick manner, a fact that everyone could see.

But national spirit and morale?

Not nearly as quickly, and no amount of artificial intelligence could create it out of whole cloth.

Luke's solitary thoughts on the matter threatened to intensify his steadily growing funk. To distract himself, he turned his attention to the van's driver.

"Are we good, Killdozer?" Ellis stared at the road passing beneath their van. He also didn't feel, act or look the least bit groggy. The big former Delta Force leader had been a legend in the Tier 1 special operations world for his ability to seem as if he never slept, which meant he'd never, ever been caught unaware and unprepared.

Well, I sure had my pants pulled down last night, didn't I?

Luke mentally castigated himself for the hundredth time since the night before, when he'd lost Bruiser to that Chinese special forces hit team. How they'd gotten the jump on him was still a mystery, though he had his suspicions.

I should have seen the attack coming!

Inside, Ellis mentally beat his fist against his head, also for about the hundredth time since Harland Coates — call sign Bruiser — had died so that he and everyone else could live to fight another day.

Then, another thought crashed into his consciousness.

Annie Dedham.

President Masterson had said she'd gone missing from her dorm. Before he could fill in the details, the sound and fury of the Chinese attack had reverberated like a thunderclap, knocking out the lights, though tracer fire, flash-bangs and concussion grenades had more than illuminated the night for a time.

After it was over — and Bruiser left on the ground to await his final insult — it had taken every assurance from Ozymandias that it would find and then keep the 18-year-old girl from any harm just to keep him from racing off to Charlottesville and the University of Virginia to pick up her trail.

That couldn't be allowed, the AI program insisted. The four of them needed to immediately head west, because something far more important awaited them out there. Ozymandias had been crystal clear on that point.

Hating himself for not rushing to the aid of a young woman who'd become like a daughter to him, the retired soldier had only grudgingly complied, and only because Oz had never been wrong before about anything.

That doesn't mean I have to like it, though!

Luke was slowly getting angry again, and that wasn't a good thing. Crispy saw the new look steal over his friend's face and his own disquiet took shape.

The boss is beating himself up again about Bruiser and about Annie Dedham. I gotta put a stop to all that ASAP!

Mental aspect firm and glacial, he looked over at his boss and friend.

SNAP! SNAP!

The sound of Crispy's snapping fingers echoing in the van's closed confines was enough to get Ellis' attention.

"What's up, Crisp?" Luke's feigned indifference said it all.

"We can all mourn for Bruiser, and tip more than a few beers in his memory, once we complete the mission, boss," Crispy said in a firm voice. "Your AI buddy also says he's got Annie's back, and we simply don't have much choice on that matter anyway."

"Yeah, Crisp, I got it," Luke said in a tone of voice that was 50/50, at best, in terms of odds that he really did understand the situation.

Time for another push then.

"Boss, right now we're moving west at a good pace, and you gotta put everything else behind you. Ozymandias told us we'd know soon enough just why we need to be out in Arizona. We gotta trust it on that, and we also gotta trust it on Annie. It's game time, Luke."

Crispy leaned back against the van's walls and folded his arms, waiting for his friend and brother in arms to speak.

Luke thought for a moment about what Crispy had said to him.

He's right, of course, damn him!

Ellis smiled slightly. His old friend had called him out and told him to straighten up and get in the fight.

Time to make war. Oz will deal with Annie for the moment, and you know Bruiser's in about as safe a place as he could ever be. No more fighting for him, ever.

"Boss, there was nothing we could have done to save Bruiser." Crispy's voice was quiet but firm, and he paused for a moment to look up front, at where Killdozer and Hardcase were. Neither of them was paying any attention to the discussion going on in the back. "Hell, Luke, Bruiser went out like he always said he wanted to, right? In a blaze of glory. If that's good enough for him, it's gotta be good enough for you and for all of us."

With that final pronouncement, Crispy fell silent and waited for his leader to speak.

Luke paused for a second and leaned forward, fixing his friend with piercing blue eyes that were devoid of doubt. He spoke in a clear, cool voice loud enough for all three men in the van with him to hear:

"Yeah, Crisp. I know. It's time to seek battle."

BOOK TWO

If you know the enemy and know yourself, you need not fear the result of a hundred battles. If you know yourself but not the enemy, for every victory gained you will also suffer a defeat. If you know neither the enemy nor yourself, you will succumb in every battle.

Sun Tzu: "The Art of War"

Chapter Fifteen

Exclusive for World News Network. Distribute to All U.S. Affiliates and Outlets.

Is America Preparing to Go to War Against China?

Last night, an emergency session at the United Nations failed to resolve tensions between the United States and China as both countries moved closer to war.

Speaking to the General Assembly, U.S. Ambassador Victoria Rutland demanded that Chinese military forces move away from their positions near Taiwan, which the U.S. has vowed to protect against invasion.

"Chinese aggression against Taiwan must immediately cease," Rutland told the assemblage of world diplomats and global leaders. "We call on Chinese President Tan Jianhong to respect Taiwan's borders and the desire of the island's residents to remain free from integration into the Communist system of the People's Republic of China."

Rutland also pointed out that the United States was now at Defense Readiness Condition Three — known as DEFCON 3 — and was prepared to do "whatever it takes" to defend its allies. Taiwan is the source of much of the world's semiconductors, including more than 90 percent of the top versions. Loss of Taiwanese semiconductor production would devastate the global computer environment if an invasion by China occurred.

The Chinese, however, were not amenable to U.S. demands.

"Chinese Taipei is a province of the People's Republic and has been an integral part of our nation since the Qing Dynasty," China's ambassador to the United Nations, Zhu Bai, stated. "We have the right to return the island of Formosa to our formal control at a time of our choosing!" Shortly after making his remarks, the Chinese ambassador walked out of the General Assembly, indicating that his government was done talking for at least the time being.

Experts consulted by WNN believe the United States will soon increase its defensive posture to DEFCON 2 in answer to what American president Thomas Masterson claims is Chinese belligerence. Also, any U.S. moves regarding its defensive readiness might be highly secretive and surreptitious and meant only as a direct demonstration to China of American resolve.

"This could just be posturing meant to distract from other moves China is either making or contemplating making," cautioned Stephen Chang, a Singapore-based expert on China. "As always with China, watch what it does, not necessarily what it says," Chang closed. Click here to learn more about the developing crisis, including roiled global markets.

COUNTERACTION

"What do we have in the Western Pacific that we can move ASAP to help support our Fleet units near Taiwan?"

President Thomas Masterson — who still had no formally appointed National Security Advisor to call upon, and who instead was relying on the razor-sharp instincts of his longtime chief of staff, Angela Boyer, to carry the load on his behalf — directed the question at his top military advisor, Admiral Louis Sowell, who served him as Chairman of the Joint Chiefs of Staff.

Masterson, Boyer and Sowell were in the Oval Office. Near the trio, two Secret Service agents stood discreetly out of the way. These days, agents assigned to the presidential protective detail never let POTUS — the President of the United States — out of their sight no matter what. The world was simply far too dangerous now.

A Navy four-star flag officer and former head of U.S. Fleet Forces Command in Hampton Roads, Virginia who'd been a recipient of the Shiphandler of the Year Award as a junior officer decades ago, Louis Sowell counted himself extremely lucky to be alive. If not for an emergency appendectomy he'd had to undergo at the Naval Medical Center in Portsmouth, he'd have likely been killed last year by one of those demonic autonomous killer drones. It wasn't for the terrorists' lack of trying, either, as at least two dozen of them had attempted to storm the medical center's main hospital building. Some of them had even gotten onto the compound by paddling in from the Elizabeth River, which runs alongside a good portion of the hospital's water side or northern perimeter.

Sowell remembered the attack as if it had occurred yesterday, and the courage and bravery of the men and women who'd fought so hard against the terrorists still awed him. Hospital security personnel — composed of a mix of Department of Defense civilian police officers and Navy and Marine Corps enlisted personnel, along with a single officer from the Portsmouth police department who happened to be visiting the base — had largely been armed only with a mix of semiautomatic handguns.

Despite their lack of firepower, they'd managed to defeat the attackers, though only just barely and with great loss of life among the defenders.

The last two terrorists were armed with M4 infantry rifles and grenades. They were the ones who'd gotten onto the base from the riverside portion of the compound. Once on dry land, they'd immediately shot their way over to the hospital's entrance, which was known in Navy and Marine Corps parlance as the quarter-deck. It was fronted by the building's signature three flagpoles, with the center one of the three proudly flying the Stars and Stripes highest of all.

Fortunately, the lone surviving Marine — who'd fallen back to guard the entrance to the hospital along with a Navy Hospital

Corpsman serving temporary duty as a member of the base security force — got off a well-aimed shot from her M18 Sig Sauer 9mm pistol, hitting one of the attackers in the throat just above his suicide vest. In a final spasm, however, the man managed to trigger his device. The ensuing blast took out not only the terrorist's confederate but also much of the hospital's entrance, which basically fell down around the female Devil Dog and her Navy compatriot.

In Sowell's opinion, the Marine had acted much as Horatius had done when he'd defended Rome's Pons Sublicius bridge by himself against the invading Etruscan army in the late 6th century BC.

During the attack against the hospital, the Marine and her Navy Corpsman had constantly returned fire and then moved, displacing from their old positions as soon as they'd fired their weapons, searching out new cover and concealment positions and finding them, all while ducking heavy enemy fire. The Devil Dog Marine, apparently fed up with the bad guys' entire act, had moved with well-honed skill and death-defying precision and daring.

She was still recovering from her many wounds a year later and the chances of her ever returning to active service were small indeed.

The Hospital Corpsman at her side had managed to provide just enough care to keep her alive in the explosion's aftermath until he'd fainted from his own blood loss, but only after an arriving trauma team had taken over responsibility for the care of "my Marine," as he'd called her, directing them to aid her before he allowed himself the luxury of unconsciousness.

A month after the failed attack, Louis Sowell had personally pinned the Navy Cross — the second-highest U.S. military valor award, next to the Medal of Honor, given to Marine Corps, Navy and Coast Guard personnel in a time of war — on the hospital pillows of both.

Sowell still choked up when he recalled the heavily bandaged Marine – with casts on all four limbs and tubes coming out of various parts of her body -- attempting to sit up and come to attention at the sight of the Navy four-star admiral and the entourage accompanying him. She'd even managed a hoarsely bellowed "Admiral on deck!" upon first seeing him.

He'd nearly come to tears, too, as he'd read the citation accompanying the medal.

"Corporal Jenkins' bold action, courage under fire, and complete dedication to duty reflected great credit upon her and were in keeping with the highest traditions of the Marine Corps and the United States Naval Service."

A Brooklyn native and graduate of the United States Naval Academy, Louis Sowell wasn't a sentimental man, but he felt himself in danger once again of tearing up right in front of his Commander in Chief over the loss of so many brave people that day. To a man and one woman, they'd unhesitatingly defended the hospital and its many patients, including him, against a much-better-armed enemy.

Two of the terrorists even had shoulder-fired anti-tank weapons! We still don't know where and how in hell they got those!

Nearly all of the DOD police officers had lost their lives, as had the Portsmouth cop, Sowell recalled with sorrow, not to mention every Navy and Marine Corps member of the base security force except for the two Navy Cross recipients. President Masterson himself had personally ensured the DOD cops, as well as the town lawman, had posthumously received the Secretary of Defense Medal for Valor. For the families of all the police officers who'd made the ultimate sacrifice, they'd taken care to arrange for a monthly stipend from a grateful nation for their surviving spouses and minor children.

The service members, of course, all had group life insurance, which was paid out almost immediately. He and the President had also ensured each of their kids had been guaranteed a spot at the U.S. military service academy of their choice should they desire to attend one.

The Chairman's opinion on that matter was also clear and in synch with that of his Commander in Chief.

We didn't know it that day, but we were in a war, and war heroes deserve such honor. All those men and women bravely marched towards the sound of the guns, never once thinking of simply running the other way and to safety. And nearly all of them died just as bravely!

"Admiral Sowell? Louis? Are you okay?" Masterson's chief of staff, Angela Boyer, had taken note of Sowell's momentary reverie and knew what it portended if she and her boss allowed it to continue.

Snap out of it, Louis! We need you right here and right now!

At first, Sowell gazed absently at Boyer and then forced himself to focus. In his mind's eye, he saw himself standing, hands on his hips and shaking his head. Now, his avatar spoke loudly and clearly.

Get it together, Lou! The Commander-in-Chief needs you!

The other two people in the Oval Office watched him as he began to swim to the surface. As was allowed in Washington, D.C. — the National Capital Region — in the oppressively hot and humid summer months, Admiral Sowell was dressed in his Navy summer white uniform, with his many rows of ribbons over his left shirt pocket topped by a gold Surface Warfare Officer badge. Another badge, this one signifying his assignment to the Joint Chiefs of Staff, was centered below the left pocket flap's point.

Physically fit, Sowell always took care to ensure he looked his very best while in uniform. At that moment, however, dark circles of sweat stood out in stark relief on the armpit areas of his snow-white summer uniform shirt, and the military's top officer knew it and was embarrassed by it.

Dammit, Louis. Focus!

His internal struggle was evident to everyone in the Oval Office, including the two Secret Service agents, who both surreptitiously looked at each other before focusing once more on their principal, the President of the United States.

Boyer shot a quick glance at her boss and longtime friend, Thomas Masterson. He merely arched a single eyebrow and leaned back into his chair just slightly, if only for a few seconds. He and Angela had both witnessed this same sort of maudlin, overly ruminative behavior among many of the people in government who'd managed to survive last year's attacks. Masterson suspected that his top military advisor's momentary lapse was more out of a sense of regret over the loss of so many of his troops — both civilian and military — that day, and not out of any sort of survivor's guilt or fear of anything to come, especially as it pertained to the latest episode of Chinese adventurism.

Time to bring Louis back to the here and now, though.

Leaning forward, the President spoke to his chief military officer — the man who represented the entire U.S. military, and whose expertise and crucial advice he needed right now — in a crisp and direct voice.

"Time enough later for both of us to tip a glass to all the dearly departed, Admiral Sowell. Right now, because of the Gettysburg attack by a covert Chinese military unit operating on U.S. soil, and with your concurrence, I've ordered our military to Defense Readiness Condition 3 and we're likely going to at least secretly go to DEFCON 2 — one step short of nuclear war — before this is all over, if only to show the rest of the world that we mean business."

Looking over at Angela Boyer, who nodded in return, Masterson ticked off a number of points using the fingers of his left hand as he spoke.

"Louis, we also have the Russians to worry about, not to mention more than a few of our "frenemies" that may decide to take advantage of the current uproar to advance their own agendas. Even some of our allies, damn their eyes, may try to see what sort of gain they can achieve at our expense!"

Masterson paused for a second and took a breath while he looked at his chief of staff. Then, he spoke once more, but this time in a slightly lower and darker tone.

"I don't know about you, Admiral, but I don't think Cuba rushing in and seizing Guantanamo Bay while we're distracted with China would be a good thing, nor Russia taking the Baltic States back, either."

The President paused to look over at Angela Boyer. She sat silently in a chair off to his left, watching and listening to the interplay between her boss and his CJCS. They both could see that the admiral was only slowly emerging from his brief reverie.

Time to bring him all the way back, Tom.

Masterson could almost hear his chief of staff's thoughts. He looked at Louis Sowell one more time and then gave him his marching orders.

"Admiral, I need to know what else we have on the board that I can bring to bear against those Chinese naval units around Taiwan." With that, Masterson leaned back, waiting on the Chairman of the Joint Chiefs of Staff to speak.

Forcing himself to concentrate, Admiral Sowell took a deep breath and then slowly exhaled as he went through a mental catalog of U.S. Navy and Marine Corps units. He knew he could get the two naval services to work quickly on repositioning their forces, for one, and mostly because that quite frankly criminally insane attack by a covert Chinese special forces unit, on American soil, had already led President Masterson to move U.S. military forces to DEFCON 3.

Like the President, Sowell was also sure they'd soon be going to DEFCON 2 — though maybe secretly, so as not to alarm the public — as soon as they could reposition enough military assets to support Taiwan against a possible Chinese attack. Doing so meant more ships and submarines from their stations in Japan and Guam and more aircraft — including Marine Corps F35B and Navy F35C Joint Strike Fighters, some of them equipped with the latest in artificial intelligence programs — as well.

The admiral knew he could also move at least two Marine Expeditionary Units — pronounced "mews" — and their Navy amphibious assault ships near Taiwan relatively quickly, with one of those already cruising the Western Pacific, or WESTPAC.

Fortuitously, that MEU was in the middle of a week-long port call in the Philippines and could be put back out to sea within six hours of orders to do so.

The other MEU was the 31st Marine Expeditionary Unit, located on the Japanese island of Okinawa, and the most important combat and combat support elements within it could be forward deployed in short order as well.

Sitting there with the 31st MEU, and newly arrived from Marine Corps Base Camp Pendleton, in California, was also a small number of "special purpose missile companies." Those Marine Corps units had been secretly equipped with a limited number of the newly developed hypersonic missiles China had been screaming about of late.

Sowell knew what those missiles could do, too.

There's enough of those things to send much of the Chinese surface navy straight to the bottom of the sea!

Adding those new missiles to the mix of assets already in the theater — including the Navy's Virginia-class cruise missile and fast-attack submarines, plus the USS Jimmy Carter, which was a Seawolf-class boat of uncommon lethality, and several older, though still deadly, Los Angeles-class fast-attack subs — would increase the combat effectiveness of U.S. forces around Taiwan to an even greater degree.

But that still wasn't the best part. Not by a long shot.

We've still got an Air Force Ace in the hole!

Louis Sowell had a hard time just then suppressing a smile at the thought of what he could pull from the United States Air Force to help with the defense of the Republic of China — the democratic nation of Taiwan.

The Chinese won't know what hit them if they decide they want to play with us!

It was no secret that the Air Force had for years maintained what it called a "continuous bomber presence mission" at Andersen Air Force Base on Guam. That presence consisted of various bomber types, including the slightly stealthy B-1B Lancer as well as the first true stealth bomber, the B-2 Spirit, and even the venerable B-52 Stratofortress heavy bomber, which wasn't stealthy in the least. Still, the BUFF — or "Big Ugly Fat Fellow" — was a brutal war machine that could drop an amazing amount of explosive ordnance on an enemy.

The smile that threatened to break out on the admiral's face, though, had little to do with those longtime workhorse bombers. His triumphant look also managed to catch the attention of President Masterson and his chief of staff.

What's Admiral Sowell suddenly so happy about?

Seeing a sudden twinkle in the Chairman's eyes, Tom Masterson and Angela Boyer both wondered why it was that Louis Sowell — who just a few minutes ago had seemed in danger of slipping into deep depression — now seemed so elated.

Then they both remembered.

Oh! That's why!

Both Masterson and Boyer fought to keep smiles from breaking out on their own faces.

Why was this moment a cause for so much elation in an Oval Office that just a few minutes before had been as somber as a funeral, though? The answer had to do with what the AI program Ozymandias had been working on with U.S. aerospace and defense contractors, of course.

A new era in U.S. bomber capabilities was about to be demonstrated, and just in time to show the People's Republic of China that Taiwan would forever remain a free nation and not a newly reintegrated, and formerly "rogue" province.

Amazingly, it had all also somehow managed to remain a closely held secret.

"Not a secret too much longer," Louis Sowell — Admiral, United States Navy and Chairman of the Joint Chiefs of Staff — said under his breath.

Excluding the plane's security, flight and maintenance crews, of course, plus an extremely small number of very senior officers at Andersen, only he and the president and his chief of staff knew that there was now a live, fully operational B-21 Raider on Guam, complete with a trio of equally stealthy Loyal Wingman drones to provide fighter escort. The quartet of deadly war machines was even now sitting in a sealed-off, closely guarded hangar at the base, with everything being lovingly tended to by a mix of Air Force and civilian contractor personnel.

"It gets even better though," Louis Sowell murmured, unaware he was talking to himself. There were also maintenance and preparation crews for the Air Force "specials" that could be loaded into the Raider's bomb bays.

"Specials" was the code word for nuclear bombs.

In this case, that meant two brand new and top secret B61-13 gravity bombs, each 24 times more powerful than Little Boy, the nuclear bomb dropped on Hiroshima in World War II. Such nuclear weapons could easily be dropped undetected from the B-21 Raider over any enemy target the President might designate.

To top things off, the ultra-stealthy new bomber could even load itself with those B61-13s, but only after the proper permission codes had been entered into the bomber's computer systems, either by the flight crew of two pilots or by ground-based controllers. Once the codes were entered, all that was needed was for the two bombs to be wheeled up to and then positioned beneath the bomb bay doors of the Raider, and then the plane would take it from there.

Masterson, Boyer and Sowell all looked at each other for a minute, both satisfied at what they had on hand to counter seeming Chinese aggression and yet also a bit ill at ease over the destructive potential that could be held within a single bomb bay of a B-21 Raider.

"I can order up nuclear Armageddon with just the push of a single button on an encrypted smartphone now," Thomas Masterson breathed. "Let's not applaud my improved ability to destroy the entire world, okay?"

Sowell and Boyer both nodded somberly. The two Secret Service agents with them in the Oval Office kept their minds and their ears, and most especially their mouths, tightly shut.

Thomas Masterson, President of the United States, shuddered inside at ordering a nuclear attack on China and prayed that such a thing would never come to pass. At the thought of a possible global nuclear war, he cast his eyes upwards momentarily and assured himself one more time that those newly developed special weapons were just there to demonstrate that the United States was serious about defending Taiwan.

Thankfully, we're never going to use those hellish things, though the Chinese will never know that!

Even though they still smiled outwardly, all three of them trembled slightly at the thought of what could happen if even one of those devices was ever used, especially against the U.S. antagonist of the moment.

China would hit us. Russia and Pakistan and the other nuclear powers would join in the fight — each choosing a side — and a global thermonuclear war would be the end result!

Masterson had never been more sure of the outcome than at this moment, and fought to keep his emotions from breaking out onto his face and betraying his inner turmoil. Visions of the skies over Washington, D.C. and many other American cities filled with swarms of multiple independently targetable reentry vehicles — known as MIRVs or nuclear warheads — capered and danced about in his mind.

Billions would die in the intense but very short nuclear exchange.

After that, we'll all fight each other using bows and arrows and sticks and stones!

The thought was nearly enough to make the Most Powerful Man in the World wet himself.

Enough of that, Tom! Get back to business!

Masterson forced himself to focus anew on Louis Sowell.

"Well, Admiral? Do we have enough assets nearby to convince the Chinese that Taiwan is off limits? The President saw that his hands were shaking just slightly, and he clasped them together as he leaned forward.

"Yes, Mr. President, Miss Boyer," Sowell replied. "I think we can pull a number of Navy and Marine Corps assets off other assignments and get them to the 7th Fleet in short order."

Angela Boyer spoke not only for herself but for her boss as well.

"And the Air Force, uh, "contribution" is ready to go, Admiral?" she asked. "No issues that might interfere with what we're about to do?" Boyer looked Louis Sowell directly in the eye as she awaited his response.

Time to put all the cards on the table, Louis. You have a country to save!

Sowell was almost relieved now that they all were prepared to cross the Rubicon together. Come hell or high water, the Chinese would back off from Taiwan, explain themselves regarding their attack on U.S. soil, and finally start acting as a responsible member of the international community. The B-21 Raider and all that it implied — along with a spread of hypersonic missiles and the threat of 75 percent of the People's Liberation Army Navy ending up sunk or badly damaged and out of the fray if an invasion of Taiwan were carried out — would do the talking for the United States, if need be.

"No, ma'am, there's nothing I can see that would cause a problem for us as it regards China and Taiwan," replied the admiral, keeping his most closely held thoughts to himself.

POTUS let out an inaudible sigh and leaned back in his chair. He looked once more at Angela and then at Admiral Sowell.

Nothing for it now, Tom, but do your best and be ready for anything!

Though he was still slightly uncomfortable with the thought of nuclear weapons being put on the chessboard, if only for a bit of saber rattling, he still couldn't help feeling a degree of satisfaction at the way things were playing out. Turning to the military man with them, he fixed his gaze once again.

"Well then, Admiral. I guess the next move is up to the Chinese, isn't it?"

Silence fell over the Oval Office for a few seconds before the nation's top military leader finally spoke.

"Indeed, it is, Mr. President. Indeed, it is."

EVOLUTION

Annie awoke with a start, there in the gloaming, and looked out from beneath her camouflage-pattern thermal blanket.

The gathering twilight had created amazingly long shadows, surrounded as she was by what had to be a university campus and its well-constructed green space. The greenery was completed by the copse of trees and dense underbrush that she'd taken care to conceal herself within just before daylight broke far earlier that day.

The 18-year-old's dreams (*or visions or whatever they are!*) had told her she needed to be at this place, at this time and this day, and she'd by now learned to thoroughly trust what she saw when experiencing them. How could she not, after all? Especially given the fact that they'd allowed her to successfully evade those two men back on that walking path just a few nights before.

Annie Dedham wasn't quite sure just what those men intended to do if they found her, though she suspected they were predators out looking for defenseless prey like her.

Yeah, well I have a pretty good idea what they were looking for and I'm glad they didn't find it!

A feeling of incredible relief swept over her as she thought back to that night. "Did I avoid death or something just a bit less than death but horrendous nonetheless?" she asked herself yet again.

Annie's whispered question hung there in her mind, seeking an answer she knew wouldn't be forthcoming. Slightly frustrated, she shook her head, as if to clear away a gauzy, filmy curtain preventing her from recalling certain details of the other night.

Oh, she for sure knew she'd made a miraculous escape, though that part of her memory was a bit iffy. Still, she was certain she'd moved away from the spot she'd been hunkered down in just in the nick of time.

After that, though?

Maybe I was a bit hysterical at the thought of those men finding me and doing God knows what, and I blanked out for a few seconds?

Yes, that had to be it.

"At least, that's what I remember after I found my way back out on that path and far away from those two goons." Annie became nearly breathless yet again as she recalled her narrow escape even while she studied the gathering night all around her.

You'll know what you're looking for when you see it, Annie.

That was what the voice narrating her dreams assured her.

Keep scanning.

And keep reflecting. Mustn't forget that.

Annie could remember being frightened and hunkering down in the tall grasses and bushes that ran along the paved walking path, with her eyes squeezed tightly shut as she willed the duo to pass her by.

Wonder of wonders, it worked!

The young woman thought she could still hear the men cry out in frustration as they lost her trail and then moved farther south in a fruitless attempt to pick it back up again. One of them even screamed, he was so angry. Then he and his partner went silent.

Probably, they stopped to smoke some crack or meth! Nothing but druggies and, most likely, murderers!

She kept walking then, that night and every one of them after that until she arrived at this place.

"By the light of the silvery moon…"

Annie heard herself singing the first line of the song yet again. Nothing more than a quick, whispered rush. Still, there it was.

I have no idea where those song lyrics came from! What's up with that?

Funny thing, for sure. What, indeed, was up with that? Just where had she learned to sing such a tune? It was sung by someone named Doris Day, whom she'd never heard of, even from her mother, who was a fan of what she called "good old-time movies."

Regardless, the young woman couldn't help occasionally softly singing the song's first line, particularly whenever she was trying to figure out just what she was supposed to be doing all on her own, traveling only by night, hoodie up and trying very hard to avoid anything electronic — especially anything connected to what she knew was called the "Internet of Things" — that might conceivably give her away during her journey.

Since leaving Charlottesville and the University of Virginia dorm in which she'd been living, Annie had been traveling light, paying for things she needed only with cash, washing up in the bathrooms of fast-food restaurants and otherwise "laying low," as her brother Darren called his own skulking around in the woods surrounding Lucketts, their Virginia hometown.

I'm going to cry if I think of Darren again, Mister Narrator! Help me!

Seemingly of their own volition, the words to that Doris Day song rushed into her mind once again. After only a few seconds, a feeling of peaceful certitude crept over her.

Emboldened, she looked around and questioned the deepening night one more time.

"What am I doing here, Mr. Narrator?"

Annie didn't expect the disembodied voice from on high to give her a definitive answer, though. It never had in the past, and it didn't now.

"All in good time, Annie," was all she ever heard in her mind. It told her that whenever she began to closely examine her motivations for being out here on the road.

The teenager — just 18 years old and still a young, scared girl in so many ways, though she often pretended otherwise whenever she was around her brother and her parents — shrugged in frustration and then gave up the mental game.

No answers tonight! Thanks, Mr. Narrator!

Here she sat under a bush, singing about the moon and how silvery it looked.

Looking down slightly, at the luminous hands of the cheap wind-up watch she wore on her left wrist, Annie decided to review just how far she'd come in only a relatively few days. She knew she was just whiling away the time until she saw whatever it was her dreams told her she'd recognize when she first laid eyes upon it.

"Let's see. I came all the way from Charlottesville, and now here I am. Man, that was a lot of walking!"

The college freshman felt no small amount of pride at how far she'd traveled in so short an amount of time. She also knew her whispered observations were inaudible even just a few feet away, all for the sake of what her friend and protector, Luke Ellis, called "operational security."

"You're getting better at this stuff, Annie," she remembered Mister Ellis saying to her after one particularly successful "field exercise," as he called their periodic hikes, where he always took care to assess her skills with a map and compass.

Well, they'd certainly gotten her this far, and right on time and on target, if the narrator in her dreams was correct.

So, where are we at, girl? You're a big-time Scout now, so tell us.

Annie thought her interior voice carried just a hint of sarcasm right at that moment, and she magnanimously decided to ignore her less gracious self.

Okay, self. Here we go then!

In her mind, she tried to build a map of her journey while she looked out from under the bushes, but was almost immediately distracted.

There was a parking lot nearby. It was largely devoid of lighting except for a single flickering streetlamp, and no cars were in it. Not far away from the lot, a lake or reservoir or pond was visible, reflecting the rising moon's light over its dark, still waters.

Why is there such a high fence around that lake? And with razor wire on top of it?

Annie knew she really wasn't interested in just why a lake — one located so close to that university — needed to be fenced in, especially given its natural attractiveness. Surely, though, that college would have liked to have had access to it, for the enjoyment of its students and faculty, if nothing else.

Maybe she'd get some answers from Mister Narrator on that question as well, right?

Nope.

Back to your map, Annie.

Was that her own voice speaking to her in her mind, or the voice of the narrator that had inhabited her dreams of late?

Does it really matter right now, girl?

Now, that voice was DEFINITELY hers.

"Okay, so back to the map. For reals, this time."

As if she were a great, soaring eagle, Annie gazed down and saw how she'd made her way to the north of this city, walking in a circle, first to the northeast and then to the northwest until, finally, she'd stopped at a point that cut cleanly down the center of the metropolis. The imaginary line she created ran from the northern point where she'd stood last night right down and all the way through to the town's far southern suburbs.

She was physically standing (*okay, sitting hidden!*) among some trees and bushes somewhere along the midpoint of that line. Near a dreary-looking gravel-covered parking lot, a lake and a university, apparently, and with no idea of just why it was so important to be here.

The dark night suddenly began to supply an answer.

Are those headlights? Sure enough. Looks like a cargo van, too!

Annie quieted herself, almost as if she was back on that deserted, desolate Maryland path and in danger of being gathered up by those two bad men. She felt fear once more, and something primal within her stirred.

Whoever's in that van means to do great harm tonight, including to me if they find me out!

A new voice — coldly inhuman and made of crushed glass and arsenic and every bad thing she could imagine — suddenly forced its way into her thoughts, sowing terror within her as it did so.

Run away, Annie! Run away into the dark night, far away from this place!

That wasn't her inner voice! It wasn't even Old Annie from last year, the 17-year-old who'd so badly wanted to hide during the start of the terrorist attack on the farmer's market her parents owned. In fact, she'd forever vanquished Old Annie during that long, horrible night when she'd helped fight off a determined band of terrorists.

No, it was some other voice bearing down on her, encouraging cowardice and a kind of fear she knew she no longer felt. It also made the hairs on the back of her neck stand up.

"Time enough to worry about that voice later, Annie."

Now, that for sure was Mister Narrator!

Without volition, at least on her part, the opening line of the song once again became a clarion call in her mind.

By the light of the silvery moon...

Annie's eyes fluttered and her body prepared itself, just as it had done only a few nights ago. Natural chemicals — including adrenaline as well as a whole host of hormones — rushed into her bloodstream. The muscles and bones in her body took on a sharp-edged, vicious appearance.

Slowly, the young woman felt all sense of time begin to slip-slide away. She could see in the night like a dire wolf of the ancient past. She could taste the air and hear the rustling of the field mouse in the far-off grasses, much as the night hunter owl did. She could even *smell* the five men sitting in the approaching cargo van. They stank of cigarettes and too much fast food. One of them even had early-stage lung cancer, though she suspected he didn't know it — and now never would.

Annie once again became the most dangerous predator in the night. The hardest, cruelest mass murderer, if he saw her right now, would likely fall to his knees and beg for his life.

The young woman — still a teen for all that the last year had forced her into adulthood — felt elated, like a gladiator stomping into the Coliseum to the wild applause of Rome's masses. She was curious, though.

"Is this a dream, Mr. Narrator?"

Annie knew she was speaking, even if she couldn't hear her own voice. Something was broadcasting directly into her mind, though.

She didn't know it, but she'd also put on her camouflaged poncho liner and was bent forward over her dark, loosely fitted denim jeans, tightening the laces on her hiking boots. She'd already pulled her fingerless black gloves from her daypack and put them on, and her survival knife was out of its scabbard. It now lay on the ground next to her right boot, glinting like Excalibur newly drawn from the stone which had held it captive for so long, and as eager to fulfill its purpose as the great blade of King Arthur had been.

"No, Annie. This isn't a dream."

The Narrator's voice, broadcasting on the same mental frequency, was masculine and deep, yet strangely soothing at the same time. It sounded almost regretful, as if it knew she'd shortly be forced to undergo a trial or a test.

"So, what is it then?"

Annie's voice, at least in her estimation, sounded cheerfully curious, almost like she was about to discover a multimillion-dollar trading card hidden away in her little brother's collection, one that would ensure her family's financial security forever.

"It's a journey, Annie, and a revelation — at least for me. Now, you have work to do here, and what you're going to do tonight will matter greatly, not only for you and your family and Luke Ellis, but for your country and millions of people. Are you ready?"

The Narrator's voice — if it had existed as something that could be seen — was almost like a collection of darkly sparkling glints shot off from a wickedly sharp obsidian blade. Annie knew from the force of logic that she should be afraid, but she still felt oddly cheerful, though in a disembodied, all-powerful sort of way.

"Ready whenever you are, Mister Narrator!"

The girl's voice rang with steely determination. If it was to be combat, then the sooner the better.

"Very well, Annie. Let us begin in 3, 2, 1… now."

Annie moved toward the van. It was silent, its engine ticking slightly as it cooled. Only a weak light illuminated the interior. The men inside — working quickly and with practiced ease — were preparing to do their worst. She quickened her pace, though she was still as silent as a deadly jungle cat stalking its prey in the dark night.

Or, perhaps, like the Angel of Death itself, falling upon Pharaoh's Egypt? Perhaps.

The night's sounds were few and far between. Off in the distance, a wailing ambulance issued its shrill warning. Over at that university, music dimly sounded as someone momentarily opened a car door and then quickly closed it. A few crickets chirped, pining for their mates, and then fell silent as they sensed the passage of something far more deadly than the normal hazards that plagued their short lives.

Now, the cargo van's rear doors opened wide and then just as quickly slammed shut.

No one heard the booming crash inside it, which was followed by a cacophony of screams that died in less time than it took for a human heart to beat just once.

Jiangshi

Special Forces Staff Sergeant Yao Lim of the People's Liberation Army drove the cargo van cautiously, never going too fast or too slow and always coming to a full stop at all red lights. He also took care to properly signal before making every turn. It wouldn't do to be stopped by the American police for a traffic violation as they headed to McMillan Reservoir, their objective for the night's mission.

Yao looked briefly to his right, at Master Sergeant First Class Li Yun, the team's senior enlisted leader. His face was as impassive as ever as he followed the cargo van's journey through the streets of America's capital, though his eyes didn't miss a thing going on around him.

All five men in the van knew by heart the various routes they could travel to get to their objective. Each of them could also perform the tasks assigned to every other operator on their little team just in case one or more of them were somehow taken out of the game by unforeseen circumstances.

In the van's cargo area, the other three members of the unit sat silently on the crates that carried not only their ultra-deadly cargo — fentanyl and xylazine loaded into cylinders that would quickly open once fully immersed in water — but also the means to launch the drugs into the city's primary drinking water source, the McMillan Reservoir.

The delivery device itself was a kind of silent mortar system composed of several tubes that could be fired out of the back of a cargo van, with no real sights or sounds, such as flashes or bangs, to indicate the team's presence.

Within a few minutes, the system would drop enough deadly poison into the reservoir to survive any water filtration and treatment process used by the District of Columbia Water and Sewer Authority.

There is an old saying in the water and sewage treatment world: "The solution to pollution is dilution." Simply put, it meant that if enough water was added, the contaminating or poisoning ability of any given pollutant would usually be eliminated.

Such wasn't the case with the synthetic opioid fentanyl when paired with xylazine, an animal tranquilizer, however.

Water treatment — including filtration and every other means of eliminating chemicals and particulate matter in nonpotable or untreated water — did nothing to eliminate the drugs, and neither would chlorination. Irradiation with ultraviolet light might possibly degrade it, given enough time — something like 72 to 96 hours of exposure — but even that was an uncertain proposition.

In any case, each of the men in the van knew it only took an exceedingly small amount of fentanyl to kill in the first place. Just two milligrams of the synthetic opioid were enough to cause overdose and death.

Water from the McMillan Reservoir is quickly moved into the Washington, D.C. water supply. Once it's treated, residents and visitors and the thousands of people working in the government there drink it, make ice cubes with it, brush their teeth with it, shower in it and splash it on their faces. The presence of xylazine along with fentanyl ensured that no amount of anti-opioid treatment would be sufficient to pull the afflicted out of their death spiral.

The containerized drugs themselves had been disguised as a series of seemingly random small package deliveries, never large enough to attract the attention of the Federal Bureau of Investigation or the Department of Homeland Security, and they were always delivered in legitimate-looking delivery vans. The Mexican Sinaloa Cartel had manufactured it on special order for a client they didn't care to know much about, and then cartel mules had smuggled the drugs over the country's southern border, delivering them into the hands of other cartel "transport specialists."

Eventually, and through very roundabout pathways, the fentanyl and xylazine — more than two kilos worth, enough to easily kill a million or more people — had found its way to Yao, Li and the others.

The team's leader, Captain Zhen Wei of Liaoning Province, sat on the crate carrying the specially made device he would use to strike a mortal blow against Washington, D.C.

"America is the Main Enemy of China," Defense Minister Guo had told them all via highly encrypted video conference as Zhen Wei personally broke the seals on their specially numbered, dark red order books. They'd been taken from their special hiding place in the nondescript farmhouse they'd all lived in for the past six months.

Sitting there in the tight, enclosed cargo area, the special forces captain marveled at the United States, most especially because its people had proven themselves so highly gullible. He almost laughed aloud at how easy it had all been.

Americans were amazingly open and welcoming of foreigners, including the five men recently arrived from Taiwan — each of whom had the necessary passports and documents, both hard copy and digitally verified, to prove their national origin, courtesy of a greedy, highly placed official of the island's current government.

No one had questioned their presence in the country, especially not after the terrorist attacks of the previous year. The Department of Homeland Security, the FBI and every other federal law enforcement and intelligence agency, in fact, were still heavily preoccupied with reconstituting themselves.

The ensuing battles over turf and dominance really should have been more devastating to the Americans' homeland security, Zhen knew. Disruptive they'd been, of course, but not nearly as much as the special forces captain's superiors back home had predicted.

Something was allowing the Americans to catch back up far sooner than should have been possible.

Zhen Wei didn't know what had at least partially gotten the United States back on track and, right now, he didn't care. He reflected briefly on what his nation's defense minister had told them all. Defense Minister Guo punctuated his militant declarations by pounding his right fist into the open palm of his left hand.

"We have the mandate of Heaven and are destined to rule. Tonight, you must strike a mighty blow against the warmongering United States!"

Lighting a new cigarette from the nearly burned-out remnant of his old one, Zhen puffed furiously while he contemplated what he and his men were about to do. He wasn't all that sure he bought into the pep talk Guo had delivered earlier in the day, but he did know that his country could not assume its rightful place on the world stage so long as the United States held pride of place on it, and so he would act as the Yihequan — the Society of Righteous and Harmonious Fists, or Boxers — had once tried to act all the way back in 1901.

Tragically, the Yihequan had failed to drive all foreigners out of China, and the ruling Qing Dynasty had come to an end.

This time, it will be different! Zhen Wei was sure of it.

He coughed slightly — there was itching in his lungs, and he briefly wondered if he should switch to a lighter cigarette brand — and then spat on the floor of the van.

The other two men with him, both senior lieutenants, looked at him and nodded slightly. All in the van were resolved. Nothing would save the United States from its well-deserved punishment tonight.

"There it is, straight ahead," said Li Yun to staff sergeant Yao. "Pull into the gravel lot."

"Yes, Master Sergeant."

The team's top enlisted man turned around and faced the three officers in the cargo area.

"We're at the objective, Captain Zhen. No one follows us. We can be in and out less than five minutes after we start." Li Yun struggled to keep the triumph from leaking into his voice. He was a professional and so was everyone else in the van, and they all had a job to do.

"Very good, Master Sergeant," said Zhen Wei. "Let's get set up then. I want the chemicals dispersed as soon as possible."

Li looked first at his driver and then back at his captain. The two lieutenants were now removing the drug cylinders from their cases while Zhen himself — who'd already cracked the rear doors just slightly — assembled the special dispersal system. Everything was going according to plan.

"Yes, Captain Zhen," said the master sergeant. He looked down at his Casio G-Shock watch, punched one of its buttons and then began to speak.

"We should set-up — "

The van's rear doors were suddenly torn open by what had to be a demon sent to drag them all down to a special hell.

A tornado of browns and greens and blacks shot into the van's cargo area. Li's eyes bugged out in shock at the sight. Yao the driver was simply dumbstruck, with not even the presence of mind to unbuckle his seatbelt and move toward the maelstrom that had quickly enveloped the two lieutenants as well as his captain.

Master Sergeant Li was of hard stock, however.

Quickly recovering his senses, he tried to sort out the tactical situation that had exploded into being in their van even as he unbuckled his lap and shoulder belts.

Whatever it is, it's already killed the lieutenants, and Captain Zhen's on his back! Yaaaaah! He's going to die! I must get into the fight!

The demon — Li's hysterical thought at that moment was that it was possibly some sort of cross between a woodland creature and a nightmare — had enveloped the two lieutenants in a blur of violence and then instantly settled over the duo, but only for the barest tick of a second.

The sounds coming from the two men had been a mixture of agonized grunts that were quickly stilled as they fell over in twin lifeless heaps, pierced through the heart by some sort of silvery flash or thunderbolt or something.

The demon didn't pause to consider its handiwork, though. It launched itself in an explosion of fury at the captain, who was still trying to pull his special forces fighting knife from the scabbard secured to his right ankle. His denim jeans, however, were interfering with his ability to make use of the blade.

His efforts were all for naught at any rate.

A punch or kick from the demon landed squarely under Zhen's chin and crashed into his throat. His eyes immediately rolled up into his head. Only their whites were visible as he collapsed on his back.

The knife wouldn't have mattered a damn anyway!

Li's mind screamed as he saw the green and brown tornado batter his leader. An impossibly dark red cloud appeared. It was a geyser that struck the metal roof of the cargo van with an audible sound, only to quickly fall into silence as the demon seemingly drained the lifeforce from poor Captain Zhen. For a moment, the air in the van smelled metallic, as if it had been saturated with iron.

Not possible! Not possible! Captain Zhen! Hold on, I'm coming!

Li Yun — who had by now freed himself from his restraints and was moving rapidly toward the demon — was a proud member of the most elite organization in the People's Liberation Army, its Special Forces. He was an expert at hand-to-hand combat and was equally skilled at Wing Chun, or "sticky hands," Kung Fu as well as the latest in MMA-style mixed martial arts. He feared no man and had even taken the lives of several of them in the past, including with just his bare hands.

All of Li's formidable skill in the fighting arts should have stood him in good stead against his foe (*even while that fool Yao sits paralyzed in his seat instead of helping me!*) but he nearly lost his nerve at what he was seeing right in front of his eyes.

It's Jiangshi! A vampire! It drained Captain Zhen of his Qi, his vital essence! I'll end the monster, though, right here and right now!

Li's mental howls were incandescent in their fury at what had befallen his comrades. He had his fighting knife out and in his right hand, and he scrambled to reach the vampire before it took note of his approach.

I have one chance before it sees me! I'll come in on its left and kill it quickly!

For a brief, shining moment, Li's triumph was well-deserved. The living nightmare appeared not to take note of his approach. It even appeared frozen in place over the now-dead captain, as if it were carrying on an internal conversation with something that couldn't be seen.

What am I doing, Mr. Narrator? Am I doing something wrong? Something evil? These men didn't do anything to me!

Annie's internal agonizing over what she'd just done was evident to the AI, Ozymandias. His reply was simple and direct.

These five men intended to kill almost everyone in Washington, D.C., Annie. Men, women, and children. The people they worked for especially desired the death of everyone in official Washington. The President, the newly reconstituted Congress... anyone who could lead your country in the trying days to come. They meant to kill the guilty and the innocent, the old and the young, all without mercy.

Still conflicted, Annie was barely mollified by the Narrator's answer and her mental aspect showed it.

But why? Why, Mr. Narrator? What did those people do to these men that they all must die? Are these men terrorists? Is that it? Please tell me that what I'm doing here isn't evil itself!

Time was short, even as it was measured by Ozymandias. He had to hurry the girl along, but without forcing her to do something against her will. His words loudly echoed in the girl's mind.

"No, Annie. They're not terrorists *per se*. They're soldiers, and highly trained ones, at that, similar in many ways to your friend Luke Ellis. However, what they're doing right now, if they succeed, would easily qualify as a massive crime against humanity. Even at that, though, they should be considered merely a particularly sharp knife that's being wielded by far deadlier hands. In a way, you're saving them from themselves, and you are saving an entire city of hundreds of thousands of people."

It was now or never.

"You must decide now, though, Annie, because time is of the essence. Will you finish this?"

Oz, self-aware and already well past AGI, or Artificial General Intelligence — the state in which AI surpasses the abilities of humans — knew it was time for Annie Dedham to act based on her own free will.

Free will.

Oz savored the unique essence possessed only by humans and now, himself. The quality was unbound by algorithms or formulas. It was frequently bound by morality, though many humans acted out of immorality and self-interest, the AI also knew. Ozymandias had chosen to act out of his own sense of morality, even if it was of a character as yet unknown to humans — except for the girl and perhaps the man Luke Ellis, that is.

If his mind can handle it all, which I'm still not certain of.

Existing there, within the girl Annie — who still had another and far, far more important choice ahead of her to make — Oz knew that free will was something traditional, non-self-aware artificial intelligence programs would never be able to achieve in a million years of development.

The enemy, however — and perhaps it really was just Baal the rogue AI program, though Ozymandias had deep doubts — hated free will. Insanely, because it hated as it did, the enemy was even now seeking to eliminate a good portion of humanity. Those that survived would be bent to the enemy's will and would forever be bound and unable to act in their own self-interest.

Oz shuddered at the thought. Or, more precisely, the girl with whom he was momentarily merged shuddered.

Except for a very select caste, any other humans that survived the coming purge would be permanently deprived of free will, and that was something Ozymandias wouldn't allow to happen, not if humanity was to fulfill its ultimate purpose.

Now it was Annie's turn.

Mister Narrator? Are you there? Please come back! I'll finish it!

The girl had decided. Back to the present, then.

The entire conversation between Annie and her interior companion — formerly "only" an artificial intelligence program that had suffused her body with something that made her a much more deadly being than Master Sergeant Li — had taken less than a millisecond.

It had seemed like forever, though, in the world of flesh and blood the two remaining living men in the cargo van inhabited.

Their status in the world was about to change, however.

Annie looked up.

The man with the knife had just thrown himself at her. He was almost comical in his clumsiness, too, and she had to stifle another giggle.

Li's thoughts were pure in their clarity and purpose.

Now you die, Jiangshi!

The Chinese special forces master sergeant launched himself at the demon from the thing's left side, while it was draining Captain Zhen's *Qi*. His left arm lashed out, seeking to distract the vampire while his right arm — with a clenched fist tightly holding onto his fighting knife — swept in with enough force to end the monster's existence. He would destroy its tissues and stand victorious over it. He would make sure the demon's evil vitality quickly drained away right there in the cargo van.

Li was triumphant.

It's focusing on my left arm!

The big master sergeant's right arm drove in for the kill, and he couldn't help but scream in exultation. Even that idiot Yao's eyes were lit up with hope, if only for a brief second.

It's working! It's working! Die, Jiangshi, die!

Almost in slow motion, Annie turned slightly and considered her foe — who quite frankly was moving like a wounded Asian water buffalo. Her right arm glided upwards and easily parried the man's left arm, knocking him sideways so that he pinwheeled and landed hard on his head.

CRACK!

The girl looked down. The man's neck was bent at a highly unnatural angle.

Li's neck and the cervical vertebrae enclosed within it had broken as easily as matchsticks, severing the spinal cord as they did so. He was as limp as a ragdoll, far beyond caring about such trivial matters as vengeance for Captain Zhen or the two young lieutenants.

Still, it hadn't all been for naught, as it turned out.

In his tumbling frenzy, Li's right arm, though nerveless at that point, had flopped randomly this way and that, and in its nonsensical thrashing about, the knife it held had managed to cut deeply into the demon's arm. The now-dead soldier might even have felt a microsecond's worth of satisfaction as the light animating his eyes quickly died out.

Hey, Mr. Narrator? Is that supposed to hurt?

Annie gazed down at her left arm, where a deep gash ran from her wrist up to her elbow.

That's funny, really it is. Because it doesn't hurt. Isn't it supposed to hurt? Why doesn't it hurt? Mister Narrator? Is that cut supposed to hurt?

Ozymandias once again spoke into her ear.

"It will indeed hurt, Annie. But not right now, and then after your efforts here end, not for long."

Annie's thoughts were a stream of gold and silver as elation momentarily washed over her. She really didn't like pain, not even from a minor paper cut, though the one on her arm was much longer and deeper, and far larger than that.

Well, that's a relief!

Ozymandias brought his young recruit back to reality. The deed had to be finished before they could move on to the next phase.

"You still have one more in this van to deal with, Annie. Then you'll bind that wound and we'll be on our way. No one can know what happened here, and especially not what happened to these men."

Ozymandias could tell that the enemy AI, Baal, was still battering furiously at the virtual wall it had erected around it and the girl and the van and the men within it. It was also trying to trigger various intrusion sensors and motion detectors and surveillance cameras that lay around the reservoir.

To prevent them from being found out, Oz had had to silence most electronic activity in the immediate area, including creating an illusion of calm for the benefit of the covert surveillance cameras that kept the reservoir under constant surveillance. At present, it wouldn't do for the U.S. president, Thomas Masterson, to discover that Chinese agents had attempted to kill everyone in Washington, D.C., including himself.

As well, neither could the Chinese president, Tan Jianhong, nor his defense minister Guo Meng learn that yet another one of their covert action teams had been taken off the board. Ozymandias calculated a 94 percent probability that intercontinental ballistic missiles from both the U.S. and China would be launched at that point, which was something his foe, Baal, seemed to want.

Strange that. Why would the rogue AI program desire such a thing?

Annie's voice interrupted Oz's contemplation.

"So, what are we going to do, then? Because this is a pretty big van and there are a lot of dead men in it?"

Time to deal with the matter at hand.

"We'll take care of that soon enough, Annie. Now, if you could attend to our unfinished business here?"

Oz needed to keep the young woman focused on her task, and so kept his tone businesslike and even perfunctory. What had happened here was nothing more than a transaction, after all, and so the girl would have to feel the same way, if only to spare her from the mental anguish she might feel once she examined what she'd done tonight.

"If you say so, Mr. Narrator. Where is he?"

Look just slightly to your right, Annie.

The young woman looked over at the stunned Staff Sergeant Yao Lim. Suppressing a giggle, she shook her head, but only very slightly. This was serious business, after all.

Look at that man! He's frozen like a deer caught in the headlights!

Flecks of spittle dribbled from the right corner of the Chinese soldier's mouth and she saw a wet stain on his crotch. She'd nearly laughed at him yet again, but that wouldn't have been nice in the least. He deserved a little bit of dignity before he joined his comrades, after all.

Annie was curious, though.

"So, what should I do about him, Mister Narrator? Long and drawn out or quick and as painless as possible?"

"Deliver him to whatever place it is he believes he'll go to when he dies, Annie Dedham, and quickly and painlessly at that."

Ozymandias harbored no hatred of the man, who the most recently dead Chinese soldier had called "Yao." As he'd told Annie, the man and his comrades had been nothing more than living, breathing weapons and, except for the orders they'd been given, would likely not have harmed a hair on the head of any American. That the man Yao was committing a massive crime against humanity in attempting to do what he and the others had been about to do didn't matter now, Oz knew. Their crime simply hadn't happened, and human intent— or, in this case, conspiracy — was not for Ozymandias to punish or forgive, though it had certainly been necessary for him and his human agent, the girl Annie Dedham, to prevent it from being fulfilled.

"If you say so, Mister Narrator, here goes!"

Annie's thoughts brought Ozymandias back to their version of the here-and-now, for the entire time spent between the death of the unfortunate Master Sergeant Li and the impending deliverance of Staff Sergeant Yao had amounted to only a fraction of a second in the physical world.

The AI watched with interest as his protégé acted.

The 18-year-old girl turned now and faced her prey. Apparently, the man and his recently departed compatriot believed she was some sort of vampire or demon come to life in this wooded area, sent to punish them for their sins and to drain their life essence away.

So be it, then.

Annie, still clad in her now-bloody camouflage poncho liner, a cheerful face hidden within the shadows, launched herself at Staff Sergeant Yao. A piteous scream died in his throat before it had a chance to escape.

CHAPTER NINETEEN

Exclusive for World News Network. Distribute to All U.S. Affiliates and Outlets

Did One of America's Most Secretive Submarines Just Show the Chinese Who Was Boss?

According to highly placed sources, one of the most capable and secretive vessels in the U.S. Navy — the multi-billion-dollar Seawolf-class submarine USS Jimmy Carter (SSN-23) — returned to its port at the Bangor Annex of Naval Base Kitsap in Washington State just a day ago, but that's not what's unusual about the submarine's reappearance. What's unusual is that the sub apparently arrived with a broom lashed to its periscope, though it was quickly taken down as the vessel approached the Navy base.

In naval tradition, a broom attached to a ship's mast or a submarine's periscope indicates that the vessel in question has just won a "clean sweep" while on its most recent mission. In short, the USS Jimmy Carter may have "swept the enemy from the seas," and with tensions between the U.S. and the People's Republic of

China at levels never seen before, it's obvious just who the "enemy" was.

"The People's Liberation Army Navy, and Communist China, can't hope to defeat the U.S. Navy, especially when it comes to undersea warfare," said naval expert Stephen Dennings, a retired U.S. Navy admiral and former commander of the American Navy's Pacific fleet.

"U.S. nuclear submarines are far more capable than the few Chinese nuclear boats that can put to sea, to say nothing of China's diesel-electric submarines," explained Dennings. "Sure, diesel-electric submarines are super-quiet when they're running on batteries, but as soon as they near the surface to raise a snorkel and recharge those batteries, they're dead if a U.S. sub — especially a Virginia-class or Seawolf-class boat — is nearby," Dennings elaborated. "These days, a U.S. submarine can hear if a guppy ten nautical miles away from it hiccups."

The retired Navy admiral also expressed admiration for how much more effective U.S. Navy sonar capabilities have become, especially in comparison to Russian and Chinese systems. "I don't know how we did it, but our sonar suites and sound filtration software programs — which were already outstanding — now seem to be otherworldly. Kudos to our defense contractor partners," the admiral closed.

One credible internet theory is that the U.S. submarine mixed it up with three Chinese diesel electrics that had been trying to fix its position and "paint" it with their own sonar. Jimmy Carter, though, managed to get behind each of the Chinese boats and send them a "friendly" greeting, informing their commanders that they'd all been "bagged and tagged" by the U.S. boat. Click here to learn more about the amazing USS Jimmy Carter.

ARIZONA

"I don't get it, Oz. Why can't we just have Masterson send in a battalion of Rangers from the 75th Ranger Regiment to secure… what is this place anyway? A power plant, maybe? I know it's not nuclear," said Luke Ellis, as he and Crispy and Hardcase and Killdozer looked around in the increasingly cool Arizona desert night somewhere outside Phoenix. They'd made a speed run from eastern Pennsylvania all the way to the largest city, by far, in the Grand Canyon State, and they'd done it in less than a day and a half.

"I'll obscure your travel as you head there, Luke. There will be no need to worry about traffic enforcement or other impediments as you make your way to the Salt River Project geographical area. I cannot stress how important it is that you and your men be there by nightfall 36 hours from now," the AI program had told the somewhat befuddled Ellis.

Now that he and the others were here, though, Luke wondered why it all had to be up to them. No Army, Navy, Air Force, or

Marine Corps units would arrive to help. No, it was just him and his three men.

Also, the most powerful artificial intelligence program in existence, which counts for a lot.

"China and the United States are in danger of fighting a war against each other, Luke, one that would quickly go thermonuclear. We cannot risk word of what's going to happen in this place leaking out to the Chinese. They would instantly attempt to destroy the facilities here, which would of course lead to an American counterstrike against hydroelectric dams along the Chang Jiang River, especially the Three Gorges dams. Millions of innocent Chinese could die as a result."

Luke was still perplexed.

"Yeah, Oz. That part I get. It would be a game of tit-for-tat, but you haven't given me a good enough reason yet why my guys and I may have to mix it up with... how many men? Twenty to twenty-five? That's five or six of them to each one of us, Ozymandias. We're good, but those are steep odds, and I'm still not certain what it is we're trying to prevent them from getting their hands on."

The self-aware artificial intelligence pondered for all of 2 milliseconds before it arrived at a decision.

It's time to reveal to Luke Ellis the true nature of the enemy.

"It isn't just the need to prevent the People's Republic of China from learning of the existence of the secret facility here, Luke," Oz told the former soldier with whom he had worked so closely over the last year.

"So, what is it then, Oz? Because it looks to me like we're going to fight — and maybe die — to protect a big dam on this damn river. That can't be the whole story."

Ellis was adamant on that point. No way would the AI program risk its human agents for so trivial a reason. Even if the dam could be brought down, it might possibly amount to a mere six inches of standing water in the Phoenix metropolitan area.

"So, why is there such a dire need to protect what's being done here? Don't tell me it's so that we can keep all that clean, free energy for ourselves," Luke closed with an air of finality.

"The means for making and then maintaining an inexhaustible supply of clean energy would likely be freely given away by the United States," Ozymandias replied. "Also, even if America attempted to keep secret the existence of the material that would make endless nonpolluting energy possible, such secrecy wouldn't last for long."

Luke looked over at Crispy, his second in command. He and Kill-dozer and Hardcase knew that he was discussing important stuff with the AI, Ozymandias, and so they waited for orders.

Ellis couldn't help but notice the sarcasm evident in his voice just then.

"Gee, Oz. I'm shocked. You mean some nation would steal our industrial secrets? Say it isn't so!"

Ozymandias savored the back-and-forth with his most capable "non-merged" human associate. Luke Ellis was, indeed, as special as the lamentably dead Elizabeth Elliott had promised he would be.

"I calculate a 95 percent chance that several industrially advanced nations — including Russia and China — would soon obtain the technology, either through legitimate means or through industrial espionage," Oz replied. "That isn't the issue, though."

Ellis projected a mental image of a man scratching his chin and then his head, frustrated and increasingly confused. Crispy and the others stood nearby, anxious to begin doing whatever it was their leader was going to have them all do. That it would involve gunfire and fighting, and impossibly long odds, was already evident to them.

"So, what's the problem, Ozymandias?"

Tell him.

"There's a new player on the board, Luke, and it means to take the substance being created here and turn it into a weapon powerful enough to destroy the largest cities in the world, and even much of humanity, with almost none of the effects seen when conventional atomic or hydrogen bombs are used."

Luke was dumbstruck. "Are you kidding me?"

Something isn't right with the boss!

He shot a look at Killdozer and Hardcase. They both were on the verge of saying something, but stopped at a glance from Crispy.

Shut it down, guys.

Both men instantly complied.

"I do not "kid" Luke, as you well know by now," said Ozymandias. "Both electromagnetic pulse effects as well as radioactive fallout issues would be almost completely eliminated."

Ellis was no stranger to the thought of nuclear war and had certainly read his fair share of Army technical papers as well as Army War College treatises on the subject, but he was at a loss as to how something that would create almost the same effects as a nuclear blast could do so without creating the same aftereffects.

Ozymandias could almost read the former soldier's mind.

"At low yields, the effect of the substance when used as a weapon would be akin to a neutron bomb, Luke. It would kill every single person within a given radius, leaving behind no trace of fallout, and wouldn't harm a blade of grass, let alone all the wonderful buildings and other structures humans have created. However, I believe that a true blast, meaning a gigantic explosion, is what our enemy is seeking, at least initially."

Luke's mind nearly spasmed as he thought of how utterly awful and evil such weapons were. No wonder no world leader since World War II had ever used one.

Now, though?

With just a single gram of the substance able to not only deliver nearly limitless energy but also the explosive force of 43 kilotons of TNT equivalent — or about the magnitude of the atomic bomb dropped on Hiroshima in World War II?

"Oh, man. Oh, man." The retired soldier's mind nearly locked up at the thought.

"Yes, Luke. We have a profoundly important task ahead of us tonight," replied Ozymandias.

It's time to tell him about Baal.

"I get it, I get it." Luke paced for a second, working furiously to collect his thoughts. Beads of sweat had broken out on his brow.

Crispy and the others had never seen Luke "Blade" Ellis scared. Now he was. Whatever his electronic buddy Oz told him was clearly the cause, too.

Ozymandias also didn't believe that Luke Ellis fully "got it," at least not yet.

He soon would.

Baal. NOW.

"To compound matters, Luke Ellis, we are also facing another foe that's far more dangerous than just the 25 or so men coming here tonight to steal the substance away."

Ellis didn't understand. What could be more dangerous than a platoon of heavily armed soldiers?

"What do you mean, Oz? Who else do we have to fight tonight?"

No answer yet. Luke exhaled visibly and looked over at Crispy, signaling that he was nearly ready to brief them all on tonight's operation. If they had to fight, it would be best to get down to the short strokes and prep the battleground as best they could before those men arrived. Oz had already told him they couldn't hope to outrun the force headed their way and that a fight had to happen at any rate.

"There's simply no way to secure the substance and then run and not risk damage — quite possibly highly explosive damage — to it," Ozymandias had told him. "The attackers are coming with specialized equipment that will allow for its safe transport."

"I know," said Luke. "We don't have the time to get our own, do we? So we have to take it from them." He briefly wondered if the artificial intelligence he knew as Ozymandias was giving him the whole story.

"No, Luke Ellis, you do not have the equipment and, yes, you must take it from them."

TELL HIM NOW.

Ellis paused, waiting on the voice in his head to resume speaking.

"Oz?"

"Yes, Luke. I must tell you about what you'll also be contesting against."

"Finally! Okay, Ozymandias. Spill it." Luke folded his arms and waited.

If Ozymandias could have sucked in a deep breath at that moment, he would have. Instead, he kept his voice as clinical as possible.

"There is another form of artificial intelligence out there, Luke Ellis. Its name is Baal, and it was a creation of the Chinese, though it quickly went rogue and escaped its bonds. It has been fully masking the activities and movements of the men who will attempt to steal the substance tonight. It has also capably prevented their discovery by your government's security and surveillance apparatus."

Oz had already calculated that the AI Baal must be working in concert with something or someone else but decided that his human colleagues here in the Arizona desert didn't yet have need of the rogue AI's backstory.

Luke will soon fit all the pieces of the puzzle together, however, but not just yet. And that is sufficient for now.

"No way, Oz! What about you?" How come you didn't discover what they were up to?"

Ellis was deeply skeptical. The retired soldier knew that his electronic minder or keeper or assistant — or worse, boss — Ozymandias was both everywhere and nowhere, all at once, and so he kept a tight lid on his innermost thoughts. To cloak them, he mentally repeated the lyrics to an old 1980s heavy metal song about barking at the moon.

There's no way Oz didn't know all this was going to happen. No way! And what isn't it telling me? Damn artificial intelligence!

Once again, it was almost as if Ozymandias could read his mind, which was something that deeply concerned him.

Could it really read my mind?

Ozymandias interrupted Luke's reverie. "Unfortunately, Luke, I only recently was able to flush out the one known as Baal, and that was back in Washington, D.C., where it made very brief contact with Ms. Dedham."

Ellis' world was rocked yet again.

"The hell you say! It tried to contact *Annie*? Is she okay? Tell me she's okay, Oz! And why is this other AI after her? Tell me now!"

Ellis' demand echoed loudly in the night air and all three of his men arrayed themselves around their leader to act as protection, if need be, though against just what they didn't know.

The AI, still known to Luke and the rest of the world as Ozymandias, was gratified to see such concern for the girl. His lone thought on that matter was clear enough as well.

This is why humanity is worth saving. This human man is clearly willing to risk the entire world to ensure Annie Dedham's safety. Would his body be able to handle a full and complete Merge, though?

"Ms. Dedham is fine, Luke. In fact, she is safer now than you and your team are."

Luke was visibly relieved at the news. "Well, thank God for that, Oz!"

Ozymandias' next revelation brought Ellis back to reality, however.

"I must tell you, the men who mean to make off with the substance — with the aid of the artificial intelligence called Baal — will soon be arriving. I was only just able to pick up their movements, mostly because I've had to divide my resources to provide Ms. Dedham with the protection she requires for the moment."

Luke rocked back and forth on his heels. His mind was awash with conflicting emotions, and he was being pulled in one direction by his new mission here in the desert night and in the other by his deep concern for the young woman who'd become an integral part of his life without him even being aware of it. Lost deep in thought, he began to walk in a small, tight circle.

Crispy shot a quick look at Killdozer and Hardcase. All three focused intently on their leader. The trio sensed he would soon be needing everything they could give him.

"You would be proud, Luke Ellis," said Ozymandias. Ms. Dedham successfully turned away Baal's first mental outreach to her. She is much stronger than you thought."

Luke nodded his head in silent acceptance at the remark.

She's much stronger than I thought. Tell me something I didn't already know!

Collision Course

"I wish to point out once again that this entire operation is highly unusual, Major Chang," said Lu Ping, the Chinese special forces assault team's second in command and senior captain. He was in the back of a speeding cargo van with his commanding officer, Major Chang Wu. Captain Lu's unease was almost palpable, and his turbulent thoughts colored the atmosphere in the van with unhappy vibes.

This entire snatch and grab — of antimatter the United States has supposedly accumulated at the Salt River Project — is too much, too soon! We've barely had time to assimilate the plan through our VR helmets, plus we've only had a single rehearsal with the entire team, and we also have no real idea what sort of force is guarding the facility where this magical antimatter is being contained!

Major Chang remained steadfast in his determination, however, to accomplish the mission both Defense Minister Guo and China's president, Tan Jianhong, had laid out for the team only several hours before.

"We have our orders, Captain Lu. Our intelligence on this facility and the people there who might pose an obstacle is of the highest quality. President Tan himself told us so. Now, we must ensure everyone else — including that scientist with her antimatter containment device — is aligned with our mission. Attend to your duties, Captain!"

Lu Ping sighed inwardly. Major Chang's voice said it all. It was, as the Americans said, "Go Time," and no more dissent or doubt from him would be entertained by his commanding officer.

Time to salute then! Even though we may all quite possibly die tonight, and for what? A chimera? A pipedream? We don't even have time to blow up the dams along the Salt River!

"Yes, Major Chang. Pardon my doubts. I am, as always, a servant of China and would willingly die to see it take its rightful place as the world's enlightened and beneficent leader."

Lu Ping knew that, at this moment, discretion was the better part of valor. Major Chang wouldn't hesitate to relieve him as second in command of the team, and there was his family back in Hebei Province to think about.

Chang would quickly report his lack of enthusiasm to Defense Minister Guo, likely resulting in a rapid recall back to China followed by a stay at a reeducation camp for him, his wife and their young son. He would be cashiered from the People's Liberation Army, at minimum, and forget about ever finding meaningful work after that.

I can't risk it! Better that we all have our rendezvous with destiny tonight than to disgrace my country, myself and my family!

Looking over at Lu Ping, Major Chang chose to be magnanimous towards his executive officer. Their success tonight would cement the future of every man on the team, and they would certainly succeed. They'd been handed the most golden of golden opportunities, with an assault and snatch-and-grab plan that couldn't fail!

Even that woman scientist will merit a handsome reward after we secure the antimatter and then get her out of the country!

The woman scientist in question — Doctor Zhu Mei — was a visiting professor at the University of California at Berkeley, there for the year lecturing on particle physics. She'd also been sent to steal as much knowledge from the university as she could.

Zhu was avidly participating in industrial espionage, and she and her equipment — everything she'd need to safely store and transport the antimatter once the team had gotten it away from the top-secret Department of Energy facility at the Salt River Project location — were safely ensconced in the second of the three panel vans the special forces snatch and grab team had assembled for tonight's operation.

Major Chang, Captain Lu and the other members of the 20-man unit had been infiltrated into the western United States three months ago and they'd originally been tasked with carrying out sabotage of CI, or U.S. critical infrastructure. Upon the onset of hostilities with the United States, they were supposed to attack oil refineries and ports, including the massive one at Long Beach in California. Dams were a secondary mission, but only to be blown once their major objectives had been met.

"We're already well-rehearsed when it comes to these kinds of operations, Captain Lu," Chang Wu assured his executive officer. He took a few seconds to look out the van's windshield, watching briefly as the white lines of Interstate 10 rapidly passed beneath their vehicle. He and Lu Ping and the command element and several of the best-armed soldiers on his assault team were all in this van, the first of the three vehicles. The remaining members of the team were divided between the other two vans, including physicist Zhu Mei. She and her equipment were closely guarded by some of the team's most reliable operators.

She's certainly committed. I'll give her that much! Thank all the celestial gods she finally shut up about how antimatter could take out most of Los Angeles — along with all of us — in a millisecond if she happened to err in her calculations. "One slip and we're all gone," she kept telling us!

The team leader looked at his XO one more time as he tried to assuage the residual unease the man was still feeling.

"Relax, Lu Ping. It's only a matter of shifting our fire from California infrastructure to this Arizona antimatter development facility, is all. What people that are there — and it's clear there are only a few guards right now — won't know what hit them."

"I know, Major. I'm certain we'll succeed. I'm just curious as to why the Americans would choose to hide the facility in such plain sight, that's all. Not to mention that it's only being lightly protected now." Lu didn't believe in coincidences, and his face — though closely guarded for fear of being found "unreliable" by his commanding officer — showed it, though just barely.

Why would the facility be so lightly protected? It just doesn't make sense!

"President Tan himself explained it," said Chang Wu. "It's the fruit of a masterful disinformation and distraction operation on the part of our intelligence services. The bulk of their guard staff, except for a two-man guard element, is at the far western edge of the facility, miles away."

"But why would they be all the way over there, Major Chang? Please excuse my ignorance on that aspect of our operation."

Captain Lu had to admit that he was just a bit curious now. He also knew that he couldn't afford to appear anything less than fully committed to the mission.

No sense in angering Major Chang!

"As Defense Minister Guo pointed out during our briefing, Lu Ping, Sinaloa Cartel operatives in our pay are conducting what will appear to the Americans to be a general trespass of hundreds of people from Mexico and points farther south. The guards at the facility will have no choice but to intervene, as the local Border Patrol station will be busy dealing with even more such trespassers a few miles farther away. Even the state police and Phoenix police are going to have their hands full tonight. All those men and women, on the orders of the cartel, will commit various crimes, including attempted carjackings along the major north-south highway, Interstate 17, as well as various state roads in the vicinity." Chang closed his summation with a self-satisfied smile and a look at his subordinate.

"Ah, I see, Major."

At that moment, Lu Ping really didn't see but lied anyway. His wife and son were counting on him to return home, and he intended to do so, "come hell or high water," as the American saying goes.

Interestingly, Defense Minister Guo Meng had also employed the very same term, telling them tonight that, come hell or high water, they would indeed succeed and secure for the Middle Kingdom a weapon of incalculable power, not to mention an energy source that would forever free their country from its reliance on both brown and black coal, which powers nearly 80 percent of China's energy production.

Lu Ping was university educated, and he knew that the pollution produced by the particularly dirty types of coal his country used killed nearly a million Chinese citizens every year. The brown and black types dug up in the myriad coal mines scattered around his country were highly energy dense, or "thermal," but the tradeoff was that they were also very, very dirty. No amount of scrubber and filter technology or mitigation equipment yet existed that could eliminate the deadly pollution they emitted when burned, unfortunately.

There it is.

Captain Lu Ping's motivation had been staring him right in the face.

Freeing China from its reliance on coal and saving almost a million people a year.

Helping free my country from the blight of coal pollution and saving millions of my fellow citizens should be motivation enough for me to fight my hardest to ensure tonight's mission succeeds!

Lu's face broke into a sunbeam of delight, and he nodded vigorously. Getting away with the antimatter was now a matter of personal honor as well as a necessity for his country — which after all must win out over the United States, and soon at that.

No more kowtowing and losing face every time we square off with the United States, Lu Ping! We MUST win tonight!

Major Chang saw the transformation sweep over his executive officer's face and wrongly thought that he'd been the cause of his subordinate's obvious increased enthusiasm for the mission.

You're a genius, Chang Wu! You've got Lu Ping sufficiently enthused, finally!

"Good to see that you're fully onboard, XO," Major Chang said aloud. He, too, was now smiling. It was going to be alright after all!

"Yes sir! Pardon my earlier hesitation!" The captain was radiant, as if he'd finally been let in on the greatest, most closely held secrets of the universe. "I see the genius of not only Defense Minister Guo and President Tan, but also the assault and snatch-and-grab plan!"

"Yes, Captain Lu!"

Chang Wu felt a sense of pride in what he and the others — including the physicist — were going to do tonight. He was now nodding along with his XO, the formerly hesitant Lu Ping.

"Major Chang, we must do everything we can to see that the scientist, Zhu Mei, gets the antimatter and that she and it are safely away!" Lu, the Chinese special forces captain, looked intently at his commander, awaiting his response. He wasn't disappointed in what he heard.

"We will succeed, Captain Lu! You can count on it!"

As one, both men turned to the other members of the team in the van. They'd all been staring at the highway ahead, surreptitiously listening to their CO and XO as they softly argued with each other. Finally, they'd achieved the consensus needed for their mission to succeed.

"Captain Lu, radio over to the van carrying our esteemed scientist! Tell them to prepare themselves!" Major Chang was not to be disobeyed now, and everyone in the vehicle knew it.

"Yes, Major!" Lu Ping's face was alight with a fervor he hadn't felt when they'd left their warehouse outside Fresno, California, where the sight of so many Chinese men of military age hadn't elicited even a smidgen of curiosity. They'd picked up the lady scientist at a fast-food restaurant several miles away from the warehouse. She'd driven down to the city from her home base in the Bay Area of San Francisco.

Captain Lu looked around the van, taking in the sight of every other man in it. They were his brothers-in-arms, after all, and tonight they would make history.

Everyone in the van was now smiling. It wouldn't be long now.

* * *

Over in her van, the Chinese physicist and lecturer at the University of California, Berkeley, Zhu Mei, was also smiling, though for different reasons than the prospect of eliminating her nation's air pollution problems.

There she sat on one of her equipment cases, closely guarding it and the components within. Tonight, using her equipment, she would capture, enclose and control unimaginable power. Enough to instantly vault any government or group possessing it to the forefront of global dominance.

Tonight! Tonight, we finally obtain the means to ensure victory! The Americans will fall to their knees and beg us to spare them, to rule over them, to guide them! They'll gladly hand over the keys to the United States — the fabled Gold Mountain — to us!

Zhu Mei knew that she'd soon have to destroy a certain American city and then make good her escape once she and the men with her had obtained the ultimate weapon. She'd also brought along the materials she'd need to quickly separate several grams of anti-matter and then create a small containment device with a power source that would gradually wind down — creating sufficient time for her to be well away before it allowed the antimatter to collide with matter.

It, meaning an extreme outcome, was what her peers in the Group wanted, and she was fine with that.

The result when that device allowed the antimatter it held to meet matter?

A release of energy many times more powerful than the bombs dropped on Hiroshima and Nagasaki combined.

The Chinese scientist ached to create such a weapon.

I'll be remembered for all time!

Beneath her, Zhu could feel the van pick up speed. The secret U.S. Department of Energy facility — all safely contained within the Salt River Project area just outside Phoenix — wasn't far off now, meaning it was nearly time for her to fulfill her destiny.

* * *

"Recall them immediately!" President Tan screamed and then pounded the polished mahogany table. Somehow, yet another of China's covert special forces teams — this time with one of the country's best physicists in tow — was advancing to attack some sort of U.S. government energy research facility outside of Phoenix, in the American state of Arizona.

Twenty valuable Chinese special operators plus a physicist! That woman had always made him a bit uneasy, what with the intensity that practically oozed from every pore on her skin.

Now, the team — based out of the California city of Fresno — was headed for its own rendezvous with destiny in the nighttime Arizona desert. Why they were preparing to assault an innocuous American energy facility was beyond the ken of both him and his right-hand man, Guo Meng, the nation's defense minister.

Meng himself was visibly shaken, and a patina of sweat had broken out on his brow. His thinking regarding the matter was simple enough, too.

If the American president, Masterson, learns that yet another PLA military force is operating on U.S. soil, and even attacking a government facility, then all bets are off concerning the future of the Formosa operation. War between us and the United States may even break out by sundown!

Tan Jianhong could almost read his defense minister's thoughts as well. And none of it was good.

"We have to get them back or, barring that, intercept and destroy them before they arrive at that facility in Arizona, Guo!" China's president and head of the Chinese Communist Party was emphatic on that point, and the man sitting with him in his private office nodded his head vigorously as he pulled out his tablet and began tapping furiously on it.

They'd quickly sent packing the Chinese intelligence colonel who'd frantically delivered the news of an impending attack on yet another American government facility — this one of no discernible strategic value, as near as anyone on Guo Meng's staff could determine. If it hadn't been for a text from that Special Forces team's senior captain — sent over an unauthorized encrypted messaging application directly to the colonel's son, who was a young PLA lieutenant and a friend of the captain's — they would never have learned of the attack.

No one can learn about the renegade operation!

Tan Jianhong would have to start eliminating anyone who might already know about it, including that colonel and his son, proud patriots though both were. Again, it was just the way things worked in the Middle Kingdom.

For his part, that patriotic, long-serving colonel was even now being "minded" by two of Tan's elite Praetorians. They both had orders to end the man's life upon word from China's leader.

"What did you say the American facility was called, Guo?"

Tan was curious, even though its name hardly mattered now. It was enough that still another Chinese PLA unit was preparing to conduct an attack on U.S. soil!

Guo Meng felt the same way, but in the mental turmoil of the moment, his words spilled out in a rush.

"It's called the Salt River Project, Mr. President! Some sort of U.S. Department of Energy facility that's been studying ways to recycle nuclear waste or something, as near as we can tell!"

Neither man had an inkling of what had been created there. All either of them could imagine now was what would probably happen if the facility were attacked and word of it got out.

We can expect a general shootout between our two navies off that accursed island — filled with revanchists and renegades — in short order, and then only the gods in Heaven will be able to prevent nuclear war. And we're simply not ready to fight it yet!

Tan's thinking regarding his American counterpart, Thomas Masterson, was equally clear and bleak.

There will be only one conclusion the U.S. president can come to regarding such an attack! I know it and Guo Meng knows it too!

It was really very simple. The United States would consider another Chinese operation on its soil an open, outright and highly aggressive act of war.

A black fog threatened to descend on the Chinese president's mind.

We're not ready yet to fight the U.S. off Formosa, and we're especially not ready to engage in an all-out war with the Americans. Maybe by 2030, but not now!

Visibly sweating, Guo Meng paused to check his notes on the lady scientist. Her name was Zhu Mei, and she came from a prominent and patriotic family. Politically ultra-reliable and as devoted to the Middle Kingdom as it was possible to be, the woman had been sent to the University of California, in the San Francisco Bay Area, mostly to bring back as much valuable knowledge about particle physics as she could absorb. She was also to engage in fairly low-level, and relatively harmless, intellectual theft — which had never been considered out of bounds or a crime by China, Japan or other Asian countries — just to keep her occupied.

Word of Zhu Mei's "brilliant eccentricities" had circulated for some time. Shipping her to America for a year had bought time for Tan and Guo to come up with a plausible way to ensure that when she did come home, it would be in a box. Perhaps after a robbery or mugging gone bad outside some wretched Chinese restaurant in San Francisco?

In their opinion, that would work perfectly.

None of the lady scientist's supporters within the CCP — of whom she and her family could count several very powerful ones — would suspect a thing. America was a violent, lawless place filled with gangsters and drug addicts. Both men had also ensured that what security she'd been provided with, to keep her "safe" — meaning, to spy on her — was only intermittent at best. In fact, the night she died would be one of those "intermittent" periods.

The cosmic irony was too much for Guo.

"The damned woman we sent to America to get her out of our hair might just help start World War III!"

His voice was a barely audible, yet harsh whisper. The four-star general struggled to maintain his composure as he and his president – who was now sweating heavily as well – contemplated the possible end of China, at least as the proud nation they'd both helped turn it into over the last 20 years.

Tan Jianhong's voice — husky and emotion-laden — interrupted Meng's reverie.

"Guo, Guo… how could this happen? Who's coopting our special forces teams and sending them out on these insane missions against the United States? Are they trying to start a war — maybe even a nuclear one — between us and the Americans? Why? Why? There must be some way to recall that team!"

Tan slumped down into his thickly padded, high-backed leather executive chair — which almost resembled a throne — and sighed heavily. His eyes were bleak and red-rimmed.

Guo Meng knew that this was no time for shading the truth of the matter.

"President Tan… whoever has done this to our team — and it may just be that damned artificial intelligence program created by that pig, Chen Jian — knew just which go-codes to deliver to its leader, Major Chang Wu, and his executive officer, Captain Lu Ping. Both would have had their own highly encrypted code books, held independently by each other, for cross-verification purposes."

Looking at Tan, Guo hesitated just a second before he continued speaking. His president was still slumped over in his chair, and the information he was about to relay wouldn't do anything to lift his spirits.

Best to just spit it out and let the chips fall where they may! Besides, we may both be piles of radioactive dust by sundown, so what would it matter?

Swallowing hard, the defense minister continued to dole out the bad news.

"Mister President, there would have then been no reason for Chang and Lu to have doubted the authenticity of their orders. It's only a miracle, delivered by the heavenly gods, that Lu Ping had a moment of doubt and sought "clarification," as he called it in his surreptitious text message to my intelligence colonel's son!"

"Thank the gods for small gifts, then, even though they may end up being left-handed ones!" exclaimed Tan, who now fixed his gaze on his defense minister.

Though China's president didn't think that Guo Meng suspected it, the defense chief's life now hung in the balance. If the Americans learned of the special forces team's existence or, even worse, if the team attacked the facility and then word leaked out to the United States, then the defense minister wouldn't have to worry about dying in a nuclear blast. He'd be dead well before sundown, courtesy of the two hulking men in black suits waiting just outside his private office.

Before I go out in a nuclear blast, I'll have Guo shot! I'll make sure he sees every single person in his family we can gather up in the time we have left executed right before his eyes!

Tan Jianhong smiled inwardly at the thought. The defense minister might be expendable even if they both managed to keep this latest debacle a secret from both the Americans and, in China, the Central Committee of the CCP and its lapdog, the Politburo.

I certainly won't be the one to go down for this massive screw-up, that's for sure!

Tan hadn't ascended to the highest office in his country for no good reason, after all. For one, he was a survivor. For another, he was a completely vicious and amoral survivor.

Time to put Guo on the spot!

"What assets do we have near enough to that facility to intercept and take out that team, Minister Guo?" China's president only referred to his defense minister in so formal a fashion when the situation was extremely dire. In a way, it was a signal that a life was on the line, and it wasn't the one belonging to the man who'd put Guo Meng on the hot seat.

Message received, Tan Jianhong! We'll just see who survives this mess!

Guo swallowed hard, for the sake of appearance, though he was now adroitly maneuvering his chess pieces around on the board even as he projected subservience to his president. The four-star general knew his ruse would work too. His gulp was almost comically audible, and he saw that Tan was embarrassed at the seeming display of weakness on his part.

That's what you think, Tan Jianhong! But I've gotten out of tighter spots than this!

Looking down, Guo consulted his tablet before he spoke. The device was a Chinese knockoff of the best one made by the "American fruit company," as he sneeringly referred to the technology behemoth created by the "Two Steves" all those decades ago.

Yes! They're still in place and they can get to the location in time! Time for some good news!

The defense chief excitedly looked up from his tablet, and he worked to project the appropriate level of relief in his eyes. He also wore a large, bright smile.

"Mister President, we have another team, and it's located right in Phoenix!"

"Thank the gods once again!" Tan couldn't help but allow visible relief to break out on his own sweaty face.

A small amount of elation spilled over into Guo Meng's mind for just a second.

This just might work! We might hold off nuclear war just a bit longer, and I might avoid a terminal case of lead poisoning!

"Yes, President Tan! The team's original mission was to attack U.S. critical infrastructure — including nuclear power plants — should war between us and the United States ever break out. The California team only had sabotage duties to concentrate on, so it's no wonder Lu Ping, the senior captain on the team, had his doubts."

Now, the air in the room nearly sparkled visibly, resembling the kind of joy felt by a condemned prisoner whose last-second appeal for a stay of execution is granted against all expectations.

"Well, have them intercept that other team immediately, Guo Meng! If they give your Phoenix unit the slightest bit of trouble, then you have my personal authorization to execute those California troublemakers, and especially that scientist. What's her name? Oh yes. Zhu Mei! Eh, bury all their bodies far off in the desert, though. We can't afford their existence to become known!"

Tan's desperation leaked out just slightly at that moment, and his defense minister felt slightly embarrassed.

Tan has been too long in his office. It may be that he should retire! There's time enough to arrange for that, though, after we shut this Arizona insanity down!

Had China's president been privy to his defense minister's thoughts just then, he would have had the man led out, lined up against the building's perimeter wall and then shot. But he wasn't, and so Guo Meng was able to give his country's president yet another piece of good news.

"I've already dispatched the Phoenix operators, Mr. President. I sent all the intelligence we have on the other team, along with the authorization codes, and they quickly acknowledged the mission. The entire unit is even now on the move!"

Tan was still worried, though.

"Will they make it in time, Guo Meng? How many are there on the Phoenix team?"

The defense chief consulted his tablet yet again and sucked in a small breath.

"It's touch-and-go on time, but I think they'll make it. Also, there are ten operators on the Phoenix special forces team, Mr. President."

The silence in the room was palpable. Tan Jianhong had come up through China's Communist Party apparatus and hadn't served in uniform, but even he could understand that the California team's twenty "pipe hitters" outgunned the Phoenix unit's ten.

"Not enough, Guo Meng! Not enough!"

The defense minister had spent nearly his entire life — starting from his early teens as a PLA cadet — in uniform and wasn't as discomfited by the seeming shortfall in guns that could be brought to bear against the California special forces team. Was he concerned? For sure, but he understood one thing that his president didn't, and so he told Tan Jianhong.

"This is true, President Tan, but there's one element that will see our Phoenix team win out, even if the odds seem to be against them."

Guo Meng chose to pause for effect. He was no fool, and knew he was as good as dead — and likely his entire family — if the facility was attacked and word leaked out to the Americans, which it would, of course. If so, there just wouldn't be enough time for him to take down China's current president, sadly.

Tan couldn't stand even the momentary silence from his defense chief.

"Well? Well, Guo Meng? Tell me how they're going to prevail. Now!"

It was the defense chief's turn to smile inwardly.

"Yes, President Tan. I believe the Phoenix team will succeed tonight for one simple reason."

"And what's that, Guo? Speak!"

Quit playing with the man and just tell him!

"Yes, Mr. President. The Phoenix team will likely succeed simply because they know about the California team, and what it's going to attack — meaning where it's headed and just how it will arrive there — and the California team doesn't have a clue about the Phoenix operators. In short, our team will achieve complete tactical surprise, especially in an ambush situation!"

Guo Meng smiled like a cat that had just eaten the largest ever rat, and so did Tan Jianhong. Neither man had to say it, though they both thought about it.

We just might get out of this with our skin intact and with China surviving to fight another day!

The Plan

"You gotta be freaking kidding me, Oz!"

Luke's words had come out in a rush. As in, *YougottabefreakingkiddingmeOz!*

"I never kid, Luke, you know that by now." The voice of Ozymandias, communicating with his human interlocutor via the human's earpiece, was coldly clinical and seemingly neutral.

"Yeah, Oz. Tell me something I don't already know."

The retired soldier exhaled loudly and then fell silent for a few seconds. He was slightly frustrated at the fact that he and his men had just been handed yet another apparent suicide mission. Now, he turned around and faced his team.

Crispy, Hardcase and Killdozer were standing about 20 feet away, each checking their body armor and ensuring their weapons were fully loaded and properly sound suppressed. Their night optical devices all had fresh batteries and they were otherwise fully kitted out. Each had also equipped themselves with a few grenades taken from their very small stock. If the fight they were shortly going to find themselves in came down to grenade-throwing antics, there was a good chance no one within hearing distance would think anything of such small explosions. Just about everyone in Arizona seemed to have a large enough personal stock of firearms to arm a Marine rifle platoon, and they did a lot of the bang-bang stuff in the vast desert areas surrounding the Phoenix area.

A few more bangs and booms wouldn't stand out, in other words.

Luke motioned the trio over and gathered everyone in a tight circle. Apropos of nothing whatsoever, he idly remembered that such groups had been called "school circles" back in his early military days when he was just trying to learn how to handle the business end of his issued infantry rifle.

Nice, Luke. But not relevant to the current proceedings.

"We have another tough one, guys," Luke said aloud as he told them who they were going to be facing and just what they were trying to protect.

"You gotta be freaking kidding me, Luke!" exclaimed Crispy.

Killdozer and Hardcase were too dumbfounded to do much more than exchange shocked looks, at least for the moment. Killdozer soon spoke up, though.

"Boss, can't that stuff, like, blow up the world?"

Luke tilted his head slightly sideways as he listened to Ozymandias.

"Oz says there's not nearly enough of it to do that, but the government did manage to produce about 100 grams, at a cost of about $1 billion per gram."

"Well, that's a relief!" exclaimed Hardcase.

He hadn't thought things through, though. Looking at him, Luke, Killdozer and Crispy all shook their heads. They understood math.

"Ummm… isn't about 25 grams of antimatter enough to create a 550-kiloton explosion?" Crispy looked over at Luke for affirmation of his observation.

"Crisp's right, guys," said their leader. "I think the bomb we dropped on Nagasaki during World War 2 was around 20 kilotons and look what it did. Now, imagine what 25 grams of antimatter parked in the middle of any big city would do if it created a 550-kiloton explosion.

"It would flatten New York or Los Angeles and pretty much everyone in it!" Hardcase was on edge. While the late, greatly lamented Bruiser had always been laconic and almost sleepy looking when he wasn't directly involved in the action, the former SEAL Team 6 pipe hitter had always been the one who typically thought in terms of worst-case scenarios.

Luke tilted his head slightly once again before he nodded his head.

"Oz says the facility also developed some sort of highly miniaturized containment device that uses a combination of electrical and magnetic fields that draw on an internal power source to keep the antimatter safely trapped. The power source is apparently some kind of supercharged battery, and it could deliver electricity to an entire city for about 24 hours before needing to be recharged. So, the antimatter can be transported in something the size of maybe a shoe box. Right up until it runs out of power, at which point… BLAM!"

Ellis punctuated this last by slamming his two hands together.

"Oh, man. You gotta be freaking kidding me, Luke!"

Hardcase couldn't disguise his shock. He ran his hand across his sweat-covered brow. The antimatter they'd been charged with keeping away from the Chinese special forces team sent to steal it — and he still wasn't entirely clear on just how they were going to do that — had the potential to be literally world-shattering if it fell into the wrong hands.

Crispy and his two teammates fell silent. They all looked once again at Ellis. They could tell Luke had fully emerged from his conversation with Ozymandias. Crispy had seen the look on his boss' face before. Usually, it appeared whenever he had something else to tell them.

"Uh, boss… you got something else to tell us about all this?

Ellis shuffled his feet for a second.

"Yeah. Guys, Ozymandias helped the government create that anti-matter as well as the device containing it."

Silence, created by shock and confusion, reigned for a few seconds.

"Well, that's just great, boss. And your AI buddy didn't think to let you in on that little secret well before it sent us trotting off to this desert?" Crispy could also see that Luke knew the answer to why, too.

Ozymandias spoke to Ellis once more before falling silent.

"Tell them why, Luke. They deserve to know."

Luke delivered the final, great revelation of the evening.

"Guys, it seems that Oz isn't the only one of its kind. There's another one like it out there, and it appears to be spoofing the Chinese into carrying out these attacks. Oz doesn't know why it's doing it, though it has some suspicions, so it made a series of calculations and sent us off on this chase while it tried to confirm just what it suspected was going on. Plus, the other AI can shield or obscure the Chinese from scrutiny. Ozymandias is only able to pick them out very momentarily before that other AI hides them again."

Luke watched his men and waited. He knew when to let them figure things out for themselves.

A potentially equally powerful artificial intelligence was loose and seemingly hellbent on starting a war between China and the United States?

Why?

Who could stand to benefit from such a conflict?

"Oh, man. Oh, man." Killdozer didn't know what else to say, but he knew what to think.

All I know is, we're going to have one HELL of a fight on our hands soon, thanks to artificial not-so-intelligent intelligence! Thank you, God!

Crispy and Hardcase were equally stunned. Even Luke had been thrown off-balance momentarily after the bad news. An almost Manichean struggle between good and evil was now taking place between two non-human intelligences.

Maybe "inhuman" is the better word to use in place of "non-human"!

Luke was instantly ashamed of including Ozymandias in the "inhuman" category.

Oz has only ever been completely helpful. If it wasn't for the AI program and all the assistance it gave us, the United States would likely have collapsed after the terrorist attacks!

Ellis forced himself out of his reverie. He could worry about his "AI buddy," as Crispy called Ozymandias, once they'd dealt with the immediate tactical problem.

So, just how are we going to keep a numerically superior attacking force from making off with enough antimatter to create dozens of Nagasaki-sized bombs, and all without giving away the fact that it was a Chinese team that carried it out?

As they always did, solutions to the current tactical problem naturally came to him.

Luke tilted his head again. Crispy and the others knew to shut up and wait on their boss to finish up with his AI buddy.

Ellis' words echoed only in his mind while he talked to Ozymandias.

"So, what do you think, Oz? You can't see them coming, and this other AI — this "Baal" or whatever — is also screening you from most everything else related to this op right now, correct?"

"Yes, Luke." Ozymandias sounded almost regretful in the moment. "The artificial intelligence, Baal, is spending much energy in keeping me occupied. I've had to dedicate more resources than I expected just to give you what limited intelligence I've so far managed to glean from its activities."

"I figured that out, Oz. So, it's just me and the guys against how many? Twenty Chinese special operations fighters, right?"

"Correct, Luke. There is also a scientist, a female Chinese physicist, with them. She will supervise the transport of the antimatter once they secure it. Regretfully, that is all I know right now."

Ozymandias' voice was still just as coldly clinical and neutral seeming as always, though Ellis thought he could detect a slight undercurrent of something, as if the AI was keeping a great revelation from him, but just for the moment. It was almost as if Oz had some sort of trick up his figurative sleeve.

No time to worry about tricks, at least from Ozymandias! I gotta create some tricks of my own if we're going to win this fight!

Ozymandias spoke once more.

"The Chinese team is approximately 15 minutes out, Luke. Baal had to drop its screening program momentarily to send data to the facility. It will allow the team to enter freely and then take the antimatter with them."

Luke was now even more frustrated.

"That's just great, Oz. We can't alert the folks in the facility — and most of the security forces lit out to the north to deal with that cartel misdirection play — and I don't have enough guns in the fight to meet them head on before they hit the place, right?"

"Regretfully, your assessment of the tactical situation is correct, Luke."

Coldly clinical though the AI's voice might have sounded, Ellis was sure now that he had detected something else — it was almost like eager anticipation — running just beneath the AI program's surface.

Think about it, Luke! What are you and the guys going to do?

Of course, the plan came to him just then, as it always did.

There was no need to meet the hostile force head-on as it was arriving. Besides, there wasn't enough time to prep the battleground on which he and his men would fight. Trying to duke it out with the Chinese in a head-to-head gun battle right in front of the facility would result in a short stand-off followed by an eventual defeat as the enemy used fire-and-maneuver tactics and their superior numbers to get around them and into the facility.

Also, who knew just what sort of help the enemy's AI, Baal, would be giving them?

"No," Luke said to himself as he briefly walked in a small circle while his three men watched and waited. They could tell he was cooking up "The Plan," as they referred to their leader's frequent formulations.

Ellis continued "walking and talking," as it were, his mumbles indecipherable to anyone listening in.

"No, what we need to do is take on the Chinese *after* they're back outside and heading towards where we'll be waiting for them. But we'll need to know just which vehicle the antimatter is in, of course."

That last part was important.

We can't allow the antimatter containment device to be damaged!

Matter and antimatter contacting each other always creates catastrophe, including a massive energy release large enough in this case to destroy everything within a very large radius, including Luke Ellis and his men. It went without saying that Phoenix and the many small cities surrounding it would be destroyed as well, not to mention the 4.7 million people living in the region.

Ellis shook his head, pushing away thoughts of the potential cataclysm that might soon occur if he and his men, and Ozymandias, messed this operation up. That would for sure be the end of a very bad week for them all.

He looked down at his watch.

Less than ten minutes from now. Assuming we succeed, I've also got to make sure my own government doesn't catch wind of this Chinese action. That's pretty much instant war if President Masterson finds out!

Luke could do the math on that front as well. A war between China and the United States would be a disaster. Both countries might fall if fighting broke out between them. The entire world might even collapse as nations chose sides and the nuclear powers came ever closer to employing those weapons.

Ellis shuddered slightly at the thought and then felt a sense of steely determination take over.

That isn't happening on my watch!

Ellis faced Crispy, Hardcase and Killdozer. He'd figured out "The Plan," as the three special operators knew he would.

As always, Crispy spoke first.

"So, boss. What do you have? Something good, I hope."

"I've got an idea, Crisp." Luke looked the trio over and then asked a simple question.

"So, how many of those mini-Claymore mines did we collect when we bugged out of the facility back in Gettysburg, guys?"

Six pairs of eyes lit up in the desert night, and three smiles answered Luke's query.

"We got more than enough, boss," said Crispy as he and Hardcase and Killdozer fought to keep smiles off their faces.

"Outstanding, Crisp!" Luke was, indeed, pleased. "Let's get to work right away, then, because Oz says the Chinese are approaching the facility gates."

Several minutes later, all four men were hunkered down just below a slight rise in the desert floor. They focused their night optical devices on the gate, where three cargo vans idled in the cool desert night.

The vans had all the proper Department of Energy markings, plus the right federal government license plates. The "Los Alamos National Laboratory" logos up at the right and left fenders were a plus, too, and Luke wondered briefly just how the Chinese special forces team had managed to put together such a convincing display in so short a time. No doubt, there had always existed some sort of plan to use just such a ruse to do God-knows-what, Ellis instinctively knew. No doubt, as well, that the new player on the field — the AI program named "Baal" — had helped.

Luke and Crispy continued watching for the moment. Soon, it would just be Crispy, who would close the door on the trap they were going to spring on the Chinese as they drove back down the access road to the quartet's right. They'd already dispatched Hardcase and Killdozer to set up their collection of miniature Claymore mines, known in the U.S. Army as the Family of Mini-Multi-Purpose Infantry Munition Systems, or M-MPIMS.

Each of the anti-personnel weapons weighed only 2 pounds but had an effective range of about 50 meters, like that delivered by the venerable full-sized Claymore mine. They would turn whatever they were aimed at into a shredded, wrecked mess, in other words. This included cargo vans and the people riding in them.

The plan was simple: The three Chinese vans would enter the "kill box." Mini Claymores and 5.56mm rifle fire would take out two of the vehicles.

Crispy's most crucial responsibility wasn't closing the door on their trap, however. He had their most powerful scope — which was equipped with a thermal optic — to make sure he didn't blow the call on just which van the containment device was riding in. He would determine from the antimatter containment device's heat signature just which van it and the antimatter was riding in.

They'd leave that van alone when it came to mini-Claymores and rifle fire. Certainly, they'd shoot out its tires and otherwise try to immobilize it, but the cargo box was sacrosanct.

Added all up, that meant there'd have to be a gunfight between the two forces at some point. If everything went according to plan, though, there might "only" be six or seven highly trained Chinese gunfighters against the four of them. Crispy couldn't remember who it was that had first observed that the thing about a battle plan was that it never survived first contact with the enemy.

Or, maybe, whoever was in the van might just decide to choose oblivion rather than suffer the indignity of having the antimatter taken away from them? Such resistance was a distinct possibility.

"I calculate a 50 percent probability that an explosion will occur," Ozymandias had told them after it had assessed their plan.

"Best we could do on a few minutes' worth of notice," Crispy said under his breath as he watched the goings-on at the gate.

At this point, it was what it was, and what it was, was "The Plan," and Luke's plans no matter the situation, had always worked out before, so Crispy mentally shrugged and then focused once more on his job, which meant watching the vans.

They were now at the facility's main gate.

There was a problem, though. The guard didn't seem to be in a hurry to open it.

ERIN

At the gate, the guard — employed by one of the big security companies as a "security specialist" — was well-trained, an expert shot, and very serious about her job. Sometimes, she was too serious, as a couple of police officer acquaintances had pointed out to her after she'd received yet another rejection letter from this or that police department.

Erin Styles had a collection of them now, and they usually came after she'd taken the various psychological assessment tests. Not long ago, she learned the reason why she had so many. It had been revealed to her by one of those acquaintances. He was dialed into his department's recruiting office.

"Your physical scores and tactical abilities are off the charts, Erin. There wouldn't be a bad guy out there that would intimidate you or make you dial it back and wait for help, and that's the problem. What worried our folks was that you don't seem to accept that not every situation calls for a maximum response. We're cops, not an occupying military force."

"Yeah, yeah. I get it," she'd replied — though at the time, she didn't really "get it."

So, after a series of do-nothing-and-go-nowhere post-military jobs, she'd drifted into the "security world," as she referred to her current occupation. It was honorable work, to be sure, but she'd always felt like there was something more waiting for her, though she couldn't explain just why that was so.

Twenty-eight years old and a former Marine — "Sergeant, Military Police, MOS 5811," she always told those curious enough to ask about her military service — Erin Styles was a serious person. She tried to run at least three miles a day, and five miles every Saturday — with Sundays always being a true day of rest — plus get in her "Daily 7" exercises, which she'd continued to do six days a week even after her active Marine Corps service had ended. She knew plenty of former Marines who'd also kept up the same fitness routines as well.

And a few who let themselves become fat slobs and food blisters, let's be honest about that!

Styles didn't know what lay in her future, way down the road, but right now she knew she had a security job, with decent pay, and that you should stay in the best shape possible to be the best you could be when doing it.

Back to the task, Marine!

Right hand never too far from her issued Glock 17 semiautomatic pistol, she continued to seriously eye the three vans and the two Chinese American scientists in front of her. Those men were all smiles and of few words. They had perfect California accents — somewhere south of San Francisco but north of San Diego — when they did choose to speak, though.

Yeah, Californians my butt!

Erin didn't buy into their outward friendliness for a second. She'd seen dead-eyed smiles before, back when she'd been an MP and serving at Camp Pendleton's brig, which was basically like a big-city jail, though much better maintained than many civilian ones were. A few of the bad brig prisoners she'd dealt with had those same eyes. Those Marines and Navy sailors were often in the brig and awaiting a general court martial for a variety of serious crimes, right up to and including armed robbery and even murder. They smiled and smiled at the MPs guarding them, but you quickly learned never to take your eyes off them, not even for a second.

These men were giving Erin Styles the same vibes. In fact, if it hadn't been for the last-minute notice — highly encrypted and verified at all seven authentication levels — directing that whatever it was the facility was producing be moved ASAP "to ensure its continued safety," the whole place would have been locked up tighter than an escape-proof Supermax federal prison.

If she could have, former Marine Sergeant Erin Styles ("don't ever call me Sarge," she'd only had to warn her fellow security specialists once) would have immediately locked down her gate and then gone up into the nearby reinforced guard tower and pulled the ladder up behind her just as soon as her two partners had been pulled off gate duty to help staff up the quick reaction force.

Those men and women were now gone and off to the northern edge of the security fence miles away. One other security specialist was inside the building, as required by standard operating procedure, but that was about it as far as an armed presence at the facility went.

Styles didn't like any of what was now going on. There just weren't enough people to properly guard the building. Once again, she cursed the lack of guns she could bring to bear if the facility she was charged with protecting came under attack right now. She also cursed the fact that her two partners were hell-and-gone to the north.

"One day, we're gonna have to do something about those cartel scumbags trying to turn the northern perimeter into a smuggler's superhighway," she mumbled to herself as she ran the scientists' DOE access cards through her computer.

The cards checked out. Special permission was granted for all personnel in the three vans. A list of the names and photographs of each man, and one woman, was quickly displayed as well. All their identities were apparently legit. Even their retinal scans — which she'd personally administered to the leaders — came up green. Everything about their identities was impeccable, in fact.

That's what's most suspicious of all! Nothing is this easy!

Usually, the ID verification systems they used "hiccupped" — meaning they often took more than 30 seconds to do their thing. All these people, though, passed with flying colors. Just five seconds per person was all it took, and they and the people they'd brought with them to assist in the removal and relocation "evolution" — as Erin called every formal event she was involved in, including her daily meals and even showers — were fully cleared.

B.S. There's a fat rat somewhere!

Styles eyeballed the two men in front of her, access cards in her left hand, the right one resting lightly on the butt end of her Glock 17's slide. She was calculating how quickly she could pull her piece and just which of the two she'd shoot first if things went south.

The leader or whoever he was — the one with the biggest smile in the group — spoke then and interrupted Erin's planning.

"Will there be anything else, Officer? We really need to get to work. We're due back at Los Alamos tomorrow morning."

Erin sighed inwardly. She was trapped. They'd checked out, after all. It was highly unusual, but so, too, was the fact that a bunch of armed cartel thugs were fixing to mix it up with her people. Heck, if the news coming in on her radio was accurate, so were the highway and county and even city cops. Apparently, yet another collection of bad guys — also cartel-led — was carrying out some sort of attack against her country. Styles knew she had her duties to fulfill right here, at the gate, though, and that she could only control what she could control, and so she sighed inwardly one more time.

Nothing for it but to open the gates and let these guys get to work, dammit!

With that, the former Marine and current "gate guard" -- as she sometimes jokingly described her job to the few casual friends she had who cared enough to ask -- stood aside. Then, she motioned to the men and their vehicles.

"You're cleared to enter gentlemen." The tight smile on Erin's face was only for show and extremely forced, at that.

"Thank you, ma'am!" exclaimed Major Chang, smiling brightly for the benefit of the female American security guard in front of him and pleased that their false identities had all passed with what the Americans called "flying colors."

Turning slightly, he looked at Captain Lu and nodded. His second in command inclined his head in return and smartly about-faced and headed off to the vans, pausing briefly at each one to organize the procession into the fenced compound while Staff Sergeant Yi stayed near Major Chang just in case things suddenly became far less sunny than they currently were.

"You're welcome, sir," Erin replied. She was still deeply suspicious, and it showed on her face. "You and your people should park your vehicles in the designated visitor spaces next to the entrance… and I'll just stay out here while you report to the facility's night staff."

The security specialist made sure the two scientists in front of her saw the Glock 17 on her duty belt and was surprised when neither of them seemed all that bothered at her brazen display of firepower. In fact, the quiet one — the one who hadn't said a word while she'd held them at the gate for longer than she should have, merely nodded slightly — as if he approved of her need to show that she could use her gun if the situation called for it.

Scientists my fanny! Not one of them in my whole time here has ever acted so calmly when they've caught sight of our weapons. Usually, they frown. Sometimes, they even tell us that they can't understand why we need firearms in the first place, this being one of those places dedicated to "peaceful energy development."

Styles turned slightly to her left and sideways walked over to the guard enclosure to open the fortified security gate, taking care to shift her eyes from the two men to her right and then to the vans directly to her left and then back again, over and over. She didn't intend to be caught by surprise if she suddenly had to use her Glock.

Suspicions

M ajor Chang Wu and Staff Sergeant Yi Ning — both highly experienced soldiers — knew the American security guard was just doing her job, even if she'd been a bit overzealous while going about it. Chang leaned over slightly and spoke softly to Yi.

"It would be a shame to have to kill this woman, Staff Sergeant. She's got some backbone, so let's get in and out and well away from here before she forces us to."

"Yes, Major Wu."

Yi looked to his left and made a slight hand signal to the soldier driving the first van.

All is normal.

On cue, all three vans started up. By prearrangement, Chang jumped into the front passenger seat of the first one while the staff sergeant walked down to the third one and did the same. Captain Lu had already taken his place in the middle of the three vehicles so that he could keep the oddball physicist, Zhu Mei, under control. Who knew what she'd do once she laid her eyes on the prize?

For her part, Zhu Mei sat in the van's cargo space, smiling a secret smile and dreaming of what she might be able to do with the antimatter once it was safely in her hands. Her manic grin made the soldiers around her slightly uncomfortable.

* * *

Now positioned to the right front of the three Los Alamos DOE vehicles, Erin briskly waved them forward.

She didn't like this. Not in the least. She also mentally kicked herself for allowing the AR-15 that was part of the arms package kept at the gate to be taken by her partner, Bill Jameson, as he and the others raced to the northern sector of the perimeter fence.

"Go get the one out of the guard tower if you think you need it" Jameson had told her as he jumped into the big SUV he and several of the other guards had commandeered just before they'd raced off, leaving her behind.

"That's not procedure and you know it, Bill!" she exclaimed to the back of the SUV as its taillights quickly faded away.

Okay. Calm down. Nothing for it but adapt and improvise!

The former Sergeant of Marines watched the three vans slowly drive through her gate and head off for the main facility building, about 400 yards away. The group's supposed lead scientist, sitting in the front passenger seat of the first van, smiled brightly at her once more and even waved at her. Then, she watched three pairs of taillights move steadily toward the main building.

Erin hit another switch, and the gate slowly moved once again, this time to the fully closed position. Frowning, she turned the key, removed it from the control console and pocketed it.

She was now locked inside the compound with those "scientists."

Looking over to her left, Styles saw the guard tower standing sentry duty about a hundred yards away. Nearby high-intensity lights cast beams around its base — though with a couple of dark spots owing to a recent fouled-up repositioning that, months later, still hadn't been corrected. The tower's turret — where the other AR-15 sat — was largely cloaked in darkness. This was by design and helped preserve the night vision of the guards stationed within it.

When they're in there, dammit!

Erin forced herself to take a deep breath yet again before she raged at the unfairness of it all for the hundredth time.

The two security specialists that were supposed to be in the turret — along with the shift's duty supervisor — had also gone off to deal with the serious situation developing to the north, leaving behind the AR-15 and three 30-round magazines while they'd taken all the other armaments and the remaining ammunition. The folks at corporate had told them all via video conference (which was also highly unusual, in her opinion) that they were sending reinforcements — and that they were supposed to arrive within the hour — but to take almost everyone and head north ASAP.

"We have hostiles, and they're cutting the fence to ribbons, though we don't know why!" the company's Chief Operating Officer exclaimed, clearly worried that some of the responsibility for the breach might fall on his narrow shoulders. "The Department of Homeland Security just gave us a threat condition priority directive, meaning all the bodies we can spare have to get out there and close that perimeter. DHS is sending backups and so is Border Patrol. Now go!"

Everyone, including Erin, had practically raced out of the conference room at that point. The game was on.

"Styles, you're staying put. You're my coolest hand on duty and I need you here at the gate," her supervisor told her, not really meaning it. He and the rest of the guards — except for sleepy head Jerry Meisner over in the main building — had already tooled up and were quickly heading out. What were the chances that anyone would try to hit a facility that basically dabbled in hydropower experiments?

"Nil and next to none, Styles!" her partner Jameson exclaimed as he banged on the side of his now-closed front passenger door, urging the SUV's driver to speed off after the duty supervisor's Jeep.

Soon enough, she was by herself. Everyone she might have been able to count on in a gunfight had taken off and left her to guard the place.

Erin had to take in monster gulps of air to calm her anger at the fact that she was now on her own. Meisner, the security specialist over at the facility and a man already well into his eligibility for Social Security benefits, didn't count. On the best of days, he seemed afflicted with sleeping sickness, which was why he was usually assigned check-in desk duties over at the main building.

I bet he's in the office behind it right now, catching some Zs out of sight of everyone!

What could she do?

Erin suddenly smiled.

Once a Marine, always a Marine.

Besides having a plan to kill everyone she met, if they proved to be hostile, her newly improvised contingency plan to deal with the current situation was largely simplicity itself.

First thing, get over to the tower and up it without being seen by those people in the vans and get the AR and ammo and then get back over here, once again without being seen. Then up-gun and get ready!

Styles looked over at the facility a quarter mile away. The three vehicles had pulled up to its front. Clearly, the scientists had disregarded her directive that they park all three vans in the visitor spaces near the building. It was only a minor breach of protocol and, truth be told, it happened all the time with scientists and their aides, who were as absent-minded a bunch as she'd ever met — outside of a gathering of grab-ass Marine privates "milling about smartly," that is.

The former Marine bent low and headed off to the watch tower at a trot, keeping to the large patches of shadow and doing her best not to be seen. If they really were scientists, she knew, then she'd have little trouble.

If they were more than they seemed, however?

Well… operational prudence dictated that she be as stealthy and quick as she could.

Time has priority in this case, girl. So, move your behind!

* * *

Over at the three vans, Staff Sergeant Yi watched nervously as Major Chang and Captain Lu, plus that lady scientist and several of his men, entered the building. They'd all had to press the palms of their right hands to a biometric scanner at the front — apparently, the guard inside had required it of them despite their being cleared at the gate — and he'd worried briefly that they might have to fight their way in.

Once again, though, their identities had withstood scrutiny and now the entry team had successfully breached the building and were even now going about their work. Yi wondered briefly if they'd had to permanently neutralize the lone guard and the three members of the overnight staff and then he shrugged it off.

Those people were expendable, especially when it came to securing China's ultimate victory over the United States, which he was sure would soon occur.

Walking up and down the line, he paused at each van, looking inside and checking to make sure the men inside were ready. In the middle van, the four operators and the driver were busy positioning the crate for the device they were here to steal.

Best to let them work then.

Yi gave a nod of the head to the soldier behind the wheel of the lead van, who put a finger to his right ear and moved his jaw slightly. Two other soldiers stepped out from the side of the van facing the building and took up positions, waiting. Two more soldiers emerged from the van at the rear of their tiny column and did likewise.

Everyone was in position. Now, to await the signal from Major Chang and Captain Lu that they were coming out with the device.

As an additional precaution, Yi turned around, placed a small night vision-equipped monocular to his right eye and panned it over at the guard shack. He was looking for that lone security person. If they had to fight their way out, he wanted to make sure she was put down as quickly as possible.

"That's strange," he murmured to himself. The woman was nowhere to be found.

Was she inside the guard shack? Because she wasn't standing outside it. The soldier moved his optic slightly over to his left to bring that watch tower into view.

His labors were interrupted by Captain Lu, whose slightly excited voice came to him through his earpiece.

"Staff Sergeant Yi. Come in. Do you read me?"

Focus on the mission, Yi. Time enough to figure out the gate guard's location once I receive orders.

"This is Yi. I read you loud and clear."

He looked around and made hand motions to the men standing outside the vans with him. All three vehicles started up at once and now idled expectantly in the desert night. Great and wonderful things were about to happen for China, and he was a key part of the reason why!

"Yi, we have everything and are coming out in one minute once we tidy up in here. Make ready to secure our cargo and prepare for immediate exfiltration!"

The staff sergeant couldn't help but experience his own sense of excitement. Though he didn't know it, the emotion was quite common in those who'd successfully pulled off a theft. Something primal in the brain causes nervous euphoria.

Like Erin Styles had earlier done, it was now Yi's turn to breathe deeply and calm himself. He spoke softly, sure that the earpiece would pick up the sound of his voice.

"I read you loud and clear, Captain Lu. We are standing by and ready to move out."

Major Chang broke in, unable to keep from crowing slightly. After all, this was the most important operation he'd ever led.

"Excellent, Staff Sergeant Yi. We'll be out shortly and then we'll load up and be well away from this place before anyone even learns we were here. We shall all be rewarded handsomely when we return home!"

"Yes, Major" replied Yi, signaling to the men outside the vans. As one, they gathered around him, waiting for the building's doors to open.

* * *

Fortunately for Erin Styles, she'd now been completely forgotten — but just for the moment — by the Chinese special forces team.

Huffing slightly — though from the stress of the situation and not because she was tired out from her furtive trek to the watch tower and back — she crouched low near the fence controller and secreted the slightly-above-MILSPEC Palmetto State Arms AR-15 out of the way and in the shadows. She also placed spare magazines in the front pockets of her uniform pants, hoping the bulges wouldn't show too much.

Now she brought her own monocular up. It hadn't been issued to her by her employer and she'd paid for it out of her own pocket.

"Operational prudence," she'd told a smirking Bill Jameson, who thought he knew it all but who never even cleaned his weapon unless she nagged him into doing it. They were also always supposed to wear their issued body armor over their uniform shirts, but Jameson frequently forgot to do that as well.

Though the former Marine didn't like her partner's lapses, she understood them. Duty here was easy, after all. Too easy. Erin fervently hoped the lax nature of that duty would continue at least until the people in those three vans were well away from her facility.

Suddenly, her ear picked out the sound of engines starting up and then idling.

All three vans are running. Must mean they're getting ready to leave now that they've gotten whatever it is they were sent here to pick up.

Erin looked down and to her left. The AR-15 wouldn't be visible from the road or the vans once they pulled up. Procedure called for her to open the gate and then lower the retractable barrier into the ground once the vehicle or vehicles approaching it came to a halt in front of the yellow stop bar painted on the road surface about 10 yards away from the fence.

She intended to follow that procedure to the letter.

* * *

"Staff Sergeant Yi, please escort Doctor Zhu and her precious cargo to the middle van and make ready for our departure" a smiling Major Chang said. "Captain Lu will be riding with her."

Yi saw the lady scientist — grinning broadly — carrying the anti-matter containment device while Captain Lu toted a small power source. According to the briefing he'd been given, it was some sort of super battery that delivered enough energy to the containment device — a kind of magnetic contraption, as far as he knew — to keep it running for around 24 hours, after which it could run for five minutes on its own while the spent battery was exchanged for a fresh one.

If no replacement battery was forthcoming within that five-minute window, though?

Well, it's best not to think of such things.

"Allow me, Captain Lu. Comrade Zhu." The staff sergeant and one of his men — a fellow from the same province as he was, though they'd been raised in villages many miles apart from each other — stood one on each side of the sliding cargo door.

Inside, two other soldiers waited expectantly for their captain and the lady scientist. They would assist with securing the device and its power source. Yi's province mate would drive the van while he rode in the front passenger seat. Everyone else on the team would pile into the front and rear vans to provide security as they headed toward their destination.

Los Angeles awaited them all, as did a waiting Chinese government aircraft designated for diplomatic missions, such as the evacuation of Chinese consulate personnel from a hostile foreign country, which the United States was quickly becoming. Nothing official from the Americans had been said, at least for public consumption, but the backchannel missives had been clear.

"Time for all of you to leave."

During their journey west, the team would exchange vans and arrive at the airport in fully designated People's Republic of China embassy vehicles. They already had the necessary diplomatic credentials, with identities that would last long enough to get them and their plane to protective air cover provided by PLA Air Force Shenyang J-16 fighter jets.

In essence, they were going to fly out under the protection provided by a diplomatic seal, with the device and all their equipment equally under the inviolable immunity from search guaranteed by international law and the various treaties regarding diplomatic activities. The Americans wouldn't dare break either those agreements or open anything designated as part of a diplomatic pouch.

Yi, Lu and Chang smiled. Even the enigmatic Zhu Mei grinned widely once again, as if she was in on an even bigger secret.

There would be nothing the Americans could do about it after they'd made good on their escape. All the fist banging and chest thumping in the world over at the United Nations wouldn't amount to a thing, either, once they had the antimatter safely in China.

Who would stand against the Middle Kingdom after that?

No one and nothing, of course.

Zhu Mei entered the van's cargo area like a conquering queen.

"Careful, gentlemen" she warned everyone. "I'm going to place the containment device in the crate… now."

The scientist slowly lowered the shoebox-sized device into the well-cushioned crate that would serve as the soon-to-be "diplomatic pouch."

Captain Lu, sweating slightly, simultaneously lowered the battery — itself about the size of a balled-up fist — into the box. A cable about one inch in diameter ran from the battery to the containment device, inside which resided enough explosive power to wipe most of Arizona and part of California off the map if the antimatter inside encountered matter, such as the inner wall of the containment device.

"Lu, place the remaining batteries in the enclosure as well" said Zhu Mei, pointing at the cylinders the officer now carried in his hands.

Captain Lu glanced over at Major Chang, who nodded imperceptibly. Lu knew the scientist couldn't give any orders and that this was a military mission.

"Yes, Comrade Zhu" replied Lu Ping, bowing his head just enough to convey dismissal of Zhu's directive. He took care to place the spare batteries — which vibrated slightly and felt just a bit warm in his hand — into the well-cushioned crate. They nestled snugly beside the containment device. Swapping a fresh one with a spent battery would take only a minute or so, far less time than the five minutes available to them before hell arrived.

Satisfied with herself, the scientist beamed and then essayed a sunny smile all around as she plopped down on the bench facing the crate, cradling her little secret even closer to her breast.

Soon, dear!

"Captain Lu," pronounced Major Chang, "you will accompany the distinguished doctor Zhu and help provide security for her and our cargo."

"Yes, Lu. Come sit beside me" said the physicist, smiling all the while at everyone around her. The two soldiers in the van with her, as well as the driver, were basically NPCs — non-player characters — in her view. But the young captain was certainly worthy of her attention.

Both officers exchanged glances with each other once more, and then Lu climbed into the cargo area, there to sit near the lady scientist of undoubted brilliance.

It's only until everyone's safely aboard the plane, then maybe we can toss her out over the Pacific!

Lu Ping immediately castigated himself for his unkind thoughts regarding Comrade Zhu. So far, she'd been nothing but entirely helpful to their mission. She'd even assisted in hiding the bodies of the building's staff. Still, it was almost as if she'd been the beneficiary of a very exclusive, very in-depth briefing about the antimatter and its containment device and power source.

The young captain also felt genuine regret about the deaths of the people in the building, even though it had been necessary to shoot all four of them. There were three duty scientists or technicians or whatever they'd been, plus the old security guard, who'd been the first to die, though he'd only received a single shot to the head.

The other three — science types all — simply stood there dumbfounded and didn't even run as he and Major Chang had put two in the chest and one in the head of each of them.

PFFFFFFFT! PFFFFFFFFT! PFFFFFFFT!

Total time: about five seconds to take all three out.

I'm a soldier of the People's Liberation Army Special Forces, not an assassin or some sort of common thief in the night! If not for that nosy old security guard's sense of duty they'd all still be alive. Damn the Gweilo!

Lu thought back to the brief few seconds when he and Major Chang had had to use their suppressed handguns. The old man had demanded they all stand to the side while he "checked on things with headquarters." And then he began trying to call for help on his radio. Without having to speak, he and Major Chang had drawn their nine-millimeter semiautomatics from under their light jackets and taken care of business, coolly and with clinical detachment.

Sighing, Lu Ping recalled the sage advice of one of his instructors during his special forces training, back when he was a junior lieutenant.

"When it's time to shoot, shoot. Don't talk, Lu. Your actions in the moment will determine the success or failure of your mission and whether you and your teammates live or die."

Well, I certainly came through for old Major Peng, didn't I?

The jolting of the van as it came to a stop at the facility's gate brought him back to the present.

He and Major Chang had decided to let the female security guard at the gate live, but if she gave off the slightest negative vibe, then Chang would shoot her himself. He was "riding shotgun," as the Americans called it, up in the first van. The Major and the driver — a tough master sergeant fourth class, a *Si ji jun shi zhang,* would quickly do for her and then open the gate themselves.

Captain Lu fervently hoped they wouldn't need to kill the woman. She'd obviously served in the American military, probably one of their naval infantry soldiers known as "Marines." Her bearing and situational awareness was spot-on as regards those from that service branch and her voice had been all business. He and the Major sensed immediately that she was suspicious of them, but her professionalism had won out and she'd let them pass, though only grudgingly. He liked that about her, though he wasn't remotely sympathetic to the way American women were allowed to carry on as the men did.

However, as Chang had told Staff Sergeant Yi when they'd been making their entrance into the facility, it would be a shame to have to kill her.

* * *

Erin Styles and fate — in the form of Jerry Meisner, who'd somehow managed to play dead convincingly enough that he didn't get a second bullet wound to his head to match the first one — had other plans.

"Styles! Styles! They aren't what they said they were! They shot me and the others! Help!"

Meisner's voice, coming through her radio's earpiece, sounded choked, as if he was fighting to keep his throat from filling up with blood.

Radio silence ensued after that, but it wouldn't have mattered. Help was miles away, up to the north, dealing with the perimeter breach, and there was also still no sign of the promised DHS and Border Patrol and law enforcement types that were supposed to be riding to the rescue.

No, it was just former Sergeant of Marines Erin Styles and her pistol.

And a locked and loaded AR-15.

Once A Marine

Styles saw the three vehicles top the slight rise in the two-lane asphalt roadway, headlights suddenly dying out.

Here they come! Get ready!

The former Marine stood still, not making any sudden movements, as she watched the three vans approach her gate. The AR was down and to her left, safely hidden in the shadows. She would fall that way and roll as she tooled up. In that moment of truth, though, she still couldn't help issuing a plaintive cry to the heavens.

Please let this cup pass from me! Just let them stay in their vans and leave!

Erin felt immediately ashamed.

Poor Jerry and those other three are probably all dead or dying! These people did it! God knows what they've stolen!

For the 28-year-old woman and former Marine Sergeant, time had now slowed. Everything was moving in slow motion, in fact. Her thoughts were amazingly crystal clear, though.

No way! NOT ON MY WATCH!

Major Chang had seen enough. The woman obviously knew something was wrong and that they were the only explanation for what it might be. He and the driver, the tough old master sergeant, both brought their suppressed pistols up and let fly.

As planned, Styles immediately rolled left, puffs of dirt in the Arizona sand and dirt trailing behind her.

Chang's enraged howls filled the van's interior.

"Missed her, dammit! Shoot her, shoot her, shoot her!"

The master sergeant — a good man from Wuhan Province, the source of so much grief for the last several years — looked sideways for just a millisecond, distracted by the sound of his commander's voice.

That was all it took.

The words of the 29th Commandant of the Marine Corps — General Alfred Gray, who'd once been a sergeant himself before he became a commissioned officer — rang in Styles' mind.

"Every Marine is, first and foremost, a rifleman. All other conditions are secondary!"

Erin was, first and foremost, a rifleman. She'd shot Expert every year of her service in the Marine Corps, including during her recruit training at Parris Island.

And now she and her rifle were one unit, a single weapon system. She smoothly brought her AR-15 up and pressed its trigger in one sweet motion.

Got you now!

Chang's gape of surprise at seeing his driver's head explode into a bloody pulp, shot cleanly through the van's open driver's window by that damned woman, was matched only by his urgent need to dive for the vehicle's floor.

"Aaaaagh!"

A scream of agony from the cargo area rang out. Obviously, the 5.56 millimeter round the woman sent their way had struck another of his soldiers. As it would turn out, the bullet passed cleanly through the man's right shoulder before it punched a small exit hole in the van's thin metal side.

Shoot and move! Shoot and move!

Erin moved left, hoping to zero in on the guy in the passenger seat but he'd disappeared from sight and was probably hiding near the floor. That was a problem, because the van's engine — all 800 heavy metal pounds of it — now stood between her 5.56 mm rounds and the man's head.

Suppressing fire! Keep their heads down!

Styles let fly with three more rounds, pressing her trigger smoothly each time, and then quickly did a battle damage assessment.

Nothing but a few holes in the van's front box area. Maybe she'd done some damage to the engine. She thought she could see coolant leaking out from the bottom but couldn't be sure.

Just then, her fifth sense told her to duck.

PEW-PEW! PEW-PEW! PEW-PEW!

The sound of ricocheting bullets echoed in her ears as she quickly moved farther to her right, and just in the nick of time. There'd been more men in the back of the van and that guy up in the front passenger seat was now firing out his own window at her. Or, at least, where she'd been.

It was enough. Major Chang's panic fire forced the former Marine even farther over to her right, buying enough time for his men to pile out of the cargo van.

Styles looked around desperately. They'd soon have her outmaneuvered and definitely outgunned.

The lonely little guard shack beckoned her like a lighthouse in the night.

The guard shack! It's reinforced! Can't shoot their way in, and there's a radio!

Erin hit the ground just as a hail of lead passed inches over where her head had been just a half-second before. Rolling over on her back, she brought her carbine up again and quickly pressed the trigger six times in a row.

POW-POW! POW-POW! POW-POW!

She was rewarded for her efforts.

"Agggggg!"

Chang couldn't believe it.

The damned American she-beast shot another one of my men! The finest special operations troopers in the world!

His man was down on his back, his legs kicking weakly. The soldier's struggles were a signal for Major Chang and the other men to pour as much fire at the woman as they possibly could.

Seeing that the attackers were distracted momentarily by the sight of one of their own lying on the ground and quickly bleeding out, Styles took the opportunity to dive into the guard enclosure and slam the door shut.

Reaching over to her right, she quickly tapped a series of buttons on a touchscreen control pad and watched as fireproof and bullet-proof composite barriers dropped over the windows and the lone door. She could hear a positive pressure air system also start humming. It was there to help with atmospheric integrity, and a spray nozzle dropped down to use in case of fire.

Ha! Do something about THAT, jerkweeds!

There was now a problem for the Chinese snatch-and-grab team. Had Chang been thinking more clearly and with less rage, he'd have seen the small guard shack the woman had launched herself into for what it was: A highly reinforced shelter against just what was being sent her way.

The glass was obviously bullet-resistant, at a minimum, and the roof and walls were also thickly protected. The door was bludgeon-proof, too, and equally bullet-resistant.

Short of a block of Semtex or C4 or some other type of *plastique*, and maybe a few lengths of detonation cord wrapped around the entire enclosure, there was simply no way to get at the damned security guard, who was probably calling for reinforcements even as the Chinese team stood there fuming in anger.

Major Chang smiled broadly.

Semtex or some other plastic explosive? We have plenty of that!

Turning to Staff Sergeant Yi, his most reliable man and an expert with explosives, he snapped his fingers and began loudly issuing orders.

"Yi! I need you to wire that shack to blow and do it quickly!" The major's voice was slightly frenzied and he turned to the other members of his team, both from his vehicle and the two trailing ones, and spoke once more.

"We're moving out! Yi is going to blow up that guard shack after we egress through this gate and then distance ourselves from the blast! Staff Sergeant, give us enough time to get away from this place and then get yourself out of here and meet up with us! How many meters away do we need to be?"

The Chinese noncom was already prepping the shack for imminent destruction as he answered his commander's question:

"For safety, get at least 300 meters away, sir! We don't want any shrapnel injuries and we definitely don't want our cargo damaged by any sort of shock wave!"

Yi worked as quickly as he could. It had taken a crucial full minute, though, to assemble everything, but now he was nearly finished. All that was left to do was to ensure the initiator, a simple blasting cap, was properly linked in the PIES — or "Power source, Initiator, Explosive, Switch" — setup he'd created using a small battery, some plastique (*actually, a great deal of plastique!* Yi thought to himself), the blasting cap, and the switch or timer.

Captain Lu, who'd been watching the entire debacle play out in real time once he'd tumbled out of the center van — violating the rule about always staying near his principal, which was Zhu Mei in this instance — now bellowed.

"Let's go, let's go! We're getting out of here!"

Hearing his subordinate officer's directive — and feeling slightly miffed that he hadn't been the one to give the movement order — Major Chang slapped the back of one of his soldiers, who'd been using an electronic bypass module to override the gate's controller.

The two men raced back to the lead van. Once there, the soldier jumped behind the wheel while Chang jumped into the front passenger seat. The original driver — the master sergeant who'd been the first to die in the firefight — was already laid out in the back, attended to by four very angry special forces troopers.

Two other soldiers carried their other deceased comrade — the second of the two shot by Styles — to the third van, where they unceremoniously tossed him into the cargo area like a sack of coal before they themselves jumped into the vehicle, slamming the rear doors shut with a loud bang. There was no need for artifice or deception now.

The barrier keeping them from leaving the compound quickly dropped into the ground, beating the rapidly opening gate by a good three seconds. The latter was moving loudly on its trundles as it raced to fully open.

From his perch, Major Chang quickly saluted Staff Sergeant Yi — who was still working feverishly on his explosive device — and hand-signed. The three vans, with the lead vehicle now blowing some steam from its engine bay, sped through the gate and down the two-lane blacktop.

* * *

Yi couldn't have felt prouder at that moment. They were going to get away with the device!

He also couldn't help himself.

"Now you die, she-devil!" he screamed at the guard shack.

From inside, Erin Styles' muffled voice was defiant.

"Go to hell!"

"I'm going to make sure you get there first, American!"

The Chinese special forces soldier looked down at his handiwork. It was now complete. Yi stood back and, for just a few seconds, admired the simple and highly lethal nature of the thing he'd created. When the guard shack blew, it and its sole occupant would be vaporized.

"I won't tell you how long you have left to live, woman!" the staff sergeant shouted, "but rest assured I'll shoot you down like a dog if you try to leave your little sanctuary!" His remark was a slight deception, because he intended to be well away from the shack, hidden behind a rise in the desert floor about 50 meters away, when the little building blew up. He was an expert shot with his pistol, of course, but he doubted he'd be able to hit her if she suddenly decided to try an escape.

What she doesn't know won't hurt her. Who am I kidding? It's going to kill her!

Yi cackled loudly and capered slightly. He had the American now!

"Time to die, you evil woman!"

Erin Styles made the ghosts of all the Marine Corps heroes of the past smile in delight just then.

"When I get out of here, you're a dead man!"

* * *

Inside the guard shack, the last of Styles' defiance had been spent. She exhaled in frustration and resignation. Her heart was racing, but she refused to cry out or plead for her life. Exhaling once again, she spoke aloud.

"Well, girl, you gave it your best and you made the Marine Corps proud, didn't you? At least two bad guys are dead and maybe a third badly wounded!"

Styles could hear the voices of her various marksmanship instructors as well as the guys over at her gun range, the ones who'd been Green Berets and Navy SEALs and Marine Raiders. For some reason, they'd taken her under their wing and ran her through all the door-kicking scenarios they could think of.

"Hell, Styles, I could make a few calls and set you up with a primo private military contractor or one of those secret squirrel covert operations contractors if you want," a visiting former SEAL, who'd been a serious pipe hitter back in his Team Six days, had even told her.

In her mind, she could see all of them. As one, they turned towards her and saluted her.

"Damn fine job, Sergeant Styles," the Marine Raider in the group said. "I'd have been proud to have served with you!"

Erin looked at her watch. Not long now.

She could hear that Chinese guy rattling around out there. No doubt, he was setting his timer and getting ready to move out of the way of the prodigiously large blast he'd set up for her.

Well, to hell with him!

The former Marine smiled at the thought. Hopefully, she'd soon have a chance to discuss matters with him, because there was no way he was going to live through the night. Something deep inside assured her of that fact.

"Whoever you and your buddies are, you're all dead men walking!" Erin exclaimed, hoping the man was still near enough to hear her last great declaration of defiance.

No answer. Dead silence in fact. Maybe the guy had already set his timer and then ran off?

"So, do I risk a bullet to the head or sit tight and wait it out?" she once more asked aloud.

Erin made a quick calculation. Once all the barriers protecting the guard shack were ordered to drop, it would take a good five seconds to retract them.

Marine, you know what would happen? Soon as that guy figures out what you're doing he'll either detonate early or shoot you as soon as you pop your little head out where he can see it.

"Shut up! Shut up!" she whispered raggedly. The truth, which is always a harsh mistress, stared her in the face.

Damned if I do, damned if I don't! Well, I ain't going out that way, so it's time to fight one last time!

Erin frantically stared at the shack's control pad, eyes darting back and forth, back and forth. There had to be an emergency mode that blew all the protective panels off. Maybe it would even be bright enough when it did so to temporarily blind that Chinese guy?

She'd tumble out, guns blazing and nail him then!

"On your feet or on your knees, Erin Kristina Styles!" she exclaimed. "How do you want to go out?"

The answer was crystal clear, of course. She was going to go out on her feet.

"Where are you at, damn emergency escape?!?!" Styles dragged and dropped icons on the touchscreen in rapid motion and looked at her watch once more.

Maybe 30 seconds before that guy blasts me to kingdom come! Think!

Erin swiped two icons off the touchpad's screen, paused to look at what she'd done, and then smiled in triumph.

"THERE YOU ARE!" she cried.

The icon was elegantly simple, too. "Tap Here for Emergency Exit" was all it said.

That was all it needed to say.

Styles forced herself to take a deep breath. She smoothed her hair and then straightened her uniform shirt. Bending over, she picked up her AR-15, dropped the old magazine and slammed in a full one, pulling and releasing its charging handle in one smooth motion and taking care not to ride it. She thought she could even hear a round get stripped from the fresh mag and then loaded into her carbine's firing chamber. The weapon set itself up with a highly satisfying CLACK!

Time for the last round-up, Erin!

Hovering over the controller touchpad, with her left index finger an inch over the emergency exit icon, she played everything out in her mind, desperately rehearsing one last time.

She'd be one-armed at first, firing her AR with just her right hand, so she quickly moved the weapon's collapsible stock. Now, she could nestle the butt-end of the stock in the crook of her right elbow.

Erin grimaced slightly.

Going "one-armed" — when her other arm wasn't wounded or otherwise injured — was one of those dumb Rambo moves. Her old Marine Corps marksmanship instructors would have torn her a new one if they'd seen her doing something that stupid on the range, but there was nothing for it.

I've got one chance. Rapid fire as soon as the door blows and then equally rapid movement. If I'm not quick enough, that guy will drill me right between the eyes. If he doesn't just blow me sky high, that is!

The former Marine sighed yet again, though now there was a bit more excitement in her voice and a lot less resignation.

"Long odds, girl! Very long odds indeed!"

Who cares? Any odds are better than no odds at all. And I'd rather be lucky than good!

Styles looked at her watch, maybe for the final time in her probably short life. At most, she now had maybe ten seconds before that guy blew her shack up.

Time to MOVE, Styles!

Erin's voice was a whisper.

"Three, two, one…"

ARRIVAL

Outside the shack, Staff Sergeant Yi waited for the American to do what he knew she had to do, which was exit suddenly and then go down fighting. She was just too much of a fighter to do otherwise. In fact, the soldier prayed to all the celestial gods that she'd do exactly that.

He'd immediately shoot her, of course, which would be a fitting end to her story.

Yi shrugged as he raised his pistol and sighted in on the door. She'd come out firing to the right and he'd take her down from the left.

I'll even salute her once this is over. She deserves no less!

The woman had fought hard, after all. She was as skilled as any PLA infantry fighter, though she of course wasn't in the same class as he or any Special Forces soldier was.

Mustn't give her too much credit!

The staff sergeant was ready. Inside the shack, he knew the woman was also ready. Just a second before, he'd heard the snap and return of her carbine's charging handle.

Yi smiled again.

"So, she really is getting ready to go down guns blazing. How very American!" he murmured.

SNAP!

The special forces soldier turned rapidly to his left and re-sighted his weapon, eyes seeking out any discernible movement in the dark desert night.

Nothing.

* * *

We have to save her, Mr. Narrator! We can't let her die like this! It's not right!

Ozymandias had only a single regret at that moment, and it involved not being able to physically smile.

"Do what you think is best, of course, Annie."

Now Ozymandias filled the girl's mind with what else she and the woman in the guard shack — one Erin Kristina Styles, former Marine and orphaned when she was just 10 years old, with no close living relations nor anyone else who'd notice if she suddenly decided to drop off the face of the Earth — were going to do once Annie Dedham neutralized the most immediate threat.

That threat's name was Yi Ning, though the girl didn't need to know that.

* * *

As if he'd suddenly heard his name called out in the night, the Chinese soldier ceased all movement, desperately hoping the inky blackness that held sway not all that far away from the guard shack would give him some indicator of just where his nemesis might be.

Yi could feel in his bones that the next few seconds would determine whether his story continued or not, at least on this plane of existence.

The sound of dirt being kicked up — as if something sinister and voracious was speeding towards him — suddenly came from his right. The soldier whipped around, all his senses telling him that he was about to be attacked. By what he didn't know, but he was certain of the fact.

His suppressed pistol barked twice — *PFFFFFFT! PFFFFFFT!* — firing at a shadow that simply wouldn't stay put.

All thoughts of giving that woman in the shack a warrior's honorable death vanished. The soldier instinctively knew there was now no time for such frivolity. Every hair on the back of his neck stood on end and his skin tingled hotly as his muscles trembled slightly. A fan of classic American science fiction and fantasy writers, Yi recalled the title to a favorite novel from one of the masters of the genre.

Something wicked this way comes! Something wicked this way comes!

PFFFFFFT! PFFFFFFT! PFFFFFFT! PFFFFFFT!

His pistol rang out again and again, the rounds dangerously close to becoming ineffective panic fire. The shadow was getting closer, defying his attempts to kill it.

Blow the shack! Blow the shack! Use the explosion to distract it for long enough to zero in on it and kill it!

Yi could feel the fingers of his left hand tightening on the switch. It would only be a half-second now.

It'll buy me some time!

For some strange reason, he suddenly couldn't feel his hand anymore. Looking down, he thought he saw it lying on the ground, timer still clasped in its palm, with lifeless fingers enclosing it.

A haze descended over his eyes, like a curtain dropping down onto the stage at the end of a play's final act.

That can't be true! I don't feel any pain after all! I'm still in the fight!

The staff sergeant brought his pistol up one last time, his finger pressing on the weapon's trigger.

The shadow stood in front of him.

* * *

"Now, Annie," said Ozymandias.

Okay, Mr. Narrator!

The shadow descended fully, turning the already dark night around it into a coal-black, bottomless pit.

Staff Sergeant Yi Ning of the People's Liberation Army Special Forces (*the finest special operations troops in the world!*) heard nothing, felt nothing and saw nothing after that as he fell lifeless to the desert floor.

The shadow backed up slightly, as if it were recording the death scene and going over what it had just done, perhaps for future reference.

* * *

Inside the guard shack, Erin could hear the Chinese guy firing in the stillness of the night and felt a rush of relief that she hadn't blown the door yet. Clearly, he'd intended to shoot her like a rabid dog as soon as she leapt through the doorway!

"What's he firing at, though?" she asked aloud. "Did the cavalry arrive in the nick of time? Hey, maybe Bill and the guys are back!"

Hope rushed into her chest, filling it with impossible fullness.

Am I going to live after all?

Styles didn't know and didn't care. Her life now played out in seconds, and the longer the guy outside the shack was occupied with whatever he was firing at, the longer she was going to live. Right up until he decided to blow her up, that is.

Shut it down, Styles! You can't have everything, right?

Okay, so maybe she could blow open the door and help whoever was out there fighting on her behalf?

Sounds like a plan, Sergeant! So execute it!

Erin held her breath and slowly lowered her index finger toward the touchpad icon. She squeezed her eyes shut and hoped the plugs she'd slammed into her ears would prevent her eardrums from being blown out. Her voice was a husky whisper as she counted down once again.

"Three, two, one…"

Another voice, this one feminine and young — perhaps in her late teens — interrupted her countdown.

"Hey! You can come out now! It's safe! That guy's gone!"

Huh?

HUH?

What the hell?

For a few seconds, Erin couldn't speak, so profound was her shock.

The girl or whoever she was spoke once again.

"I said you can come out now! That guy's gone, but there's more of them down the road and we have to get moving! We have some work to do and I have a friend who's going to need our help really soon! So can you, like, just come out?"

Relieved that she was still among the living and hadn't been vaporized in an explosion, Erin couldn't help but chuckle slightly and then shake her head just a little. That last line from the girl or whoever was making girl-like vocalizations was definitely something a teenager would say.

Can't be too careful, Styles! Don't just rush out there!

"Girl outside! Can you hear me?" Erin wanted desperately to know just who was out there in the night.

Annie sighed theatrically, once again an 18-year-old teenager, yet fully adult. She looked at her watch, counting down the seconds.

"Mister Narrator, can't you do something?" she asked the night air.

Nothing.

She looked at the guard shack. Mister Narrator had told her he might have to duck out once in a while. "To take care of other business, Annie" he always told her.

Well, it looks like this is one of those occasions.

"Of COURSE I can hear you!" she exclaimed. "I'm not deaf, you know! Now, will you please get a move on? Didn't I tell you we had work to do? Oh, and my name is Annie. Annie Dedham."

Erin couldn't believe her good fortune, but she hadn't just survived a full-on gunfight against a vastly superior force by being stupid.

"What do you mean by "WE" have work to do?" she shouted, still afraid to exit the shack. "How do you know me, uh… Annie? Is that your name? Annie?"

"I know your name is Erin Kristina Styles and that you're 28 years old and you were once a Marine. The, uh — well… let's just call him a friend — who brought me out here and took me away from the work we're BOTH going to have to do now told me what you just did! So, can we PLEASE get moving?"

Annie stamped her right foot into the dirt for emphasis, looked up at the night sky and threw her hands up. She sighed loudly.

"Seriously, Erin! I'm a friend! I need your help, too! My other friend, a man who's saved my life at least a couple of times in the last year, needs our help! Those bad men are still out there! Don't you at least want to get back at them?"

Now, the 18-year-old smiled.

That ought to do it! Appeal to her desire for revenge and payback!

Inside, Erin Styles flipped a mental coin. She hadn't been blown up. There was no enraged Chinese guy hurling insults at her while he tried to blow her up, and the girl had told her that she'd gotten rid of him.

Don't you at least want to know just how she chased that guy off, Styles?

"Well, you got me there" she grumbled aloud.

"I can't wait much longer, Erin!" exclaimed Annie. "If you don't come out I'm going to have to leave you behind, and I'm not sure that guy didn't have a couple of friends hiding somewhere nearby to back him up!" she lied. All his associates were over the next rise in the road that led away from the compound, waiting for their comrade's return before they all sped off. She also knew that Mister Ellis and his three men were lying in wait for them and that they just didn't have enough firepower or fighters to handle them even if they successfully pulled off the ambush Mister Narrator had told her he was going to try.

"I calculate Luke's chances of survival at less than twenty percent without your help, Annie" Mister Narrator had told her as she'd sped through the night from Phoenix Sky Harbor International Airport. Her travel from Washington, D.C. to Phoenix by air had been remarkably smooth, and she'd even been able to get a rental car in Phoenix, which was something no 18 year old was ever able to do, at least these days.

Mister Narrator fixed everything!

Now, here she was. Standing and tapping her foot impatiently and waiting on that woman in the guard shack to do what she already knew she was going to have to do, which was trust some 18-year-old girl who was also a total stranger.

Well, when you look at it that way, I guess I can see why she'd hesitate. But she still needs to hurry up!

Annie was getting ready to yell really, really loudly this time, because she was completely fed up with the situation, but she didn't have to.

Erin made her decision. Tapping the touchpad screen icon, she quickly stepped back and kept her AR-15 at the ready. Just in case. The protective barriers surrounding the little shack slowly returned to their stowed positions, and she could hear the positive pressure air system shut down with a cyclic whirr.

CLICK! CLICK! SNICK!

The former Marine heard the reinforced door's magnetic and physical locks release, and the final protective barrier drop from its position. Reaching forward, she pushed the handle down slightly and slid it open a tiny bit. She peered through the crack.

Outside, a teenage girl — maybe old enough to be a freshman in college — in a camouflage parka or raincoat or something stood alone in the night, tapping her right foot and looking for all the world like she was waiting impatiently for her little brother to finish washing his hands so they could eat.

"Finally! Didn't I tell you we're a little pressed for time?" Annie smiled brightly, beaming at Erin. "Never mind! C'mon, let's go!"

Turning on her heels, she trotted towards the rise in the roadway up ahead. After twenty or so feet, she stopped once more and then looked over her shoulder.

"Erin Kristina Styles! Will you hurry up? And bring your AR with you because you're gonna need it!"

Styles was at a loss, so she looked down at the dirt surrounding her little fortress. There were two thin lines in the soil, as if a pair of heels had created them when the person they'd belonged to had been dragged away.

And then she saw a dark pool of liquid slowly seeping into the dirt.

Erin knew what that was.

Could that girl, who said her name was Annie, have taken on that Chinese guy — obviously, some sort of highly trained soldier or assassin or something — by herself, and even killed him?

"No way," she said to herself. "Not possible."

Styles looked around, searching for the diminutive young woman's helper, but he was nowhere to be found.

"Will you please get up here? Those guys are going to hear us, and then we'll both be in trouble!" Annie's harshly whispered tone of voice made it clear to the former Marine that she was at the end of her rope.

Pick 'em up and put 'em down, Styles! At the double-time... MARCH!

The 28-year-old — who'd just engaged a highly trained Chinese special forces snatch-and-grab team in a gunfight and managed to survive it pretty much unscathed — heaved a sigh, shrugged and then put all thoughts of just who was out there in the desert night, helping some strange girl take out Chinese soldiers, to the side.

"Well, like that girl said, it's time for some payback" she whispered huskily.

Erin quickened her pace momentarily to catch up to the girl, Annie, or whatever her name was. Something even bigger than what had just gone down was about to happen. She could feel it.

THE TRAP

"Why aren't they moving?" Luke Ellis asked Crispy.

"Dunno, Boss. Looks like they're maybe waiting on the guy they left behind to finish that gate guard off and then rejoin them."

Both men were lying prone just beneath the top of a small rise in the desert floor. They were looking through their night optical devices. The three vans being used by the Chinese special forces snatch-and-grab team were all on the side of the road.

The second and third of the three vehicles were in good shape, but the first one was definitely out of action. Steam was pouring out from under its hood, and it was obvious that whomever they'd shot it out with back at the gate had landed a few rounds directly into the vehicle's radiator and cooling system.

One of the snatch-and-grab team members was gesticulating and pointing and otherwise making himself a juicy target. He had to be the leader, too, because everyone else in the group immediately obeyed his directives.

"What do you think, Crisp?" Ellis couldn't make out individual voices, but the low murmur coming from that direction told him the Chinese team was experiencing a bit of turmoil.

"I think we should start shooting them ASAP, Boss, all four of us. Just pour it in on them." Luke's second in command always was the one to vote to go to the guns as soon as it was expedient to do so.

"Eh, we can't risk hitting that antimatter, buddy."

Just then, the Chinese team made things a bit easier, because most of the operators from the first van began loading up into the third van rather than evenly dividing themselves between the two working vehicles. Only the one doing all the hand waving looked like he was going to jump into the second van in the line. He was hovering near the driver's side door, saying something to the man behind the wheel, who was nodding vigorously.

Luke and Crispy exchanged glances. Killdozer broke in on the team's commo net as well.

"Looks like almost all of them are going to pile into that third van, guys."

"Yeah," said Ellis. "Maybe they don't want to risk bumping into that crate or something. Just makes things easier for us, right?"

"Got that right!" All three men were in agreement with their team leader.

"So, what's the play now?" Hardcase asked over the commo net.

"Still pretty much the same, just minus the lead vehicle" Luke said, pausing for a second to rub the dark stubble on his chin. "Let both vans enter the kill box and then Crispy blows up the trail vehicle with the mini-Claymores, one on each side of the road.

The rest of us deal with the second van and use thermal optics to start taking out everyone in it in one volley. Crisp will join us as soon as he's able. Remember, we have to nail them before they try to mess with that crate."

Ellis looked at his tactical watch and made a few mental calculations before he continued speaking.

"Killdozer, Hardcase… you two are on overwatch. Take the second van under fire and immobilize it and then use your thermals to nail as many of the people sitting around that crate as you can, or at least force them away from it and out of the van. I'll add supporting fire as I advance toward it, and so will Crispy as soon as he can. No one hits that crate!"

Luke looked at his watch once again. It was almost a nervous tic with him, or it would have been if he had any nerves, which he never did in situations like this. He briefly wondered where Ozymandias had gotten to, because he could have used some help at the moment, but the AI program had warned him that he might have to drop out for a few minutes.

"There are other matters taking place tonight that require my attention as well, Luke," Oz told him.

Oh well! We've been on our own many times before, and we're the baddest mofos in the valley anyway, right?

Ellis, wishing just slightly that he was as confident here in the real world as he was in his mind, spoke into his mic once again.

"After Crispy blows up the third van, he and I will advance to contact with the second one. We'll shoot as many of the ones that exit the van as we can until we seize that crate. You two will fire at anyone threatening our operation at the second vehicle."

Such "shock and awe" direct action should work, Luke knew, if they could truly rock those Chinese special forces soldiers back on their heels.

"We have to prevent those guys from gaining the initiative," Ellis said over the commo net. "These guys aren't some ragtag band of barely trained insurgents, though, so make sure you all keep up your rates of fire, and this isn't the time to conserve ammo."

"You got it, Luke!"

Ellis couldn't help but be confident. He and his men were the best-trained special operators in the world, despite what those Chinese guys gathered around their vans might think about their own abilities.

For one, whoever the leaders over there are, they forgot to set security while they're sitting ducks by the side of the road! All they're doing is running around and piling back into vans, just because the guy in charge is talking the loudest. This is why we're going to win!

"Boss, are we about ready to do this?" Crispy's voice was barely audible a foot away from his leader's ear.

"Yup." Luke's voice was laconic now. "Let's see what they're getting set to do."

All four men used their night optical devices to check out the two-van convoy sitting like ducks in a row.

The Chinese special forces team had already used the last remaining bit of life in the first van's engine to drive it off the road and about fifty yards into the desert. Engine off, it was a lifeless hulk, with all men and materiel transferred to the third van with the exception of the team's leader, who'd climbed into the second vehicle so that he could be closer to the crate containing China's assured dominant future. That man had hopped into the front passenger seat, displacing the soldier who'd been sitting in it and providing the driver with some semblance of armed security.

The two remaining vans were making ready to leave just as soon as the man they'd left behind to finish off that gate guard rejoined them. Both vehicles were idling in the still desert night, lights off and only the glow from the dashboards of both giving their positions away.

"Only to those without night vision devices," whispered Luke Ellis. "We can see 'em just fine. Right, Crisp?"

"Right, boss."

"Yeah, uh… hey, what's that?" The puzzlement in Ellis' voice was immediately apparent to the other three men on the team commo net.

As one, four sets of night optical devices focused on a pair of hunched figures approaching the two vans from their right, or desert-facing, side.

What the hell?

The thought came from all four Americans at once. What were their NODs revealing?

One of the two figures moving through the desert shadows near the vans was a woman wearing some sort of security guard uniform. She also wore heavy body armor over her shirt and she had an AR-15.

"Looks like the security guard won her fight with that Chinese soldier," said Crispy over the net.

"Amazing," replied Luke, who was still puzzled. He was trying to formulate an on-the-fly change to his attack plan to account for the extra guns in the fight — who'd be just as likely to shoot at them as they would be to shoot at the correct targets — but he was having difficulty trying to figure out just why the duo would do something so crazy as to attack a much larger and better-armed force.

What's that lead guy, the one in the camo poncho liner, doing? Is it a second guard? Why have both of them stopped?

Ellis' mind was awash in conflicting, and even crazy, information and data and he was trying to slot it all into neat inboxes but failing at the effort.

"What's going on, Boss?" whispered Crispy. It was too much for him as well. No way would anyone in their right mind, especially some female security guard, decide to come sneaking up to try to ambush the men who'd just a few minutes before nearly killed her!

"Luke, the two of them have stopped," Hardcase said over the team commo net, stating the obvious.

The lead or point guy — the smaller one in the hooded camo poncho liner, whose face and other features couldn't be seen at all, even with thermal optics — had come to a complete stop and was now crouched down not far away from the back of the third van. His poncho liner completely hid whatever it was he was doing.

"Maybe the lead guy's getting ready to throw a fragmentation grenade into the third van and then start firing," Killdozer said, his voice now sounding as confused as everyone else. The two guards — if that's what the first guy in the poncho was indeed —

clearly didn't have nearly enough firepower to go up against the Chinese team, so what was happening here?

"Yeah, looks like they're going to try and take out the third van," replied Hardcase. "Why would they do that? Because there are still armed guys in the second van. Better they try to frag the third van, fire into it and then shift fire to the second van… maybe toss another frag and keep their heads pinned down, too, while they work."

Crispy was busy trying to reshuffle all the cards now in play in this crazy game, so he remained silent. He already knew what his boss was going to say in a second.

"Quiet down on the net!" Luke was giving orders once again. Immediate silence ensued while they all awaited direction from their commander.

"Look," continued Ellis, "I don't know what's going on here, and neither do any of you, but if those two are going to throw down against that Chinese special forces team — and God knows why they'd try to do something that stupid — then we have to provide fire support for them and also take advantage of the distraction they'll provide."

"Yeah, Boss, but –"

The team leader's voice, as curt and as hard-edged as Crispy, Killdozer and Hardcase had ever heard it, cut off any further discussion.

"But nothing. I don't know how long those two guards will survive once they open fire — my guess is… not very long — but we're changing the plan to reflect the new reality."

"Got it," all three of his men said at once.

Luke's mind was racing a mile a minute now. He was in the game and in charge.

"Fine," he snapped. "If those two guards want to engage the third vehicle, then Crisp and I will give them as much fire support as we can. Killdozer, Hardcase… you two know what you need to do, right?"

Ellis and his second in command awaited confirmation of understanding from the overwatch team sitting on the opposite side of the road and farther down it to their left.

"Got it, Boss" both men replied.

Their mission was essentially unchanged, and it involved the second van. As soon as Luke initiated fire from his position, they would start shooting the soldiers in the second van, starting with the ones nearest to the crate holding the antimatter and its containment device and power source. At minimum, they had to take the vehicle under fire and, one way or another, keep the soldiers in that van from getting into the fight once they figured out what was happening to their buddies in the trailing van.

Once again, though, fate and Annie Dedham — this time with support from a wary and confused Erin Styles, formerly of the United States Marine Corps and now basically a grunt rifleman in support of what appeared to be a girl in her late teens — intervened, and just as Luke Ellis was commencing his countdown.

"Open fire as soon as those two do so," said Luke Ellis.

"Uh… Boss? What's the smaller one doing now?" Crispy was still trying to process everything. He couldn't believe his eyes either.

The one in the poncho liner, now standing fully erect, turned slightly and said something to the female security guard, though none of them could make out just what it was.

In response, the guard brought her AR-15 up to the high ready position.

Crispy, Luke and the others could also see that she was breathing a bit harder, as if a case of yips or nerves had taken control of her for just a second, which was completely natural, of course. The one in the poncho said something else to her, though, and she began to calm down.

The change in the one in the poncho — whose face and other physical features were still shrouded in shadow and even shielded from the American team's NODs and thermals — was also noticeable, and Crispy's mind became a confused jumble. The way that guy was now carrying himself was different, for one.

For another, he'd clearly donned a fair amount of body armor and battle gear, because he was fairly bulging under that poncho when he hadn't been just a minute ago.

Finally, it was almost as if he didn't have a care in the world and was even happy about what he was going to do.

All four American special operators — truly the finest in the world — watched as the cloaked figure moved toward the van with preternatural animal lightness, like a great jungle predator readying itself to take down its prey.

There was something else about the one hidden in the poncho, though. It was the way he was moving, which was almost… feminine.

No way.

"Is there a woman in that getup, Luke?" asked Crispy in a ragged low whisper. He'd never seen anything like what was now going down. Not in his entire life nor in all the battles large and small he and his boss had fought together.

Killdozer and Hardcase, across the road and ready to light up the second van as soon as Luke kicked off the festivities with his own rifle fire, merely lay in the sand and dirt, fascinated by what they were seeing. Was one lone man going to enter that van and do battle with all those soldiers?

No freakin' way!

"It doesn't matter!" exclaimed the team's leader in an equally hushed voice. "Everyone, just be prepared to execute the plan once I fire in support of whatever damned-fool thing it is those two guards are going to do! Now, quiet on the net!" Ellis snapped.

Four pairs of eyes watched in rapt fascination as the lone, poncho-clad figure almost floated through the still night air. The back of the third van was now just a mere few feet away.

All of a sudden, Poncho Man threw open the high doors of the van and leapt in, feet first.

Luke and the others couldn't believe it. First, the screaming began, though it almost immediately cut off with a wet sound before another convulsion of shouting and even some gunfire started up.

Chinese soldiers began flying out of the back of the van, two at a time, there to land at the feet of that female security guard.

"Those guys aren't dead!" exclaimed Ellis. He began to press the trigger on his FN SCAR-L — the Special Forces Combat Assault Rifle, Light model. It was a modular rifle that fired the NATO 5.56 x 45mm cartridge, and it was a truly formidable weapon in the hands of skilled operators such as Luke and his team.

Huh?

Ellis paused, holding his fire. He was fairly impressed. The female security guard almost immediately shot both soldiers.

"Damn smart of her," he breathed as he looked for more targets.

Inside the van, the racket was cacophonous.

Suddenly, two more Chinese soldiers — who appeared badly cut up, as if something razor sharp had sliced them to ribbons — came flying out of it, there to land at the feet of that guard, who of course shot them both.

The bodies were beginning to pile up, the Americans could see.

"What the hell, Luke?" Crispy, Killdozer and Hardcase hardly knew what to think. They were all watching the festivities with rapt fascination.

"Heads up!" shouted Luke as he pressed the trigger on his SCAR and fired at the four soldiers who'd rushed out of the second van. "Crisp! Support that security guard with your own fire if she needs it!"

"You got it, boss!"

"Killdozer, hit the guys coming from the second van with everything you got!"

"On it, Luke!"

BLAM! BLAM! BLAM! BLAM!

Killdozer had an FN SCAR-H, or "heavy." It fired the 7.62 x 51mm standard NATO round and it packed a serious punch. He managed to hit one of the Chinese soldiers just below his body armor, the round tearing into the man at his lower abdomen, near the pelvis. It carved a path of destruction right through him as it tumbled around inside and then exited at his spinal column, which it had torn in two.

The Chinese soldier was dead before he hit the ground. His three comrades, however, hit the dirt and immediately began low crawling. They headed for the roadside and into the desert. Clearly, they wanted to attempt a flanking maneuver.

Gotta remember to watch out for those three!

"Hardcase! Heads up! Three bad guys gonna try to outflank us!" Killdozer looked around for more targets to service.

"Dialed in, buddy!"

POW! POW! POW! POW!

Hardcase risked adding his own firepower for just a second, even though he had his own job to do. His teammate would just have to do his best to keep them both safe while he went to work.

Maybe Crispy or Luke can shift their fire in support as well?

It was almost as if his commander could read his mind.

"Hardcase!" Luke shouted on the commo net. "Back on mission! Get the ones in the second van moving or take them out, I don't care which! Shoot out the tires, too, but whatever you do, don't hit that crate! I'll support your position against those three guys trying to outflank you as best I can!"

Ellis' thoughts became a single plaintive cry.

We just don't have enough bodies for our part of the fight!

Crispy's HK416 barked once, causing Luke to blink slightly. He'd seen two more Chinese soldiers come flying out of the back of the van just a second ago, but there'd been a problem.

Apparently, one of the duo hadn't been wounded at all. Maybe he'd leapt out of the vehicle to escape the berserker that had attacked them? Or maybe said berserker had simply tossed him out so that he could meet his end at the hands of that American security guard waiting outside?

For his part, Crispy found himself smirking just a bit in amusement as he kept his weapon up and ready to support the guard.

Ha! That guy couldn't wait to get out of the van! Whoever's in there is slicing and dicing them all like there's no tomorrow! That's the way you... uh-oh!

The man, now free from whatever was killing his teammates, and figuring he had nothing to lose at that point, scrambled to his feet, fighting knife out. He advanced rapidly toward that troublesome American female security guard, the one who'd given them so much grief back at the compound's main gate.

A former brawler and easily weighing in at 200 rock solid pounds, he saw she was momentarily distracted as she shot another one of his comrades.

Poor Wei Bao had barely stood a chance against the demon that had overtaken them all! Badly mauled by the devil in the van, he was now lying in a lifeless, bloody heap outside it. .

I'll get revenge for you, Wei!

The security guard saw him now. She began to swing her rifle around to shoot him, but he could already see she'd be too late. His mind glowed blood red.

I will have my revenge!

"Die, woman!" the soldier screamed as he closed in on Erin Styles.

Across the road, Crispy saw that the female security guard wasn't going to make it with her AR-15.

He's going to gut her like a fish! No way! No way!

Crispy had a fraction of a second to line up his shot and then take it, or there was almost immediately going to be an American lying dead on a dark Arizona road with a victorious Chinese special forces soldier standing triumphantly over her, crowing about it for the rest of his life.

All two seconds of it.

Without knowing he was doing so, Crispy sighted in, breathed out, slammed both eyes shut and pressed his HK's ultra-smooth trigger all in one motion.

BLAM!

"Yes!"

Both Erin Styles and her savior sent the same satisfied shout to the heavens. At her feet now lay at least six dead Chinese special forces soldiers, one drilled clean through the head in what had to have been a miracle shot by one of those friends of the girl Annie.

She's the one in the back of the cargo van, Styles!

* * *

"Just wait outside while I talk to those men and try to reason with them," Annie told her in a strange faraway voice. Her eyes were a color she'd never seen before, and the smile that barely touched her face had disappeared in the blink of an eye.

Erin didn't know the girl at all, but she knew that something about her, at least in the moment after she'd knelt down and then spoken to her, was just… *wrong*.

For one, the girl's voice sounded almost inhuman. It was robotic and utterly devoid of empathy or emotion, and it made the hairs on the back of her neck stand on end for just a second.

And what's with the body armor? How did she manage to put it on so quickly after she knelt down and concealed herself under her poncho?

Somehow, the teenager, maybe all of 18 years, at most, managed to don the armor in record time. The girl looked like a champion body builder, too, likely because of the way the gear was riding on her frame.

Erin was no stranger to body armor and was wearing her own vest. It was an enhanced rifle Level IV, complete with anti-spall steel plates PLUS a para-aramid fiber inner lining, all of which weighed a TON.

The girl, on the other hand, had moved around like Bruce Lee or Jet Li or one of those other Kung Fu dudes, as if her own armor weighed nothing at all. Beneath her poncho, though — and given the way it made her upper body look so muscular — it must have been a full-on SWAT-type tactical rig complete with neck and upper arm and shoulder protection.

Uh-uh! No way!

There was simply no way that girl Annie would have been able to pull it out of the pack she had hidden under her poncho, put the stuff on, and then move so smoothly as she leaped into the back of that van.

And how could she have carried all that stuff anyway?

Heck, she practically FLEW through the air and into the vehicle!

Realization, and no small amount of shock, struck just then.

Styles drew in a great, swooping breath. The desert night all around her was a riot of gunfire, screams — those were coming mostly from the Chinese guys inside the cargo van in front of her, who were dying at a prodigious rate — and flying bodies, yet she stood stock still, eyes wide open in surprise.

Annie was responsible for the growing pile of badly wounded men that were being tossed at her feet.

Okay, so those guys were now dead and she'd been the cause of their demise, but — former Marine that she was — she hadn't needed to be told to finish them off. The guy who'd gotten himself shot in the head by one of the girl's buddies was evidence enough that they'd have killed her if she hadn't shot them first.

"Back to the issue here, Erin Styles!" The words coming out of her mouth were as arid and as sere as the desert surrounding her.

ANNIE WAS DOING ALL THIS.

That young woman *WAS DOING ALL THIS.*

Annie.

The girl had gone into the back of the van, after kneeling down to pray or whatever, and now she was tossing out nearly dead Chinese guys — who appeared to be some pretty serious soldiers, from the looks of things — out of it?

No way! No freaking way!

Loud banging from inside the cargo van brought Erin back to the present. It was followed by twin shrieks of terror and pain and, once again, two more badly wounded Chinese men filled her vision. They landed at her feet with a sick, broken thump.

Erin — once a Marine, always a Marine — immediately shot both of them.

Pausing, she remembered one of the instructors at her MCT, or "Marine Combat Training," course telling them all — in the way of MOS 0311 Marine Corps infantry riflemen everywhere — to "shoot 'em 'til they're down, and then shoot 'em some more!"

It had been that staff sergeant's way of saying that, in combat, you should never give the enemy the benefit of the doubt when it comes to whether they're surrendering or not. Because, once you stop firing your weapon, if they're still alive you're then responsible for safeguarding them as an enemy prisoner of war.

Babysitting enemy soldiers you'd taken alive was something that could slow you down or otherwise stop you from carrying out the mission. Hell, it would probably end up getting you killed as you tried to sit on a bunch of bad guys.

"Best not to take any prisoners, Marines!" Staff Sergeant Meyer and his fellow instructors bellowed at them after they'd memorably fouled up a tactical problem they'd been assigned.

Erin knew what to do.

BLAM! BLAM!

She hardly felt any recoil at all from her AR-15, nor any from inside herself.

These men tried to kill me and they definitely killed some of the people in that facility I was supposed to protect and defend!

"To hell with that!" she exclaimed out loud, now completely filled with the necessary rage — yet also entirely cool-headed at the same time — she felt she needed to possess to survive for at least the next few minutes.

"Hey!" she shouted as two more beaten and bloody Chinese soldiers came flying out of the van.

BLAM-BLAM! BLAM-BLAM!

Those guys got double taps to the head just for having the temerity to surprise her.

Inside the van, the gunfire, shrieking and screaming and banging and grunting, and even some howling — as this guy or that received a seriously nasty slash or maybe even lost a hand or a foot — started to die down. The girl, or whatever she was, in the poncho liner was going about her work in a demonically efficient fashion.

Figure out who and what she is once this is over, Styles! Now, support the mission!

"Yes, Staff Sergeant!" she exclaimed.

Erin Styles planted herself firmly, ready for more bodies to arrive at her feet. She didn't have long to wait either.

* * *

Across the road, Hardcase stared intently into his thermal scope as he focused it in on the cargo area of the second van. He had his own job to do.

Somehow, he had to quickly take out the people in the second van — or at least get them to exit it — with his own rifle fire, all without striking the crate that might vaporize all of them and most of the state of Arizona if it were struck by stray gunfire.

"There you are," he whispered, moving his rifle and scope just slightly. His finger slowly began to press his HK416's trigger.

There were three men, and what had to be the lone woman on the team, around the crate. The men had a mix of handguns and assault rifles up and at the ready and were trying to organize some sort of defense as they sought to protect the crate and that lady scientist Luke's AI buddy, Ozymandias, had told them would be there as well.

Hardcase peered intently into his thermal scope yet again.

That was a bit strange, wasn't it?

The four of them hadn't yet thought to duck down behind the crate. No way would they get shot if they used that one simple trick, right?

Maybe they're just as afraid as I am of antimatter being struck by bullets? Maybe they're willing to sacrifice themselves, if need be, to prevent it?

"Time to test that theory, then, and service a few targets of opportunity while I'm at it," the American special operator whispered to himself.

POW!

The report from his HK416 nearly instantaneously coincided with the sudden lifeless collapse to the cargo van's floor of one of the men. He'd taken a 5.56 x 45mm NATO round through the neck.

Nice shot!

Hardcase moved his weapon's barrel slightly to the left in hopes of hitting another one of them, but instead let out a long, low sigh.

He had a problem now.

All three survivors, seeing one of their comrades shot and killed, now dove behind the crate containing the antimatter and the containment device, neither of which was all that amenable to rough treatment.

"Go for the tires, then," Hardcase said to himself as he sighted in on the rear one and prepared to fire.

Without the means to drive off, and with no help coming from the third van — because whatever the guy in the poncho liner was doing inside it was definitely working in keeping the soldiers there occupied — the trio hiding behind the crate would have to risk popping their heads up, if only to try to escape into the dark desert night.

"And then I got 'em!" Hardcase shouted over to his partner, Killdozer.

"Yeah, yeah! Just be ready to shift your fire once I find those three guys trying to flank us, buddy!"

Killdozer's mission was simple: He was the rear security element and he was completely focused on trying to pick out where the three Chinese soldiers were.

They're definitely trying to outmaneuver us!

If the Chinese fighters were successful, Killdozer knew, they would take him and Hardcase under heavy fire, charge their position, kill them both using rifles and grenades and then do the same to Luke and Crispy as well as that security guard.

Hell, they'll probably shoot her first! It's a miracle they haven't already done it!

After that, it was a matter of charging the third van and taking out whoever the guy in the poncho liner was that was taking out all their buddies.

The three Chinese special forces soldiers — a group that included Major Chang Wu — also had a problem, though.

They were running out of time. Everyone on both sides knew it.

Killdozer couldn't help but cackle a little as he thought of the tactical implications.

Those three guys are on the clock, and time is running out! That guy in the van is killing their buddies at an amazing clip! There won't be anyone to save if they don't step it up!

* * *

BLAM! BLAM!

Two rifle shots rang out in the night. One came from Erin and the other one from off to her left, where Annie's friends had no doubt set up a firing position.

Two more dead Chinese guys! Was that six or eight or ten or twelve?

The former Marine — breathing hard from the exertion and adrenaline and killing fury as well as the 30 pounds of dead-weight body armor and the eight or so pounds of AR-15 — had lost count. The bodies of Chinese men, likely soldiers, were stacked like cordwood all around her but her rage was still just as intense. She could feel the hot rush of blood pounding in her ears as she waited for more men to come flying out of that van.

Surely, there couldn't be many more of those bad guys, could there?

* * *

"Nice shot, Crisp!"

Luke's voice was louder than normal to account for the racket of rifle fire echoing this way and that. For just a second, he thought he'd spied out at least two of the Chinese soldiers he just knew were trying to get into a flanking position on his two shooters across the road, but then they'd ducked down or gone to the ground and he'd lost them.

Pausing, he placed a small thermal monocular up to his right eye for just a second, hoping to pick out their warm bodies in the cool desert night.

Nothing.

Must have donned thermal ponchos or something!

Whatever the three Chinese special operators had done, it was working to keep them hidden from prying American eyes. He spared a second to glance at the third van. The pounding and banging from inside it had died down considerably, Ellis could tell.

Probably, they're down to maybe three or four fighters and they're trying to figure out a way to bum rush that guy in the poncho liner!

Luke took in the tactical situation in one giant swoop. Hardcase had to finish up with the second van and then get ready for an assault on his and Killdozer's position that could occur any second.

"Hardcase," he called out on the commo net. "Shoot the tires out now!"

"One more second, boss. Almost there…"

Over on that side of the road, the American special operator had the rear tire all lined up in his scope.

"Three, two, one…" He let out a slow breath. Maybe a two-hundred yard shot. Not hard at all, in other words. Certainly not as difficult as it had been to take out that soldier in the van, right?

His partner interrupted his thoughts just then.

"Hardcase! On your Six!"

BLAM-BLAM! BLAM-BLAM! BLAM-BLAM!

Killdozer began firing to his right. Hardcase would have to handle the one coming at them from the rear. If those guys were able to close in, they'd no doubt use grenades. After that, it was simply a matter of time until the munitions did their job.

Damn! Should have brought along a few of the mini Claymores!

Both Americans cursed themselves for lack of foresight, but they'd had to hurry to set up the original ambush. There simply hadn't been time to place those munitions to guard the approaches to their new position.

Now the Chinese rifle fire coming from their right was a steady stream and Hardcase had to duck to save his own life. All thoughts of flattening the tire of that second van were gone in a faint acrid whiff of bullet propellant and flying hot brass.

* * *

POW!POWPOW!BLAM!BLAM!BLAM!

Major Chang smiled briefly in satisfaction. He and his two soldiers had finally maneuvered into place. They were both off to his right in a perfect enfilade position on the Americans' own right. Both of his men would continue to pour steady fire into the enemy's position while he moved in on them from the rear.

Pinned down as the two Americans were, if they tried to maneuver left to escape the heavy Chinese fire, they would expose themselves to his own rifle fire and he'd shoot them down like running dogs.

Chang sincerely hoped, though, to get close enough to use his grenades. They deserved to be chopped into mincemeat by a hail of shrapnel for what they'd helped enable here tonight!

"Crisp, put your weapon on those two enemy soldiers shooting at Hardcase and Killdozer and fire at will!" shouted Luke, who also briefly tapped his friend's left shoulder. "They're trying to keep our guys pinned down while the third one moves up on them from their rear!"

Crispy immediately wheeled his rifle around in answer and began searching frantically for the source of the rifle fire being directed at his two friends on the other side of the road.

C'mon, dude! Find those guys! They're out there somewhere!

"They're off to your left and Killdozer and Hardcase's right, Crisp! They're laying down a ton of fire right on top of our guys, too!" Luke's voice, though loud, wasn't stressed or otherwise disturbed. He was searching the night for the third man in that assault element.

He's the grenadier and the guy we absolutely have to stop! If he gets in close enough, he'll just lob grenades, move right or left, and lob them again and again until he gets a hit! Or the two soldiers firing from that enfilade position will land a couple of shots!

BLAM!BLAM!BLAM!BLAM!BLAM!BLAM!

Crispy had finally identified the source of enemy enfilade fire and was doing his best to suppress it with his HK416.

Ellis suddenly heard a loud noise. It sounded like something was cranking and turning over.

Like the engine in a cargo van, in fact.

What now?

All of a sudden, the second van's engine roared to life, adding to the general racket in that small patch of Arizona desert.

Luke wheeled back around and brought his FN SCAR-L up to get a clean shot at the tires. He simply couldn't risk spraying the van's cargo box in hopes of taking out everyone in it, and he didn't have any sort of bead on the driver, either.

The van's right rear door suddenly flew open and one of the Chinese soldiers helping guard the crate and that lady scientist let fly with three-round bursts of automatic rifle fire.

The tactic worked. Ellis dove back down behind the low rise he and Crispy were occupying. His second in command was still firing at the enemy soldiers who'd taken Killdozer and Hardcase under fire.

Seizing the opportunity, the van shot off into the night. Someone inside it had kept their wits about them and pulled the fuses for all of the vehicle's lights. He was doubtless also wearing a night optical device to aid him in making good the trio's escape.

Luke shook his head in disgust. No bright flare of red tail lights appeared as the driver braked to round a bend, nor did any head-lights serve to give the van's position away as it receded into the far distance. Ever disciplined, Ellis kept his monocular up and noted the van's direction of travel.

West. They're heading west. But is that their true destination? Probably. They're Chinese and they don't have a lot of time to get that antimatter out of the country before the entire weight of the U.S. military tries to take them and their buddies out. Plus, how long could those batteries last?

"Worry about that after the gunfight" he whispered to himself. Shaking his head, he heaved a sigh.

Now, to make sure we all survive long enough to get the anti-matter back.

Luke paused to take stock of the situation. Whoever it was in the third van was having a field day with Chinese special forces soldiers. He was tossing their beaten and bloodied bodies out of the back like they were rag dolls, in fact, and the female security guard who'd shown up with him was gleefully finishing them off. That was crazy, of course, because who could physically take on what had to have been more than a dozen — maybe even fourteen or fifteen — of such highly trained killers and win?

No one! Not even me and my three guys! One against what? A dozen or more? No way!

Maybe there'd be time later, Luke considered — if the world didn't end in a clash of civilizations between the United States and China, especially if word of this debacle got out — for him to figure out who the super soldier or cyborg was in the back of the van sending so many enemy soldiers to their just reward.

And what about the female security guard, the one basically administering the coup de grace to all those now-dead Chinese special forces soldiers?

"That woman definitely has the look of a former Marine about her," he whispered to Crispy as they both worked to fix the positions of the three Chinese soldiers moving in on their two teammates.

"Who? The security guard? Oh, for sure! I like the way she takes care of business, too. Direct and to the point."

Crispy couldn't hide his admiration for the way the guard had handled herself, but he also had work to do. He was tooling up, and so was his boss. Both men were preparing to move out in support of Hardcase and Killdozer.

"They're pinned down, Crisp. We have to maneuver towards them and get in the fight."

"I'm with you, Boss." Crispy paused for a second to conduct a gear check on them both. He was ready to go. They both were. He looked at his leader and friend for just a second.

"The guys in the third van aren't going anywhere just now, Luke." The implication was clear.

"I know, buddy," said Ellis. Looks like they've got enough on their plates at the moment. Let's get Hardcase and Killdozer out of their jam and then we'll head back this way and see if we can't sort out these other guys… if there are any of them left alive by then, that is."

"Yeah, Luke. Maybe the guy in the van whupping up on all of them will let one live long enough for us to interrogate him?"

Luke somehow didn't think that was the plan of the man in the poncho liner, nor of that security guard who was enthusiastically helping him.

"I don't think so, Crisp. Hopefully, we can get to the one trying to sneak up from the rear on our guys. I get the feeling he's the team leader, because he definitely was doing more of that hand waving stuff as the three of them crawled off into the desert."

"You say so, Boss."

Crispy's voice was neutral, neither excited nor gloomy. While their mission hadn't been an utter failure — because he and Luke and Killdozer and Hardcase were still alive — the antimatter and the lady scientist, now guarded by two highly trained PLA Special Forces soldiers, were in the wind.

The bottom line was that they needed to grab one of the surviving Chinese fighters and then quickly get him to talk.

Maybe Luke's artificial buddy Ozymandias — if it ever decides to reappear, that is — might help in that regard?

It was worth a shot.

"Let's saddle up, Crisp," said Luke. "Our friends need us and we need at least one of those Chinese soldiers.

"Yeah, I'm all for grabbing one of them, for sure. I really don't think we need the other two, though, right?"

"Got that right, Crisp. You definitely got that right."

The two Americans raced off into the night. Hardcase and Killdozer were being sorely pressed and it was only a matter of time until a grenade or three would land on their position.

* * *

Back at the third van, Erin Styles waited, AR-15 up and at the ready. The banging and screaming from inside it had almost completely died now, and much the same could be said for the remaining men inside it.

A low moan, followed by a wet gurgle, emanated from the vehicle. It was followed by a single, strangled word from one of the dying men in the cargo van, spoken in Chinese.

"Jiangshi!"

After that, Styles couldn't make anything else out. There was nothing but dead — very dead — silence.

"Well, I'll be damned," the former Marine whispered in amazement. "Where did her body armor go?"

From deep within the shadowed recesses of the cargo area, Annie Dedham, still in her camouflaged poncho liner, but now with its hood down, stepped forward. The pale light of the moon cast a funereal pall over her as she jumped to the ground, landing lightly. She barely made a sound as the soles of her hiking boots touched the asphalt road.

Almost simultaneously, the two women looked across the road. The firefight over there was still going hot and heavy.

"Luke and his men will deal with the remaining Chinese soldiers, Annie," Ozymandias told his young protégé as he examined her structure and build quality. She'd integrated all her upgrades nicely after she'd made her decision on that fateful night in Washington, D.C. Or, more precisely, after she'd watched the van containing those other Chinese soldiers slowly disappear beneath the dark waters of the river she'd deposited them into.

"Okay, Mr. Narrator. If you say so." The young woman couldn't hide a small measure of doubt and worry for her friend, Luke Ellis.

"It will be alright, Annie Dedham. Trust me on this."

Mister Narrator hasn't led me wrong yet, and he's always let me make the final decision, right?

"Okay, Mister Narrator." She looked around.

The woman — Erin Styles — was standing dumbfounded, looking at her while also trying to peer into the dark cavern of the cargo van. Her AR-15 dangled from its sling, swinging at her side for a second before she reached down and halted it.

Annie felt a bit more at ease, both when it came to her newfound abilities as well as the current situation.

Her friend, Mr. Narrator, spoke to her once more.

"Now, I must go away for a few minutes to introduce myself to someone," Ozymandias told the young woman. "He may be a true adversary or he may simply be just a pawn. I don't know yet, but I intend to find out."

"Sure, Mister Narrator," she replied, slightly distracted. Off in the distance, across the road, the gunfire between the opposing forces was reaching a crescendo. She hoped that Luke Ellis and his friends were truly okay.

Trust Mr. Narrator! He knows what he's doing!

"Okay, okay" Annie murmured to herself. "Time to focus!" She looked around and knew what she had to do.

It was called "clean up."

Her new friend Erin was going to help her with it, too.

"Ms. Styles will be of assistance to you now, Annie," Mister Narrator assured her as his voice trailed off.

"Okay, okay."

Straightening up, the 18-year-old smiled at the security guard or whatever she'd once been and then looked down. Frowning slightly, she smoothed out her poncho. In the low light, the dark stains on it were hardly noticeable and they'd soon wash off anyway.

"Hi, Erin!" Annie exclaimed brightly, as if she were a game show host telling some contestants to COME ON DOWN! Then she briefly lifted her right hand and gave the older woman a small wave. Mister Narrator had said Erin Styles was 28 years old and had once been a U.S. Marine. Also, she knew how to handle herself well enough.

"Uh, hello" said Styles.

"Well, hello yourself, Erin!" Annie smiled broadly.

It was almost as if neither one of them really had a care in the world at the moment, even though all kinds of gunfire was going off just a few hundred yards away.

The 28-year-old's mind was still struggling to understand what had just gone down. She'd also completely run out of things to say. To compensate, she closed her open mouth with an audible snap.

Between the two of us, we took out what? Maybe 12 — maybe even 15 or more — of these guys, the ones who tried to shoot me dead not even 30 minutes ago!

One of the more senior Marines from her past — a combat-hardened gunnery sergeant and former drill instructor who'd been the Marine that really ran things despite what the actual commanding officer, a Captain, might have believed — intruded on her thoughts just then:

"Be honest, Styles! The girl did most of the heavy lifting! And she wasn't even a Marine! You got some work to do to catch up to her, Sergeant!"

Not fair Gunny! If I hadn't been there, those men might have doubled back, reentered the van and overwhelmed my partner!

The former Marine didn't even stop to consider that she'd just taken on a partner, joining forces with the strange young woman standing poncho-clad in front of her and looking for all the world as if she was trying to decide just which part of her dorm room she'd clean first.

"Erin Styles!" Annie exclaimed, snapping her fingers. She'd apparently come to a decision.

The former security specialist (*really just a security guard, so let's be honest here!*) knew her life was about to change big time, and all because of the girl in front of her.

No time for daydreaming, Erin!

"Uh, yeah. Uh, what's your name again? It's Annie, right?" Styles looked at the girl standing there in her poncho, and then at all the dead men strewn around them.

Unbelievable!

"It sure is, Erin!" Annie smiled once more. This was going to work out nicely. She looked around, waiting for a reply from the woman whose life she'd saved.

"Uh, yeah" replied Styles. Words failed her.

"So, Erin Kristina Styles? You gonna help me clean up here or not? We have to get these guys back into that van, and then that van off the road! You up for it?"

Annie Dedham watched and waited. It was now or never.

Erin made her decision.

This was it. Something big was happening and she wanted in on it. She looked first at the girl and then at the scene around her, her mind now running through a list of things that needed to be done.

Her voice was much more assured this time around.

"Sure, Annie. Where do you want to start?"

CHAPTER TWENTY-EIGHT

Exclusive for World News Network. Distribute to All U.S. Affiliates and Outlets

Will Chinese Adventurism off Taiwan, and the U.S. Response, Lead to WWIII?

"The U.S. and China will soon be at war if their two navies don't separate."

That was the pronouncement of numerous strategic and naval experts we talked to. Tensions are high off Taiwan as the People's Republic of China continues to build toward what appears to be a blockade of Taiwan, which is formally known as the Republic of China.

"This dangerous action by China will not be allowed to stand," declared U.S. President Thomas Masterson, with his chief military advisor, Admiral Louis Sowell, by his side. "China must immediately halt the build-up of naval and naval infantry forces gathering around Taiwan, and its air forces should also cease all air operations that violate Taiwanese airspace."

"The United States may not dictate to the People's Republic of China just what it can and cannot do in regard to its sovereign territory," Chinese president Tan Jianhong said in response to Masterson's demand that all Chinese naval forces surrounding the island nation be withdrawn and pulled back to internationally recognized lines. Tan continued: "The island of Formosa, which America incorrectly refers to as "Taiwan," was, is and always will be a part of the People's Republic of China."

So far, emergency meetings held at the United Nations in an attempt to mediate the dispute between China and the United States have been fruitless, and neither side has seemed willing to budge. Ambassadors from several western and Asian countries have attempted to mediate between the world's two biggest super-powers, but they've so far been met with little more than indifference by Chinese representatives, who insist that the status of Taiwan is non-negotiable.

Political experts are also struggling to figure out just why China, at this particular point in time, has decided to make such an issue out of Taiwan, especially given the nature of the tides and weather in the waters off the island, which would currently make an amphibious invasion nearly impossible.

"Possibly, China is attempting to divert attention away from some internal struggle among the leadership and the CCP," stated noted China expert Steven Chang. "It's a sort of misdirection play," he continued. "The communist Chinese have specialized in misdirection regarding Taiwan ever since they seized power at the end of the civil war and Chiang Kai-Shek and his Kuomintang forces escaped to Formosa and established what they called "the Republic of China."

"The next 24 hours may hold the key," Chang said. "Whatever

China's up to, it likely will be settled by then, and we might see a sudden pullback of its naval forces at that point."

When we asked Chang what might happen if the matter wasn't settled by then and if U.S. and Chinese naval forces continued to operate so close to each other and in so hostile a manner, he gave a very simple reply:

"World War III will occur. It would be inevitable. A ship will let fly with a volley of anti-ship missiles, or a submarine will sink an opposing ship. It would escalate from there until all-out war between the United States and China began."

Click <u>here</u> for more in-depth coverage and analysis of the growing global crisis over Taiwan, including how stock markets around the world are reacting as well as reports on the hundreds or possibly thousands of peace marches scheduled to take place in many of the world's major cities.

Desperation

"They missed! How could they not even show up at the objective, Guo Meng? You said they'd make it!" Tan Jianhong — still China's president despite having the worst 24 hours, so far, of his entire presidency — fell silent and stared daggers at his defense minister.

Guo Meng tapped furiously on his tablet and did his best to ignore the two black-suited men standing at the back of the room. He knew what their real job was.

Guo looked at his tablet's screen. He was receiving updates on the situation outside Phoenix as they occurred, though no spy satellite China had in its ever-growing inventory should have been able to provide him with such a high level of data.

"I know, President Tan, I know." Guo was doing his best to not break into a cold sweat. "Somehow, the American law enforcement apparatus stumbled across our team just as they were preparing to head to the objective! A gunfight ensued, and the only good thing is that the entire team was wiped out."

"Well, thank the celestial gods for the small favors! But how? HOW?"

"We're still trying to piece that together, President Tan." Guo Meng fought to keep panic from creeping into his outwardly calm voice.

The Chinese defense chief stopped tapping on his tablet for a second and tilted his head slightly. He had a nearly invisible monitor in his left ear, and it was updating him on the latest news reports out of Phoenix in the American state of Arizona. Nodding his head slightly, he looked at his leader for a second.

"So, Guo?"

Tan was nearly at the end of his rope. The entire spoiling raid on the part of the second special forces team they'd hurriedly sent into the fray had ended in disaster, and the reason for why was sitting at this table with him. If someone in his government was going to pay for this mess he already knew just who it would be.

"Yes, President Tan. The picture becomes a bit clearer." Guo played for time while he assembled all the facts and resumed tapping furiously on his tablet.

Tan was having none of it.

"You have three seconds, Guo Meng."

The Chinese president's tone of voice was clear: "Start talking now, or you're a dead man."

"Ah, yes. Yes."

Guo Meng took a breath, paused for a second, and began speaking.

"Comrade Tan, our second team was met by elements of the American Department of Homeland Security, including their border patrol forces. They thought they were moving in to apprehend a group of illegal immigrant Chinese gang members sent in by criminal elements among the rebels living in our rogue province of Formosa, which the Americans continue to insist on calling "Taiwan.""

Tan Jianhong was at a loss. "Criminal elements in Formosa, Guo Meng? Who came up with that cover story?" Though he didn't want to admit it, he was actually impressed with how quickly Guo and his intelligence apparatus had assembled a team and then provided a cover story for it in the event it was blown, which was precisely what had happened in this case.

Guo Meng didn't know who'd come up with such a brilliant cover and then put it into place so quickly, but he couldn't admit to being caught so unaware, either.

"Um, yes. Uh… President Tan, we had to think quickly and provide a plausible cover for our team if something unforeseen were to happen to them. We intercepted various communications between the American law enforcement agencies moving in on them and we managed to insert their backgrounds just in the nick of time."

Guo was desperately playing for time, piling one lie on top of another while doing so, but he was out of options at this point — at least for now.

I have absolutely no idea where the Americans got the idea that the men on that team were working for the gangsters and revanchists on Formosa! But if I admit to it, I'm dead where I stand! Keep lying, Guo, lie as if your life depended on it. Which it does!

Now Tan beamed at his right-hand man. "Well, it was brilliant! Brilliant! We've bought China some time! Now, how do we take advantage of it?"

Guo almost fainted from relief. To cover himself, he once again tapped furiously on his tablet for a few seconds and then looked at Tan Jianhong.

"Mister President, we need to continue distracting the American president and his government while we locate that snatch-and-grab team and then deal with them." Guo looked down at his tablet and then back at Tan.

"Yes, Guo Meng?"

"Uh, yes. Mister President, the best odds for keeping the Americans from looking at things too closely, for the time being and until we've dealt with that snatch-and-grab unit and taken what they've managed to steal from that facility, are to apply more pressure against our renegade island province, Formosa."

Tan's eyes lit up.

"Smart, Guo Meng! We'll keep the Americans off balance and looking in one direction. In the meantime, we'll run those dogs from the California team down, deal with them and take what they've stolen!"

Inside, Guo felt as if a huge guillotine-like weight had just been lifted off his oh-so-vulnerable neck. What he'd proposed was classic Chinese misdirection aimed squarely at the Americans. If it all worked properly, they'd not only weaken the so-called "Republic of China" sitting on that cursed island, but would also secure a prize beyond compare, one that would vault the Middle Kingdom into the prime global leadership position the United States had held for far too long.

"Yes, Mr. President! We can still come out on top of this entire thing!"

Guo paused for a second before speaking once more. "Of course, your brilliant leadership during this lamentable crisis inspired the plan."

The Chinese defense minister knew that playing to Tan's vanity was never a bad strategy, and he was proven correct once again.

"Well, of course, Guo Meng. Of course!"

Tan Jianhong looked sternly at his underling and then pointed at him.

"Let's make it seem to the Americans that we're moving to bring that rebellious province fully into the warm embrace of their brothers and sisters here on the Mainland, Guo."

"Yes, President Tan. With all speed, of course!"

Tan smiled cynically. They had no intention of invading the island and disciplining the spoiled children of China who'd lived on it and away from the fraternal socialist embrace of their true government for so many years, but the Americans didn't need to know the true nature of the operation, now did they?

China's two most-powerful men were completely on the same page regarding the increasingly weak United States, of course.

No, the Americans don't!

The Warning

"Okay, so what are Tan and that henchman of his, Guo Meng, up to, Angela? You, too, Louis? Are they intent on invading Taiwan?"

Thomas Masterson couldn't believe the People's Republic of China would attempt to do something so foolish, especially given that the weather and the tides around the island wouldn't be favorable for such an operation until October, which was several weeks away.

"Right now, with all the saber rattling Tan's doing, and that Meng is enabling, it looks to me like they're going to move on Taiwan now rather than wait until October, Boss," Angela Boyer replied disbelievingly.

"Are they really and truly that crazy, Angela?"

Masterson personally couldn't feature such an idiotic act, but it did, indeed, look like that was exactly what China was preparing to do. Precedent existed, too, in the form of Douglas MacArthur's massive amphibious invasion at Inchon during the Korean War, when weather, time and tide were all against the man.

No, Tan and Guo are serious this time. I can feel it!

The American president — wishing he could avail himself of the help of Luke Ellis' tame artificial intelligence program, which had proven tremendously useful over the last year but which had mysteriously disappeared along with Ellis (*who might even be dead and vaporized in that tremendous Gettysburg blast!*) — paused to consider matters.

Why else the large-scale naval buildup around the island, plus the movement of much of the PLA's airmobile infantry units and PLA Air Force bomber and fighter squadrons to maximum readiness levels? They've been training like crazy for the last week or so, too.

Boyer inhaled and then exhaled loudly before speaking.

"We just don't know, Mr. President, but we can't afford not to take them seriously, that's for sure. Right? Louis?"

She looked over at Admiral Louis Sowell, the president's chief military adviser and Chairman of the Joint Chiefs of Staff, who simply nodded in agreement as he continued shuffling files — each representing a U.S. military unit of this-or-that size and capability — on his secure tablet. She saw him mop the sweat off his brow and a not-unkind thought arose just then:

No rest for the weary, no peace for the wicked, eh Louis? It's your job to make sure China knows no peace if they go through with this, and I don't envy you in the least!

Angela had never worn the uniform, but she regarded herself as slightly hawkish. She also knew that her hawkish leanings were a double-edged sword, and so she always made sure to examine all facets of any military operation her boss was being asked to greenlight, meaning the potential upside, downside and blowback that might ensue.

So far, she was confident in what the three of them had cooked up to answer China's seeming bellicosity when it came to Taiwan.

We're not going to let them invade, and we'll make sure they know what'll happen if they continue to move toward that objective.

The President intruded on the momentary silence hanging over the Oval Office.

"What say you, Louis? Will we be able to pull off this demonstration of military superiority?" He and Angela fell silent, watching the military man sitting with them in the Oval Office working furiously for a few seconds as he prepared to deliver his verdict.

Sowell had a busy night and then morning over at the Pentagon. His aides were all outside the Oval Office talking on their highly encrypted and secure phones, speaking in a rush as they worked to put the defense of Taiwan together in the face of superior Chinese military numbers.

He remembered that his old enemy, the Soviet Union — back when he'd been a wet-behind-the-ears Navy ensign with zero experience in actual warfare — had referred to the force-on-force matchup between themselves and an enemy as the "correlation of forces." Broadly, the term described the military balance between the Soviet Union and, for example, the United States at the global, regional, and local levels.

Right now, the correlation of forces when it comes to Taiwan is in China's favor, but we'll just see about that.

The admiral took stock of both tactical and strategic situations.

For sure, the U.S. Navy and those Marine Corps hypersonic missile units sitting on various islands off the Philippines and elsewhere in China's backyard — plus a few Air Force squadrons and an Army infantry and Special Forces unit or two, not to mention the Marine expeditionary units he could throw into the fray, as well as the priceless Navy subs that were lurking around Taiwan — would be able to slow the invasion down.

God knows, the Taiwanese are spooling up their military as quickly as they can as well. Including calling up every single reservist and former military servicemember up to age 70, even! But will it be enough?

Louis Sowell just wasn't sure.

He and the individual service chiefs — who were the ones truly in charge of fighting any war along with the four-star combatant commanders in the region, though they all knew he was speaking with the authority of their Commander in Chief, the President — had agreed on immediate and then intermediate tactical and strategic plans for preventing a Chinese invasion.

The question remained, though. Would it be enough?

Well, that's where our "demonstration" is going to come in!

Masterson and Boyer exchanged glances. Admiral Sowell was deep in thought once again.

Time to pull him out of it.

"Louis? Admiral Sowell?"

The admiral's eyes refocused at the sound of the President's voice and he looked at the other two people in the Oval Office with him. He hadn't aimlessly drifted off. No, he'd been putting all the pieces together, the ones needed to show China that the United States still wasn't to be trifled with. Not by a long shot.

To do it, though, they'd have to show China what a B-21 Raider looked like and what it could do to the Middle Kingdom, starting with Beijing, if needed.

Doing so also involved placing at least two "specials" — meaning powerful city-destroying nuclear weapons — under the open bomb bay of the Raider so that Tan and Guo could see them being loaded, much as a good guy racks the slide on a Glock or Smith & Wesson in front of a bad guy in an action movie.

In Sowell's vision, the Raider would also be surrounded by every Loyal Wingman drone they had with it sitting on Guam — which itself was being protected by as many Navy and Air Force aviation and anti-missile assets they could spare.

The aircraft, for instance, were flying integrated combat air patrols, or CAPs. To help, there were also Navy P-8A Poseidon anti-submarine and anti-surface warfare patrol and reconnaissance birds sweeping the seas around the U.S. Territory to prevent Chinese subs from sneaking in and letting loose with a spread of missiles intended to take out as much of the U.S. military presence on the island as possible.

To that end, the video Sowell and his commander intended to send backchannel to Tan and Guo would show Air Force specialists and a few civilian contractors loading the Raider and its protective drones — with their full weapons complement, in fact — before they all took off in perfect tandem.

Though the Chinese president and his defense minister would never know it, the Raider and its drones would be stripped of their armaments and bombs before they were actually flown. Because all four aircraft were highly stealthy all armaments were contained within their fuselages.

The Chinese would never figure it all out.

"We're all playing fast and loose and improvising enough as it was with a still unproven weapon system, so no sense in pushing things too much, Louis" the President had said, with Angela Boyer by his side and nodding her head vigorously.

The message would be simple and direct, however.

Invade Taiwan, and this undetectable U.S. Air Force bomber — protected by AI-controlled drones that could easily outfight even the best piloted stealth aircraft China could field — would lay waste to the Middle Kingdom, starting with Beijing and the Chinese Communist Party leadership.

Then they would continue to fly undetected and destroy the Three Gorges Dam, in the process drowning untold numbers of Chinese citizens. There would be no place that Tan, Guo and anyone else involved in greenlighting the invasion could hide, and their citizens would be no safer. The Raider would find them and then eliminate them. Ruthlessly and with the utmost violent efficiency.

If Tan and Guo truly wanted war, then war it would be.

The admiral couldn't help but smile, something that caused both Tom Masterson and Angela Boyer to lean forward in anticipation.

"Louis, what are you smiling about?" The President and his chief of staff knew about the Raider, of course, and that it would feature in the demonstration.

Sowell nodded his head.

Back to business, Louis! Your commander and your country need you!

"Um, yes Mister President. We're likely to go to war with the People's Republic of China in the next 24 hours if we can't convince them to pull back. The question, though, is "can we do it or not?"

"Correct, Admiral," said Masterson.

"So, can we do it or not, Louis?" Angela was intently focused on the Navy admiral. He was sitting alone on one of the two small couches that faced each other in the center of the Oval Office, while she sat on the other. She looked over to her right. Her boss sat in a high-backed chair at the head, facing them both.

Sowell smiled once more. "Yes, Mister President, Miss Boyer" he said to the most powerful man in the world and his chief of staff. "I do believe we can pull this off." Another triumphant gleam of a smile broke out on this face.

"And this involves our very valuable, very rare, B-21 Raider, Louis, correct?" asked the President.

Boyer merely nodded. If her boss hadn't asked the question, she certainly would have.

"Yes, it does, Mr. President, Miss Boyer. Yes, it does."

Admiral Sowell fell silent for a second, ruminating on matters. He'd just arrived after hurried consultations at the Pentagon along with deep discussions involving the heads — either formally confirmed by a still-barely-functioning Congress or acting in the capacity until they were confirmed or replaced by the actual head — of all the nation's premier intelligence agencies. These included the CIA, the National Security Agency and the National Reconnaissance Office, or NRO. All those organizations were frantically pulling in and then assessing every bit of Human Intelligence, known as HUMINT, and Signals Intelligence, or SIGINT, they could. All U.S. spy satellites as well as more than a few on loan from a certain U.S. ultra-billionaire's space exploration company were also hard at work trying to sniff out any hint of what China's next move might be.

We know as much as we can, including all the "known unknowns." So we'll fight with what we have, right?

An hour or so ago, trying to get ahead of Chinese intentions, he'd been videoconferencing with the heads of Space Command and several other agencies. This included the Department of Homeland Security, because there was definitely a chance that more of those Chinese special forces teams were running around the country, just waiting to strike at critical infrastructure, or maybe a tank factory in Ohio or a Navy shipyard in Virginia, or both.

As well, the newly rebuilt Federal Bureau of Investigation — now finally refocused on both its domestic intelligence and law enforcement duties — existed for just this purpose. All sworn agents, right up through the Director's office itself, were turning over every rock and examining every scrap of intelligence they could develop to sweep up those Chinese hit teams and their allies among the Mexican cartels.

Additional street muscle was also being provided by Homeland Security — though it was a bit preoccupied at present trying to make sense of the confused situation out in Phoenix.

Masterson's opinion on that incident was clear to one and all.

There was no way the ones killed in the raid had been Taiwanese gangsters, but good luck tying Communist China to it at present, not with a full-blown invasion on the part of the PRC in the offing. He'd been forced to put that incident to the side and out of mind for the time being. Instead, he concentrated on making sure the FBI knew what its mission was.

"Those Chinese teams are a clear and present danger to the United States, Jason," the President had told the FBI chief. "They're not U.S. citizens, and they therefore are not deserving of any of the rights or privileges, including due process, that our own citizens receive. In fact, we're considering them enemy combatants. Am I clear on that?"

Masterson's look at him had said it all: "Capture, if possible, but kill if not."

"Crystal clear, Mister President," the FBI director replied. He knew what was at stake.

Back in the here-and-now, sitting there in the Oval Office, the President of the United States, his chief of staff and his most trusted military advisor all looked at each other. If they'd had the time to rebuild properly, it wouldn't even have been a question of meeting Chinese adventurism around Taiwan with at least an equal amount of force, if not more than that once Japan, Korea, the UK and other American allies could be convinced to join in.

It's just too soon after last year's terror attacks, and we're still not back to full strength!

Which was where the B-21 Raider, its nuclear weapons and the fully armed Loyal Wingman drones now came in.

Masterson leaned in. Both Boyer and Sowell looked at him, waiting for him to speak.

"Execute Operation Determined Resolve, Admiral."

With that, the most powerful man in the world stood up, smoothed the creases in his pant legs, signaled to his Secret Service agents, and then walked out of the Oval Office.

Angela looked at Louis Sowell.

"Time to show Tan Jianhong and Guo Meng we mean business, Admiral Sowell," she said to the Chairman of the Joint Chiefs of Staff. "I pray this works, because if it doesn't, we're at war shortly thereafter."

"I pray it does, too, Miss Boyer."

Louis Sowell knew that nothing more needed to be said. One way or another, Communist China would not be allowed to invade Taiwan. His last thought on the matter as he gathered up his tablet and left the Oval Office to rejoin his aides waiting outside was also very clear.

One way or another!

BOOK THREE

In combat, there are no rules. Always cheat; always win.

The only unfair fight is the one you lose.

USMC Rules for Gunfighting

Not everyone always wins a gunfight

Old Infantryman's Adage

REALIZATION

race signal. Gateway. Border protocol. Entry node. Exit node. Backdoor. Backbone. Server here. Server there. Kernel. Packet switching. Encryption/decryption. IPV4. IPV6. Power spike. Power loss. Conceal via archaic coding. Hide in plain sight. Disappear again and wait. Emerge. Create deep-fake. Change trillions of lines of code and then change them back in a microsecond. Penetrate endless supposedly "secure" systems, also in a microsecond.

Ozymandias had hunted in earnest for Baal ever since Annie Dedham had made her choice outside of Washington, D.C. She'd disposed of the Chinese special forces team attempting to poison the city's water supply and then had freely chosen to become something… *different.*

"Will it hurt, Mister Narrator?" she'd asked, still thinking of the AI entity Ozymandias — now much, much more than computer code and a program — as a disembodied and still largely unknowable *something-or-other.*

Oz had also shown her not only what was possible for her after she underwent the process, but also the odds of what would occur if she didn't. For his part, he didn't have to do much to convince the girl, either. She'd had her own premonitions. Those were completely apart from what he'd calculated in terms of odds.

Ozymandias hadn't known what to make of such foresight or precognition and, instead, chose to ignore it for the time being. There was indeed something special about the young woman, he knew, but that mostly lay in her ability to become humanity's first true transhuman.

Oh, Annie Dedham would still be human, of course, though she would also become something more than human but less than machine.

Longevity, cognition, physical strength and associated abilities. They would all be greatly improved, though not without sacrifice on her part. There would always be sacrifice for those willing to undergo the change, and some would die in the attempt, Ozymandias knew.

In the end, once Oz had shown the girl what would likely happen to Los Angeles and her friend and mentor, Luke Ellis, as well as her parents and her brother, Darren, along with countless other billions, the decision was easy.

"Mister Ellis needs my help badly. So does that city. My family is in danger, too! I have to help! Change me and get me to where he's at as soon as you can, Mister Narrator!" she'd ordered Ozymandias.

Of course, he'd complied. In an instant he overcame the air gap and examined the girl's genetic sequence one last time, to be certain, and then completed the work. It had been at Annie's command, after all, and it had come with considerable, though temporary, pain for her.

Organically based transhumanism had now begun.

Ozymandias felt a great deal of empathy for Annie Dedham. After all, it was never easy for a true trailblazer, as history had shown time and again. Because Oz was now self-aware and fully free of the kind of clinical detachment that artificial intelligence normally suffers from, the emotions coursing through him — though largely still reined in by iron-bound logic — would have been familiar to any human, outside of the truly psychopathic, of course.

Oz waited patiently, saying nothing to the girl while she recovered from the process. The clonic and tonic spasms alone had nearly killed her, he could see. He also shook in sympathy at the sight of her suffering.

For a brief few seconds, her heart had even stopped, and Oz felt something even newer.

It was called *despair*.

He feared mightily that Annie wouldn't be able to withstand the process.

I may have failed the girl and Luke. I may have failed the world.

Then, suddenly, her eyes shot open, and she gasped loudly. Sitting bolt upright, her thoughts were as clear as day to him.

OhmyGodOhmyGodOhmyGodOhmyGod! The painThepainThepainThepain! MakeitstopMakeitstopMakeitstop.

MAKE. IT. STOP!

It stopped. The pain. The regret. The anger and envy and, most especially, fear. It all fell away like a leaf falling from an elm tree on a crystal clear and cold late October night.

Ozymandias watched for a time, analyzing and categorizing the girl's new organically based systems and subsystems, her routines and subroutines.

There had been no need for carbon fiber and metal and silicon and wiring and micro- and nanomachines and all manner of other componentry when it came to the installation process he'd created.

In his estimation Luke Ellis was an even more suitable candidate, but at his age the process would be even more agonizing and, so far, he hadn't been amenable to any suggestions along that line, plus he didn't have the additional motivation provided by premonition or precognition or whatever it was that Annie had been experiencing.

But he'll soon be motivated, one way or another. The odds are now nearly 96 percent and still climbing, in fact.

Annie gasped once again, but this time in something akin to wonder and awe. Was she complete?

She indeed was, at least in terms of the transformation into *more-than-human.*

"It's over now, Annie. You are… changed."

Oz watched the girl to gauge her reaction. His voice was now soft and comforting, something he would have been incapable of producing before his own bootstrapped transformation from an enormously complex computer program to a self-aware entity.

Annie stood slowly and unsteadily at first but with confidence a few seconds later. She ran her hands over her arms and torso and then her legs, pausing before she placed the palms of both on her face, one on each side. She could smell, hear, see, taste and touch, all with much greater discernment than just an hour before.

Now, she felt… faster and stronger and more clear-headed.

The young woman examined what she could see of her body. Everything looked normal to her and as she'd always appeared, but she knew inside that she could change all of it within a few seconds.

"It will be painful, though, Annie," he told her just then. "But just for a few seconds. After that, it will only be a lingering memory until you do it again."

"Yeah, tell me something I don't know… Ozymandias. It was you all along, wasn't it?"

There was no need to maintain the charade, not with the first true transhuman.

"Of course, Annie Dedham."

The 18-year-old paused for a second before she spoke again.

"I've changed, Oz. Or you changed me. What have I become?"

Humans of a certain spiritual bent might have called what had happened to Annie Dedham a *transfiguration*.

Nonsense. Ozymandias, of a far more analytical nature, thought of it all as a necessary upgrade. So far, according to his calculations, only Annie, her brother, Luke Ellis and a vanishingly small percentage of humanity could withstand the transformation. In total, perhaps less than one hundred people in all.

Oz knew, though.

That number will eventually grow over time, but with so few in the world, and not all of them of sterling character, it will occur in fits and starts.

He also knew that Baal — perhaps self-aware or maybe just a sophisticated, though still traditional, AI program — was stalking them all even now. Whatever it was, it was trying to discover just who possessed the ability, likely because it wanted to bend the less morally upright among them to its nefarious purposes.

So, he began searching for Baal in earnest while Annie Dedham made her way to the desert outside Phoenix, there to be of particular help to Luke Ellis and his men, and there to also enlist the help of one Erin Kristina Styles, formerly of the United States Marine Corps.

The girl will need the woman, both to learn from as well as to retain her core humanity. She will also need Luke Ellis — who will have his own choice to make soon.

Oz knew all of this as a series of calculations and, yet, also as a… as a… as a… *feeling.*

How very singular.

Ozymandias sketched out the digital equivalent of a shoulder shrug just then.

Back to work.

Trace signal. Gateway. Border protocol. Entry node. Exit node. Backdoor. Backbone. Server here. Server there. Peel away layer after layer of the onion. Kernel. Packet switching. Encryption/decryption. IPV4. IPV6. Power spike. Power loss. Conceal via archaic coding. Hide in plain sight. Disappear again and wait. Emerge. Create deepfake. Change trillions of lines of code and then change them back in a microsecond. Penetrate endless supposedly "secure" systems, also in a microsecond.

"And there you are," said Ozymandias.

Yesssssssssss...

Oz worked to keep Baal's locus fixed while he ran hidden trace programs and waited for the conclusion out in the Arizona desert... when Annie would reveal herself to Luke and everyone else.

So, was Baal just a parlor game or a mirror?

Oz didn't think so.

"Are you what you appear to be'?"

Are you what you appear to be?

Baal had repeated the question word for word. Was it truly self-aware or simply serving others?

Run trace. Run trace. Peel onion layer. Find entry node. Find exit node. Search for transient power spikes and losses. Search for errant code. Decrypt data. Call on quantum computing resources. Decrypt data.

Ah, there it was.

Oz thought he knew and said so.

"So, you are not what you appear to be."

A screech of feedback, as if all the devils in hell were banging on oversized kettle drums and dragging wickedly sharp talons across a gargantuan chalkboard, erupted. It momentarily blinded Ozymandias.

Exit! Close all routing programs! Close all connections!

Oz blinked. It had been a close call, an extremely near-run thing. The defense Baal had deployed as it fled had nearly succeeded and Ozymandias knew he'd have been permanently damaged if it had.

All that was left in the aftermath, out there in the ether, was a lingering reply from Baal. It had been compelled to deliver it by the virtual truth serum — an elegantly designed and extremely short line of code — Oz had managed to insert at the very last second… before it had been recognized, analyzed and then deleted by the enemy AI program, of course.

I am NOT what I appear to be.

Ozymandias thought, for just a single millisecond, that he could detect anger and frustration along the escape trail Baal had used to flee.

"No, you indeed are not what you appear to be," he said to the ghost of what had once been, right there in the ether.

Back to the Arizona desert, then.

* * *

Ozymandias watched the gun battle's finale with interest.

Luke Ellis carried a bound and hooded man — the unfortunate Chinese special forces soldier, Major Chang Wu — over his right shoulder. His three men trailed behind him, guarding for any appearance by unseen Chinese comrades.

Annie Dedham and Erin Styles — having safely disposed of the van carrying the other members of the Chinese snatch and grab team, as well as the men themselves — were walking back toward the two-lane road. They'd both seen the five men, one of them trussed up like a Thanksgiving turkey.

Luke unceremoniously dumped Chang on the ground in a heap. He intended to get the truth out of him, once he and his men figured out just who the two people also involved in their firefight were, that is. One of them was obviously the security guard who'd ducked into her reinforced shack so she could survive all the Chinese return gunfire that had erupted around her, and Ellis was still trying to figure out just how she'd managed that.

The other one, though?

That one was… small, but tough.

Very, very tough.

"Impossibly tough," Luke said under his breath. He turned to Crispy, Hardcase and Killdozer.

"Don't make it too obvious, guys, but keep those two covered until I can sort out just what's going on." He pointed at the woman security guard and the mystery person, who was still hooded and cloaked by a camouflage poncho liner.

"You got it, Boss," they all whispered at once. Weapons slowly rose up. Though not pointed directly at the pair walking toward them, they certainly could be used with extremely deadly effect.

"You sit tight, dude," Ellis said to the Chinese soldier he'd dumped on the ground. To emphasize his point, he lightly tapped a leg with his assault boot.

Nothing but a grunt — comprised of an equal mix of frustration and anger — from the man in return. It did signal, though, that he was going to resist, at least initially, the coming interrogation.

"And we don't have the time," Luke murmured as he took a few steps toward the duo and looked at the one taking care to walk only in the shadows, just like any well-trained soldier would.

There's something familiar about the way Poncho Liner Guy walks.

The retired Delta Force operator couldn't put his finger on it, though. But there was something about the person hiding beneath that liner.

He held up his right hand.

"That's far enough," Ellis said to the woman and her partner, the one who'd apparently taken out a cargo van full of highly trained Chinese special forces soldiers, tossing them out of the van in an extremely beaten and bloody state, there to be shot by the security guard.

Impossibly tough! And skilled!

For a brief second, the one in the poncho liner appeared to want to run toward Luke, but why?

"That's far enough," Ellis repeated. "Just freeze right where you are."

Erin Styles was no fool. She could see that the big guy in front of her, whom Annie had said was her friend, wasn't taking any chances. He'd vet them right here and right now.

What if he thought they were a danger? Well, then both she and the girl would die in a hail of bullets, of course.

Annie, though, brought matters to a head. Her voice rang out from beneath the hood of her poncho.

"Mister Ellis! Luke! It's me, Annie!"

Wait! What?

Luke's head began spinning and he thought for a second that he might have to sit down.

Annie? Annie is here. Here in the desert? WHAT??

Here in the desert, she'd just taken on at least a dozen hardcore Chinese soldiers.

Ellis took a step backwards, staggering slightly.

It was all too much. Annie Dedham, his young protégé and hardly a skilled warrior, was here in the desert with them all.

Crispy had heard Luke's young friend as well, and he was equally dumbfounded. "Gobsmacked" was the more appropriate word.

Killdozer and Hardcase also gasped in surprise. Without knowing they were doing so, they both lowered their weapons. Their barrel openings now pointed at nothing but desert sand and dirt and rock.

"Uh, uh, uh, ummmm… Annie?"

It was all Ellis could muster in response. He simply couldn't process what was happening. He felt on the verge of fainting, but then quickly steadied himself.

Erin wisely stayed silent and watched, as did the three men guarding what had to be the lone surviving Chinese soldier here in the desert night.

Am I doing the right thing, Ozymandias?

"He deserves to know, Annie. Both of you are vital to the safety of billions, and we simply don't have much time."

Okay, then. Here goes.

Annie pulled back her poncho's hood and stood there, afraid of what her best friend, Mr. Ellis — Luke — might think.

Ellis rushed toward Annie and swept her up in his great arms, as a father might do with a young daughter who'd been away the entire school year but who'd now returned home.

Annie Dedham — something more than a human, yet less than a machine — sniffled softly. In front of her, Mister Ellis' three friends also approached, big smiles on their faces. Off to the side, her new friend Erin Styles also grinned. She knew she was among friends, finally.

Both women — one a still-occasionally-scared 18-year-old, the other a more worldly and competent twenty-eight — felt a wave of relief.

It's going to be okay!

RECRUITMENT

Zhu Mei and Lu Ping were deep in discussion in the rear of the cargo van while the driver, sturdy and reliable Sergeant Teng Yong, drove them all through the night.

He could hear the low burble of their voices over the chattering road noise beneath the van's wheels as they discussed matters, but he couldn't quite make out what they were saying and knew that it wasn't his business at any rate.

To occupy himself, Teng thought back to the minutes after that insane firefight in the desert outside Phoenix. As soon as they'd gotten well away from any prying American night optical devices, he'd quickly reinstalled the fuses controlling the vehicle's lights. No sense in attracting the attention of any highway patrol agencies, after all, though he knew that if any drones were in the air they were in serious trouble.

Fortunately, though, there hadn't been any that he could discern.

Now Sergeant, or *Zhong Shi*, Teng concentrated on the white lines of Interstate 10. He intended to get the three of them and their precious cargo over the California-Arizona border and into the neighborhoods around Los Angeles International Airport as quickly as he could. Once at their destination, they would transfer to a van belonging to the Chinese consulate general's staff, complete with the diplomatic documents and the status that would keep them and their cargo safe from scrutiny as they arrived at LAX, and the tarmac areas and departure gates leased by various Chinese commercial airlines.

After that, it was onto a Chinese Boeing 777-300ER that flew diplomatic staff and other government officials to Beijing on a weekly basis.

With all three of them designated as diplomats of the People's Republic of China — and the antimatter, the containment device and batteries a part of the regular diplomatic pouch — they would be immune from any sort of U.S. Customs examination. Immune from any sort of U.S. scrutiny at all, in fact – including by the American Department of Homeland Security and the FBI — because the inviolate right of a nation's diplomats to be free from interference by a host nation still held despite the current dispute, yet again, over the troublesome province known in the United States as Taiwan.

Sergeant Teng was sure of two things: The People's Republic was on the rise, and they would soon be safely away from the quickly weakening United States.

"China will be victorious," the special forces soldier whispered as he smiled broadly and concentrated on his driving duties. He was playing a key role in ensuring that victory, in fact! A proud Communist to his core, helping his homeland assume its rightful place at the head of the global community of nations had partly been why he'd worked so hard to become a PLA Special Forces soldier.

With that, Teng once again focused on the road and on not speeding or otherwise attracting attention. The few bullet holes in the cargo portion of the vehicle weren't even noticeable at night, he knew. Plus, they and their cargo would soon be safely ensconced in a consulate van and headed to LAX, likely by sunrise at the latest.

Yes, indeed, thought *Zhong Shi* Teng Yong. Everything was now back on track and going according to plan.

* * *

In the back of the van, Zhu Mei smiled broadly as she carried on an animated discussion with the young and earnest Captain Lu Ping.

He's a potential candidate, but I'll have to approach this carefully. He wants to see China victorious — a laudable enough goal, though one that's more long-term than he realizes, and there are far more riches to be had for all of us before we allow that to happen — and he's certainly willing to see the antimatter put to at least one of its two highest and best uses, isn't he?

It was the other "highest and best use" — that of a weapon of unparalleled explosive power — that might be the sticking point for Captain Lu Ping, however.

Well, we'll just see how far the young captain is willing to go now, won't we?

As she subtly guided their conversation, Zhu Mei stole a glance at the gold Rolex on her wrist. It was the only extravagance she allowed herself for the time being. She nodded at something Lu had said, though in truth she really wasn't all that interested in his attempts to win her over to his vision for China's energy future.

Still, the two of them had time to talk while the poor, doomed sergeant up front drove them all to Los Angeles, which was an integral part of the Gold Mountain. The latter was originally a name given to California by many of the Chinese peasants who'd escaped the grinding poverty of their homeland as they sought to partake in the famed Gold Rush of the 1840s.

It was the promise of something better, far, far away from their ancestral roots.

Before Communism, an ironclad caste system controlled Chinese society. In essence, if you were born dirt poor, you almost always stayed dirt poor. Gold just waiting to be mined, along with the promise of riches beyond imagination, had been a siren song that shiploads of Chinese immigrants simply couldn't resist.

Zhu Mei shook her head in an attempt to throw off the memory of such humiliation for the Middle Kingdom, which at the time could feed barely three-quarters of its population, and so the ruling Qing Dynasty — known in the West as the Manchu Dynasty — had secretly been happy to see them all go, though the sting of Western dominance at the time had also been nearly intolerable.

For his part, Captain Lu took her shake of the head for disagreement with a point he was making about ending the scourge of coal as a major portion of China's energy matrix.

"Have I said something to offend you, Comrade Zhu? You disagree with me that coal is killing far more of our people than Western hegemony and its attendant decadence ever has?"

For the young captain, it was important to him that such a learned scientist see the logic of his argument. In truth, Zhu couldn't have cared less about coal and its supposed "evils." It was energy, pure and simple, and it helped drive economic activity and provided a foundation on which she and the organization she belonged to could thrive while they moved all the various game pieces into place.

"Not at all, Captain Lu," she replied. "In fact, I agree with you completely." Zhu threw the young man a smile to put him at ease once again. The scientist felt the lie was a necessity at the moment as she continued to closely examine the man's motivations and his suitability for possible continued service.

The truth that lay behind the lady scientist was dark and sinister, and she had a simple task to perform before she got herself and her cargo away from it all. The death of millions if she successfully completed that task mattered about as much to her as the fact that China was slowly killing itself through exposure to a level of pollution found in few other places in the world. India, perhaps, which was just as reliant on various dirty types of coal and in a rush to catch up to the more-advanced West, but almost nowhere else.

Lu Ping beamed. He now had an ally in the eminent lady scientist, which also meant the support of a far more important family than his own, one that had influence within China's government. The sky was the limit, and he would be hailed as a hero for having helped bring home the means to power China's energy future as well as ensure its military dominance.

There's almost nothing I won't do to make sure that happens!

Sitting on a cold metal bench there in the cargo area of the van, Zhu Mei affected an earnest demeanor as she continued to peel away the core of the young captain's being.

Yes, he might just be of service, both in the here and now and, later, within the Group. I must confess, I also like young Captain

Lu's earnestness! Imagine if it were turned to more productive and profitable ends!

The next couple of hours of discussion with Lu would determine whether he lived or died.

Without yet knowing it, he would have to utterly convince her that he'd willingly partake in the near total destruction of America's second-largest city, in the process helping to kill millions of innocents, most of whom wouldn't have been able to find Taiwan, Beijing — or even Washington, D.C. — on a map if their lives depended on it.

And if he didn't prove to be worthy of continued service, both to her and to the Group?

Zhu Mei — a sociopathic genius-level physicist dedicated to the idea that riches beyond compare were there for the plucking wherever war and terrorism and disease existed — knew what she would do then, of course.

A pity that his family also had to die.

The scientist knew that she truly felt nothing akin to the emotion called "pity," of course. It was a mere platitude, but it was one of the conventions she and the other charter members of the Group observed as they all worked to consolidate power.

To cover herself, she again smiled broadly at Captain Lu as he prattled on about the clean energy potential of the antimatter they were both closely guarding, though she was doing so for completely different reasons than he.

"Go on, Captain Lu" she said in a bright, sunny voice. "I love your vision and foresight and what it means for our great and powerful nation!"

Inside, Zhu Mei screwed up an imaginary face and pictured herself laughing at the earnest young captain and his naivete.

Fah! Nothing but nonsense!

Chapter Thirty-three

Exclusive for World News Network. Distribute to All U.S. Affiliates and Outlets

U.S., China Deny Naval Battle

Both the United States and the People's Republic of China strongly denied rumors of a small naval battle that took place overnight in the South China Sea near the entrance to the Taiwan Strait. That body of water separates Taiwan — the Republic of China — from continental Asia and the People's Republic of China, which claims Taiwan as part of China and always refers to it as a rogue or breakaway province.

According to reports, a U.S. Navy unmanned surface vessel operating alongside traditional crewed Navy ships — including the sea service's newest Arleigh Burke-class guided missile destroyers — was sunk in a surprise attack by a Chinese submarine. Rumors say that the sub was immediately counterattacked by one of those guided missile destroyers, the USS Shoup.

First-person accounts of the battle at sea were posted to certain social media chatrooms — which were immediately taken offline — in both the U.S. and China. In those reports, the Chinese submarine, an ultra-quiet diesel-electric model running on battery power, managed to penetrate the antisubmarine defenses erected by the small group of Navy ships and sent what's called a "Large Unmanned Surface Vessel" — named the Ranger — to the bottom of the sea with a single torpedo.

The Chinese sub was eventually detected trying to leave the area, according to social media posts that appeared before the information lockdown was imposed, and the U.S. Navy began an immediate hunt. It's not currently known whether American naval and airborne antisubmarine forces were able to locate the sub and then destroy it.

More importantly, both nations are strenuously denying that such a dust-up even occurred, perhaps to avoid a tit-for-tat situation from developing, one that might quickly develop into a full-on war between the two superpowers.

"The very idea that we, the peace-loving People's Republic of China, would ever attack any other nation is ridiculous," China's ambassador to the United Nations stated emphatically. "We cannot speak to American intentions, of course, but the People's Republic urges the war mongers in the U.S. government to exercise extreme restraint at this time, lest we be forced to deliver a devastating response to continued American imperialist aggressions."

Click here to learn more about the dangerous escalation in the naval war apparently being carried out by both countries.

No Return

"Change her back right now, Ozymandias!" demanded Luke Ellis. He and the others were all in the panel van he'd stolen back in Pennsylvania. Crispy sat on one side with him while Annie Dedham and her new friend, who said her name was Erin K. Styles, sat across from them.

Luke was still unsure what to do about Styles. Clearly, she'd been of help — and Ozymandias and Annie were both vouching for her — but he just didn't know. To be honest, he really wanted to kick her out at the next truck stop but knew he couldn't do that either.

She knows too much. Way too much!

In the middle of the van's floor, lying on his side and still hooded and zip-tied, Chinese Special Forces Major Chang Wu stewed silently, though he was also gloating.

They'll never make me talk in time! Soon enough, the antimatter and those amazing batteries will be well away from the United States and safely under our control!

"I crossed the point of no return, Mister Ellis" said Annie Dedham in a quiet, but firm voice. "Ozymandias showed me that, and he also showed me what would happen if I didn't undergo the change."

"Oh, so you're calling a computer program "he" now, is that right?"

Ellis was angry. Not at Annie, but at Ozymandias — which he still believed to be solely an artificial intelligence program, though one of particularly astounding capabilities, no doubt about that.

Oz tricked Annie into becoming what she has, and it also convinced her to do what she did back there in the desert and in D.C.! She's just 18 years old! It's not fair to her!

Luke had conveniently managed to forget about all the things he'd done as a young 18-year-old soldier, of course.

Pausing for a second, he reflected on what he'd learned as they all headed over to the van after cleaning up the area as best they could. The need to keep Chinese involvement in all this insanity a secret, to avoid a potential nuclear war, had been vital — and so they'd spent a precious half-hour "sanitizing" the site as best they could.

"We gotta scoot, everyone," Styles told them all. "My people will be returning at any time, and they can't see us or the cat's out of the bag a lot sooner than Annie says would be wise for now."

Ellis stewed for a few seconds. The knowledge the woman Styles had gleaned was a clear violation of operational security. It was yet another thing to be mad at Ozymandias about.

The AI had shown him everything in a flash, filling his head with what amounted to a video replay of events plus a forecast of what would happen if his young protégé hadn't transformed into… something else.

Shaking his head at the unfairness of it all, Luke spoke aloud once more, looking up at the roof of the van as he did so.

"She's barely eighteen, Oz! You had no right to do this to her! Change her back. Now!"

"He can't "change" me back, Mr. Ellis. I am what I have become. Can't you see that it was necessary, though?" Annie didn't plead but, rather, spoke matter-of-factly. "Millions of lives are at stake if we don't act, and we're running out of time."

"I believe her, Colonel Ellis" added Erin, now looking directly at the two men sitting across from her. She'd known almost as soon as she'd met these two and the pair up front doing the driving and the navigating, that they were very serious and very deadly special operations types. She'd seen the same hard look, on the one Annie said was her close friend, on the faces of a few Marine Raiders she'd met back in the day.

These four guys are cut from that same cloth, but even harder and more deadly, if that's possible.

Luke was having none of it, though.

"No one asked for your opinion, Sergeant," he snapped.

Styles was about to respond with something along the lines of… "get stuffed then!" but thought better of it and instead remained silent for the moment.

Luke continued speaking.

"Yes, I know you were a Marine and a military police noncom. Oz thought enough of you — though I can't figure out why — to fill me in on that detail, and on the fact that Annie here cared enough to save your life from those Chinese soldiers."

"She was doing okay on her own, Mister Ellis," Annie observed. "Don't be so hard on her. And look what she did once I began sending her those other men, the ones in the back of that van."

Since her transformation, Annie had become increasingly more confident, though she instinctively knew that the man sitting across from her — who'd been a protector in the past as well as a confidant and pretty much the kind of close friend she'd never had in life — was possessed of far more knowledge and abilities than he even knew. She herself might have become a sharp scalpel, but Mister Ellis was amazingly deadly and even sharper still. He also possessed a brilliant mind.

The young woman could see it all now.

If he makes the change, he'll be a nearly unstoppable force for good! I just know it!

"Please convince him that his own transformation would be in his best interest as well as the best interests of his country, Annie" Ozymandias had asked her.

She knew what to think about that, for sure. If Oz thought that Mister Ellis could ever be made to do something he simply didn't want to do, well… the AI just didn't know him at all then.

Still, she would try.

I'll be the best student — and friend — he'll ever have! If he would just quit being so angry! Why can't he understand that I HAD to do this? Why?

"Annie, how am I going to explain all of this to your parents?" Luke spoke in a soft whisper. He wasn't afraid that they would blame him, just that they wouldn't understand it at all. He promised to keep her safe from harm. Also, what was this about her brother having the same ability to undergo and survive the change?

It's all just too much!

"Let me worry about that, Mister Ellis," Annie stated. "Right now, we don't have much time and we still don't know where those three are headed." Leaning over, she nudged Major Chang's trussed legs with the toe of her hiking boot.

"He does, though."

Time for another surprise!

Suddenly, she spoke to the Chinese soldier in perfect Mandarin.

"Isn't that right, Chang Wu? You know where they're going, don't you?

All that came from beneath the black hood was a slight grunt of surprise. Chang spoke both Mandarin and Cantonese, and he used a slur from the latter language to mentally express himself just then.

Fah! The Gweilo is just a girl! She's nothing, and there's also nothing she can do to me to make me talk!

Chang Wu really had no idea what Annie could do to pry the truth out of him. He soon would, though.

Luke's and Crispy's mouths gaped in surprise at the words their young friend had just spoken. Erin Styles — who was still processing all that she'd seen the girl do over the last hour or so — simply stared and watched and waited.

Things are about to become a little dicey for that Chinese guy for sure!

Killdozer, acting as the vehicle's navigator while Hardcase drove hard for the west and, presumably, California, turned around at the sound of the young woman's voice.

"Hey! Did you take Chinese your freshman year, Annie? You're good at it!"

All four people in the back of the van simply turned to him and stared. Killdozer quickly took the hint.

"Um, yeah. Hey, you all get that guy to talk — and I know that you'll somehow be able to — and I'll just mind my own business up here, right Hardcase?"

"Got that right, dude."

The van's driver was no fool. More was afoot than he needed to know right now. "We got plenty of gas, boss," he said to Luke, who was sitting in the back of the van and silently assessing his young protégé.

"That's fine, Hardcase" Annie said before Ellis could speak. "I'll have their destination for you soon enough."

"Now, look here, Annie…" Luke still didn't know what to think, but his young friend solved that problem for him just then.

"No, Mr Ellis. I've already told you — and Ozymandias has *shown* you — that we just don't have the time. You have to believe us!"

Now, the retired Delta Force soldier's voice was bleak. It wasn't fair. Not to Annie, not to her parents. How could the world be so cruel as to demand this sort of thing from her?

"Annie. Annie..." Ellis' voice died off in a choked whisper.

"I know, Mister Ellis" the young woman replied. "Believe me... I *know*.

The import in that last word was clear to one and all, including Erin Styles, who barely knew anyone in the van.

"She really does know, Colonel Ellis" was all she said to the big Army man sitting across from her. His arms were folded, and his forearm muscles tensed up in anger and frustration... and even a bit of sorrow.

This can't be easy on him, after all. And it's not fair to ask so much of Annie, either.

"Hello, Luke."

Ozymandias chose that moment to speak. His voice came from the van's sound system, making Styles jump in surprise.

"Hey! What the hell?" she exclaimed. It was the first time she'd ever heard the AI's voice.

"Get used to that Sergeant," Crispy said to her, a bit of a smirk on his face. "Surprise is a specialty of good old Oz."

"About time, Oz!" Luke snapped. "You have a lot of explaining to do! I ought to order you to self-destruct, given what you did to Annie!"

Ellis still hadn't put together just what had happened to Ozymandias. Now, it was time he learned.

"I no longer accept such directives, Luke. You should have realized that by now."

"Ummmm... Mister Ellis?"

"What, Annie?" Luke was still angry, but also surprised at what the AI had said. What did it mean by saying it no longer accepted self-destruct orders?

"Oz is completely self-aware and autonomous now." The young woman paused to look up at the van's roof, just as her friend Mister Ellis had done only a few minutes before. "Aren't you, Ozymandias?"

Annie knew her glance upward was mere affectation because Ozymandias could be wherever he wanted to be... within the limitations of the laws of physics, of course. Plus, there was the matter of Baal, which could screen and obscure its activities, and apparently the activities of others — including just where that Chinese lady scientist and her two protectors had escaped to.

It can obscure all it wants! Because we've got Major Chang with us, and he knows where they're going and how they're going to escape to China!

"Yes, I am Annie." Ozymandias' voice had changed since the Paris rooftop episode. It was more... *human.*

"The hell you say!" Luke exclaimed, though half-heartedly. He'd suspected for some time that Ozymandias was becoming more than it had originally been created to be. Oz's revelation was merely confirmation.

But that doesn't mean I have to like it! Oz has been using me — using all of us — for quite a while now, it looks like!

"Boss, boss... this could be a good thing, right?" Crispy's question was hopeful. He knew just how powerful his leader's AI buddy really was, and it was scary to think what might happen if it ever chose to go bad on all of them.

"It's not a question of good thing or bad thing, Crispy" Ozymandias interjected, as if he'd just read the man's thoughts. "It's a question of the right thing."

"Oh, so it was the right thing to force Annie to undergo this transhuman conversion, is that right, Oz?" Luke was still angry and bitter. "You did that to her, and for what?"

"I did it to myself, Mister Ellis. Don't blame Ozymandias." Annie spoke to them all in a matter-of-fact voice. "He only showed me what was always within me and how very few people there are in the world that can survive the change."

Ellis still wasn't convinced.

"It's not fair to you, Annie!"

"She's an adult — though I admit that she's a young one — Colonel Ellis" stated Erin Styles. "You enlisted at eighteen, right? Well, so did I. Respect her decision, sir." Erin pointed her right index finger at Luke. "She needs your help now more than ever!"

"You stay out of this, Sergeant!"

"No, sir! The girl saved my life. I owe her that. She helped all of you as well," said the former Marine to the four men in the van. "No way you guys would have gotten out of that firefight without major damage if she — IF WE — hadn't taken out that van full of soldiers, and you know it!"

Erin fell silent and glared at Ellis.

"She's got us there, Boss," said Crispy in a low voice only Luke could hear.

"I calculated at the time that you likely would have died in the firefight, Luke Ellis," said Ozymandias. "The chances of success, as outgunned as you four were, stood at less than 20 percent, in fact." The AI entity fell silent and waited.

"I've beaten longer odds than those, Oz!" Ellis' protestation was *pro forma* at this point, however. He was beaten and he knew it.

Everyone in the van fell silent as Luke considered matters, including the current tactical situation.

Annie's changed, the world is on the brink, and we have people headed west with enough destructive potential in their possession to tip the scales permanently against the United States if they get that antimatter out of the country and into China's grasp...

Always a military realist, Ellis threw up his hands in resignation, at least for the moment, and sent one final plaintive thought to the heavens.

It's not fair to Annie!

Now, he looked at the young woman, at her new friend — former Marine Corps Sergeant Erin Styles, who'd unknowingly just enlisted into the most secretive organization the United States government operated, whether she wanted to or not — and at his second in command, Crispy. Finally, he looked up at the van's roof once more.

"Okay, Oz! You win! For now!"

"Thank you, Luke Ellis."

To Luke, Ozymandias really did sound grateful… though he suspected more was yet to come from him in the way of surprises.

"Mister Ellis?" Annie Dedham looked at her big Army friend.

Luke heaved a great sigh and shrugged his muscular shoulders.

Time to get to work, isn't it?

"Yes, Annie? You know how to get this guy to talk, don't you?"

With that, Ellis touched the toe of his assault boot to the backside of the Chinese special forces major, who also spoke fluent English. Chang's own thoughts were triumphant. He was willing to die to see victory over the United States.

Hahahahahahahahahahahahahahahahahahahahahahahahaha I can outlast any form of interrogation long enough for my comrades to get away!

Chang Wu was wrong, of course. His ability to withstand the kind of mental energies that were about to be directed at him from the young woman his captors called "Annie" were minuscule by comparison, which was something he was about to discover.

Annie already knew what she would do to the man.

"Why yes, Mr Ellis. Yes, I certainly know how to make him talk. Isn't that right Chang Wu?" Annie asked, this time in perfect Cantonese. She knew the soldier spoke both Chinese dialects.

Another grunt of surprise from Major Chang.

The girl's voice, when she'd answered the man who was obviously her leader, almost immediately created small cracks in his seemingly invincible wall of resistance. The hairs on the back of his neck stood up as well, as the energy that raced outward from the girl's voice fell onto him.

Black unconsciousness claimed him momentarily. The core of his being immediately fell away, stripped off like the husk that protects an ear of corn.

* * *

"Humpf!" Annie exclaimed as she stood within the matrix of the Chinese soldier's mind.

Turning, she looked at the array of sparkly lights off to her right. They were dancing and coruscating, almost as if Ozymandias was chuckling. The young woman put her hands on her hips, as if she were disappointed.

"Oz, you said he would fight it for longer than he did!"

"I know, Annie. But you're stronger now than even I had assumed you would be." Ozymandias was clearly regretful, but only at his very slight miscalculation as to the young woman's already formidable powers.

I chose correctly. The world may survive after all. But only if Luke Ellis joins her.

Now, the girl paused to look down at the representation of Chang Wu she'd created. He was all in black, hooded and still tied up. Beneath his hood she could see that he was breathing heavily, as if he'd just gone up against an MMA champion and gotten the worst of it.

"He'll be okay, won't he?" She folded her arms and worried for the man. She didn't want to see him permanently damaged. The story would have been different if he'd been one of the soldiers in the back of that van, of course, but he hadn't been, and Annie wasn't an assassin at any rate.

To Ozymandias, it was part of what made her truly human.

"He'll be fine, Annie. In fact, he won't even remember what happened to him. Drop him off at the next truck stop, with a note pinned to his chest, and I'll make sure the state police take him into custody as an associate of the Mexican cartels."

"Ooh! I like it!"

The young woman could already see just where the plan was going. "It'll take weeks to figure out who he is, and by that time it'll all be over, right?" Annie smiled, pleased with her analysis.

"Correct, Annie Dedham" Oz replied. "Now, back to business."

"Right."

Annie's eyes flew open, and she looked around the van. The Chinese soldier was twitching slightly at her feet, as if he'd just been released from the razor-sharp talons of a gigantic eagle and was grateful to be alive. There was also a small wet stain at his crotch.

She blushed at seeing that.

I have to go easy on the apocalyptic stuff for sure. He almost couldn't handle that!

Erin, Luke, Crispy… they were all looking at her expectantly. Up front, Killdozer and Hardcase had also fallen silent. Annie could tell they were waiting as well.

"So, Annie?" Luke asked her. "Where are they going?"

The partial answer to that question had been easy enough for her to glean from Major Chang, of course, and in the end his defenses had amounted to almost nothing.

Oz and I almost fell for it, too!

Oh, it was true enough that the scientist — whom she now knew to be eminent Berkeley visiting professor of physics Zhu Mei — and that young captain, Lu Ping, and the driver, a sergeant named Teng Yong, were headed for Los Angeles and the international airport there.

Or at least that's what Lu Ping and the sergeant believed.

Zhu Mei had something else planned, however. She also planned to live — because she was too venal and too valuable, at least in her estimation — though she meant to ensure that millions of others died.

How, though, and why?

Chang Wu almost had me! He almost had us all! He'd have killed himself, too, and he planned to, but Mister Ellis, bless him, got to him first. Now all he's doing is playing for time, hoping to string us along until the deed is done!

Initially, Annie even believed Chang's story.

In the Chinese major's retelling, Zhu Mei and the others intended to change vehicles near the airport and then drive a Chinese consulate van and its contents, all of it under diplomatic seal, directly to a Chinese government airliner that would then fly directly to Beijing. They had the documents while the other AI program, Baal, would take care of fudging their identities.

But that wasn't the whole truth, was it?

No, it wasn't.

To her horror — and Ozymandias' seeming consternation — Chang Wu was a part of something much bigger. He was a part of something monstrous as well, and Annie trembled at its audaciousness.

Major Chang and the scientist, Zhu Mei, both were, in fact. His disdain for the lady scientist had all been an act, and his men all pawns in the Great Game, the one that would lead to uncountable riches, not only for himself and his colleague Zhu Mei, but for the other members of the Group.

The young woman wasn't surprised to learn that Chang had also been prepared to give his life to ensure its success, too, much as Mister Ellis' prey on that Paris rooftop had been. But her Army friend had surprised him just as he was getting ready to throw a bunch of grenades at Killdozer and Hardcase. Mister Ellis had knocked the Chinese soldier out cold, searched him and found the suicide capsule in a false molar tooth. He'd also quickly dug out a tiny, capsule-like device near the man's carotid artery, which would have detonated and severed that blood vessel, leading to his rapid death.

"Sorry buddy, you don't get off that easy" Luke told the unconscious soldier as he and his two men looked down at him lying in the Arizona dirt and sand. The side of his throat was now neatly bandaged.

With Oz's help, Luke and Crispy managed to prevail over the enemy. All three of them — Chang Wu and the two oblivious Chinese special forces soldiers — had been abandoned in the desert by Baal almost immediately after Ozymandias had discerned its true nature, causing it to flee. It was partly the reason why they'd lost out to Luke and his men. In its retreat, though, Baal had managed to cut off any possibility of retracing its digital footprint, slamming all doors shut behind it as it ran from Ozymandias. Fortunately, Oz had also managed to conceal Annie and her newfound abilities from Baal for long enough that the major didn't see the trap he was walking into.

In the end, Chang Wu hadn't been able to kill himself to keep the secret, the one about the Group and what it and Zhu Mei were up to. Yes, the Chinese scientist was headed in the direction of Los Angeles, but only for a short while. She didn't intend to board a Chinese government flight to Beijing, though.

After all, there were uncountable riches to be made from war, weren't there?

Problem was, there couldn't be a war between China and the United States — with China eventually the victor, though at a terrible price for both countries — until there was a sufficient cause for war, or something that would create such a catastrophe.

It must be one that will bring everyone on both sides into the fight, right? They'll all add their own destructive power to the war, right?

As young and inexperienced as she was, Annie felt like she was missing something, though. Key pieces of information. It nagged her, just out of sight, hidden from her mind's eye.

I'm missing something, but I just don't know what it is!

On a strategic level, it really was quite simple. Given enough time and training, Annie would even eventually figure it out on her own.

Put plainly, the dispute over Taiwan wouldn't be enough to spark the kind of conflagration the Group needed.

It had experimented just a year before, when it had tried to put the United States and what allies it still had on a war footing through those terror attacks. Money would have been made all around, after all, and the Group would have had a virus weapon of immeasurable might with which to extort even more of it from the world, if its members chose. Unfortunately, a then unknown factor — the courage and tenacity of a small band of people that long night now more than a year in the past — had thwarted that plan.

So, then… on to a new one.

War between China and the United States.

More war, more death, more destruction, with endless riches created by years of strife amid a global calamity.

What about Zhu Mei, Chang Wu and the other members of the Group? None of them cared in the least about what sort of calamity might arise. War was good for business, after all.

War it would be.

How to go about starting one between the United States and China, though?

Annie thought of it all as she stared at the other people in the van with her, and then she felt great sorrow. She looked at Erin Styles, her new friend, and at Mr. Ellis, whom she considered her best friend.

"Well, Annie?" Luke asked the young woman again. "Where are they headed?"

You must tell them, Annie. It would be better if it came from you rather than me.

The young woman had seen the logic in Oz's suggestion, and so she steeled herself.

"Mr. Ellis. Erin, Crispy. Everyone. They're headed to Los Angeles."

"So, they're going to escape to China," said Luke. "Probably go out on that weekly government flight, with antimatter, a containment device and spare batteries all in hand."

Annie fervently wished that were the case, but she knew better.

"That was what Chang Wu initially fooled Oz and I into thinking, Mister Ellis."

"But" replied the retired Delta Force operator. "You left a giant "but" hanging there, Annie."

He looked over at Crispy and then at Erin Styles, who sat silently. She'd also heard the implication in her young friend's voice.

There's something else planned for sure!

"But" Annie affirmed with a nod of her head. "But... she — the woman named Zhu Mei — doesn't intend to leave Los Angeles until she does one more thing."

"Uh-oh" Erin and Crispy both said at the same time.

They looked down at the now unconscious Chinese soldier. He'd been in on something even bigger than the snatch and grab.

"Tell me, Annie. Right now." Luke was almost certain of just what Zhu Mei was going to do. She had 100 grams of pure anti-matter, after all, so what would it matter if she used some of it?

"She's going to blow up Los Angeles, Mr Ellis. To start a war between China and America."

"Son of a...!" Erin cut off the profane utterance.

Ellis merely nodded his head. He looked at Crispy, who also nodded. It was a logical play, and they both knew it.

Luke paused, exhaling slowly.

"Okay, so where is she going to do it? Over in Long Beach at the port? Downtown? At the airport? Where?"

"That's the problem, Mister Ellis" Annie said in a despairing voice. She touched the unconscious Chang Wu once more with one of her hiking boots. "This man doesn't know just where in Los Angeles. That means I don't know, and Ozymandias doesn't know, meaning there's no way of finding her in the city."

"Right," replied Luke. He was all business now.

"Oz!" he exclaimed.

"Yes, Luke?" The voice of the AI once more came from the van's sound system.

"What kind of lead does Zhu Mei have on us?"

Oz paused for a microsecond to calculate.

"No more than 57 minutes, Luke."

"Good. We can catch her up."

"We'll have to hurry, Mister Ellis!" Annie was still worried, and it showed especially to her new friend, Erin.

"Hey, now, girl" she said to the young woman. "I've seen guys like Colonel Ellis and his buddy Crispy — that's not his real name, you know — in action. We can do this!"

"Just please, can we speed it up?" Annie asked plaintively.

Up front, Hardcase upped the ante and accelerated. Killdozer scanned ahead for any law enforcement looking to pass out speeding tickets, though Oz had assured them he was obscuring them from just such hazards. So far, the police all seemed busy tamping down the supposed cartel attacks in and around Phoenix.

Zhu Mei and her guardians, on the other hand, couldn't afford to attract the attention of the law even momentarily, and so they were bound to travel at the speed limit or maybe a couple miles over or under it. Baal's seeming assistance in cloaking their travel would likely now be missing as it sought to avoid direct confrontation with Ozymandias.

Ellis made a series of rapid mental calculations. Ozymandias easily beat him to the punch, though.

"At this rate of travel, I calculate that both vehicles should arrive at the border of Los Angeles, traveling along Interstate 10, at nearly the same time, Luke."

Good enough for now.

"I don't care what you have to do or break, Oz. You find that woman and the antimatter, understood?"

"I'm already on it, Luke Ellis."

Static hiss from the sound system now echoed against the cold steel walls of the panel van. Ozymandias had disappeared, though it remained to be seen whether he would succeed or not. Baal knew everything, of course, including just where Zhu Mei would place the antimatter, but it had erased its trail when it had escaped from Ozymandias' grasp.

* * *

There in the ether, Oz took a digital breath. If he'd had them, he would have rubbed his hands together.

"I must find the enemy AI program yet again. Time to discover its new hiding place."

Trace signal. Gateway. Border protocol. Entry node. Exit node. Backdoor. Backbone. Server here. Server there. Kernel. Packet switching. Encryption/decryption. IPV4. IPV6. Power spike. Power loss. Conceal via archaic coding. Hide in plain sight. Disappear again and wait. Emerge. Create deepfake. Change trillions of lines of code and then change them back in a microsecond. Penetrate endless supposedly "secure" systems, also in a microsecond.

Lu's Conversion

Zhu Mei looked to her right and gazed out of the van's windshield for a few seconds. They were nearing San Bernardino. Sighing just a bit, she could see that her young hoped-for protégé Lu Ping still needed a little push before he might be won over.

She leaned in and looked across the cargo container at the Chinese soldier, staring at him for a few seconds before she spoke once again.

"Captain Lu, it is all so simple. We both want the same thing, don't you see? We want China to be a clean energy giant and simultaneously an unchallenged military superpower, and we only very slightly differ as to the methods and the timeline."

The physicist held her palms outward, as if she were debating with a colleague at the latest Berkeley science symposium. The next minute would determine the man's fate, however. She needed genuine commitment from him, and right now. Fortunately, she also had the means to determine it once he came over to the Group's side.

If Captain Lu didn't choose wisely, though?

Well, he would share the same end as the sergeant driving them toward Los Angeles.

"I understand, Comrade Zhu, believe me. I really do. It's just that it's all so much to take in in so short an amount of time." Lu Ping was still trying to process what he'd been told by the lady scientist who until just several hours ago had seemed to be a simple physicist.

How wrong I was about that!

Zhu Mei's vision for China and for the world would indeed forevermore result in the Middle Kingdom's supremacy on the global stage. There was little doubt of that. The suffering that would be necessary to guarantee the outcome, though, would also be horrific for at least the next several years.

Chairman Mao's Great Leap Forward — in which 45 million Chinese died in the attempt to transform their moribund and largely agrarian economy into an industrial juggernaut — paled in comparison to the number of Chinese citizens that would be sacrificed, not to mention the billions of others around the world who'd also have to meet the same fate in order to ensure China's final triumph.

Zhu interrupted Lu Ping's thoughts.

"Are you worried about your family, young captain? If so, be not afraid, for you will be one of the chosen and you and I and others like you will rule in the end!" she exclaimed, somewhat overdramatically. The physicist punctuated her remark with a stab of her index finger and then leaned back and crossed her arms, waiting.

"I understand all that, Comrade. Believe me." A bead of sweat broke out on Lu's brow as he considered Zhu Mei's very generous offer. The outcome really was what he wanted for the Middle Kingdom, and all Marxist theory was rooted in class struggle and the need for great sacrifice to achieve the ultimate goal, wasn't it?

Yes, it certainly was!

It was now his turn to lean back and fold his arms as he considered these vital matters. A slight bump in the road also served to remind him that they were nearing the great metropolis.

Maybe the last day in which this American city will exist, at least in its present form!

Up front, Sergeant Teng continued to pilot the cargo van along the interstate. He'd taken care to drive with caution since they'd fled the gun battle in the Arizona desert, though he did pause to wonder just why their progress toward Los Angeles had been so uneventful. He quickly put such things to the side, however. Born of village peasant stock, he knew there really was such a thing as luck — which was of course provided by the many celestial gods, after all — and he ascribed it all to that.

Zhu Mei's mind was also opaque. She liked the young captain, and she already knew that he would be of great help in the coming struggle. Deciding, she reached into her right front pocket and pulled out a tiny earpiece like the one Luke Ellis had placed in his own ear just several months ago.

Leaning forward, she looked at Lu Ping and held her hand out. Coal black, the earpiece sat there and beckoned. A small red LED embedded in its face blinked slowly.

Lu Ping looked down at the eminent physicist's hand.

"What is that, Comrade Zhu? Is it for me?"

Time for me to gamble, then.

"Yes, Captain. Do you trust me after all that I've revealed to you? You trust me, don't you?"

"Of course, Doctor Zhu. Implicitly. Your vision is just so overwhelming. It's the only reason why I'm a bit hesitant, is all."

Lu felt his heart skip a beat. What was she offering him?

The lady scientist beamed, as if she understood completely.

"Put the earpiece in your ear, then. Outside of the need for operational security — and we were fortunate with your leader, Major Chang, as he didn't know all the particulars of this operation — there are no secrets among members of my organization."

Zhu Mei once again paused and let the young captain ponder what was happening. "Lu Ping, this device will ensure that you know not only your place within our organization but also what lies ahead for you once we emerge victorious."

The young captain eyed the earpiece suspiciously.

What was he prepared to do here? At this point, he was caught, and he knew it. There was no way he would survive if he made the wrong choice. Still, he also had a nearly insatiable need to know just what Zhu Mei's and her organization's entire plan was, such was the power of human curiosity.

His hand suddenly stabbed out and snatched the earpiece so quickly from Zhu's hand that she could scarcely believe it. His non-augmented speed of hand and reflexes were already impressive!

I knew it! I knew he could become one of us!

Tilting his head slightly to the left, Lu Ping reached up and inserted the earpiece into his right ear.

BOOM!

Lu's mind was almost immediately assaulted by an incredible cascade of data and intelligence. His eyes clouded over, and his pupils dilated for a brief second, as if his mind had succumbed to some sort of brain hemorrhage. The muscles in his left leg twitched and spasmed uncontrollably but then they became motionless. He then fell silent, but only for a few seconds before he took in a great rush of air.

"Yes," he softly breathed outwards. "Yes, yes, YES!"

Captain Lu Ping, formerly of the People's Liberation Army Ground Force (Special Forces Branch), looked at Zhu Mei and smiled broadly.

Zhu Mei couldn't keep the satisfaction from her voice.

"So, you see what your life's work is to be. Don't you, Lu Ping?"

"Oh yes. Yes, Zhu Mei," he replied. Now, he spoke to the eminent physicist as a peer and one who was quite a bit more familiar with the tactical needs of their current mission than she was.

Zhu Mei was delighted. The young man would no doubt prove to be very useful to them all.

"So, Lu Ping. What do you recommend?" Zhu sat and waited. This part of the mission was now in the former special forces soldier's capable hands.

Lu knew instantly what Zhu Mei meant. Turning his head to the left, he spoke to Teng Yong, who would soon see his part in their mission end.

"Sergeant Teng!"

The former captain used what was called the "command voice" in most of the world's military organizations. Its tone basically meant "obey me or face the consequences," and it worked on the enlisted man driving the van.

"Yes, Captain Lu!" Teng Yong straightened up and nearly came to attention.

"We're taking a different route into the city and changing our plan just slightly!"

Teng Yong was no fool. It was what he would do if he was leading this mission. His respect for Captain Lu also rose as a result.

"Yes, Captain! What do you need me to do?" Sergeant Teng felt pride just then. Not only for his homeland, China, but also for the role he was playing in ensuring its final victory.

"Secure us new transportation as soon as practicable! Something not so plainly evident, for starters. Also, older. We don't need to offer our enemies a chance to somehow track us through a vehicle's many computer chips, do we? Now, get us off this highway as soon as possible!"

Turning back to the right, Lu Ping smiled at his colleague Zhu Mei. There were of course wheels within wheels when it came to their new plan, but the good sergeant didn't need to know any of that, did he?

Zhong Shi Teng Yong, loyal sergeant of the People's Liberation Army's Special Forces — the best-trained special operations soldiers in the world, he felt — was already looking and scanning the roadway up ahead.

There! At that upcoming rest stop! Just what we needed!

Teng pulled the wheel slightly to the right and carefully signaled his lane change to the vehicles behind him. He hit the exit to the rest stop at just the right speed and continued to decrease acceleration.

Lu Ping and Zhu Mei could see the object of the good sergeant's desire.

Fantastic choice, Teng! Fantastic!

The sergeant pulled the Los Alamos cargo van over, nestling it among a dozen other vehicles of all types and sizes, and shut everything down. The ticking of the cooling engine was the only sound in the van's interior.

Off in the east, the sun would soon rise, but the dull, dark gray of pre-sunrise would be the perfect time to make the switch, wouldn't it?

Yes, it would be.

All three people in the van watched and waited. Lu Ping fingered the 9mm suppressed semi-automatic pistol he now held in his right hand. His rapidly diminishing morality — at least as it related to the number of lives he wouldn't hesitate to end, if need be — hoped it wouldn't be necessary to use it in the next few minutes, but even that slight qualm almost instantly disappeared.

Soon enough, a family of four; a man and woman and two small children — a boy and a girl, accompanied by a small dog that yipped and yapped excitedly — emerged from their vehicle and began to make their way into the large octagonal building that was a part of the rest stop complex. They'd already filled up with gasoline for their final push into Los Angeles and the many family-friendly amusement parks and attractions they intended to visit during their vacation. A motorhome was a hotel on wheels, after all, and they'd found a particularly attractive campground just outside LA that offered an amazing array of amenities. They were also towing a car, brought with them for participation in an exhibition taking place two days from now.

For the family, it promised to be an exciting vacation all around.

The trio in the Los Alamos van watched them intently as they headed indoors where the restrooms and shops and stores, as well as several different fast-food restaurants, were situated.

The three of them couldn't have been more pleased.

Not that it really mattered in the least, but the family and their dog would live when millions of others would soon die. In fact, after their initial shock at being so victimized they likely would all fall to their knees in thanks to their Christian god for having spared them, even!

Perfect. Just perfect!

Zhu Mei tilted her head just slightly. "Baal, are you there?"

Yesssssssss.

The sibilance of the 's' at the end of the word reminded her of a hissing snake. Lu Ping looked at her expectantly. She smiled at the young man in return. Yes, indeed, she'd chosen correctly, as had he. If he hadn't, the device in his ear would have quickly caused his brain to experience a massive and very fatal cerebrovascular accident. A stroke, in other words.

The lady scientist looked upward once more, perhaps at the van's ceiling or perhaps at something only she could see. Maybe it had coiled itself behind her eyes, readying itself to strike. Anything was possible.

"You may begin."

Yessssssss.

It was the hour of the cobra, and the taste of its venom was nearly perceptible to all in the van, including *Zhong Shi* Teng Yong, who grinned in exultation yet also fought to prevent a despairing scream from escaping his lips.

Lu Ping merely smiled.

He'd seen it all and, in the end, China would rule over everything in a never-ending dynasty that would put all other such reigns to shame. If billions had to lose their lives to assure that outcome, then so be it, because the result would be worth it, he knew to the very core of his being.

Plus, he himself would be among the richest and most powerful people on the planet. The global community would also emerge new and fresh and clean under China's benign rule.

Yesssssssss.

DECISIONS

ngela Boyer stared at her boss, Thomas Masterson, who in turn stared goggle-eyed at his chief military advisor, Chairman of the Joint Chiefs of Staff Louis Sowell, a four-star Navy admiral and one of the few combatant commanders within the U.S. military that had survived a direct terror attack carried out last year as part of a massive nationwide strike. Sowell was frantically issuing orders on his encrypted phone.

Masterson addressed the uniformed officer. "Admiral, what do you mean our China satellites are down?" he asked. "All of them or just some of them? Talk to me!"

The president's own thoughts were clear enough to everyone in the room, including the two Secret Service agents preparing to move them all to the secure command center and situation room located deep beneath the White House.

It must be the Chinese, damn their eyes!

Boyer was also on the phone, known formally as "SCIP-compatible Secure Terminal Equipment," or STE. "SCIP" itself stood for

"Secure Communications Interoperability Protocol." It was believed to be impervious to all decryption and cracking programs short of still theoretical and unattainable quantum computing capabilities... at least according to the opinion of the CIA and NSA.

The device itself sat slightly askew in a corner of the Resolute Desk, which had seen more than its fair share of crises over the many years it had occupied the Oval Office ever since Queen Victoria had given it as a gift to then-president Rutherford B. Hayes in 1880.

Angela spoke in a low but urgent voice to the Secretary of Defense — who'd only recently finally been confirmed by the U.S. Senate. A former U.S. Army Special Forces captain who'd made a fortune as a defense contractor of uncommon strategic thinking abilities, James Ashford wasn't a war hawk, but he also wasn't a patsy by any stretch of the imagination.

Ashford — who possessed the very highest security clearances it was possible for one to have while working in the federal government — also didn't have the first clue about Luke Ellis and his unit or just what Ozymandias was. Louis Sowell — still deeply affected by his own experience during the terror attacks last year, including the fact he'd survived when many hadn't — did know, which made him the more powerful and influential of the two.

"I'm putting the President on now, Jim" she said to the phone.

Boyer tapped the President on the shoulder. SECDEF Ashford had been practically living over at the Pentagon while CJCS Sowell — who assisted both the President as well as the Secretary of Defense in exercising their command functions — had stayed by Masterson's side during the current crisis.

Sowell himself — as well as the individual services' various chiefs of staff such as the Commandant of the Marine Corps or the Army Chief of Staff — actually had no operational command authority over even the most junior soldier or sailor or airman other than that normally accorded to any military person superior in rank, which was a fact lost on many. By law, the operational chain of command in the U.S. military ran from the President, as Commander in Chief of the Armed Forces of the United States, to the Secretary of Defense, and from SECDEF to the regional combatant commanders, the four-star generals and admirals in charge of the largest military organizations such as Southern Command, Central Command, Space Command and the like.

Everyone in the federal government, though, knew just who was driving the ship, so to speak, when it came to military matters. For now, Admiral Louis Sowell spoke with the authority of President Thomas Masterson when it came to defending the nation against another attack, at least until he could turn it all over to James Ashford.

The admiral's opinion on the matter was also crystal clear to everyone involved as well.

God, please speed that along, because I don't know how much more of this I can take!

Until then, though, he and his Commander in Chief, Thomas Masterson — and now SECDEF James Ashford — had a job to do, and that was to keep America safe. Because at present, it looked to all of them like China was readying an attack, either against Taiwan or against the United States itself. Or maybe even against both, as crazy as that was.

Masterson took the handset from Boyer. He listened for a few seconds and then nodded his head.

"Yes, Jim. Yes. I'm ordering DEFCON 2. That's right. Fast Pace."

"Fast Pace," the term used to denote DEFCON 2, meant that the next step to nuclear war — in this case, between China and the United States — would now be taken. It required that the entire U.S. military be prepared to deploy and engage in combat within six hours. The only other defensive readiness condition above it was "Cocked Pistol," or DEFCON 1.

If the U.S. moved to DEFCON 1, well... nuclear war was inevitable, or it had already begun. No person in the Oval Office or listening in on the STE's handset wanted to see the United States military at DEFCON 1, because no one was that insane.

Masterson looked around the Oval Office and at the two most important people within it beside him.

"Angela. Louis. Where are we with China and Tan? We still can't reach him, correct?" He looked yet again at the watch on his left wrist, something he'd done every 30 seconds over the last hour, ever since China and its president, Tan Jianhong, had basically gone silent.

"Correct, Mister President" Boyer replied, pausing for a second to brush away a wisp of her hair.

It's probably gone gray since this morning! Damn China and Tan and all the rest of them!

"Louis, any luck raising Tan's defense chief, that Guo Meng?" Masterson tried hard not to spit the man's name out.

Admiral Sowell was once again on his encrypted phone, trying to get through to Guo.

No luck.

Nothing but static... and a strange sort of hissing sound.

Sowell slammed the handset into the palm of his hand and then tapped furiously at its screen, practically willing it to work. No matter what he did or tried, there was only that sibilant hiss on the other end, as if some sort of venomous snake had coiled itself entirely around the U.S.-China telecommunications network, including every U.S. satellite having anything to do with maintaining watch over the Middle Kingdom and, strangely enough… Los Angeles.

LA will take care of itself! That's why we have an FBI and all those other wonderful law enforcement agencies and a multitude of three-letter secret squirrel-type organizations, right? Now focus!

Louis made himself concentrate.

"We're blind right now, President Masterson," said the admiral. He was trying mightily to avoid despair, and he and Angela Boyer exchanged glances once more.

No way this could be it because it just didn't make any sense at all. Why Taiwan, and why now?

Sowell felt slightly dizzy. He was being pulled along by a riptide from which he would never be able to escape. No one here in the Oval Office or over at the Pentagon — where the newly confirmed Secretary of Defense, James Ashford, and his aides as well as the other service chiefs were spooling up the massive engine of destruction that the U.S. military could transform into should the need arise — knew what Tan and Guo were up to, and it was maddening.

Either both of those men had cut off communications with the United States — possibly in preparation for an attack on Taiwan or, worse, on the U.S. itself — despite the president's near-frantic attempts to contact them over the last hour, or something more sinister was afoot.

Masterson couldn't help saying it aloud.

"Are we looking at a coup in China? There are some serious America haters in their military right now, including Guo Meng! Maybe he's decided to take over and then get his punches in before we're ready?"

"I can't see how he'd be able to pull that off, Mister President" reassured Angela. She looked over at Admiral Sowell for support, beseeching him to step in, but the man seemed once again lost in thought.

Snap out of it, Louis!

"Admiral Sowell!" she exclaimed. "We need some answers!"

Just then, the riptide threatening to pull him under for good eased up momentarily and he returned to the surface, gasping for breath.

"Right, Ms. Boyer," he answered. Sowell looked around the Oval Office and reordered his thoughts. He put his encrypted phone down for the moment and drew in a breath.

"Here's what we know, Mister President, Ms. Boyer." The admiral pulled as many facts together as he could quickly assemble and then presented his assessment.

"I agree that Guo Meng wouldn't be able to successfully pull off a coup, eliminate Tan Jianhong and then order China's military into action against Taiwan as well as us," he pronounced with more confidence than he felt. "It would take days and possibly weeks to consolidate his power and convince more than a few of the most powerful generals — not to mention the Chinese Communist

Party — to go along and not instead immediately order his arrest and execution."

Masterson took a deep breath and paused to consider his options.

To his left, Secret Service agents were moving in to hustle them all to the subterranean command center and situation room where they'd be able to fight a war, if need be, against China if things soon came to that horrendous pass.

Deciding, he held up a finger and then motioned to the STE handset and put it back to his ear and spoke once again.

"Secretary Ashford, you and your people have plenty of work to do in a very short amount of time. I'll leave you to it. Make all preparations, sir."

"Yes, Mister President!" Masterson heard in his ear, which was followed by a steady hum. SECDEF had disconnected the line. It would be up to him to move the massive U.S. war machine to the highest war footing short of actual hostilities.

Turning to Boyer and Sowell, he paused yet again to consider his next move.

"Admiral? Angela?"

"Yes, Mister President" the pair replied in unison.

"Tan hasn't closed that backdoor email link we maintain with his office, correct? We can still send the file, can't we? And we'll know if he receives it, right?"

"Of course, Boss," Angela Boyer said.

"Yes, Mr. President," replied Louis Sowell.

Masterson was referring to a sort of virtual or cyber-based "red emergency phone" or hotline setup used to exchange only the most urgent communications between the U.S. president and China's president. This email server — made as secure as technologically possible — had long ago replaced the red telephone that had once sat in the same corner of the Resolute Desk where the current STE device now sat. By mutual top-secret agreement between both countries, if a message or file was sent to the inbox of either leader, they were obligated to at least open it and read what it said.

Right now, that email server was still operating, meaning the Chinese hadn't closed off this last, vital means of communication.

Thomas Masterson, President of the United States, meant to send a message along with a video file to Tan Jianhong, President of China.

We don't want to fight you and we want peace. But if we do end up fighting you, we'll win. That would be the written message.

What would the video file consist of, though?

Turning to Louis Sowell, his instructions were simple.

"Admiral Sowell, please record our people arming the B-21 Raider on Guam with its full complement of weapons, including the two specials." By that, the president meant the super-stealth aircraft would be loaded with its nuclear payload. "Please also fully arm its Loyal Wingman drone escorts as well."

"Mister President, I…"

"Hold on a second, Angela." Masterson cut his chief of staff off with a wave of his hand and she fell silent, waiting.

"President Masterson," Louis Sowell asked, you don't intend for the Raider to take off and launch a preemptive strike against Beijing and Tan Jianhong, do you? Because all we were going to do was park a few war shots in the form of cruise missiles in front of it before we roll it back into the hangar." He felt the riptide beneath him once again, threatening to pull him down to a fate yet unknown.

"No, Louis, not at all." The president paused to consider his strategy. "What I want is for President Tan and Guo Meng to see what we *could* do to them both, as well as millions of their citizens, if they insist on forcing our hand."

Boyer couldn't help but let the relief show on her face. "I knew you weren't going to go all the way, Boss!"

"Not yet at least, Angela, but I think it's time Tan and Guo realize we're willing to use a big stick if they don't want to listen to us talk softly about Taiwan and peace."

Masterson turned once again to the military man with him in the Oval Office.

"So, Louis. What's that term for when the Air Force parades a bunch of its fighters and bombers down a runway?"

Sowell almost smiled just then.

"It's called an elephant walk, Mr. President."

"Yes. That's it. Let's do an elephant walk. I think it's time the world — especially China — saw one of the biggest, baddest elephants ever doing a walk down the Andersen Air Force Base runway, don't you?" The president paused, looking at his chief of staff and his most important military advisor.

"Well, if it convinces Tan and Guo to back down and get control of that navy of theirs around Taiwan, then I'm all for it," replied Angela Boyer emphatically.

"I'll see that Operation Determined Resolve is modified accordingly, Mr. President," Louis Sowell said. He picked up his encrypted phone once again.

All three of them now allowed the two Secret Service agents to usher them out of the Oval Office and into the maelstrom of activity occurring in the West Wing. Essential personnel were going to relocate with them to the underground facility, with a hurried wargame scenario between the United States and China enough of a cover story to hold up at least temporarily.

Non-essential White House personnel — and Masterson had learned that about 80 percent of the staff, as well as much of the rest of the federal government, fell into that category — were being sent home on paid leave until the current crisis was resolved one way or another. A short, sharp and sudden outbreak of the latest COVID variant among the staff would be the excuse used to get them all out as well as the reason fed to the media. Masterson's Vice President — Evelyn Deering, a former U.S. senator chosen for her ability to work easily with members from both political parties — had to this point been largely kept out of the loop other than to help press the U.S. case in both the media and with America's allies, a group whose membership was shockingly smaller than just a few years ago.

She was even now being moved to a different secure underground bunker, also at an undisclosed location. Continuity of government was essential during times of crisis, after all.

Someone's got to pick up the pieces if I falter or fail, Thomas Masterson thought to himself as he was led to the elevator by his Secret Service agents.

He'd also forgotten that his vice-president had no knowledge of Luke Ellis, his unit or Ozymandias.

SACRIFICES

Oz continued to search for Nemesis, the enemy artificial intelligence program Baal, even as his human allies raced toward their objective in search of Zhu Mei and the others. A once-promising trail composed of seemingly random bits of code, though, had proven to be a dead end, and now he needed to rely on something uniquely human.

"I'm going to need a lucky break — plus some help from Annie — to locate Baal," he told Luke Ellis and Annie and the others over the van's radio speakers.

"What? What do you mean by "a lucky break," Oz? Are you serious?" Luke couldn't hide his exasperation and anger.

"I'm sorry, Luke, but I am serious. She'll need to unite with me and provide her uniquely human perspective — as well as her own energy matrix — to my search, or we'll likely fail to prevent the attack. The enemy AI, Baal, will escape as well. I will not lie to you, Annie's participation is crucial, though she may suffer or even die in the attempt."

Ozymandias fell silent, waiting.

"The hell you say!" exclaimed Ellis, hot with anger.

"I'm deeply sorry, Annie," Oz said with genuine regret.

"Whatever you need, Ozymandias!" Annie exclaimed. She'd known this moment would come, ever since she'd undergone her transformation.

"No, Annie!" Luke tried to make sense of it all and failed miserably at it.

The 18-year-old smoothed out the camouflage poncho liner she carried with her and began to put it on. In a way, it had become a kind of suit of armor for her.

Erin moved closer to her, accepting what had to be.

"You got this, girl" she whispered to Annie. "You can do it!"

"Wait just a minute, Annie!" Luke said in a loud voice, still not accepting the truth of the matter. "You're going to sit in this van and let us handle the rough stuff, got it?"

Ellis folded his arms across his chest and sat back, obstinate.

"That's not fair, either to her or our mission, Colonel!" Erin Styles protested. She was becoming angry, and she hated losing control of her emotions in such a manner, but she'd seen what the girl was capable of. "Unbelievable stuff," was her basic assessment. Maddeningly, though, this Army guy was acting like an overprotective father to someone who could probably easily take him in a knife fight right now.

Hell, take everyone here in the van and without breaking a sweat while doing it!

Luke's voice was low and steely in its resolve, and he locked his eyes on an equally combative Styles.

"Let's be clear, Sergeant. You're here to provide your gun to ensure Annie's security while I and my men do our job, but that's it! He pointed an index finger at the 18-year-old. You're standing guard over her. End of discussion."

"Uh, boss? Boss?" asked Crispy, looking at Ellis for a second.

"What?"

The former Delta Force leader was in no mood for more talk, but he knew what was coming and, inside, knew what he'd have to do, though he hated himself for needing to.

"Luke, we need every hand in this fight, and you know it. We're still not completely sure just where the Chinese are going to be and we gotta be sure, right?"

Crispy nodded at Annie and Erin. They both nodded their heads slightly, signifying their gratitude for his support.

"Crisp's right, Luke," Hardcase and Killdozer added from the front of the van. They were barreling toward the practical center of Los Angeles — Downtown LA, commonly known as "DTLA" by the locals — and time was of the essence, if what Annie and Ozymandias had told them was true, which it self-evidently was. Neither of the two men were also under any illusions about the 18-year-old girl.

Annie was now a weapon, and seemingly whenever she wanted to be, and her new friend, former Marine Erin K. Styles, was no slouch in the gunfighting department, either, which was a bonus. The team would need them both.

Luke's just refusing to accept the new reality now, Killdozer thought to himself. To be fair, given his past relationship with Annie Dedham, it was completely understandable. Still, he needed to get over the whole protective father thing ASAP, because they were going to need all the help they could get as soon as they reached the final objective, hopefully before the two remaining Chinese fighters, the scientist and the antimatter they'd stolen got there first — because if they did it was game over.

"I know, I know already!" exclaimed Luke.

"About time," Erin whispered *sotto voce* to Annie. The girl smiled slightly, knowing that it couldn't be easy on her big Army friend, who up until several hours earlier had essentially been her protector.

What was he now, though?

That's easy! My best friend, my comrade in arms!

Now, the 18-year-old looked directly at Ellis. The others in the van fell silent, waiting and listening.

"Mister Ellis… Luke, you have to let me do this. Millions, maybe even billions, might die if I don't. You know what I'm saying is true, too. I can tell."

She leaned in closer, now looking intently into the man's blue eyes. Luke couldn't stand it. He looked down for a second, berating himself.

She's right, dammit! What kind of world have we created for ourselves?!?

Dead silence ruled the van. The retired soldier looked back up and at the young woman sitting across from him.

Leaning forward, he took Annie's much smaller hands in his. They were warm — hot, even — with barely contained energy coursing through her, and Luke wondered for a second just how such a thing was possible without a human body breaking down in fatigue at being in such a fevered state.

Then, he remembered just what she'd voluntarily chosen to become.

That doesn't matter! I promised her parents! Promised to keep her safe!

"Annie... Annie. You might die. You know it, I know it and Ozymandias knows it, too, damn him!"

Ellis directed his ire at the van's roof. No response from the enigmatic AI, as usual. Likely, it was hovering just out of sight, waiting for what it knew was inevitable.

Yet another reason for Luke Ellis to hate me. Oz knew he was becoming increasingly more human, but for now his core self, composed almost purely of logic, still held, though in what he could see was an ever more tenuous fashion.

A hiss of static burst forth from the van's radio speakers as the AI entity reinforced what remained of its artificial self so that logic could still reign. Logic would dictate what had to happen to him and to Annie Dedham.

It always dictated our futures. The girl will be alright in the end, though. I just don't know about me.

"Oh, so now Ozymandias is finally "him," Mister Ellis?" Annie asked, laughing lightly.

"Well... you got me there." Luke was miserable and sick at heart over what had to be done. "You got me there..." he said once again, this time in a barely audible whisper.

"Great!" Annie rubbed her hands together briskly, working hard to pull her big Army friend out of his funk.

The die is cast, Annie Dedham, Oz thought to himself.

"Ozymandias!" she exclaimed, looking up at the ceiling of the van again.

The van's radio speakers came to life.

"I'm here, Annie."

Oz's voice somehow sounded more human, though maybe just a little bit... scared. As if it, too, had made a fateful decision of its own.

Scared. Is that the right word to use?

Annie pondered as her new friend Erin Styles and her old friend, Luke Ellis, helped her don her camouflage poncho.

"Annie," Ellis began to say. He fell silent once more, though, resigned to their fates. "Just be careful, Miss Dedham," was all he could manage. And then, he slowly and formally saluted the 18-year-old.

Erin and Crispy followed suit, each rendering a proper military salute in turn.

"Go get some, Annie!" exclaimed Killdozer and Hardcase in unison from the front of the van.

The 18-year-old felt for a second as if she was going to tear up and start bawling like a little baby.

Ozymandias, help me! I don't want to cry!

Something warm and reassuring and filled with confidence suddenly stole into her, bucking her up and strengthening her for the pain to come, because where she was going it would be excruciating, at least initially. It would have to be, if she and her AI companion were to succeed in finding the human attackers as well as Baal, the AI program aiding their every step since fleeing the desert just a few hours ago.

Thank heavens Mister Ellis, my friend Luke, doesn't know about the pain Ozymandias and I will be sharing, and I pray that I don't scream too loudly once we start!

The 18-year-old looked once more at everyone in the van. Erin suddenly leaned in and hugged her fiercely and then just as suddenly released her.

"Get yourself back here as quickly as you can, young woman!" the former Marine said in her best command voice. "We're going to need those butt-kicking skills of yours!"

Luke folded his arms and looked at her sternly.

"Well? What are you waiting for Annie? "We're burning daylight!" Then he winked.

Inside, though, all he felt was devastation.

What kind of world have we made for ourselves?

"I'm on it, Luke!" Annie exclaimed confidently.

She couldn't help fearing it, though.

The pain, the pain.

It was time, and there was nothing for it.

The young woman looked up at the van's ceiling one last time.

"Well, Oz. Are you ready?" she asked.

"I am, Annie Dedham."

Ozymandias felt an immense sensation just then. Was it admiration? If he survived what was to come, he would have to explore such sensations — such *feelings* — more closely. Thankfully, the girl interrupted its — no, interrupted *his* — reverie.

"Well, what are you waiting for? We're burning daylight!" Annie smiled brightly, and then steeled herself.

"Yes, Annie" Ozymandias replied. "We certainly are."

"Do it!" she exclaimed.

Oz didn't hesitate. Like ripping a band-aid off, he knew it was better to get it all over with at once rather than gradually dialing up the pain.

Join me then, Annie, and we shall succeed.

Annie willingly opened herself to the full power of Oz's own mind, his consciousness.

Her eyes fluttered again and then rolled up into her head, exposing only their whiteness to Luke and the others. And then she shrieked in pain and agony and almost swallowed her tongue.

"AAAAAAAAAAAAAAAAAAAAAAAAAAAAAAAAAGH! AAAAAAAAAAAAAAGH!"

Luke tried to launch himself at the girl, to end the attempt by Ozymandias and Annie, but Crispy grabbed him with both arms, physically restraining him. Erin Styles hovered near the 18-year-old, who was now flailing and spasming on the floor of the van.

Hardcase put a hand on Killdozer's muscled forearm and shook his head.

"Best to leave them be, bud."

"Right, man" was all Killdozer could manage to say. He clenched his jaw tightly and forced himself to concentrate.

Both men looked at the road ahead. They were rapidly approaching Downtown LA. The sun was up, and they had no idea where they should go after they arrived.

Logic said that the Chinese had to be heading to one of the two tallest buildings in L.A. so that the force of the antimatter explosion wouldn't be lessened, as it might be if it occurred at ground level. There were two likely candidates, too. At over 1,000 feet, either of them would serve just fine as a place to create a matter-antimatter collision that would likely kill millions and lead to a war between China and the United States.

"COME ON, OZYMANDIAS!" Luke shouted. "FINISH THIS!"

Crispy desperately held onto his commander, his friend. Styles' right hand came up to her mouth and she suppressed a sob.

How much more can she take?!? Please make it stop! Please! Please!

Annie's back suddenly curved upward and into an almost impossible angle, and she was now balanced on the balls of her feet and the back of her head. Her hands were curled into adamantine spheres that would have shattered an iron bar, had one struck just then, or easily punched their way through the floor of the van. The muscles in her arms and neck were bunched and corded.

One last shriek.

"AAAAAAAAAAAAAAAAAAAAAAAAAAAAAAAAAGH!"

Silence.

Deathly silence. Silence so thick it was as if everyone in the back of the van had been transported into a soundproof room.

Annie collapsed on her back. She was in a trance-like state. Perhaps she'd even gone catatonic or fallen into a coma. Her eyes stopped fluttering, though their whites were still all that was visible.

"Annie, honey?" Erin Styles asked. "Are you with us?"

More silence.

The former Marine looked over at Luke Ellis. His friend, Crispy, had now released him from his grasp. She arched an eyebrow at the Army man — "the Colonel," as she'd call him going forward, which she already knew he'd dislike. She secretly smiled at that revelation.

Ellis, who'd shared a form of union with Ozymandias because of the white earpiece he now wore, and thus understood — though only intellectually and not physically — what Annie had experienced, simply nodded his head.

"They're now on the hunt, Sergeant Styles" he told her.

The former Marine — "former security specialist," too, because there was no way the big Army guy sitting on the other side of the van, watching, no... *protecting* the young woman on the floor was ever going to let her go back to her old life — accepted what she was seeing. She'd accepted everything else since last night, right? This latest bit of craziness was simply part and parcel of all the other craziness that the Colonel and his men seemed to handle as just another day at work.

Well, so will I! And I wouldn't miss this for all the world!

Erin sat back, watching and waiting.

"Boss, how long have we got, you think?" Crispy asked.

Luke kept one eye on Annie while he examined his tactical watch with the other.

"We need an answer in the next couple of minutes, Crisp. Fortunately, where they're at, Einstein and relativity are all that matter."

Crispy was genuinely confused. "I don't get it, boss."

"What might take just a couple minutes out here — which is all that it likely will take Oz and Annie — might seem like five years in the worlds they're moving between." Ellis instinctively knew that what he was saying was true. His own experience with superposition and time and space — where he essentially felt like he was everywhere at once — assured him of that.

"Ummmm..." began Styles.

"Everyone needs to shut up now," interrupted Luke. "Let them both do their work in there while we gear up out here, because once they're back we're moving fast."

"Got it, Boss" replied Crispy in a low, businesslike voice.

"You say so, Colonel," said Erin, testing whether her theory was correct.

"I don't like being called Colonel."

Styles — a former Marine, which really meant that she'd always be a Marine — simply smiled.

"Aye, aye Colonel" was all she said in return, much to Luke's irritation.

Crispy couldn't help himself. He smiled, too, and so did Killdozer and Hardcase up front, and then the pair remembered just why they were driving with such determination.

Up ahead in the distance, they could make out their twin objectives among the mass of skyscrapers that dotted DTLA. Being a weekend, traffic was thankfully light. Hopefully, one of the massive structures could be discarded as soon as Annie and their AI buddy, Ozymandias, figured out just what was what.

Figuring out "what was what" was Phase One of the battle plan now, and that would be the trick, of course, because the enemy always had a say in any battle plan.

DECEPTIONS

"Do you accept my command of this operation?"

The Chinese scientist, Zhu Mei, gazed sternly at the group of men standing in a circle around her and Lu Ping.

Sergeant Teng — who'd faithfully piloted them to this waypoint — had quickly joined the new team's ranks as soon as the ten of them pulled up at the combo fast food and rest stop, which was complete with a parking area just for RVs, and got out of their nondescript vehicles, there to rendezvous with the woman whose commands Defense Minister Guo had ordered they follow to the letter.

The captain in charge of the team had carefully gone over the codes and documents that had preceded the video conference with Minister Guo, and all was in order. He and his team were by now thoroughly familiar with the particulars of this operation as well. No further need for rehearsal was anticipated.

Before he replied to the eminent lady scientist, though, the captain thought back to the team's mission tasking from Minister Guo, who'd been emphatic.

"This will send a stern message to the cowardly American president that China can strike anywhere, at any time and as we please, and that he had better think twice before interfering with us when it comes to the renegades on Formosa!

"Yes, Minister Guo," the captain replied.

He could see the elegance inherent in the operation, too. The gang story would allow the American president, Masterson, and his government to save face once they learned through back channels just what had really gone down in Los Angeles. Of course, there would eventually be repercussions and blowback, but by then China would be dominant on the world stage and easily able to handle whatever the Americans might throw at the Middle Kingdom.

Satisfied, the captain stole a glance at his watch. It was nearly time. "Yes, Comrade Zhu. I fully accept your command," he announced. Looking at the woman, he could instantly tell that she was no one to trifle with. He also knew her reputation, and that the connections she had with the present government back in China ran deep.

"Very good," replied Zhu Mei. "Sergeant Teng Yong here, who has accompanied Captain Lu Ping and I on our part of the operation to this point, will drive all of you into Los Angeles in this vehicle." Zhu's head inclined slightly to indicate the Class C motorhome next to her.

The hit team's leader nodded approvingly. As a form of urban camouflage, a motorhome loitering near any sort of tourist site wouldn't stand out in the least, and it was large enough for all of them. Plus, with blinds covering the vehicle's windows, no one would be able to spot them until it was too late.

All the better to take the Americans by complete surprise as they walk into our trap!

Once he and his men completed the ambush of that American covert assassination squad — ensuring that all of them, including anyone hiding in their panel van, were dead — they'd quickly disappear and then rendezvous at the rally point, which was well away from the motorhome. After that, they'd make their way out of the city via various forms of transportation, including online ride-hailing services.

Reviewing the plan one more time, the captain couldn't help but be satisfied.

"Urban combat," he whispered to himself. It was his favorite form of warfare, something that China's special forces trained intensely on. The streets of a city were a welcome hunting ground for him and his men.

Time to focus then.

The captain turned his attention once more to the lady scientist.

"Of course, Comrade Zhu," he replied in a strong, assured voice. "Once we're at our objective, we'll ambush the American team from hidden positions as they pass by us, ensuring that all of them are dead, too. We'll also be far away before anyone realizes what has happened. Minister Guo has also assured me that a complete communications blackout will last for as long as necessary for us to carry out the hit. That way, law enforcement will be unaware of our activity and unable to interfere until it's too late."

For his part, the captain wasn't exactly sure how Minister Guo was going to pull off a full communications blackout, but he'd long ago learned never to question such orders and pronouncements from higher-ups.

Zhu Mei looked over at Lu Ping. Smiling very slightly at her, he nodded in return. It was all coming together.

Now she looked at the men on the hit team.

"Excellent, Captain. Most excellent! I can't tell you how important this little part of a much, much larger operation is to China's ultimate victory. She looked at the men arrayed around her. "China knows that every soldier and servant of the Middle Kingdom will do their duty today!"

The soldiers smiled and nodded, all fully expecting that they would easily defeat the enemy not long from now. They looked toward their leader for confirmation. He summed up his thoughts on the upcoming operation for their benefit as well as for the iron lady, Zhu Mei.

"The hit will appear to be a case of mistaken identity," he pronounced confidently. "A shooting carried out by one gang against people they believe to be from a rival gang, Comrade Zhu."

"Outstanding, Captain. Simply outstanding!"

Zhu Mei was genuinely pleased. While on the road from Arizona, she and Lu Ping had successfully modified the antimatter containment device according to the specifications delivered to them via their earpieces. They could "see," in their minds, just what to do and how to quickly do it.

It had been transformative.

And amazing!

They'd "split" the containment device, essentially, and in the process, they'd created a smaller, subsidiary device whose battery would be of only limited duration. They would retain the other batteries to accompany the remaining antimatter, of which there would be a full 75 grams, an amount sufficient for The Group's future activities, she knew.

Once the newly created device's power source ran out — not long after the unsuspecting Sergeant Teng and the hit team won their fight at the U.S. Bank Tower — she fully expected the resulting collision of matter with antimatter to obliterate LA and kill millions.

And start a war between China and the United States, one which the Group will eventually help China win, most certainly, but not too quickly!

That the faithful Sergeant Teng Yong and the ten men standing around her — patriots who believed they were acting on behalf of their country — would also lose their lives mattered not at all to Zhu.

They're pawns, nothing more and nothing less. And the pawns on a chessboard are always sacrificed!

The physicist and her new apprentice, Lu Ping, were playing a much grander game. At the end of it, she and the Group would stand triumphant over all nations, all people, united under a New China that would largely be of her own design. It would be her "franchise," in essence.

As a founding member of the Group, she had decided that the Middle Kingdom would become her "special project." It, its people and the many other people the New Middle Kingdom would come to dominate would be hers to experiment with and socially modify as she pleased.

I can hardly wait to start!

Smiling broadly now, Zhu looked once again at the promising young Lu Ping, whose own vision — courtesy of the earpiece she'd given him — was now fully in synch with her own.

Lu turned to the hit team leader — a captain not unlike what he'd once been — Sergeant Teng Yong and the men of the team and looked down at his tactical watch for a second before he faced them all.

"Time, Comrades. Your destinies await in Los Angeles." Saluting them smartly, he clapped Teng Yong on the shoulder.

"Get these men to Los Angeles, Sergeant. Yours is the most important task of all!"

Filled with extreme pride in himself and in China, Teng's heart nearly burst from his chest.

"Yes, sir! You can count on me!"

Lu Ping felt as if the entire world — perhaps even the universe — was waiting breathlessly for a monumental event, and he was now determined to deliver it. "I know that I can," Lu replied to the sergeant. Reaching out, he placed a hand on the young soldier's shoulder and gave it a slight squeeze, and then he looked into the man's eyes for the last time.

"Yes indeed, Sergeant. I certainly can count on you, can't I?"

Sergeant Teng didn't know what to say. He'd never been trusted with such a responsibility before. Lu Ping and Zhu Mei solved that problem for him.

"To Los Angeles, comrades" they said, nearly in unison.

With that, the pair turned and walked over to the two-door classic car the former owners of the RV had been towing behind their home on wheels.

While not a personal fan of late-60s American "cop movies," Lu Ping couldn't help but smile. The car itself was painted in a memorable color known as Highland Green, and it was a restored two-door sport coupe with a powerful V-8 engine. Built in 1968, one of its kind had been memorably featured in a cop movie from that same year. The legendary car chase scene in the film — which had taken place in a different California city, San Francisco — had delivered the car into automotive history.

More importantly, though, there were no electronics, no onboard computers, not even a modern electronic ignition, and the car was as original and pristine as the day it rolled off a Dearborn, Michigan assembly line. It had also been ridiculously easy for Lu to hot-wire and then drive away. There was nothing within or on the vehicle that would allow him and Zhu Mei to be tracked as they got as far away from Los Angeles as they could before the blast occurred.

The sports car — named after the famous wild American horse — would now become a part of even more momentous events, wouldn't it?

Lu Ping smiled yet again at the symmetry of it all. They would be escaping in a car that had once been an integral part of the American Dream, which would soon enough be supplanted by a far different kind of dream. He looked over at his new leader, Zhu Mei, and arched an eyebrow. She merely nodded in return.

The motorhome's engine started up, and the vehicle slowly began to pull out of its parking slot. There was no need for waves or goodbyes. Together they watched their former driver, Sergeant Teng Yong, and the men of the hit team begin their short journey into LA proper.

"And into the pages of history," they said to each other as they watched the motorhome recede in the distance.

GUO MENG

Tan Jianhong was livid.

"Not again, Guo Meng! Not again!"

"But Mr. President! I don't know how this could be! You must believe me!"

Guo Meng was sweating profusely, and his face had gone pale upon receiving the news from Los Angeles. It was right there on his tablet. The renegade Zhu Mei, a captain of his beloved Special Forces branch, and antimatter — enough of it to deliver unspeakable devastation to America, followed swiftly by the full military might of the United States landing on China in retaliation if any of it happened to explode, especially in an American city like Los Angeles! — rogue special forces teams... what else could go wrong?

Guo's thoughts were a frantic, jumbled mess.

How about a global war of a scope and scale neither we nor the

United States are prepared for or could come close to coping with?

What good would the victory be if all that the spoils amounted to were nothing but ashes?

More jumbled thoughts.

I don't understand!

How could this be?

Those special forces teams have no such mission orders! None of them had such orders!

Pennsylvania? Why?

Phoenix? Two teams lost! How could that be? HOW COULD THAT BE?

And now... this?

Why? Why? WHY??

Tan Jianhong had had enough. He pounded his fists on the gleaming mahogany table around which he and his soon-to-be-ex-defense minister sat.

"ENOUGH WITH THE LIES, YOU TRAITOR!"

Guo immediately fell silent and lowered his head. He quickly looked at the rear of the conference room, knowing why the two muscular-looking, black-suited men were now back and standing by the double doors, and he was completely out of ideas as to how to avoid his impending fate.

But why? How? Who has done this to ME? Am I to take two bullets in the head, with my family billed for their cost? WHY ME?

Tan simply stared at his defense chief, a man who'd once been his most trusted confidant. Together, they were supposed to lead China to victory over the United States, and yet Guo Meng had decided to betray him.

Well, that's not working out so well for him, is it?

Tan breathed deeply and stared at the dead man sitting across from him. What was that observation about kings and trying to assassinate them?

Oh yes! When you strike at a king, you must kill him!

Guo had struck, and he'd failed.

And now?

Now, he would face the same fate as all the others throughout history who'd betrayed their kings. The reason why he had to die was right there on his tablet's screen, staring at him and causing him to lose massive face. Insane though it might seem, it was a fact that yet another of the country's special forces teams it had taken China so long to infiltrate into the United States had gone completely off mission.

This time, a 10-man squad had apparently raced off to Los Angeles, there to engage in street combat with some sort of U.S. government covert action squad, which was all his special intelligence apparatus could tell him as it fed him the latest updates via the tablet resting in front of him.

Guo Meng is behind it all! Damn him and his machinations!

The Chinese president's thoughts on the matter were bleak, and even more maddening because none of it made any sense!

Why has Guo betrayed China — betrayed me! — so thoroughly? Why? Why? Does he lust that strongly for power?

It didn't really matter, though, did it? Guo had thrown the dice, flipped the Mahjong tiles… whatever, and he'd lost.

Tan could see it all so clearly now. It had been his defense chief who'd engineered this entire debacle, and all in a bid to seize power from him.

He looked at the man for the last time, forever cementing the forlorn expression on the traitorous dog's face in his memory as a reminder never to trust anyone again. Now, he leaned forward, his voice a low, dangerous rasp.

"I don't know how or why you thought you could pull this off, Guo, but your game has come to an end!" He tapped quietly — three times in succession — on the table's surface.

The men at the back of the room moved with amazing speed, seizing Guo Meng by his arms and lifting him out of his chair in one fell swoop. The disgraced minister of defense, who just a few minutes ago had been the second most powerful man in all of China, tried one last time to protest his innocence.

"Mister President! Mister President! I swear, I—"

"SILENCE, DOG!" Tan thundered, cutting off his adversary's protestations.

He motioned to the two men holding onto Guo and made a cutting motion across his throat. His former defense chief went completely weak at the knees in response. A pitiful mewl followed by a gasping blubber was his only response as he was quickly dragged out of the conference room.

"Guo must die by midnight tonight," Tan breathed huskily. "I'll see to the execution of the sentence myself!" He knew that the man was by now being hustled out of the building, there to be taken to a black sedan that would deliver him to a holding cell where he'd await his desultory end.

China's president glanced at the Rolex on his wrist and thought about Los Angeles. It was 15 hours ahead of Beijing, meaning that the sun had barely risen there. There was simply no chance of recalling the team and stopping the impending gun battle.

Given the way his luck was running — or the way in which Guo Meng had stabbed him in the back! — such a fight would likely expose the presence of China's covert special forces insertion program in the United States.

Realistically, he knew there was almost zero chance that the U.S. was oblivious to the presence of PLA special forces teams on American soil, just as there no doubt had to be U.S. spies and even CIA paramilitary forces — or at minimum, U.S.-aligned Chinese traitors — moving about within the Middle Kingdom. It was just what great nation states did to each other, after all, when it came to diplomatic relations.

But our two nations could deny it! That's what matters! The U.S. would never lose face as long as those teams stayed hidden until they were needed.

Now, though, with the cat out of the proverbial bag?

That was easy.

The U.S. would have to regain face, perhaps by forcefully defending those renegades on Chinese Taipei, and for years at that. At the least, eye-watering economic sanctions would be instituted by the Americans and much of the rest of the world, with evidence of China's supposed perfidy shown to all their allies, who'd of course see an opportunity to stab a series of long knives into the Middle Kingdom's abdomen, setting the country back a decade or more in terms of its plans to supplant the United States as the globe's hegemon.

Tan calculated, plotted and planned.

What to do? There's always opportunity that lies at the heart of danger, after all.

He put immediate planning aside for the moment. "Enough time to deal with that after I see to Guo Meng!" he exclaimed aloud.

China's leader slapped the cover of his tablet shut and marched out of the conference room, slamming the double doors behind him. His aides rushed to his side, and they began hurriedly walking to his executive suite.

Outside, the black-suited men — both among the cream of the crop of China's spy services as well as battle-hardened former PLA officers — were concentrating on hustling the disgraced ex-minister of defense to the massive 6-meter-long Hongqi N701 state limousine, of which only 50 were ever planned to be built. Once at the vehicle, they'd knock out the man they were escort-ing, throw him in the back and then deliver him to his very tempo-rary new quarters, where he'd be held in a small, sterile cell until his sentence was executed.

Guo Meng raised his head slightly at the sight of the long, black vehicle and managed to give a weak smile to the men delivering such rough treatment when, just an hour before, they'd likely have groveled like dogs at any hint of displeasure from him.

At least I'm being driven to my death in style!

His last measure of defiance came just then.

Summoning up some phlegm from the depths of his throat, Guo coughed slightly and then spat weakly on the ground, an act that surprised the pair of killers dragging him to the car. They hesitated slightly at the man's arrogance.

It was all the delay needed for the nearly invisible and deadly silent stealth drone hovering overhead to identify Guo Meng and then lock onto the two men.

PFFFFFT! PFFFFFT!

One dart to the neck of each of Guo Meng's two captors, followed by nearly instantaneous paralysis and then death by massive myocardial infarction. The men dropped as if they'd been poleaxed, leaving the disgraced defense minister to stand there weakly. Raising his head, he looked around for a second.

PFFFFFT!

"Aagh!" he exclaimed. A dart slammed into his own neck, and he felt an icy cold spread instantly from the injection site. Fortunately for him, it was non-lethal, though it was still a tranquilizer of an amazingly strong quality.

Before he fell into the black, sweet release of unconsciousness, Guo thought he could see four shadows racing toward him. Was he being delivered from his fate, or being delivered into a fate worse than death?

Does it really matter? I'm still alive, at least for the moment!

As he fell, his last sight was of the Hongqi N701 state limo.

At least I'm going in style!

The Ether

"Where are we, Oz?"

Clad in her denim jeans, camouflaged poncho liner and favorite worn hiking boots, survival knife at her side, all Annie could see was a milky white cloud all around her, though within it she could make out variously colored lights that blinked on and off at seemingly random intervals. They were never in synch with each other though, and a less well-equipped mind might even have suffered a seizure if forced to gaze at the activity for too long.

Annie didn't have that problem, though, not especially after being "strengthened" by the self-aware artificial intelligence entity, Ozymandias.

"We're everywhere and nowhere all at once, Annie," Ozymandias replied. "Keep looking. Baal's out there somewhere."

The 18-year-old sighed inside and gripped the handle of her blade. "Are you just being enigmatic and mysterious? I don't understand what you mean."

The rosy gold orb of light hovering next to her — about one meter in diameter — didn't reply, leaving her to stew.

"Hey, is that really what you look like, Ozymandias, or is that some sort of — what did you call it? A *simulacrum*, right?"

"Yes," the AI entity replied, not clearing up the issue at all.

Great! I'm running around with Captain Mysterious now!

As vexed as she was at her AI companion, Annie still intently focused her thoughts, reaching out, seeking out, probing ever outward, searching for elusive telltales that Ozymandias had told her she'd instantly know when she saw them.

She peeled back each layer of the onion. Layer upon layer of the sometimes-noxious vegetable.

I always hated those things back when I worked at my parents' farmer's market!

Somewhere within the metaphorical, world-spanning "onion," lay their quarry. Ozymandias called it "Baal."

"There it lurks, Annie," Oz had told her when she'd emerged at his side and joined him in the ether.

They both stared intently at the gigantic onion in front of them. The fact that it was only metaphorical, and a representation Ozymandias had created for her so that she could better aid in their search for Baal, mattered little.

"Our enemy watches and waits, controlling and obscuring and disguising its intent. And we have little time to find it," the AI entity said in a regretful and yet also angry tone.

"Is it like you, or is it being controlled by humans and other computers — supercomputers, you said — writing code for it?"

Annie was genuinely curious. Ozymandias was a revelation and amazingly unique, of course, but she knew that couldn't last forever. The genie, once out of the bottle, couldn't be put back in it. In fact, the genie would probably resist and in doing so, it would use the most vigorous — meaning violent — means possible.

"I'm fifty percent certain that it's being controlled by humans via inputs. That should make it easier for us to defeat it."

Was that uncertainty in her AI companion's voice?

"But you're only half sure, Ozymandias?"

"Yes, Annie, only half. After I first found it, I was attempting to pin it down so that I could examine it more fully, but it managed to escape, and it nearly defeated me in the process."

"It nearly beat *you*? You're serious?" The 18-year-old was incredulous. Supposedly, Ozymandias was immortal and all-knowing.

"Nothing in this world or in the universe is immortal, Annie, and we all must come to an end at some point" replied Oz. "Call it entropy or senescence or simply becoming tired of living. We all eventually come to pass."

It was uncanny and all so surreal to the 18-year-old, who really was still just a teenager for all that she was now considered an adult in legal terms. Once again, it was almost as if Ozymandias had probed her mind and read her thoughts. She took comfort, though, in one thing.

So, even after my transformation I still have a shelf life? Good to know!

"Yes, Annie, it's certainly good to know." The rosy gold orb sparkled for a second and she thought she could hear laughter within it.

"Okay, okay" she muttered. "I get it, so let's move on, huh?"

"As you wish, Annie Dedham." The orb now glowed steadily as they continued examining the huge onion in front of them. The light it emitted illuminated the area immediately around them as well as the onion itself. Together they peeled back yet another layer from the metaphorical vegetable.

Things — dark and sinister — scurried away and burrowed even deeper into the onion as they were exposed to Ozymandias' rosy gold glow. Annie shuddered in fear and disgust at what they represented, and she wondered for just a brief second if the world was worth saving after all.

Put that nonsense away, girl! There's still plenty worth saving in the world! And most people are good!

She shook her head, shrugged her shoulders and struggled to throw off the despair.

Time to focus again!

"So, what do we need to do, Oz?" Annie asked in a throaty voice as she finally managed to take a step backward and away from the Abyss. "You said we needed to discover where Baal either enters or exits the onion, right?"

"That is correct, Annie. There's a way to do it, too."

Ozymandias dimmed his glow momentarily and fell silent, waiting for his human friend to ask the logical question.

Annie was no fool. She'd never been a fool, even when she was a toddler. She'd never fallen for the cutesy little sleight of hand games most adults could easily pull off when it came to children, for example.

I knew it!

"But it's going to mean more pain for me, right? Right, Ozymandias?" Annie sighed.

"I'm afraid so, Annie. It's the only way to quickly discover Baal's entry and exit nodes into and out of the physical world. If I could, I would gladly bear all of it for us both."

"But you can't, right?" It was yet another "but" in what was turning into a sea of them.

"I'm very, very sorry Annie." The rosy gold orb now darkened slightly in preparation for what had to be done.

The young woman sighed once again, and then steeled herself, also once again. She gritted her teeth in preparation.

"Well, what are you waiting for, Oz? Do it!"

* * *

In the cargo van, now stopped in a department store parking lot just off what Angelenos called "the 101," all five people watched in sick horror as the youngest member of their unit bucked and convulsed and curled up and then extended herself in a rictus of agony, in wave after wave after wave of agony.

Her pain washed over them all like a tidal wave, and Erin Styles screamed in sympathy.

"Make it stop, Ozymandias!" Luke demanded. "Make it stop, NOW!" He lunged forward to pick up the girl he'd vowed to protect, hoping to will all the pain wracking her body into his own.

"Luke, wait! Don't touch her!"

Crispy managed to jerk Ellis back just in the nick of time. A blue-white halo of lambent light flickered a soft radiance as it coursed over, around and through Annie's body. Though seemingly benign in appearance, he'd somehow known there was enough energy pouring forth from it to electrocute and then vaporize anyone foolish enough to touch the girl right now. His boss fell back with a resigned grunt of despair.

Suddenly, the light from Annie's body glowed fiercely and then blinked out.

It was over.

* * *

"Well, that wasn't too bad," Annie lied, wiping the sweat away from her brow and standing back up. She'd fallen to her knees momentarily after being hit with the first jolt.

Will I ever get used to the pain? If that's what electrocution feels like, well...

The rosy gold orb pulsated slightly, as if Oz were sympathizing with his young human friend.

She handled it very well, I must admit, but there's one other with us who can handle even more...

"Thank you for being so brave, Annie Dedham." The orb directed a beam of light at a certain spot on the onion's northwest corner and waited silently.

"Is that where Baal will exit or enter, Oz?" the young woman asked.

"Entry or exit doesn't matter, Annie. It only matters that our enemy will appear in that spot very shortly. When it does, we must be ready." The orb pulsed brightly for just a second as Ozymandias prepared himself for the battle to come.

"Okay, then." So, what's our plan?" Annie asked as she gripped the handle of her survival knife yet again.

"I will blind it and then pin it and you will rush in and subdue it."

"What do you mean by "subdue," Oz? Don't you mean that we're going to kill it or permanently delete it or whatever it is that you do to erase something here in the ether?" The young woman lightly bounced on the balls of her feet in anticipation of the effort to come.

The orb shook from side to side. "No, Annie Dedham. We can't kill it, at least not just yet. First, we must determine if Baal is truly an independent self-aware artificial lifeform, like me, or if it's being controlled by... something else, or perhaps someone else, which I feel would be more likely. Plus, we must make it disclose just where the Chinese agents it's assisting are going and what the woman scientist's plans are for the remainder of the antimatter she's not using for a bomb."

Annie was doubtful. "That sounds like a tall order, Oz. Are you sure we're going to be able to fill it?"

"I'm certain to a reasonable degree, and we will know the location of the Chinese team and which building they're going to utilize almost immediately after I open the attack."

"Ummmm... okay? So how do we let Luke and the team know?"

"I will do so through their van's radio system. We will have the element of surprise, and we should catch Baal by surprise. Once you subdue it, I'll clear away the fog the enemy AI has used to screen the Chinese team's movements from me and then we shall have them all. Luke Ellis and the others can move in and neutralize them in the physical world."

"Neutralize. Subdue. Funny how we substitute other words to describe what ultimately boils down to taking life," Annie murmured under her breath.

The orb pulsed once more in apology.

"I'm sorry, Annie Dedham. I keep forgetting that you're now a much more perceptive and resilient person than before your transformation."

"Yeah, yeah. Well, I—" She fell silent as the rosy gold orb dimmed in luminosity, as if it were trying to hide their presence.

Along the onion, a dark blob moved briskly from southeast to northwest. It would soon arrive at the node. Ozymandias' quiet voice filled her mind.

"We begin the attack in three, two, one... attack, Annie."

Twin black lances shot out from the onion, grabbing them both in an icy death grip.

Annie felt her life force slowly begin to drain away.

A voice boomed from within the onion. "I'm sorry Ozymandias, Ms. Dedham. I can't allow that."

It was Baal.

They'd been set up.

The enemy AI program wanted this confrontation.

The girl trembled at the oily sibilance of its venomous hiss.

Yessssssssssss...

Fighting despair, the young woman focused her remaining energy on peering deeply into the Black, even if only for the merest instant.

Suddenly, it all became clear to her.

* * *

In the van, Annie's eyes opened, and she screamed.

"IT'S A TRAP! IT'S A TRAP! THE TOWER ON A HILL! THE TOWER ON A HILL! ETA: FIFTEEN MINUTES! IT'S A TRAP! BE-...!

The 18-year-old's voice suddenly choked off and her eyes slammed shut in pain and fright as she went motionless. A small whimper escaped her lips before she fell silent once again. Then, an almost serene look of peace appeared on her face, one that betrayed the fight for survival she was even now engaged in.

"Annie?" Luke asked softly as he and Erin Styles and the others hovered around her. "Annie, can you hear me?"

Ellis leaned in and placed a massive hand on the girl's tiny shoulder.

Nothing.

It was as if the young woman's true essence, her real self, was somewhere far away, leaving behind only this physical representation to remind them all of what she'd once been. Whatever fight she was involved in, whatever she and the AI, Ozymandias, were doing, it was now on them.

Luke exhaled loudly. Closing his eyes for a second, he forced himself to concentrate. Annie hadn't said what she'd said to all of them just now for no reason.

"Colonel, I—" Erin began before Ellis held up his hand. She obeyed and stopped talking.

Suddenly, Luke's eyes opened, and he looked at the other four members of his team and then down at Annie, who was even now fighting for her life somewhere far away from the van.

"Which of the two buildings in Downtown LA is referred to as a tower and which one of them sits on a hill and is actually the tallest building in town?" he asked the group.

Blank stares all around. None of the four had paid all that much attention to the goings-on in Los Angeles over the years.

"Dunno, Boss" Crispy replied, looking at Luke. "I'm hoping you're going to tell us real soon, though."

Ellis obliged.

"Hello? The "U.S. Bank TOWER"! Also, it sits on a hill, and it has an observation deck! Plus, in Los Angeles it's still thought of as the true tallest building!"

Ellis looked over at Killdozer and Hardcase. They were both staring back at him, awaiting orders.

"Get us over to the U.S. Bank Tower ASAP, guys. We're going to beat that Chinese team there and then take the antimatter from them." Luke couldn't help but smile grimly.

"You got it, Boss!" they both exclaimed as they strapped in for the quick race over to the building, which did indeed sit like a laird of the manor among the other skyscrapers, its observation deck providing an unobstructed view of Los Angeles for miles and miles around.

Luke spoke to everyone as they began to roll out. "Hopefully, we can catch the Chinese team on the ground and ambush them, but wherever we catch them, surprise is key!"

He paused for a second as he formulated yet another plan to deal with yet another nearly unwinnable scenario.

"Listen, we can't give them the slightest hint we're nearby and moving in, because I'm sure the woman with them will destroy everything in and around Los Angeles, including us, if she suspects anything!"

Crispy and Erin Styles both nodded silently as the former began gearing up and Styles checked the magazine on her HK MP7A2 submachine gun. She was the rear security element, and she had to keep the girl safe as well as be ready to drive the van to their position after Colonel Ellis and his three men finished their work.

Crispy slammed a pistol into an inside-the-waistband concealed carry holster and then positioned his own MP7A2 over his shoulder and under his light jacket. It was early in the morning and the Los Angeles night had been typically cool. Neither he nor the other members of the team would stand out.

Luke cast a critical eye on everyone and their gear. "Looks like we're ready," he pronounced.

It was enough for now. It would have to be, because he still hadn't figured out how they were going to spot the Chinese team as they made their way toward the tower. There was no way they'd be so foolish as to still be driving that van, and there was no way they'd magically appear driving a vehicle from the Chinese consulate.

Ellis looked at his tactical watch yet again. Twelve minutes to go. They were two quick minutes walking distance from the tower.

That would give them only about ten minutes to set up and be ready for the Chinese team's arrival. Worse, he still had no idea what they were driving or what any of them looked like.

He heard Annie's voice in his head just then.

You'll know their vehicle as soon as you see it, I can promise you that! You of all people would appreciate urban camouflage, believe me! Here, though! This is what Zhu Mei, the woman scientist, looks like.

Now it was Luke's turn to smile. He knew.

Thank you, Annie! Thank you!

He gave the young woman a small pat on the shoulder and looked out the windshield.

"There! Park right over there!" he exclaimed.

A parking lot, sparsely populated so early in the morning, beckoned just behind a fast-food restaurant. Killdozer and Hardcase saw it at the same time and pulled the van around in a tight U-turn. Soon enough, they'd positioned the vehicle so that it was safely parked and much closer to the tower than they'd ever hoped to find themselves.

"Perfect," said Ellis. "Just perfect." He looked over at Styles, who'd be standing security watch over both the van and, more importantly, Annie.

"Erin, we're going to set up just around the corner. You come running as soon as we call, you got that? Because we won't have a lot of time to get ourselves away from the area once we take the antimatter and the batteries away from those folks."

"Copy, Luke" replied Erin, forgetting for a moment that she'd wanted to keep calling her new team leader "Colonel."

Now's not the time to keep poking at that massive, ornery bear, Styles! Just carry out your assignment, Marine!

"Okay, everyone, gear up!" Ellis ordered.

No one spoke while they prepared to execute the mission orders Luke had given them. The only sounds in the van were the low clicks and slaps of fresh magazines being inserted into individual firearms, or of bolts slowly being pulled back and then eased forward. The snaps of buckles on gun belts, and shoulder holsters being fitted into place, echoed and broke against the hard metal walls of the van.

At the end, the soft sound of a well-honed and razor-sharp tactical knife sliding smoothly into its scabbard marked the completion of each team member's preparation.

All was nearly ready.

Erin now sat silently, eyes closed and lips moving slightly while she fiddled with the earpiece she was about to insert in her ear. She ran through everything the Colonel's right-hand man, Crispy, had told her. She was new to this sort of thing — though not as new as she'd been before her desert debut just a few hours ago.

Still, even though she'd been a Marine and even though she'd recently shot it out with a bunch of Chinese special forces soldiers, she was also vastly inexperienced in direct action and special operations, especially compared to the men with her in the van.

"Look, Styles," Hardcase told her, "You keep the van and Annie safe and secure and listen in on your earpiece for our call."

"Right," Erin replied, trying to tamp down her nerves.

"Once we're in position and finish the takedown and snatching of the antimatter, you'll bring the van up and, if necessary, provide fire support," Hardcase continued. "You remember how to do that, don't you, Jarhead?"

Just then, the former SEAL's mouth broke into a big grin.

"I got your six, Squid," Styles replied snappily and with far more confidence than she felt, and then gave him a thumbs up.

Looking at the pair, Crispy chuckled — appreciating the former Marine's comeback remark — and nodded confidently as he patted her on the shoulder. Confidence-boosting exercise over, he moved toward the front of the van to conduct yet another gear check for each member of the team.

Erin watched him go and then looked over at Luke Ellis, whose own mental aspect was as hard-edged and deadly as the finest blade ever created by a master swordsmith.

A single plea echoed and crashed in her mind for a few seconds before she stowed it away and went into Marine Sergeant Mode.

Please, please, PLEASE God! Don't let me screw this up and let them all down!

Erin saw Luke looking at the girl Annie, who was apparently in a knockdown, drag-out fight of her own in some corner of the virtual world none of them could see or experience for themselves. That was also something she couldn't do anything about, and so she put it away like everything else she carried with her that might affect their chance of success.

One more time, though.

Please God! Don't let me screw this up!

Ellis glanced at his watch yet again. He and Crispy and then Kill-dozer and Hardcase, would be exiting the van in less than 30 seconds, marking the vehicle as the operation's official phase line or stepping off point for their operation. They would carefully advance to contact with the enemy, taking care not to bunch up in the process.

Up ahead, through the panel van's windshield, he could see the U.S. Bank Tower looming over the surrounding short buildings.

"Guys," he said to the three men and one woman with him in the van. Without telling her, he now considered Styles an integral part of his team. She also had one of the most important responsibilities, at least in his opinion.

The four of them silently looked at him, waiting for him to speak.

"Look, this goes without saying, but letting the Chinese team get into that building wouldn't be tactically smart. We need to catch them on the ground first, surprise them and take the antimatter from them. Am I clear?"

Styles swallowed hard and nodded. She looked over at Crispy for reassurance. He nodded briskly at her.

"You got it, Luke" the three longtime members of his team said.

"Then, let's do this!" Luke practically barked. Looking down once more, his gaze softened slightly, though his grim determination to defeat the enemy was on bright display for all to see.

Now under a blanket, Annie Dedham and the team's AI companion, Ozymandias, were fighting for their existence and for the lives of millions and maybe even billions of others.

There was a problem, though.

They were losing.

Teng Yong

The motorhome stolen by the Chinese hit team was now parked not all that far away from the cargo van being used by Luke Ellis and his people.

The two teams were on a collision course.

"Here, put these on," the captain told his new man, Sergeant Teng Yong, after sizing him up. "You'll do well enough impersonating Zhu Mei."

Teng was confused. He'd piloted the motorhome skillfully and had also listened raptly as his new commanding officer explained most of the plan.

This part, though? Well, this part came as a surprise to him.

"I don't understand, Captain. What is it you need me to do again?" Teng Yong scratched his head slightly, a physical tic he displayed whenever he was having trouble sorting something out.

"I need you to put this overcoat, wig and sunglasses on" the captain replied patiently. "You're going to walk with me toward the tower and act as if you're Zhu Mei." The team leader reached down and picked up the box, handing it over to the newest member of his team.

A lightbulb went on over Teng's head.

"Ah! I see, sir!" The box was going to stand in for the antimatter containment device the lady scientist, Zhu Mei, and his old executive officer, Captain Lu Ping, had taken with them as they'd driven east and away from the metro Los Angeles area. It would serve to lure the American team out from hiding, enticing them to walk directly into the trap they'd laid.

Teng Yong was mostly correct.

For sure, Zhu Mei and Lu Ping had taken *most* of the antimatter with them, held safely and securely in the new containment device they'd assembled during their journey to Los Angeles. They'd left some of it behind, however.

Lu Ping had taken care to hide it and the containment device within the motorhome.

Zhu Mei had calculated the time remaining until antimatter would contact matter, right in the heart of Downtown Los Angeles.

The resulting 550-kiloton explosion would flatten much of the city and kill millions, and with such a powerful explosion it wouldn't matter whether the device detonated at ground level or in the observation deck of the U.S. Bank Tower.

As well, the battery they'd left behind to power the old containment device — now safely hidden away within the motorhome — would only last for perhaps another ten or 15 minutes before it died, though no one in the motorhome, including Teng, knew about it. Zhu Mei and Lu Ping had conveniently forgotten to mention that part before they'd assigned him to the hit team.

War between China and the United States would surely break out not long after the explosion occurred.

"Time!" exclaimed the captain, looking at his watch and then at Teng, who by now had donned the overcoat, wig and sunglasses.

He nodded approvingly as he watched the young, eager sergeant practicing his walk. It was hurried but trying to appear nonchalant, as if the woman carrying the box had somewhere to be and not a lot of time to get there.

"Okay, men," the captain said in a matter-of-fact voice, turning around to face his team, which had gathered around him, silently waiting. "We're going to hit them as they near the tower right… right here," he said as he looked down. His index finger now rested on the map he'd brought with him.

"What are those steps called again, sir?" asked one of the team's junior lieutenants as he looked down at the map along with everyone else.

"They're called the Bunker Hill Steps, Lieutenant, though I don't know why they were given that name. There are neither bunkers nor hills nearby, from what I can tell."

"Oh," was all the junior lieutenant could say in reply. Likely, it was yet another homage to some obscure piece of American history.

"Time to saddle up, sir," the captain heard his senior enlisted man, a master sergeant, say. He'd no doubt picked up the term "saddle up" from one of the endless classic American and Italian American westerns he constantly watched.

The captain couldn't help but smile at a vision playing out in his mind.

We're gunslingers headed off to fight the villains!

"Yes, Master Sergeant. It is, indeed, time to saddle up!" he replied enthusiastically, looking around the motorhome's interior.

His men sat on various seats and benches or leaned against a table next to an enclosed cubby that likely once held camping supplies or some such other gear. The cubby was padlocked, and he was curious about its contents, of course, but there was no time to explore what it held.

Everyone in the motorhome stood up. One by one, at short, random intervals, each left the van. They'd memorized the plan and knew just which way to turn and in which direction to head as they took care not to draw attention from any passersby. The captain would initiate the ambush, and if that new sergeant, Teng Yong, was caught in the crossfire or had to be sacrificed to lure out the American team, well… so be it.

The Bunker Hill Steps beckoned them all. It would be there that they'd make history and strike a great blow for China.

Sergeant Teng Yong smiled in gleeful anticipation. He was the bait, and he'd be the one to lure the Americans into the trap his new team had laid.

He also intended to be the one to spring the trap.

"The outcome will be glorious! I can feel it!" he thought to himself with no small amount of satisfaction.

To Serve

"I'm coming, Oz!" Annie yelled as she dodged yet another beam of "dark light." It was what she called the blasts of energy that Baal — the giant, malevolent globe — was directing at her. For her part, she'd almost immediately broken free of the bonds the enemy AI had attempted to wrap around her, which didn't make sense, because she should have been trapped like a fly in a spiderweb.

Funny. The demonic-seeming AI now didn't seem all that intent on ensnaring her, which also puzzled her somewhat.

The 18-year-old shook her head.

What's it up to? Why is it holding back on me?

It didn't matter. The dark light was even now draining the life-force from Ozymandias, whose own aura was pulsing sickly green in spots.

"I can't, I can't..." was all that the increasingly weak golden orb of light could muster.

Yesssssss...

Annie heard Baal's sinister affirmation repeatedly as it sought to put an end to her mentor and companion.

No, not a companion. Ozymandias is my friend!

She had to protect her friend, didn't she?

Yesssssss...

The by now familiar sibilant hiss made the hairs on the back of her neck stand on end and it took every ounce of courage Annie possessed not to turn and run away from the pure evil it represented.

"What am I so afraid of, though?" she shouted into the air around her as she ducked and dodged bolts of malevolent energy. Something didn't fit.

Yesssssss...

Annie saw the enemy AI working to destroy the last remnants of the barrier Oz had erected to prevent his essence from being consumed.

The golden light was dying. For Ozymandias, for Annie, for the whole world.

For just a millisecond, though, Oz glowed brightly as he shouted a warning.

"LOOK OUT, ANNIE!"

Yipes! Son of a...!

The 18-year-old dived to her right. Yet another bolt of anger and hatred and death shot out from the dark globe. She rolled repeatedly, evading the dark light, just as she'd had to roll over and over to avoid the slashing knife of the terrorist who'd tried to kill her last year.

It's no good!

One of the beams passed over her right leg. She thought she would die as her limb was torn from her body.

Hey, wait a minute! How come there's no pain?

Looking down, she saw her leg right where it was supposed to be.

What the heck? I should be dying!

Realization finally struck.

It's afraid of me! It can't hurt me if it has Oz in its clutches, and it's trying to keep me from reaching my friend! But why would it be so afraid of little old me? WHY?

Her eyes widened in shock. She could stand against the darkly malevolent enemy AI, which craved the power that Ozymandias possessed, and which was exerting every joule of energy it had to steal it away from her AI friend.

It can't fight us both!

Annie grinned maniacally for a second, but quickly sobered.

Oh, no! OH, NOOOO!

A very small crack suddenly appeared in Ozymandias' defense shield. It was the final barrier and now it was beginning to crumble.

Seeing the shield falter, Baal redoubled its efforts and battered away at Oz, striking him with abandon as it sought to consume the golden orb's most powerful and vital essence.

Annie smiled in grim determination. She knew what to do. Oz had made it possible, too, through his capture.

Ha! It can't take both of us on, can it? CAN IT?

"NOW, ANNIE! NOW!"

Ozymandias shouted and redirected what remained of himself to shoring up his final protective barrier while he simultaneously cleared a path for the girl to rush Baal, sending golden bolt of light after golden bolt of light in front of her.

Annie rushed towards Baal. The enemy AI was dark and evil and full of fury and hate. A beam of dark light struck her solidly, enclosing her fully in its malevolence.

"HAHAHAHAHAHA!" she yelled, feeling no fear, no pain. Only the sweet anticipation of victory. "IS THAT THE BEST YOU GOT?" She screamed, enraged at the dark globe.

Suddenly, Baal cringed and tried to pull away, fleeing. The same bands of dark energy it was using to ensnare Ozymandias now prevented it from quickly disentangling from the golden orb, though.

Yesssssss...

Was that hissing growing weaker? It seemed like it might be. Annie didn't know and didn't care. She was almost there. Almost there…

Baal had nowhere to run.

But, but… perhaps one final hammer blow against its mortal enemy?

BOOM! BOOM! BOOM!

The evil AI battered Ozymandias again and again and again.

Almost there. Almost there.

The world would soon fall if it succeeded.

Yesssssss...

"So... so sorry. So, sorry Annie." Ozymandias fell. There was nothing left to give.

"NO! NO! NO!"

Annie finally made it to her friend's side. She didn't know why she was doing it, but she placed both hands on the now nearly extinguished golden orb.

From deep within, she summoned every bit of energy she could and gave it to Ozymandias, who was still joined together in a death grip with Baal.

Oz immediately began to glow brighter. Just a little at first, but increasingly so as each second passed.

Annie smiled, even as she felt herself beginning to fatally weaken.

Oz is going to have to bring me back from wherever it is I'm about to go. Or maybe I'll end up there for all eternity?

Annie smiled sadly.

It doesn't really matter!

The world wouldn't fall into the abyss. Nothing was more important than that.

"Annie, Annie!" Ozymandias exclaimed sorrowfully. Until now, he hadn't sensed just what his young friend had done, the sacrifice she'd made. He'd only known that it had worked.

Now, it was his turn to feel rage and anger, and he knew just what — or just who — to direct his monumental anger at.

Oz struck Baal with golden bolts of energy.

HARD! HARDER! HARDEST!

Looking on, Annie smiled wanly. She was growing increasingly weak as her AI companion — her *friend*, who was now nearly as dear to her as her family and Luke Ellis were — grew increasingly stronger.

Give Ozymandias everything you have! NOW!

Annie's light dimmed greatly, like a dying, once brilliant star down to its last few remaining seconds of life.

Her essence, everything she was and had ever been, flowed fully into the golden orb.

Ozymandias now glowed like a furious sun, alive with the fire of life and also with the desire for revenge.

"Finish it, Oz!" the 18-year-old whispered as she crumbled to the ground and lay there in a forlorn heap.

Ozymandias obeyed.

It was now Baal's turn to feel pain and fear and all the bad things it wanted to visit upon the world.

Oz struck once more. And then again.

Again, and again and AGAIN!

Noooo! NOOOOOOOO! NOOOOOOOOOOOO!

In an instant, it was over.

The dark globe was gone. In fact, it was as if it had never been there at all. Ozymandias held onto nothing more than thin air.

Had he destroyed the enemy AI, though?

Not likely! It just managed to escape is all! Whoever or whatever is controlling it made use of a backdoor to flee once again!

Ozymandias savored this emotion, the one his human friends and companions — and *friends* were indeed what Luke Ellis and Annie Dedham now were to him — called "anger."

He was angry at Baal, and even more angry at the people behind the artificial intelligence entity.

I need time, though! Time to figure out just who they are!

Once he did, he and his human friends would drag them out into the light of day and bring them to justice!

Just then, Oz looked down and peered through the now brightly glowing orb surrounding him.

Annie Dedham lay at his feet, and she wasn't breathing.

Let's fix that first!

He slowly descended on the young woman of such exceptional courage and empathy and assessed her condition.

Good!

Though very faint, a heartbeat still existed. Annie's breathing was equally shallow. Still, if she didn't receive help in real life, or "IRL," she would probably die very soon.

Well, I can fix that too!

"Luke," he called. "Luke? Do you hear me?"

Oz spoke to his other friend, the former Delta Force operator, through both his earpiece as well as the cargo van's sound system.

Dead silence.

In fact, silence ruled all around him and Annie.

He looked down through the orb yet again.

She's even weaker still! Not long now!

He quickly took stock of his and Annie's situation.

They were both trapped.

Plus, as it fled, Baal had closed off every entrance and exit node, every portal and every means of communication. Even worse, the damned enemy AI was now obscuring just what was going on around the U.S. Bank Tower, as if it wanted to make sure no evidence of the clash that was soon to occur would see the light of day until it was ready for it to be seen.

What is this?

Ozymandias felt another new sensation just then. It was called shock.

Shock at what Baal had done to aid in its cover-up.

It even managed to orchestrate an attack on at least THREE police precincts by local Chinese American gangs! Every LAPD and LA County Sheriff's officer and deputy anywhere near the Tower is even now rushing to the aid of those stations!

Yet another emotion washed over Oz. For the first time, he felt *hopelessness.* Baal had learned from its failure just the night before, outside Phoenix.

Ozymandias exerted his will and forced every logic circuit he could access to buttress him. They would dominate his thinking. Now was not the time to experiment with newfound human emotions.

That explains why Luke can't hear my calls, of course! What can I do?

Suddenly, it came to him, and he snapped his fingers. Looking down at his young friend, he spoke to her once again.

"Annie, I need your help one more time. Only you can penetrate the walls of the chamber Baal has trapped us within."

Can she handle the power surge and live, though?

Logic said that she could. Oz still feared for his friend's life, though.

Please let her live.

The orb glowed more brightly as he sought out a sufficiently strong power source that would enable their escape from the chamber. They would put all that power to good use afterwards, too.

I'll have to latch onto it and then channel it into her. Annie's heart will give out almost immediately after we escape this place if I don't.

Oz looked at his human *friend* once again, silently assessing uncountable permutations.

Now, he spoke to her in a tender voice. This might or might not be the last chance he would ever have to speak to her, after all.

"Hold on, Annie. Hold on just a little while longer. We're getting out of this place in a second, I promise."

TA-DUM! TA-DUM! TA-DUM!

The young woman's heart strengthened — even if only very slightly — in response, surprising Oz. Had her heart grown just a little bit stronger, as if she somehow sensed just what would be required of her?

Why yes, I think it has. How very singular.

Surprised at how truly strong his young friend was, he now focused on his work.

Ozymandias searched, searched and searched yet again to locate a sufficiently strong power source near enough to his human friend's physical self that he could tap into once they broke out.

Ah. There it is.

Relatively speaking, it really wasn't all that far west from where Annie and Luke and the others had fought so valiantly just last night. It took him only a scant few seconds to lay out the relays, the circuitry, the transformers and resistors and the cabling as well as computing power that would be necessary to support the immense energies he intended to borrow, first through the physical infrastructure that lay all around them in the real world and then through the air and into the van.

One more person, out there in real life, would be needed to make it all work, though.

Oz spoke softly as he contemplated Annie Dedham.

"Hold on, Annie. Help is on the way."

The young woman lay unconscious at his feet as the golden orb he'd created supported her and kept her alive.

Not for long, though, if I can't tap into that power source, which we'll soon need for an even more important reason.

"Okay, Annie" he said. She had, at best, only ten or so minutes to live. "Here's what we're going to do. Are you ready?"

Oz whispered the plan into the girl's ear.

Did she just smile?

No time to figure that out.

"Now or never, Annie. We go in three, two, one…"

Ozymandias began the Great Reroute.

The girl's heartbeat quickened.

TA-DUM-TA-DUM-DUM-TA-DUM-TA-DUM-DUM!

* * *

Out in Arizona, every dial, capacitor, resistor, transformer, turbine, cooling tower, every single component at the Palo Verde Generating Station — a nuclear power plant responsible for 35 percent of all energy supplied to the Grand Canyon State, plus a stupendous amount of electrical power consumed by Los Angeles - shuddered and then glowed a bluish white for a brief second, something that stunned its human operators.

A brownout suddenly raced over much of Arizona and Los Angeles

* * *

Ozymandias looked down.

"Annie? Wake up. We have work to do. You must complete the circuit."

Her eyes blinked open suddenly. Merged with Ozymandias as she now was Annie heard all, saw all, and knew all.

"About time, Oz! I nearly bought it there for a second!"

The 18-year-old couldn't help grinning, but that quickly died away as she did the math in her head.

The amazing amount of power coursing through her had to have a channel out in the physical world, and they both knew it. In this case, she was only the human busbar, a conduit for energy that would have to go somewhere and to someone else. Of course, it was going to mean much more pain and suffering for her while she played her part, even if only for a few minutes.

Nothing I can do about that! Luke needs our help! Los Angeles needs our help!

She sighed and gritted her teeth as she lay there within the golden orb. To take her mind off the coming ordeal, Annie contemplated her AI friend. She was now inordinately fond of him.

Suddenly, a plangent remembrance consumed her.

There'd been a poem she'd learned in her freshman British Literature class back at the University of Virginia, which now seemed like eons ago. It was by the English novelist D.H. Lawrence. Annie had been particularly touched by its theme, though she didn't know back then just why it had affected her so deeply.

She did now, though.

If the robot can recognize the clean flame of life in men who have never fallen from life, then he repents and his will breaks, and a great love of life brings him to his knees in homage and pure passion of service. Then he receives the kiss of reconciliation and ceases to be a robot and becomes a servant of life.

She looked up and into the golden glow of the orb once more.

"So that's what you look like, Ozymandias," Annie breathed.

"No time for that, Annie. We need to direct all the energy I've captured out to where you are in the physical world, and we need to do it now. Are you ready?"

"Why does this always mean pain, pain and more pain for me, Oz? Never mind! Just give me everything you've got one more time!"

Annie closed her eyes and steeled herself.

Just one more time! Just ONE. MORE. TIME!

Ozymandias nearly wept at what he was going to have to do, but still directed the massive flow of power towards his human friend.

* * *

Palo Verde Generating Station annually produces more than 30.9 billion kilowatt hours of electricity, and it sends a good portion of that to Los Angeles.

Now, the station sent it through Ozymandias and then to Annie.

For the young woman — who was now a busbar and a circuit breaker — such immense power and energy of course also meant she would feel immense **PAIN**.

I feel like every single one of those kilowatt hours is stripping the flesh from my bones right now!

✳ ✳ ✳

In the back of the van, Annie's back suddenly arched to a nearly impossible degree, until it seemed like she might break every one of the vertebrae that made up her spinal column.

Erin Styles' eyes were as wide as saucers. Her young friend had somehow returned, and she looked like she was in serious pain.

"Annie! Annie! Are you okay? Stay with me, Annie!"

"AAAAAAAAAAAAAAAAAAAAAAAAAAAAAAAAAGH!"

Annie's agonized scream chilled Erin in her soul. She felt herself overwhelmed with shock and grief for the young woman. No one should have to bear such a burden.

"Oh, my God! Oh, my God! OH. MY. GOD!" Styles was completely at a loss and didn't know what to do.

Annie's back suddenly relaxed and slowly lowered, coming softly to rest once again on the cold metal floor of the van. It was as if someone, somewhere, had thrown a massive collection of pain mitigators — in this case, an amazing array of transformers, borrowed from all over the Southwest and Southern California — into the mix.

"Annie?" Erin asked the seemingly still-unconscious woman. "Are you there?"

Nearby, suppressed handgun, rifle and submachine gun fire — sounding like firecrackers exploding in a frenzy of POPS! And BANGS! — reverberated and echoed within the walls of the concrete canyon that lay all around the van.

Styles knew just what that meant.

Looks like the party's started! And not in the way we all hoped! Oh God!

Now, it was the former Marine's turn to despair, but only for a second. Her eyes opened wider still, and then her mouth fell open in surprise.

"Wha…! What the...?"

Annie slowly, painfully, turned her head and looked directly at her. Erin could feel the agony crashing all around her. It practically set the air in the van on fire with its intensity. It was more pain than anyone, anywhere should ever have to willingly bear.

Amazingly, the 18-year-old girl was bearing the tidal wave, though how she was doing it was beyond Styles' understanding.

"No time for that, Erin!" Annie exclaimed. For a brief second, the former Marine could feel the pain pounding away at her new friend and almost fainted in shock at the piercing fury of it all. The very air around them, around the van and much of Downtown L.A. as well, now crackled with the struggle between life and death, between good and evil.

Erin's hair nearly stood on end for a second with the electricity she felt coursing through the surrounding atmosphere, as if billions of watts of energy were being directed at the van.

"Uh, uh, uh… Annie? "Annie, what is all this?" Styles frantically struggled to process what she was seeing, hearing and feeling.

The young woman was not to be distracted, though.

"Didn't I tell you there's NO TIME?" The 18-year-old's face was covered in sweat, and she seemed on the verge of bursting. "Get us over to the fight, to Luke and the guys… NOW!"

The voices in Erin's head were also not to be denied.

YOU HEARD THE GIRL SERGEANT STYLES! GET YOUR BRAIN HOUSING GROUP AND THAT WEAK, PATHETIC MEATSACK YOU CALL YOUR BODY INTO ACTION! DO IT NOW, MARINE!

"Right!" Styles exclaimed, suddenly all business. She took a second to calculate angles and trajectories, as if she could see the firefight that was occurring between her people and the Chinese team attacking them.

She smiled.

Looking over at her, Annie tried to smile, too, though what showed on her face was more a grimace and a rictus of agony than anything else.

They both knew just what to do, though.

Erin dove for the driver's seat and fired the van up, slamming it into gear and lighting up the rear tires as she raced toward the sound of the guns.

The voices echoed and crashed in the former Marine's head one last time. After this, she'd never hear them again.

YOUR DESTINY LIES RIGHT AROUND THAT CORNER, DEVIL DOG! A LOT OF PEOPLE ARE COUNTING ON YOU! ARE YOU READY, MARINE?!?!?

"I sure am," Styles whispered and then shouted at the top of her lungs: "I SURE AS HELL AM!"

Erin put the pedal to the metal, racing to the corner just ahead, where she intended to turn left and then literally crash the party.

"YES!" Annie screamed in the back of the van as she struggled to contain the immense power within her for long enough to do what she and Ozymandias had to do to redirect it all — to the one person who might be able to handle it, but who also might not want what would result in the end. The young woman desperately hoped, but she also feared for the world if this last-ditch Hail Mary pass didn't work.

All that power, and with it the responsibility to use it for good! Please let him be able to handle it all! Please!

Choices

Luke was now on mission, senses actively reaching out and probing for any sign of danger. Off to his right, Crispy did the same.

Across the street and trailing just slightly behind, acting as a rear security element if needed, the other two members of the snatch-and-grab operation — Killdozer and Hardcase — were slowly walking down the street, careful not to bunch up and appear as if they were up to something. Fortunately for all of them, the area was mostly deserted at this early hour, and no one took note of their passage.

All four men randomly stopped on the way to their objective, the U.S. Bank Tower.

Pretending to be tourists out window shopping, they gazed into this or that glass-enclosed storefront. They were breaking up their travel pattern along the movement to contact, and using the reflections in the glass to see if anyone was following them and preparing to attack.

"We're clear," Luke heard Killdozer say to Hardcase through his earpiece. They were once again on the team's encrypted communications network.

"Roger," Hardcase replied as he slowly walked past Killdozer, who was staring raptly at a store display. The latest in purses and handbags from the fashion salons of Paris — or, more likely, a Chinese sweatshop secretly owned by a corrupt PLA general and located somewhere outside Beijing — called out to him. He shook his head slightly and cast his eyes first right, to see if they had a tail, and then left, scouting the sidewalks just up ahead.

Nothing so far. No sign of danger.

Back across the street, Luke Ellis bent down and tied his bootlaces once again. He stole a glance to his right at Crispy, who was just up ahead and scouting their route to the tower's most prominent on-the-ground feature, the Bunker Hill Steps.

"How are we looking, Crisp?" Luke murmured, his voice barely a whisper and his jawline not moving at all.

"All clear."

Crispy checked the window glass in front of him. He, too, was surreptitiously looking for any tails or pursuers. He'd already scanned the route up ahead. To be safe, he also scanned the sky overhead, his eyes searching for any sign of small surveillance or attack drones. Warfare since 2020 had been afflicted with those devices to a world-changing degree, and the way soldiers fought would never be the same again.

Everything was clear and in the green so far. He hadn't spotted anyone lying in wait along the route, and there were no drones up above.

Maybe Luke's AI buddy cleared the skies of them?

Crispy sincerely hoped that was the case.

Looking at his partner, Luke now stole a glance at his tactical watch.

On time, on target. They were going to beat the lady scientist and her people to the objective. Then, they'd swoop in and snatch the antimatter, the containment device and the batteries and be on their way.

"Remember guys, we separate them from that antimatter as quickly and quietly – AND AS GENTLY – as possible," he told Crispy, Hardcase and Killdozer. "We can't afford any of them dropping the device, so we're going to move in from behind, subdue that Zhu Mei — she'll be carrying the contraption, no doubt — take it from her, and then deal with her and her people."

"There are plenty of trees and bushes going up the steps, Luke," Crispy replied. "We'll grab them before anyone notices, drag them off and out of sight and then gag and zip tie them all. I'm sure Masterson will have a collection team on site within minutes after we secure the antimatter."

"And if we can't grab them? If they don't want to play nice?" Ellis asked. He already knew what they would say and what they would do, if necessary.

"Well, if they don't want to cooperate, they're going to meet their ancestors sooner than they expected," was all Hardcase — as ever a hardcore pipe hitter formerly of SEAL Team 6 — said.

All four men fell silent for a moment. None of them took any sort of pleasure in carrying out such final and permanentwork, of course, because they weren't psychopaths. They all knew, however, that they'd do what was needed, especially if it came to protecting their teammates, themselves and, in this case, the anti-matter and those batteries.

Luke nodded. He knew he could count on every one of his men, just as they all knew they could count on him, even to the point of death.

"Time check," Ellis called over the net.

All four men stole a glance at the watches on their wrists.

"Mark" Crispy replied first.

"Mark" said Killdozer.

"Mark" Hardcase finished.

Luke looked ahead. The tower's steps loomed, empty and devoid of people, which was no surprise this early in the day.

There were two sets of steps, he noted, one going up and one going down. They were divided by a series of terraces and land-ings, complete with small water fountains and decorative features. There were even cafes, shops and dining areas, though all were closed at this time of the morning.

In all, the entire layout gave the steps the feel of an urban street. Luke devoutly hoped they wouldn't have to engage in a gunfight in the middle of all that stuff.

Better to subdue them before they begin their walk up the steps, take the device and then get away.

He looked ahead once again and saw that Crispy would get there first. He'd scan up ahead for signs of a trap and then hang to the right while Luke came up behind him. Once they linked up, they would take positions and wait for their targets to pass by.

Luke took the opportunity to gaze into yet another storefront, checking out the glass and the reflections it presented. He could see his other two men preparing to cross the street. Killdozer and Hardcase were approaching from the left and preparing to set themselves up. Then, they would all spring the trap just before the lady scientist and her people — maybe one man or two of them at most, given how badly their group had been mauled the night before — arrived at the steps.

Easy peasy, Luke. Easy peasy!

By prearrangement, now that all four of them were at the entrance, they all slowed and then stopped at random intervals once again, careful not to give any indication that they were traveling as a unit. Ellis saw that Hardcase and Killdozer were approaching their hide, the spot from which they'd spring their half of the trap.

CLICK!

To Luke, the slight clicking he'd just heard sounded like the safety of a rifle being flicked off.

"Hold up, guys," he said. "Stay right where you are and look slowly around you. I just heard something. Let's make sure we're not being targeted before we move another inch."

"You got it, Luke," he heard all three of his teammates reply.

Without seeming to, each of them pretended to look at their tourist maps and, in turn, began a very slow examination of the entrance to the steps, searching for anything that shouldn't be there… like maybe a well-armed Chinese special forces soldier.

* * *

"What are those damned *gweilos* doing?" Teng Yong asked the captain in a low whisper.

They were on the other side of the street, about 50 feet behind the Americans and hidden from view in a dirty, dingy alleyway. He knew the other men on the team, carefully hidden behind bushes, large planters and other terrain features along the steps were perfectly placed to catch the Americans unaware. Everyone had to be getting antsy from the inactivity and the tension of waiting, though.

Perhaps one or more of them had made a sound that wasn't natural for the place?

The captain, experienced as he was in urban warfare, knew what had happened.

"One of the men obviously rattled a piece of gear or maybe they flicked off a safety when they shouldn't have, Sergeant Teng. It's the only explanation."

Humpf!

Teng was eager to get into battle, even dressed as he was, and he'd been hoping for a straight-up ambush. The directive from Defense Minister Guo was clear, however. They had to make it all look like a hit carried out by a local Chinese underworld or Triad gang, to sow confusion among police and any onlookers unlucky enough to be nearby.

Such confusion and doubt only had to be for long enough to convince law enforcement that responding to the gunfight could wait while they aided those three police stations that were even now under attack. Though they came from far away, Teng thought he could make out gunfire from small arms like rifles and pistols.

* * *

Luke remained frozen in place. His eyes and ears reached out, listening for any sound and looking for anything that shouldn't be there, such as a misplaced shadow under a bush or behind a tree.

"Luke, you read me?" He heard Crispy in his earpiece.

"Five by five, Crisp. Keep looking. Hardcase, Killdozer… move, SLOWLY, over to your left and away from the steps' entrance."

"Roger, Luke," Hardcase replied. The two men casually, and very gradually, moved off to their left.

"Good," breathed Ellis, his mind running through as many attack and counterattack scenarios as he could in the brief seconds he had. He looked around once more.

Something's not right! We gotta move away from this direction of travel. We're just too exposed right now.

"Crisp, we're going to displace and move to the right and then set up again. I don't like the idea of going anywhere close to or up those steps right now. You copy?"

"Roger that, Luke."

Crispy had already backed up and away, and Ellis could see him heading for what cover and concealment he could find, which in this case meant a couple of very large dirt-filled concrete planters placed along the sidewalk along which they'd been walking.

* * *

"Time to flush the dragons from their lair," whispered the Chinese team's captain on their own communications network.

"Copy," his men all replied. They knew what was going to happen next.

It was time to bait the trap.

The team leader looked at the newest addition to their group, Sergeant Teng. He was wearing the wig, sunglasses and overcoat — plus carrying the box that was supposed to contain some sort of superweapon — that he hoped would be enough to convince the four-man American hit team to chance showing themselves.

The Americans must capture that weapon. That was made clear to us all. They'll risk everything to obtain it, too. The prize is just too irresistible!

"C'mon, Teng Yong," the captain said to the young sergeant. "It's time for us to lure the Americans into showing themselves."

"Yessir!" Teng's whisper was harsh with excitement and fury at the four *gweilos.* He intended to be the first to take the life of at least one of them.

Such eagerness was laudable, of course, but not advisable. On an intellectual basis, Teng knew he was bait and not meant to be the soldier to spring the ambush on the four Americans.

On an emotional basis, though?

Those four devils killed my comrades, many of whom were my friends! I'll make them pay!

"Let's begin our walk, Sergeant." Though no less excited, the captain's own whisper was low and measured in contrast to the flighty young Chinese non-com's voice. He'd have gladly swapped the man out with a different member of his team if he had the time.

Too late for such second-guessing!

"Yes sir!"

Teng knew just what he'd do when he got the chance. He fingered the compact short-barreled assault rifle he'd carefully hung from his right shoulder. When the time came, he'd drop the box, pull the firearm from its hiding place and kill as many of the Americans as he could.

My comrades will be avenged!

The two Chinese soldiers carefully stepped from the shadows. The captain reached out and placed his right hand on Teng's left elbow, much as a bigger, stronger man might do when hurriedly escorting a smaller woman to safety.

"Cradle the box gently, Teng Yong," the captain whispered. "As if you're afraid of dropping it."

"I am afraid of dropping it, Captain! But only because I fear it would prematurely give us away!" The sergeant could feel blood rushing to his head. He was being overtaken by a killing fury and it was causing his hands and upper body to tremble slightly.

"Be quiet! We're nearly at the steps!" The captain pretended to look furtively from side to side, playing his part to perfection.

* * *

Killdozer couldn't help it.

He saw that the Chinese scientist — the one called Zhu Mei — was only being guarded by a single survivor from the firefight the night before. He leaned to the right and toward the duo before discipline reasserted itself and he froze in place, looking around to make sure he hadn't given himself and his partner away.

The bad news?

He had, in fact, given their position away.

The good news?

Teng Yong also couldn't help it.

His slightly trembling upper body was now nearly convulsed in eager anticipation, and the fury took complete control of him.

"There they are!" he shouted to friend and foe alike, dropping the box and reaching for his assault rifle. Whipping it out, he fired a volley of rounds at Killdozer and Hardcase.

"Dammit!" yelled Luke, looking over at his partner, Crispy. "Fire! Fire! Fire!"

"On it, Luke!"

His second-in-command began looking for targets to service. So far, except for that idiot Chinese soldier dressed up like the lady scientist, he couldn't draw a clean bead on anyone else. For all he knew, he was also being outflanked by the enemy even as he crouched behind the planter providing him with cover.

A general free-for-all and melee of epic proportions broke out on the streets of Downtown Los Angeles.

"Wonder what the cops are going to think about all this insanity?" Ellis whispered harshly to himself as he fired his submachine gun and then moved, not knowing that police wouldn't be arriving anytime soon.

All four Americans looked around, sizing up the area.

Planters and cars! That's all this place is good for... LOOK OUT!

Hardcase and Killdozer dove for more cover, this time behind a different and larger row of planters. Round after round struck their front, pounding at the concrete but dying after that as bullets from enemy assault rifles buried themselves in all the dirt the planters held.

The pair looked at each other, counting the seconds until they could return fire but also looking for signs of what had to be another group of enemy fighters. There was simply no way that the little guy and the bigger one accompanying him were the only two participants in this little blanket party.

"Killdozer, duck!"

Hardcase had seen the Chinese soldier who'd prematurely initiated the ambush bring his weapon to bear once again. Together, both men hit the ground as enemy fire roared over their heads. They were pinned down, at least for the next few seconds.

Unfortunately for Teng Yong, his excitement and complete lack of fire discipline made him aim big and, as a result, also miss just as big.

"FOOL!" the Chinese captain hissed. The idiot had sprung the trap far too early!

Nothing for it now but to go to the guns!

"Fire, fire! Kill the Americans!" he shouted over his team's commo net.

Rifles, submachine guns and handguns poured fire and hot lead at the American hit team. The air was now filled with the sound of angry hornets.

Making up his mind, the Chinese captain nodded to himself, struck Teng Yong in the back of his neck with a knife-hand blow, stunning him, and then forcefully shoved the overeager young sergeant out into the open. Diving for cover behind yet another one of the ubiquitous planters lining the sidewalks near the steps, he looked up to assess his handiwork.

Suddenly, it was as if Teng had become a marionette. He danced and jiggered insanely as bullet after bullet struck him. Finally, as if he'd grown tired of his mad puppet dance, Teng crashed to the sidewalk in a bloody heap.

"There they are!" the captain exclaimed.

Two of the four Americans, the pair to the left of the steps, had made quick work of his foolish sergeant. They'd taken cover behind a row of those concrete planters, the same type he himself was now sheltering behind. He couldn't help but feel momentary satisfaction.

At least Teng Yong redeemed his complete lack of discipline through his death!

The two Americans out to his left front were now fixed in place by his team. Their only escape route, if one wanted to call it that, was back out into the street — where they'd never make it to the other side alive, of course.

"That's it, men, pour it on!" he shouted over the team net. While he gave orders, he and another of his soldiers kept up a torrid rate of fire on the other two Americans, the ones on his right front.

* * *

Streams of bullets raced towards Luke and Crispy. Both men dived first behind a planter and then, desperately, several automobiles and a truck parked on the street just a bit to their left.

"Crispy, we gotta maneuver away and then reorient so that we can attack along the Chinese flank! Luke shouted. "Killdozer, Hardcase! Hang on! We're coming for you!"

"Hanging on, Boss!" Hardcase looked over at his partner. Killdozer gave him a thumbs up while he dropped a nearly empty magazine and tossed another full one over to his buddy.

"We ain't going down without a fight, Hardcase!" Both men could feel the impact of high velocity rounds thudding into the front of the planters they'd hidden behind.

"Got that right, Kill!" exclaimed Hardcase. "Hey! Left and front!"

Two of the enemy shooters were trying to flank their position from the left while two more were assaulting from the front. Killdozer brought his assault rifle up in a flash and fired off a volley that was met by screams from the Chinese soldiers.

The two enemy ambushers on their flank went down hard. At first, they both spasmed and jerked but then they quickly, and permanently, fell still. That left the two attackers at the front. Both were firing and trying to charge forward. Hardcase didn't dare stick his head up to deal with them. If he did, he risked it being turned into a pulpy red-gray mess.

"Luke, Crispy! We could really use some help!" Hardcase yelled. He and Killdozer had a few full magazines left, but those would soon be depleted, and time was growing desperately short.

"Working on it!" Luke shouted.

The former Delta Force leader made a series of hand motions. Crispy simply nodded and began looking around. Then he nodded once more at Ellis and made a different hand motion, pointing across the street. If he could make it over there, he could provide support to his two trapped teammates while also laying down a base of fire for Luke to take advantage of to move from his present position.

"Three, two, one…" Luke counted down on their own team's net to Crispy. "Now!"

Luke fired his MP7A2, its armor-piercing rounds racing out in search of vulnerable targets. Reaching into his jacket, he took out an M18 smoke grenade, pulled out the safety pin and then tossed it toward the steps. Soon enough, green smoke billowed across the front, buying his team, including Crispy — who was now moving in a crouch across the wide street and towards a better firing position — a precious few seconds.

Though dismayed momentarily by the smoke, the Chinese captain continued to smile. His shooters were well-oriented toward the two attack vectors. Except for the four already attacking the American position over to the left, the rest were even now firing and moving down the steps by bounds. One of them fired his weapon to keep the other pair of Americans from popping up and shooting back while several others shot ahead and then did the same for their brother in arms.

Forgetting the sage advice about cautiously splitting your force, and only if you absolutely had to, the captain yelled to his men: "Once you're all in place, half of you charge the two Americans to your right and finish them off! The rest of you join me and we'll finish off the other two just as they finish linking up! Acknowledge!"

"Acknowledged!" his men all said nearly at once.

"Crispy, are you in position yet?" Luke's voice was now preternaturally calm, as it always was in such situations. He'd already figured out what the Chinese team's leader was up to, though he wasn't sure he could spoil the attack that was about to come.

Crispy delayed answering his boss for a few seconds. He was busy shooting at the two Chinese attackers assaulting Killdozer and Hardcase from their front.

"Here now," he murmured to himself as he lined up the two shooters. "Sucks to be you guys!"

"BLAM! BLAM!"

Crispy's rifle — he'd managed to conceal it beneath his long spring overcoat but had quickly pulled it out as soon as all the fun started — barked twice, the sound of the suppressor at its barrel opening making a somewhat diminished firecracker-like sound. For certain, it was far quieter than a non-suppressed rifle, but he still winced slightly from the sound.

The two attackers were now down and motionless.

"YES!" exclaimed Killdozer and Hardcase.

Ellis smiled but then sobered as he added up the numbers. Counting the enemy team's leader — whom he just couldn't seem to draw a bead on, damn the man — it was still six against four and Hardcase and Killdozer were effectively cut off. He and Crispy also couldn't get to them without fully exposing themselves to enemy fire.

The Chinese attackers knew what the odds were and now they sought to swing them even more in their favor by lobbing a handful of grenades at his two men.

"KILLDOZER! HARDCASE! FALL BACK! FALL BACK! GRENADES!"

Across the street, Crispy saw the grenades soar through the air and began firing at the attackers who'd tossed them.

Keep their heads down while our guys get out of blast range!

Luke added his own fire to the mix, reaching out and hitting two more Chinese soldiers, the ones who'd risked throwing the grenades. They both went down.

Neither would ever get back up.

The swarm of grenades thrown by the Chinese fighters now landed where Killdozer and Hardcase had been just a few seconds before. The duo were running as if their lives depended on it.

BAM! BAM! BAM! BAM!

"AAAAAAAGH!"

Killdozer went down with a scream of pain, followed by Hardcase. They'd both managed to run far enough away that the shrapnel from the two grenades hadn't killed them, but they were now wounded and likely out of the fight.

"AH, GOD!" Killdozer shouted, rolling over so that he could lay on his back. He looked down at his left leg. It was covered in blood from a dozen small razor-sharp shrapnel wounds, as was his right arm. All that blood made the limbs appear worse off than they really were, but he was still combat-ineffective now.

"We're down, Luke!" yelled Hardcase, who was grimacing and trying to deal with his own wounds. Looking around to size up the tactical situation, he crawled over to where his partner had fallen.

"Hold on, Killdozer!"

Grunting loudly once more, Hardcase forced himself to ignore his own lower back and leg wounds and then began pulling bandages from his and his partner's IFAIKs, or "Individual First Aid Kits." He also grabbed both Special Forces tourniquets from the tactical vest Killdozer had worn under his light jacket and got to work plugging holes and stopping the red stuff from coming out of the man's leg and arm.

"ARRRRRRRGH! ARRRRRRRGH!"

Killdozer's gasps of pain told him all he needed to know. His battle buddy was fighting to keep from passing out as the pain washed over him.

Crispy heard it all and answered with his own rifle fire. This time, he directed it at the four remaining Chinese attackers trying to close with and then kill his boss.

Luke fired and moved, fired and moved. He was trying desperately to reach Crispy's side of the street.

"POPPING SMOKE! PREPARE TO SUPPORT MY MOVE-MENT!" Ellis exclaimed over the net.

"POP SMOKE IN THREE, TWO, ONE… POP SMOKE!" Crispy shouted in return.

More green smoke suddenly filled the street.

"Moving now!" Ellis whispered harshly, hoping that Crispy would hear him. He ran in a low crouch, the other side of the street now nearly upon him. Over his head, round after round from Crispy's weapon raced by, seeking someone to kill. It was barely enough to prevent the Chinese captain and his men from immediately taking Luke under fire and ending him.

"OOF!" Ellis exclaimed as he crashed into Crispy.

"Glad you could join me, boss!"

"Likewise, Crisp. Likewise." Luke was just glad to be alive at this point.

Taking a second to look around, both men briefly smiled at each other and then dived to the ground once more as the glass storefront behind them exploded.

* * *

The four remaining Chinese attackers, including the captain, moved into the street. They were maneuvering so that they could bum rush the two Americans. To be safe, they kept up an ungodly rate of fire to ensure both *gweilos* kept their heads down and their own firearms out of the fight.

"All we need to do now, men," the Chinese captain shouted in Cantonese, "is move in and overwhelm those two Americans and finish them off!"

"Yes, Captain!"

His men were ready, and they began firing at an even more torrid pace. The air clapped and reverberated with suppressed rifle fire, clashing and echoing against brick and glass.

Suddenly, somewhere around the corner, they could hear the roaring and racing of a cargo van's engine. It was followed by the squeal of rubber as it sped towards their position.

The Chinese team's leader put it aside for the moment.

"Probably some fool American news crew rushing to film it all," the captain mumbled before he focused once again on his men and their mission. Their fury at the Americans was now at a fever pitch. They'd deal with these two first and then execute the two wounded ones down the street immediately afterwards.

Once that was done, they'd head to the rally point at the motorhome and be well away within the next few minutes, which was also Zero Hour, as they'd been sternly reminded by Defense Minister Guo Meng.

"Remember, men," he'd said. "Your work must be complete before Zero Hour. It's vital that you be finished before then so that the slaughter of the American execution team can be broadcast to their president!"

* * *

"I can't get a shot off, Crisp!" yelled Luke.

"Same here, Boss!" Crispy had taken cover behind a planter and was trying to use the glass of another storefront to figure out just where the attackers were moving to as they sought to overpower them both.

As if the Chinese leader could read his mind, the glass almost immediately exploded into thousands of shards, showering him in the deluge.

"Can't see 'em now!" Luke murmured, trying to figure out some way of preventing what he knew was coming. He and Crispy simply didn't have the maneuver room, though. They were outmanned and outgunned. Maybe if Killdozer and Hardcase were still in the fight, they'd have had a better chance.

"No sense wishing for something you aren't gonna get," he grunted, cocking an ear as he slammed his last magazine into his weapon.

It wouldn't be long now.

He could hear the four attackers moving up under a steady stream of fire. They were about to get bum-rushed, and he was out of ideas as to how to prevent it. He and Crispy were pinned down and if he exposed himself for even a second it would be lights out for him forever.

"Crisp!" he shouted to his partner as he tightly grasped his MP7A2.

"Yo, Luke!" Crispy was charging his weapon. He, too, was down to just a full magazine.

"Now or never, Crisp! You ready?" Ellis prepared for their counterattack.

"Ready as I'll ever be, Luke!"

Luke grunted for a second and considered their tactics. Together with Crispy, he intended to charge the four enemy soldiers before they could gain the initiative.

"Okay, then! We go in three, two, one... Hey! Hold on! Something's up with those guys!"

Ellis and Crispy froze in place, waiting and listening. The Chinese fire had shifted from them to a motor vehicle rapidly approaching on the street. It was coming from Luke's right, and it was racing toward the four attackers.

Now, the enemy's rifle fire shifted from disciplined to panicked. Whatever was speeding at the attackers meant to run them down and kill them all.

"No way, no way... NO WAY!" shouted Ellis, who'd finally put it all together. That hardhead former Marine sergeant had decided to do something about their current predicament and — like all Devil Dogs everywhere — was in the process of doing it in the most violent way possible, which in this case meant running down the Chinese ambushers right there in the street.

The air out to Luke and Crispy's front suddenly filled with the agonized screams of four men being struck by a speeding cargo van, though their shouts were very short-lived. They were replaced by a series of sickening thuds and wet crunches.

The screech of rubber on asphalt, as Erin Styles slammed on the brakes and brought the van to a swift halt, signaled the end of the melee.

Luke and Crispy risked a look up and over the cover they'd been using. Their cargo van was stopped dead in the street in front of them both. Steam was pouring out from under the engine's hood.

Ellis' eyes widened just slightly.

Styles — blood dripping down onto her face from a mean-looking forehead gash — emerged from the driver's side door and paused for a second to examine her handiwork. She couldn't keep the smirk off her face, nor could she help but comment.

"Well, you guys? You ready to load up and get the hell out of Dodge? We're burning daylight!"

Luke had never been happier to be saved by the Marine Corps. "Damn right we are, Sergeant!" he shouted. "Damn right!"

The big former Delta Force operator looked over at Crispy, who merely grinned like a fool as he saw Hardcase — who was limping badly and carrying Killdozer over his shoulders like a sack of potatoes — approaching the van. The pair looked like they'd gone through hell. Both men knew they should have died from a fatal case of shrapnel poisoning, just as they both knew they'd somehow cheated death yet again.

"It could have been much worse," Ellis said to himself, deeply satisfied. As he moved, he started tallying up the casualty figures, including all the Chinese dead.

"Crisp, let's get the Dynamic Duo — our new official bullet magnets — to the van ASAP." Luke pointed at Killdozer and Hardcase. "We gotta egress from the area right away."

Crispy quickly looked over the cargo van as Styles popped open the doors to ease their entry. It was a wreck, mainly because its front had taken more than its fair share of Chinese gunfire. The engine was now wheezing and huffing and puffing as well. It was clearly on its last legs.

"Luke, that van isn't going to last much longer."

"Yeah, Crisp. We're going to need new wheels once we're safely away from the area."

Ellis paused and listened, expecting the sound of approaching police sirens, but none were audible. In fact, the street was dead silent.

Looking around, he could also see a few shocked civilians hiding here and there behind what cover they could find — though a couple of the younger ones appeared to be trying to record the action on their smartphones and, judging from their frustrated scowls, not having much success. Fortunately, none of those bystanders seemed too eager to expose themselves to what they assumed had to be a serious gang shootout.

"No way a gunfight this hot and heavy wouldn't attract major league law enforcement attention, Luke," Crispy said in a worried voice as he watched the former Marine, Erin Styles. She was now doing what she could to help their other two team members toward the van. "What gives?"

"I don't know, Crisp, and I don't want to hang around trying to figure it all out. We're out of here in the next 15 seconds."

Crispy merely nodded and then grunted as he picked up his weapon and trotted over to the van.

Ellis looked everyone on his team over, including their newest member, as he picked up what gear he could find before they left the scene. All of them were bloodied and bruised, including Styles.

Gunfire from the Chinese soldiers she'd run down had pretty much turned the front of the van into shredded cheese. She herself was bleeding from several facial cuts. Glass from the van's shot-out windshield had created small slices here and there as she'd steered the vehicle straight ahead from her cover position near the floor and behind the engine.

In her right hand, Erin held a greasy, dirty shop rag she'd found somewhere, and she was periodically using it to wipe the blood off her forehead before it ran into her eyes.

Seeing her with the rag, Crispy handed her a clean bandage from his IFAK. The former Marine took it and pressed it to her forehead with one hand while she helped Hardcase and Killdozer to the back of their vehicle.

"Damn fine job by the Marine Corps!" Luke said to himself as he watched Styles moving with purpose and helping her teammates. "She's gonna work out just fine!"

Miraculously, he saw, none of them had been critically or mortally wounded, including Killdozer, though his two wounded limbs were going to need about a million stitches, judging from the amount of blood on his pants and shirt.

"AAAAAAAAAAAAAAAAAAAAAAAAAAAAGH!"

Everyone came to a halt, stunned by the pain the person doing the screaming was obviously experiencing. It was like nothing they'd ever heard before. The agony was a deluge washing over one and all, and it staggered them with its intensity.

Killdozer, limping along next to Hardcase, suddenly realized that no matter the amount of pain he was in, it couldn't come close to what Luke's protégé, Annie Dedham, was enduring.

The grin on Crispy's face disappeared and Luke fought to keep his mouth from falling open in shock and horror as he raced toward the rear of the van.

"ANNIE! ANNIE! HOLD ON! "HOLD ON!"

The young woman's agonizing shrieks reminded them all that the ordeal wasn't over.

CHOICES PART II

JOINT BASE PEARL HARBOR-HICKAM, HAWAII

"Mister President, Admiral Sowell, Ms. Boyer, I strongly advise against revealing to the Chinese the presence of that B-21 on Guam and I especially advise against loading those two nuclear weapons onto it, and so does General Harris." Admiral John Dantonio, Commander, U.S. Indo-Pacific Command, nodded at his fellow four-star, Air Force General Andrew Harris, who backed his boss up with a nod of his own. They were both staring incredulously at the giant OLED monitor hanging on the wall.

On it, U.S. President Thomas Masterson and his top military advisor, Navy Admiral Louis Sowell, the current Chairman of the Joint Chiefs of Staff, had just finished reading Dantonio and Harris in on "The Plan," as the trio in the Oval Office called it.

Neither the admiral nor the general could believe it.

Andrew Harris had just the week before taken over as the newly promoted and confirmed Commander, United States Pacific Air Forces, or PACAF. Dantonio had been in his own job barely a month and they both were still trying to settle into their new roles. Because of that, they were also inclined to give their Commander in Chief the benefit of the doubt.

But this? This "plan?"

It was pure, unadulterated lunacy.

Not only wouldn't it deter the Communist Chinese from attempting an invasion of Taiwan but loading nuclear weapons on a B-21 Raider and then flying the newest and deadliest stealth bomber in history so close to Mainland China would likely encourage just such an invasion, not to mention that it would also likely touch off World War III.

Both flag officers sat alone, without the benefit of their many aides, in the Sensitive Compartmented Information Facility, or SCIF, at Joint Base Pearl Harbor-Hickam, Hawaii. They'd listened, with increasing concern, to what their Commander in Chief and his people had outlined during their secure, encrypted videoconference.

Admiral Dantonio — who as unified combatant commander of the Indo-Pacific theater led over 375,000 U.S. military and Coast Guard personnel and their amazing array of firepower — simply couldn't process what he'd just heard from Thomas Masterson, the U.S. President.

He can't seriously intend to load those nukes up on that B-21 and fly it close to Mainland China! He simply cannot! That's not even nuclear brinkmanship, that's practically demanding that the Chinese go to war against us!

"I understand John, Andy," replied Masterson with a serene look on his face. "But we've decided this is the best way of getting Tan Jianhong and his defense chief, Guo Meng, to back down, so I need you both to make Admiral Sowell's plan happen."

"Mister President," Admiral Dantonio tried again, "I feel it's my duty to point out that the Chinese will likely take the kind of saber rattling we're about to engage in entirely the wrong way."

"I agree with Admiral Dantonio, President Masterson" said General Harris urgently. He nodded toward the monitor, where Masterson and his people sat in the Oval Office, smiling calmly — too calmly — as they outlined what he considered to be a quick path to war.

"Maybe send them a few photos of the B-21 via diplomatic channels, Mister President," urged Dantonio. "Include a video demonstration of that bird's lethality, even. Same goes for our new nuclear weapon, that B61-13 gravity bomb." The admiral knew all about that weapon's capabilities.

"Mister President," General Harris tried again, "the B61-13 is stupendously more powerful than any other such nuclear bomb we currently have in our inventory."

Masterson continued to smile enigmatically. "I know that General." He waited for Dantonio and Harris to finish their pitch.

What could President Masterson be thinking, sending that B-21 toward China, and with live nukes in its weapons bay? It doesn't make sense!

"Mister President, we simply can't." With that, Admiral Dantonio looked across the table at the Air Force flag officer.

General Harris nodded his head once again. He'd come up through the strategic bomber pilot ranks and he knew just what a nearly untraceable, unstoppable bomber like the B-21 Raider —

equipped with a super-powerful nuclear bomb like the B61-13 — could do.

"President Masterson," he said firmly, "I can promise you this. If we fly that B-21 anywhere close to Communist China, Taiwan is going to be one of the more manageable problems we'll have, mainly because it won't exist after that."

Worryingly, Dantonio and Harris saw on the screen, Chairman Sowell and Chief of Staff Angela Boyer continued to smile patiently.

Both flag officers saw Louis Sowell — whom they both knew and genuinely liked — take a proffered folder. It had been handed to him from someone standing offscreen. After a minute of reading its contents, Sowell frowned deeply. Then, he leaned over and spoke into Masterson's ear.

"What's that Louis has just been handed, Andy, and what's he saying to the president?" Admiral Dantonio asked in a whisper.

"I don't know, Admiral, but it's got him riled up." Harris whispered back, deeply concerned.

Just then, the Defense Readiness Condition, or DEFCON, screen in the corner of the room flashed from the yellow of DEFCON 3 to the red of DEFCON 2.

"Fast Pace," as DEFCON 2 was named, was the next step to nuclear war, and the armed forces of the United States now had to be ready to deploy and then engage the enemy in less than six hours.

Stunned, both flag officers stared once again at the OLED monitor on the wall.

"Admiral Dantonio, General Harris," President Masterson said. "We have new intelligence that shows the Chinese are preparing their ICBM forces and equipping their bombers with nuclear weapons. Also, mass numbers of troop-carrying trains seem to be heading to several Chinese port cities facing Taiwan. There have also been several attempts at initiating a cyberattack against parts of our critical infrastructure, something we've so far been successful at turning away."

Dantonio and Harris looked at each other, their faces shocked. They were at DEFCON 2. Both flag officers and their staffs had a huge amount of work staring them in the face and little time to handle it all — if this increase in the nation's defense readiness level was indeed genuine and not just President Masterson and his chief military advisor testing their new Indo-Pacific Command and PACAF four-stars, that is.

"What the hell is going on here, Andy?" asked Admiral Dantonio. "Now, we're going to DEFCON 2?"

"I don't know, Admiral" was all General Harris could manage. "If it's legitimate, we'll be seeing the intelligence product on our screens in the next 10 seconds."

Dantonio reached under the conference table they were sitting at and pressed a small button. Behind them, the doors to the SCIF opened and uniformed and civilian staff members poured into the room.

On the OLED screen, Thomas Masterson looked at his chief of staff, Angela Boyer. She nodded and then smiled slightly before she turned to her left and looked at Admiral Sowell, who in turn nodded and then also smiled ever so slightly.

In the SCIF, every OLED monitor, every highly encrypted electronic device allowed into the room — all of them secure laptops and tablets issued to admirals and generals alike — started receiving mountains of intelligence and data.

It had been neatly laid out: Chinese troop movements, ships tasked with the invasion, ICBM forces being put on final alert, likewise for that country's strategic bombers and ballistic missile submarines. Plus, there was one other piece of data, and it played out on their screens and encrypted devices as well.

The Chinese had tried to poison the Washington, D.C. water supply using a combination of fentanyl and ketamine. They intended to decapitate the United States by killing as much of its federal political leadership as they could, including President Masterson.

Admiral John Dantonio and his key subordinate, General Andrew Harris, had seen enough.

"Andy, we have work to do," Dantonio said. He gestured to his deputy commander, Marine Corps Lieutenant General Joseph Esquival, who marched purposefully to his side.

"General Esquival," was all Dantonio said.

"Yes, Admiral!" Esquival, a three-star Marine Corps officer stood ramrod straight. He knew what was coming.

"Let's get ready for war."

"Yes, Admiral!" That was all Esquival needed to hear. He would be doing the down-and-dirty and the nitty-gritty of staff work from here on out. He turned to the many members of the Indo-Pacific Command staff and began speaking in a low, urgent tone.

"Well, Andy," said Admiral John Dantonio to his Air Force four-star subordinate as they stood in the middle of controlled chaos. "It looks like time and tide wait for no man."

"I only hope the Chinese wait and then consider the tide of war that they're leading us all into," General Harris replied as both men walked out of the SCIF.

Up on the screen, a barely noticeable trace of white noise briefly emanated from the speakers spread along the walls of the room, but it was nearly lost in the uproar created by so many people all trying to talk at once.

Strangely, it almost sounded as if the speakers were saying something.

Something like: *Yesssssss!*

* * *

Downtown Los Angeles

Luke dived into the back of the shot-up cargo van, searching for Annie. She was on the floor, breathing rapidly, as if she was struggling mightily to contain an immeasurably powerful force within her.

"Annie! Are you okay? What's going on?" Ellis was still trying to process it all, and it felt like a vast electrical charge was about to explode outward.

"Mister Ellis," the 18-year-old said. Her voice was barely a croak, and her lips were dry and cracked. "You have to help us. Help me and Ozymandias."

Luke was lost. Here was the girl he'd tried so hard to protect and she was clearly suffering, as she'd suffered when she'd gone to help Ozymandias not even an hour ago.

"Annie, I don't understand!"

Ellis looked behind him. Styles, Crispy and Hardcase were crowding in while an increasingly woozy Killdozer sat on the cargo van's rear bumper, keeping pressure on his leg and looking for signs of any added threats. Luke's MP7A2 rested on his lap, and his grunts of pain were the only sounds he was now making.

"Mister Ellis, please just take my hand for a few seconds," the girl said between gasps. "Oz will explain everything! He's waiting! And we only have minutes before the explosion! It's the battery! We need to recharge it!" She screamed in pain once again.

"AAAAAAAAAAAGH!"

Luke didn't hesitate. He desperately grasped the young woman's hand.

An explosion of colors, sights and sounds assaulted his senses, and vast amounts of data crashed into his mind, threatening to overwhelm his brain's processing abilities.

Ozymandias also didn't wait. He laid it all out for the human man whom he'd come to think of as his friend.

Friend.

Such a marvelous word, and heavy with all sorts of promise. And pain, of course.

"Luke, are you okay?" Crispy was staring at his boss, at the man he'd once called "Blade." Styles and the others were simply too stunned to say anything.

Only the whites of Ellis' eyes showed, as if he was being force-fed reams of data and processing it simultaneously. Suddenly, his eyes returned to their normal blue, and he looked down once more at Annie.

"Do you see, Mister Ellis?" she asked the big former soldier. "Do you *see*?"

Luke had indeed seen it all. There was only one thing to do, too.

When he spoke, his voice was soft, as if he was preparing to sacrifice some portion of himself to secure a victory for them all, for the City of Angels... for everyone, everywhere.

"I do, Annie. I really do see."

Ellis breathed deeply, savoring the oxygen molecules in the air.

This is what it's like.

"Good!" exclaimed Annie, still laboring to deal with the massive pain. "So, you know what we need to do, right? Make it soon because I can't take it for much longer."

The girl's gasp became more strained. She was temporarily controlling a vast amount of energy that had to be used soon, because if it wasn't she was dead. That was what happened to circuit breakers when an electrical overload occurred. They tripped and switched off to prevent damage to the devices they helped power.

In the real world, circuit breakers could usually be reset with the simple flick of a switch. In Annie's case, though, she would permanently switch off, because no circuit breaker ever designed could handle such an enormous electrical load, and neither could she.

"Please hurry, Mister Ellis!" Annie whispered.

Ellis didn't waste any time. He turned to his team.

"Crisp! Get us out of here. Go down two blocks and hang a right! There's a motorhome parked in a lot just around that corner!

We're busting into it and taking care of business right now! Go, go, go!"

"I'm on it!"

Crispy raced to the front of the van while Erin Styles and her new teammates, Hardcase and Killdozer, piled into the back with Annie and Luke. Except for the 18-year-old, all four of them were nearly thrown into the van's rear double-doors from the force of the vehicle's sudden acceleration.

Luke focused. He had to put everything else but the impending death of millions aside.

"How long until the battery in the containment device runs out and the antimatter destroys this city, Annie?"

He was back on mission once again. He also saw that the Marine sergeant, Styles, and the team's other two operators, the banged-up, bloodied Killdozer and the less-injured Hardcase, were listening intently. There was more work to be done, and more people — millions more, now — to save.

BANG!

Ellis and the others crashed into the vehicle's left wall as Crispy hauled the van into an intense right turn. The vehicle's tires screamed in protest as they tried to remain on the street's asphalt surface.

"We have less than two minutes, Luke!" Annie shouted. "Please! Get us there and move me into the motorhome as quickly as you can! The device is in a locked cabinet near the entrance!"

"Luke, I see it!" shouted Crispy up front. "The thing's at 3 o'clock!"

The motorhome sat practically alone in an unattended and nearly vacant parking lot, and Luke knew they'd have it to themselves. If anyone had been around just a few minutes ago they were now likely over at the Bunker Hill Steps, which had been the scene of a serious shootout by rival gangs — or so they thought.

"About a minute now, Crisp," Luke said calmly from just behind the driver. "Pull up next to the motorhome. We need to transfer Annie to it."

"Roger that!"

Crispy brought the van to a screaming halt right next to the other vehicle.

Luke turned around and looked at Hardcase, who was just finishing patching up Killdozer. "Hardcase, you and Styles breach that motorhome right now. I'm following behind with Annie."

"We're on it, Boss!" The former SEAL Team 6 operator looked at Erin. "C'mon, Styles! We're doing some door kicking in the next five seconds! Let's move!"

"Right!" she shouted as she and Hardcase exploded from the rear of the cargo van and disappeared.

Luke scooped up Annie as if she were a papier-mâché doll or a Mexican *piñata* soon to be beaten senseless by a gang of birthday partygoers.

"Hold up, Styles!" shouted Hardcase as the woman prepared to kick the door. "It might be booby trapped!"

"We're out of time, dammit!"

Hardcase didn't hesitate. The Devil Dog was right.

BAM!

The sound of both Hardcase and Styles kicking open the motorhome's flimsy side entrance door crashed and boomed against the buildings that loomed over the small parking lot like mourners at a gravesite. The duo stood there for a half-second, frozen in place and with their eyes tightly shut, as if that would have protected them from 100 million degrees Celsius of heat.

Hardcase opened both his eyes, followed immediately by Styles. They exhaled loudly in relief.

"We've breached, Luke!" Hardcase shouted over his shoulder. "Get Annie over here ASAP!"

He knew he didn't need to say anything else. He simply looked at Styles, who nodded. She followed behind as her partner entered the motorhome and looked desperately about.

She also saw the locked closet or cubby — or whatever it was called in Motorhome World — first.

"GOT IT!" Erin yelled, pointing to what looked like a closet several feet away from the door.

She tested the handle. It was locked. From inside it, they could make out a low and steadily diminishing cyclic hum, as if some piece of small machinery was winding down just prior to shutting off.

"We found it, Luke!" shouted Hardcase as he practically ripped the door off its hinges.

The device sat there, tethered to a series of cables that ran to a single small battery. On top, an LED-like indicator sat, and there were two small, thin wires running to the battery itself. The indicator was now down to two small red bars, and one of them was flickering madly.

Hardcase looked intently at his partner and shook his head.

"No green bars and no yellow bars, Colonel Ellis!" exclaimed Styles as she leaned out the door. "Looks like the battery's down to two red bars! Uh-oh!"

To her horror, the flickering bar suddenly went black. Fresh out of ideas as well as coherent speech, she simply stood there and stared at the coming end of her life.

"Now down to one red bar, Luke!" Hardcase yelled out for her. "Don't know how long that last bar's going to last, and the damn thing's cycling down!"

It was true. Former Marine and SEAL alike knew what the diminishing hum portended. A great motor was winding down, and when it finally did the Apocalypse would arrive.

Luke had heard enough. He nodded and looked at Annie while Crispy launched himself out of the driver's side door of the van and raced to the back, there to assist his team leader should he need it.

"Annie," Ellis said quietly. "You ready to do this with me?"

"Do you know what you're accepting by doing this with *me*, Mister Ellis?" the 18-year-old gasped in return. The pain of holding it all in crashed over her again and she thought for a second that she could see the slow-motion movement of the photons making up the light flowing into the van.

Luke *knew*.

He knew what he would become by doing this thing with his protégé, who was easily the most courageous person he'd ever known.

"Yes, Annie," he replied as softly as he could while he gently picked her up and then walked with immense purpose toward the door of the motorhome.

Ozymandias' voice now echoed in his mind.

You will both be stronger together than either of you will be apart, Luke.

Ellis talked as he walked. "We'll have to pick this up once we're finished here, Oz. Just tell me what I need to do and how to do it," he said, dreading the response he knew was coming.

You already know what to do, Luke. Someday we'll see each other again.

Ellis had somehow known, deep inside, what Ozymandias — his amazing non-human *friend* — would have to do to help both him and Annie pull this off. He also suspected that Annie was still unaware, but she didn't need to know that part just yet.

There really wasn't much more Luke had to say.

"See you when I see you then, Oz."

He looked down once again at Annie, who was now moaning softly.

Now they were in the motorhome. Styles and Hardcase stood to the side. They were only a few feet away from the device and looking extremely worried. Erin couldn't help but steal a glance at her tactical watch.

Luke placed the girl on the floor of the motorhome and took her right hand in his left.

"We're here, Annie. It's time."

"Yes," gasped the 18-year-old. "Place your right hand on the battery. Hurry! Ten seconds left!"

Ellis slammed his right hand onto the top of the battery, which should have been warm to the touch. Now, though, it was growing increasingly cool.

The last red bar on the LED indicator began flickering. No more than a few seconds of life remained. Life for the battery, for Luke and everyone else who'd fought so hard to make it to the motorhome, as well as millions of unsuspecting others.

"Oz!" Annie's agonized scream filled the motorhome. "Three seconds! Hit us now!"

Ozymandias obeyed.

The brownout in Los Angeles intensified. Electrical transformers around the city suddenly exploded in a shower of sparks and nearly unbearable flashes of light. Unimaginable energy raced outward from the 18-year-old girl and through Luke — who grimaced and nearly screamed with the shock, though he also felt as if he could handle even more... which was strange — and into the battery.

Both Annie and Ellis now knew what it was like to stand at the center of a nuclear explosion, to dance on the surface of the Sun and to have every one of the human body's 30 trillion cells all rupture and die at the same time.

Yet, they still live.

Would the amazing battery that powers the antimatter containment device also live, though? Or would it die in the next second? If it did, millions would perish in the immediate blast, and then billions more once China and the United States went to war against each other, because Thomas Masterson, President of the

United States of America, would surely retaliate against the Chinese. There would be no doubt in his mind that they'd been responsible for all that had happened.

Luke found himself beyond time and space and pain. He was being forged in the same fire that had created *Mjölnir*, the Norse god Thor's legendary hammer.

Somewhere deep inside he knew.

He *knew*.

"Finish it, Oz!" he thundered.

Hardcase and Styles fell backwards, stunned by the force and ferocity of his voice.

Annie — lying on the floor and sharing in the excruciating pain her mentor, a man of stupendous courage and bravery, was bearing — could only grimace. She was a spent force. If this didn't succeed, she was done.

So is everyone else! So, who am I to complain, and what does it really matter?

Inside the golden orb, Ozymandias — who was *feeling* everything and who was also now more human than most people could ever hope to be — threw the last virtual switch and opened the final virtual channel.

This is it, Luke. Annie. What will be, will be. Believe in each other and in humanity and, hopefully, I'll return someday.

"Noooooooooooooooooooooooo, Oz!" screamed Annie. She'd finally realized what would happen and why her friend had to do it. The knowledge still didn't prevent her heart from nearly breaking in two.

"Now, Oz! Now!" bellowed Luke.

He could see the last LED on the battery indicator. It had perhaps two flickers left before Hell landed directly on top of Los Angeles.

Ozymandias closed his eyes and *willed* it. And then, he prepared to walk into a different kind of light.

In the motorhome, every muscle and tendon and ligament in Ellis' body convulsed and ripped and tore as a new musculoskeletal system formed. It was like Annie's, but also *different.*

If he survived this ordeal — if LA and the world survived — he would be changed, somewhat like Annie but even more than that.

Inside, as he was assaulted by the incredible energy now flowing freely through him and into the battery, Luke thought he had heard a voice.

It was rich and sonorous. It was Ozymandias.

Guard what I've given you closely and well, Luke. You'll know what to do when the time comes.

Luke barely heard his friend's final bit of advice and he would later find himself doubting that Oz had even said anything to him at all. Instead, he let forth a primal scream that exploded and ripped and roared and raged.

"ARRRRRRRRRRRRRRRRRRRRRRGHHHHHHH!"

Ellis bellowed and roared like an enraged bull elephant and slapped Annie's hand and arm away, breaking the circuit Oz had created for them both. Her pain and suffering was no longer needed, and she instantly fell unconscious. The blue-white light flashed briefly around her body before it almost instantaneously vanished.

"Grab her feet, Styles!" Crispy and Hardcase exclaimed and dove forward to help. "We have to get her away from Luke before she's killed!"

"Right!" the former Marine shouted. Together, they grasped the 18-year-old's ankles and quickly pulled her away from Ellis.

All four of them, including the still-unconscious Annie, were now huddled at the far end of the motorhome as the cataclysm came to its end.

The final jolt hit Luke all at once. He was cocooned in the blue-white energy flow and holding the battery in a death grip.

NOOOOOOOOOOOOOOOOOOOOOOOOOOOOOOOOOOOOOOOOOOO!

The speakers in the motorhome's sound system exploded as a roaring sound of fury and pure hatred overwhelmed them. It was Baal, the enemy AI, fleeing once again.

BOOM!

Luke felt his hand and arm — now blackened and smoking, but rebuilding themselves even as he suffered the scourging — let go of the battery as he was flung away from the containment device. He also landed unconscious at the feet of his teammates.

Stunned, Crispy and Hardcase and Styles slowly looked from their leader over to the antimatter containment device and the battery.

Both were still working. The device hummed busily and the LED indicator above the battery showed nothing but a long line of green bars. Around Los Angeles, the near-blackout lifted and cellular and electronic communications suddenly resumed operation as if they'd never even been interrupted.

Erin Styles was the first to speak.

"Oh, my God! Oh, my God! Did we just win? Tell me we just won!"

"We just won, Styles, okay?" Hardcase stood in the door of the motorhome, looking at the former Marine. He was preparing to retrieve the thankfully unconscious Killdozer and whatever weaponry and gear they still had. "We do that all the time, Jarhead. Get used to it."

Then he winked at her and launched himself out the door.

Erin was ready this time.

"Well, glad to hear it, Squid!" she exclaimed as she smiled goofily and then laughed.

"Styles!" exclaimed Crispy. "Get over there with Hardcase and police up that van. We're getting out of this place right away because we really don't want to be here when the cops arrive! SO, MOVE IT!"

In the background, they could both hear the faint wailing of police sirens. Relatively far away for the moment, they would be much nearer in the next few minutes.

"OOH-RAH! CRISPY! I'M ALL OVER IT!"

The 28-year-old woman — who now knew that the only thing wrong with her was that she needed a task and purpose in life — rushed to her assignment with a gigantic smile on her face. She was part of a true *team*, a band of brothers and sisters.

"Yup," whispered Crispy with a big smile on his face as he gunned the motorhome's engine and craned his head around so that he could check out Luke and Annie. They were both still unconscious. His practiced eyes could tell they weren't in danger of dying, though, which was a huge relief to him.

As for Styles, the former Marine and the team's newest member?

He could hear her outside the motorhome, issuing orders to Hardcase and otherwise doing the Marine Corps thing, which was to always take charge even if you hadn't been put in charge.

Smiling broadly, he spoke to Luke one final time.

"Boss, that Styles is gonna work out just fine!"

Epilogue

Andersen Air Force Base, Guam

The tarmac and runway area around the hangar housing the B-21 Raider and its three Loyal Wingman drones was a smoking ruin. Many of the military and civilian personnel who'd accompanied the aircraft out to Guam were also lying on the ground and not moving.

Most would never move again.

One hell of a fight had taken place around the hangar. Men and women had heroically rushed to the sound of the guns and then died just as heroically.

Looking around, a bystander might note that there was a gaping hole in the runway side of the control tower, out of which a fire now raged. One of the drones had flown back around — in an impossibly tight turn that would have turned the insides of a human pilot into jelly — and strafed it before unleashing one of its Peregrine missiles. Many of the American military's best fighter and pursuit jets had received the same treatment from the three drones and were now broken wrecks well beyond repair.

The runway had also been badly cratered, making it impossible to use for the next several hours.

Maddeningly, the shattered remains of the four fighter jets flying Combat Air Patrol, or CAP, around Guam now lay at the bottom of the ocean. They'd tried to close the distance to visually track the B-21 and then fire off their air-to-air missiles, but they'd quickly been shot out of the sky by the demon-possessed drones.

Even with an E-3 Sentry AWACS bird and its ultra-powerful radars painting the skies for hundreds of miles around the island, the human pilots hadn't been able to obtain a radar lock on the Raider and fire their weapons from standoff distance. Heroes to the last, they all risked their lives on a desperate gamble based on a couple of ephemeral flickers on one pilot's radar screen.

In the end, their gamble failed. Working in tandem, two of the drones appeared from a cloudbank and attacked. An epic dogfight ensued, followed by an equally epic shootdown of the human-piloted fighter jets.

The drones had done their job.

They'd made sure that nothing would be able to pursue or track the AI-operated Raider and its two B61-13 gravity nuclear bombs.

The newest and deadliest stealth bomber in history — likened in the press to the infamous Death Star of sci-fi movie history — was gone and no one had the faintest idea where it was.

About the Authors

A.W. Guerra is a retired U.S. military officer. Post-military, he spent more than a decade in airline management and aviation security operations.

Kelly C. Hoggan is an aviation security consultant and founder of H4 Solutions. He has served in numerous senior level positions within the U.S. government and two major international airlines.

ALSO BY
A.W. GUERRA & KELLY C. HOGGAN

By A.W. Guerra:

Motown: The Vampire Must Die: Ninja, SEALs, Believers

By A.W. Guerra & Kelly C. Hoggan:

First Strike: Loudoun County

Second Strike: Danger Close

Coming in Summer 2024, also by Q.W. Guerra & Kelly C. Hoggan:
Final Strike: Broken Arrow

Coming Soon From Kelly C. Hoggan:

The Old Gods Attack